A VERY
MERRY
MARGARITA
MIX-UP

BRITTANÉE NICOLE

Copyright

A Very Merry Margarita Mix-Up © 2022 Brittanee Nicole

Cover Design by Ink and Laurel
Formatting by Cover 2 Cover Author Services
Editing by VB Edits
Content/Beta Edit by Brittni Van

DEDICATION

For my daughter. Mackenzie, may you always find magic in the
simple moments.
I love you!
XOXO,
Mommy

Magic…

You may have to squint

You may have to close your eyes

You may have to look quickly

But…

If you pay attention

It's there, subtly

There is magic in every day

In every moment

In every person you meet

Look for it and once you find it

Embrace it and nurture it

So the rest of the world can find it too

-K.M. Brady

Author of Perfectly Imperfectly A Mess

A VERY MERRY MARGARITA MIX-UP PLAYLIST

1. Last Christmas by Wham
2. My Gift Is You by Gwen Stefani
3. Cozy Little Christmas by Katy Perry
4. Happy Christmas by John Lennon and Yoko Ono
5. It's Beginning to Look A Lot Like Christmas by Michael Buble
6. Santa Tell Me Ariana Grande
7. You Make It Feel Like Christmas by Gwen Stefani and Blake Shelton
8. Christmas Tree Farm by Taylor Swift
9. Underneath the Christmas Tree by Kelly Clarkson
10. Like Its Christmas by Jonas Brothers
11. Rocking around the Christmas Tree by Brenda Lee
12. The Christmas Song by Shawn Mendes and Camilla Cabello
13. Baby It's Cold Outside by Michael Buble and Idina Menzel
14. All I want for Christmas is You Mariah Carey

PROLOGUE

SHAWN

"Shawn, there's mail for you!" My sister Charlotte hollers from the kitchen, her chocolate lab Charlie trailing behind her as she delivers the oversized box to the living room.

I rub my hands together, watching her bring the box closer to where I sit on the couch. My best friend's girlfriend is a writer, and she sends me her favorite books monthly. A care package of sorts. She always includes some type of sage advice along with the books.

Don't forget: oral a day will keep the doctor away.

Shawn, remember: you can't have your cake and eat it, too, but you can always eat—

"What are you smiling about?" Charlotte asks, pulling my focus from the book box created just for me.

I laugh. "You do *not* want to know."

She rolls her eyes. "You're weird."

That's true. We've been having the same conversation since we were kids. I grab my keys from the table and use the edge of one to slice open the tape that holds the cardboard tabs shut, already excited to see what Tessa sent. It's packed full of books, but on top is a white envelope. My name is scrawled in Tessa's exaggerated handwriting with a big heart next to it. I slide my finger under the flap of the envelope, careful not to rip the contents, but as I lift it up, a familiar paper-thin green object slips out and floats down, landing on my lap.

"What's that?" Charlotte asks, watching my every move.

My heart pounds in my chest. Without picking it up, I know exactly what it is. Last year, I spent time working at a bar in Tahoe called the Silver Lining. The women who own it started a tradition of sorts. The walls behind the bar were covered in dollar bills. Patrons would write their wishes—for themselves, for friends, for family members—on greenbacks. And over that year, I witnessed quite a few of those wishes come true. Each one was *after* the dollar fell.

I don't believe in magic, but it was interesting to watch.

I'm the type of man who takes charge. Who believes if you want something, you make it happen. *You* make the change. It's how I ended up in this town after my baseball career ended.

I spent a year at the bar in Tahoe shortly after I left baseball, but I was just biding my time. Figuring out my next step. When I witnessed my best friend Ryan finally go after the girl he'd always wanted—after his wish fell, of course—I knew it was time for me to do something about my stagnant life.

So I made a wish. The one that is currently sitting on my lap.

I wish for a mix-up.

I made a wish because my best friend Ryan wouldn't leave me alone until I did. But why ask for a mix-up when I could make one happen?

I took things into my own hands and joined the fire academy. Trained for months, passed, and moved to Bristol, Rhode Island, to be closer to my family.

All quite the mix-up from my previous life. The one where I was a professional baseball player making millions and living in Los Angeles.

But then I'd let my life grow stagnant again. There was no opening at the fire department here. Charlotte's fiancé mentioned an opening at a bar, and suddenly, I was living in my sister's basement, working behind a bar, and doing the opposite of what I'd set out to do.

I scrub my hand over my face. *I really hadn't taken charge of my life at all.*

Sucking in a breath, I pull Tessa's letter from the envelope. This note is only one line. Four words.

It fell. It's time.

I lift the dollar bill and study it. What kind of mix-up are we talking about here? My job? My living situation? Or maybe, just maybe... Nah, I'm getting ahead of myself. If I want to make a change, I have to do it myself. And right now, I'm late for work.

JULES
ICE CREAM
SUPER PREMIUM ICE CREAM
SUPER PREMIUM ICE CREAM

CHAPTER 1

JULES

"I think I screwed up."

"You didn't screw up. You're just taking a breather," my best friend assures me.

Right. A breather. I look out at the bay and take a deep breath. My sisters were raised here. They have probably stood in this exact spot. Maybe gone boating with the father I've never met. "What am I doing here?" I ask, more to myself than to Amy.

"You're looking into your past. Maybe reconnecting with your family." She sighs on the other end of the line. "Jules, you don't need all the answers right away."

"My mom *kidnapped* me, Amy. I'm not reconnecting with a family I lost touch with. I'm showing up in a town where no one knows me, to find a family that doesn't even know I exist. What if—"

She cuts me off. "Your mother may be a piece of work, and lord knows we've had our differences..." She chuckles.

I join in, thinking of how my best friend drives my mother crazy.

"But she didn't kidnap you. She worked out an arrangement with your dad."

"Yeah, they divided us like we were dang golden retriever puppies. You take one, I'll take two, and never again shall they meet. Like, who the heck does that?"

"Other than the parents from the *Parent Trap*?" Amy teases. "Yeah, I don't know. It was kind of shitty."

Exactly. I kick at a rock resting a few inches in front of my toe, and it skids into the water.

I arrived in Bristol, Rhode Island—my birthplace, apparently—earlier today. I don't have a plan. I turn back to face the ice cream shop that drew me here.

Jules Ice Cream.

A letter from a grandmother I'd never met with a picture of this shop started all of this insanity. I'd run away from my life, my job, and my mother for an ice cream shop.

As if reading my thoughts, Amy asks, "Have you gone in yet?"

I finger the key in my pocket. "No. It feels scandalous to walk in."

Amy blows out a breath. "First of all, it's sugar, not sex. What could possibly be scandalous about sugar?"

"Not the ice cream shop. It's facing the life that my mother stole from me. She took me across the country to raise me and left behind my older sister and my *twin*. Amy, I have a twin sister I've never met. This is insanity!"

She sighs again. "I know. Do you want me to fly out? I'll be on the next plane."

I shake my head, my hair whipping in the wind. "I need to do this on my own. I don't even know if Hailey knows about me."

The second I learned of her existence, it was like this piece I'd been missing finally clicked into place. All my life, I had felt not quite whole. Not quite right. Something, an ache, an uncertainty, always existed. And now I understand why. The person I shared DNA with, who lived with me for nine months inside my mother and spent six months sharing a room and even a crib with me—a fact I only know because my mom begrudgingly showed me the pictures when I discovered the truth—*she* was what I was missing.

Hailey.

And Caris, my older sister.

Sisters. *I have sisters.*

My blood pumps in excitement again.

"So what's your plan? Are you going to show up at their bar and say *surprise*?"

I laugh. "I can't wait too long. You saw her Facebook picture. We're identical. In a small town like this, it won't take long for people to talk. And I want her to hear it from me first. Unless she already knows."

"No way!" Amy says vehemently. "I don't believe for a second that your twin could know you exist and not seek you out."

Unless she doesn't want to know me. Maybe she hates me because my mom chose me. I wish she hadn't. I wish I had grown up in this idyllic town with sisters. I wish my mom had taken off on her own. That makes me a monster, right? Wishing my own mother had abandoned me rather than bringing me along for her insane adventure to win over Hollywood.

Newsflash—she didn't make it. Unless marrying the first man with a big enough wallet to support her and her child is considered making it. That's unfair of me though. My stepfather is amazing. He made up for all the things my mother lacked. Unfortunately, he didn't make her happy either, so now he's remarried and has a new family, and mom is on husband number three. He's not so great.

Feeling overwhelmed, I kick another rock and stare out at the sea. It really is beautiful here. In front of me, sailboats bob in the water, and their colorful sails billow in the wind.

It's like a quaint town out of a Hallmark movie. A perfect place to grow up, to raise a family, spend your twenties, discover yourself.

When I first arrived, I drove by bars and restaurants up and down the main road—Hope Street. How freaking cute is that? *Hope Street.* I've been here for mere minutes, and I already love everything about this place. I don't know what I'll do when it's time to return to my normal life in LA.

"I gotta go, Amy. I'm going to check out the shop and then get up the courage to go to the restaurant. Or maybe visit my grandmother."

That's probably the safer option. At least *she's* expecting me.

"All right, but my offer stands. If you decide to stay, I'm flying out. It'll be like college again!"

Amy and I were roommates in college, and we've been best friends since grade school. She's like a sister to me. I imagine if the shoe were on the other foot, I'd be terribly jealous of her newfound sisters, but she's been nothing but wonderful.

"I'll call you tonight. If—and it's a big if—I decide to stay, you're more than welcome to come."

She claps on the other end of the phone. "Oh! Road trip! I really hope you stay. This is going to change your life, Jules!"

Her energy and positivity balance perfectly with my reserved, rule-follower nature. My deep auburn hair and freckles fit my subdued personality, while her strawberry blond hair and perfect pout match her big personality. Her outgoing disposition makes it easy for her to make friends. Things are more complicated when you're an introvert like me. I've spent my life relying on her to introduce me to people and bring me out of my shell. Honestly, if I stay here, I'll need her.

But my life is in LA. *"We'll see. Love you."* I hang up and tip my face to the sky.

I need a sign. An indication that I'm not making a massive mistake by moving across the country, leaving my life, my job, and my crazy mother behind.

The wind behind me blows wildly, and my hair whips around like I'm caught in a tunnel of air. Tingles race down my back and straight to my toes. I turn from the shore and watch as a tall man approaches me.

My breath stops.

He is *gorgeous.*

Beautiful. Better looking than any man I've ever seen. Tall, broad shoulders, dark hair rustling in the wind, and chocolate-brown eyes that make my knees weak.

But it's the way he looks at me, with determination, *with purpose,* that takes my breath away.

He walks toward me without hesitating, his eyes never leaving mine. And before I can react, he grabs my hips, searing my skin where his fingers meet the exposed strip between my shirt and my jeans. He tilts me back, with one arm cradling my waist while the other moves behind my neck. After a split second of hesitation, he looks into my eyes, then presses his lips to mine.

18

CHAPTER 2

SHAWN

The wind whips almost violently as I walk toward the dock, late for my shift. November snuck up on me this year. Soon, the stores will be decorated with Christmas wreaths, and lights will glitter like stars in the sky. The bar will see fewer tourists and more locals. Everything will change. Except me.

It fell. It's time.

Tessa's words haunt me. She's right. It is time.

As another gust of wind pushes across the bay, and a newspaper blows out of an old man's hand. He reaches for it, but the wind makes it dance right past his fingertips and straight into my chest.

He winces apologetically as I try to piece it back together for him.

"Not a problem," I say, staring at the newspaper, twisting it until the pages are all facing the right way. "Not sure what you were reading—" I stop when my attention catches on the inky-black letters I've been waiting for.

Now Hiring. Bristol Fire Department.

It's time.

"That's okay, young man. I was just about to throw it in the trash.

Do you want it?" he asks, eyeing me, a flicker of recognition lighting his gray eyes. "Hey, aren't you—"

Before he can say anything further and remind me of who I used to be, a famous baseball player with the entire world at his fingertips, I fold the paper under my arm. "Thank you. I'm late for work, but I appreciate it. Have a good day."

I walk fast so he doesn't have time to respond. I'm almost past the dock when the wind kicks up again. I fold the paper over a few more times and put it in my back pocket, not wanting to risk the breeze stealing it again. When I look up, I'm struck by the most beautiful sight.

Standing on the dock, her red hair whipping around, her head turned up to the clouds, as if making a wish, is Hailey.

It fell. It's time.

The words echo in my mind as I take her in.

I have to make my move. *This* is the mix-up I've been waiting for.

When my friend's eyes meet mine, they soften in a way they never have, not while looking at me, at least. When I approach, Hailey doesn't smile or tease me about being late like she normally does. She just waits for me to reach her, and when I do, I don't hesitate. I take her in my arms and stare into her hazel eyes—I'd always thought they were brown, but they're closer to a gorgeous green, like the evergreen Christmas tree we decorate every year at my parents' house—then she lifts her chin just slightly, and it's enough to signal that she wants me to kiss her. She *wants* this as much as I do.

My lips mold against hers, and she moans into my mouth before she slips her tongue against mine, opening for more, and that damn near makes me pick her up and take her back to my place.

But I don't. I dip her, *romantically*, sweetly, showing her I can be the guy for her. I can be the one she's been waiting for, because she's definitely the girl I've been pining after for months. The one I can't stop thinking about.

She lives in my dreams, in my thoughts, and I can't get over the feel of her in my arms right now.

I pull back. I don't want to get ahead of myself. I want her to know that I'm interested in more than just the physical. She's constantly bringing men around the bar, and I want her to know that I'm not like that. I won't be another guy who cycles into her life and then disappears. We're friends first, and soon, I hope we'll be a lot more.

Hailey looks at me with shock on her face and brings her hands to her lips. "What the—" she starts before I interrupt her.

"Don't say anything. Just…*that was perfect.* I've wanted to do that for so long. Meet me for dinner tomorrow night. Roberto's. Seven o'clock. If you show up, I'll know you want to give this a shot. If not, no hard feelings. We'll go back to normal. Like this never happened. Okay?"

Her green eyes cloud, and her brows pull together in confusion.

I squeeze her hand to reassure her. "I really hope you show up." Leaning in, I tip her chin and kiss her softly again. "I'm ready. I hope you are too."

CHAPTER 3

HAILEY

Could this day possibly get any worse? The keg Shawn brought up last night tastes off, and the meat delivery company called to tell me they're delayed. Plus my grandmother has summoned me to the estate for some unknown reason.

"I don't have time for this!" I scream, kicking the keg and shrieking because I'm wearing sandals and that hurt like a bitch. I'm bitterly holding on to the last bit of warm weather before winter comes and steals the only happiness I have left.

"Whoa, Hailes, what are you doing?" My best friend, Amelia, whips me around to face her and frowns down at my bleeding toe. "Stay still. Let me get something to clean that up."

She grabs the first aid kit from under the bar as I sit on the cooler and hold my foot up for her to bandage.

"Thanks," I mutter, biting my lip to keep the tears at bay. I don't cry. Neither does Amelia. We're stone-cold bitches. Or at least we used to be. She's been an emotional basket case since her secret husband came back to Bristol. I'm glad they finally stopped fighting what the rest of us knew was inevitable.

"Is there a reason you're beating up the keg?" she asks, squatting beside me and biting back a smile.

I elbow her, almost knocking her on her ass.

"Hey, I'm trying to help you!"

I laugh. "No, you're making fun of me."

"Because you got into an unwinnable fight with an inanimate object. A big, heavy, inanimate object. Seems kinda like bringing a knife to a gunfight."

I roll my eyes. "Okay, Taylor Swift."

One side of her mouth quirks up. "Seriously, what's going on?"

I huff. "The keg is skunked, we're out of burgers and the meat won't be here until tomorrow, and to top it all off, you're all smiley and won't tell me why."

"I'm sorry, Hailes. I'll call Shawn and ask him to grab burgers on his way in. Tom's should have enough to get us through the night." She ignores my dig about her happy mood and gets out her phone.

I just want her to admit she's back together with her ex. I could use something happy to focus on.

Everything else is falling apart. Managing a restaurant is hard enough, but managing one on the water in Bristol, which is almost always a mob scene because of the incredible views our spot offers, is something else. We have to be prepared for everything. Dinner crowds, college kids, late-night music fans, big drinkers. You name it and our bar has it.

"Thanks, Ames." I stand and inspect my big toe, which she's wrapped tightly. I've got to change my shoes, or I'll be subjected to a lecture from my grandmother about how impractical I am. I'll never hear the end of it.

When I come back with more appropriate foot attire, Amelia is humming to music with a big smile on her face again.

"Seriously, you need to tell me what's going on," I beg.

"Just happy is all," she replies, shrugging. She's driving me nuts. "Get out of here. Isn't it your day off?"

I wish I was on the schedule today. Then I could ignore my grandmother's edict. "Yes, but I've been summoned by my grandmother. Not exactly something I'm looking forward to."

Amelia nods just as my older sister, Caris, walks up the stairs, her blond hair pulled back tightly. I rarely see her during the day since she's so busy with her new winery and the matchmaking business that operates out of it. Everything Caris touches turns to gold, it seems. "Hey, Car. Were you summoned to grandmother's as well?"

She nods and presses her lips together. "Yes, but I have to stop at the hospital to drop off something for Dad before I head over. Want to ride with me?"

My stomach squeezes at the mention of Dad. "I was there earlier. Maddox will think I'm stalking him if I show up again," I reply.

Caris huffs a laugh. "That's why I'm here. Maddox said he wouldn't hate one of our burgers."

I wince. "Ugh, we're out of burgers."

The last thing I want is for Caris to know that I've screwed up something else, but I can't exactly hide this. It's not my fault that the meat is delayed, but that's not how it looks. I run the bar, and she handles everything else. Her law firm, the winery, the ice cream shop, *and* Dad's care. While she handles all her responsibilities with grace, this damn bar throws me for a loop regularly.

My sister turns to me and cocks her head to the side, her lips tipped in a frown. "We don't have burgers?"

I grind my teeth. "I've got it covered. Shawn is picking some up from Tom's. He'll probably be here in a half hour, so if you want to wait…"

She nods and heads for a stool at the bar. "Yes. Maddox never asks for anything."

I bite the inside of my lip. No, he doesn't. Her best friend—one of the best-looking men I've ever seen—is a giver, not a taker. Since

our father's stroke last year, he's been handling his care on top of his regular patients. And he does so without complaint. Probably because he's always been in love with Caris.

Maddox spends almost every holiday with us. He even subjects himself to Sunday dinners with my grandmother. I can't imagine a man would do that for anything less than love. If only Caris realized what's right in front of her. He would give her everything if she'd see him for what he was.

I'm not bitter or anything.

"All right. I'll see you back at the ranch, then," I say, infusing the words with a positivity I don't feel. I don't know why I'm in such a funk. Not much gets to me, but I'm off today. Like something is in the air. Things just *keep* going wrong, and something tells me the burgers and skunky beer aren't the end of it.

Summoning my inner goddess, I let out a breath and smile as I walk out of my bar. *Things are going to get better. They couldn't possibly get worse.*

CHAPTER 4

SHAWN

Walking on a cloud, I hum as I carry the bags of burgers toward the entrance of the restaurant. Nothing could ruin my mood right now. Before I made it to work, I received a text from Amelia that Hailey needed me to pick up meat from the market. Apparently, I left her tongue tied back at the docks, so I shouldn't be surprised that she didn't ask me to do it herself. I shocked the hell out of myself as well.

Then, as if the Gods were really shining down on me, I ran into the fire chief at the grocery store. He's still got the application I submitted months ago on file and told me to come in for an interview tomorrow.

Everything is falling into place.

The dollar fell and I'm getting my wish. I shake my head at the ridiculous—but maybe believable—scenario as I open the front door.

The chef meets me when I step inside. He wears a big smile on his face and helps me carry the meat in. "Poor Hailey was a mess earlier. Thanks for grabbing this."

When was she here? And why was she a mess?

I shake the concern from my head. I'm *not* overthinking this. I overthink everything. Charlotte and I have that in common. My mind starts to race, and suddenly, I've taken a little thing and made it so much worse.

"No problem, Chef. I'm going to head upstairs and see if Ames needs anything. I'll see you in a bit."

He nods as he continues unloading the groceries.

I take the stairs two at a time, excited to tell Amelia about the kiss. She and I grew close after her brother Jack proposed to my sister this past summer. We grew even closer when she asked me to be her pretend boyfriend so that her ex-husband would leave her alone. I'm pretty sure it backfired since he hangs around the bar even more now than he used to, but I don't think she minds anymore. I'd bet money they're back together by Christmas. The fake dating also seemed to bother Hailey. It was the first time I really thought we'd have a shot. And now we just might.

"Ladies, I finally made my move!" I say with a big smile, grabbing Amelia and spinning her in a circle.

She laughs and smacks me as I put her down. "What move?"

Caris leans across the bar with her hand under her chin and a devious smile on her face. "A move on my sister?"

I don't even try to hide my excitement. "I saw her down at the docks about a half hour ago. She looked so beautiful. Took my damn breath away. And I thought to myself, *what am I waiting for*? I walked right up to her, turned her around, and told her I'd been dying to do this for weeks. Then I dipped her and kissed her. And she kissed me back!"

Caris and Amelia look at one another, brows furrowed almost identically, and then Amelia turns back to me. "This was a half hour ago?" She looks above my head at the clock.

I follow her gaze before replying, "Yup. I kissed her and told her to meet me for dinner tomorrow night at Roberto's. If she shows, I'll know it was more than just the most earth-shattering kiss I've ever experienced."

30

Amelia looks at Caris again and nods with a smile plastered on her face. The girl doesn't smile. Not like that anyway. When she smiles, you feel it in your bones because they're so rare. Hmm. "Right. Wow. Well, that's great, Shawn. The keg is empty. Can you grab one from downstairs?"

I dip my head in an *at your service* gesture and leave the ladies to gossip about my news. It took me long enough, so it's probably a shock. But I'm tired of waiting around for my life to change. I'm doing what I set out to do when I moved back home. I'm taking control of my life.

JULES
ICE CREAM

SUPER PREMIUM ICE CREAM

SUPER PREMIUM ICE CREAM

CHAPTER 5

JULES

So this is how the other half lives? The address my grandmother provided brings me to what can only be described as a mansion. It's like I stepped back into the Gilded Age. I half expect Daisy and Gatsby to make an appearance. The emerald-green lawn rolls down to the bay in splendor with not a single blade of grass longer than the next. Like someone wanders around measuring the exact height and trimming pieces that dare to stand above the others. In the distance, a white tent billows in the wind. I bet if I walked back there, I'd find a dance floor and a chandelier. I'm not sure if my grandmother has a party planned or if this entire scene is regularly set up on her property. Maybe she's a partier. Maybe she hosts events weekly. It gives my heart a pang to think that while I lived without any knowledge that these people existed, they continued to live opulently and celebrated life on the regular. So much for wondering if they were pining after my existence.

The mansion is constructed of light gray stone, and the blue bay beyond is visible through the grandiose windows that line both the front and the back walls. Pausing to buy myself a moment of courage, I pick up my phone and flip it into selfie mode. I can't imagine I'm dressed up enough to meet my family.

Family.

I've only ever had my mom. It's odd to think there are other people out there who share my DNA.

Sisters. Not just people. A father. And a grandmother.

Maybe more. I have no clue if my father remarried and had more children. I could have half-siblings as well. As if Amy can sense my spiraling, a text pops up, stopping me from focusing on how my hair is frizzy and unkempt despite how I attempted to tame it in the car, and how my freckles are peeking out from the makeup I expertly applied at the airport when I landed this morning. Even my green top looks wrinkled. I don't look anything like the daughter of Helene Kingsley. She'd be mortified if she knew I was meeting my grandmother dressed like this.

There's nothing more important than lipstick and cleavage, my mother always says. *You have to know when to show it. With men the answer is* always, she'd say with a laugh. *But raise it up if you're dealing with a woman.*

My top has a simple bow that ties at the neck. No cleavage. Mom would be happy.

Amy: You look beautiful. They're going to love you. Call me when you're settled, and my offer still stands. Say the word and I'll be on the next plane.

I'm smiling at Amy's sweet words when the door swings open, revealing a man standing across from me. When I look up, startled, I almost drop my phone.

"Can I help you?" he asks.

I have to bite back a giggle. He's dressed in a three-piece suit and looks down his nose at me like I'm a peasant before pulling out an honest-to-goodness pocket watch. I'm about to call him Watson when a small woman with a cane appears behind him, and I lose my voice.

"Well, don't just stand there, Bernard. Let the girl in." Her voice is shrill. It doesn't fit her small stature at all. But she stands tall, even in her petite frame, and the way the man straightens at her tone adds to her prim stature.

The most shocking part of her appearance, though, is her red hair. It's almost the same shade as mine. After a lifetime of wondering, I can finally see where I get it from. My mother would be green with envy. Her hair is almost all gray if she doesn't dye it regularly, but one look at this woman tells me there isn't anything fake about her. Despite the fact that my grandmother obviously has money, she doesn't involve herself with frivolous things like Botox or facial cream, if her wrinkles are any indication. I can practically hear her saying, "Dear, humans are meant to have wrinkles. It's a sign of aging and nothing to be ashamed of."

We've only shared letters back and forth for the last few months, but in this moment, it's like I've known her my whole life. She holds out her arms and her eyes get misty as she takes me in. "My Jules. My God, you are gorgeous."

Tears prick at my eyes. *My Jules.* Family. A grandmother. I rush past Bernard and hug her, leaning slightly, but since I'm not tall, it's not much of a reach. The unexpected punch of expensive perfume mixed with cookies floods my nose, making the tears fall faster.

"It's so nice to finally meet you," I say, remembering my manners as I pull away and curtsy.

Her eyes light up, and Bernard snickers behind me. Yeah, I just freaking curtsied at my grandmother like she's royalty and I'm a peasant. Fortunately, she bites back her own laugh, holds out her arm for me, and turns toward the patio. "Come on, dear, let's get reacquainted over tea."

Once we're seated and the tea has been served, she gets right down to business. "Are your things in the car? I've had Bernard set up the guest bedroom, so we'll have him grab everything and unpack for you." She looks at me over her cup of tea expectantly.

"I didn't bring my things. Or a car. I figured I'd stay in a hotel. I didn't want to assume…" I drift off uncomfortably.

She tilts her head and regards me. "*Assume*? You're my granddaughter. Of course you'll stay here. Both of your sisters will be required to live here for the duration of your stay so that you can all get reacquainted. All my girls under one roof." Then, as if she hasn't made her point, she lifts her face to the sky. "As it should have been all along."

I'm not sure what God has to do with her anger. He wasn't the one who separated us. It was my parents and their crazy scheme to divorce without co-parenting. It stings even thinking about the man who so easily gave me up. At least I know it wasn't my grandmother's idea.

"What about my father?" I ask. The man shouldn't deserve even a moment of my concern, but I can't help but ask.

Her brows furrow, but she relaxes the wrinkles before I can read her expression. "He's indisposed at the moment. I'm afraid you won't be able to meet him just yet."

Figures. The man probably doesn't want to meet me. Can't face his mistakes. Well, I don't want to meet him anyway.

"That's okay. I can stay at the hotel. I'm only here for the weekend anyway. No sense in uprooting everyone for me."

Her teacup clatters to the table and she stares me down. "But you've only just arrived."

I bite my lip. "I have a life back in California. I can't stay here indefinitely." That's an exaggeration. I hardly exist in California. I'm between jobs and living with my mother. And outside of Amy, I doubt anyone will miss me.

My grandmother smiles, as if she's in on some secret. "Just wait until you meet your sisters before you make any long-term decisions. I have a proposition for all three of you, but I don't want to share the details until they get here."

My chest tightens. I was prepared to meet my grandmother, but I didn't know I'd be meeting my sisters today. I'm not ready. I would have dressed up. My hair is a mess, and I'm not even wearing lipstick. A girl *needs* lipstick for something like this.

As if my inner thoughts are written across my face—I turn as red as a tomato when I get flustered, so they practically are—my grandmother reaches across the table and takes one of my hands before I can twist them anxiously. "They're going to love you. Hailey is a bit flighty and quick with her tongue, but it's just her defense mechanism. She's never known the gentleness of a mother. And Caris—she's poised. Holds the weight of the world on her shoulders. But spend time with them and you'll see how kind and spirited they are."

I find myself biting back my own retort. They grew up without a mother, so I should go easy on them? Well, I grew up without all of this. Without family. But my grandmother isn't to blame for that. Neither are my sisters. And I'm sure she didn't mean anything by it. Besides, my mother raised me never to speak back to my elders. I'm certainly not going to disappoint her now.

"Lovely. Do you have somewhere I can freshen up before they get here?"

"Of course. I'll have Bernard show you to your room."

CHAPTER 6

HAILEY

I pull up to the estate in my dirty, old, deeply offensive vehicle. That's what my grandmother thinks anyway. I called it lived-in, but she's never liked my Jeep. Unlike Caris, who picked a brand-new Beamer for her seventeenth birthday, I went to the dealership myself and bought the Jeep Wrangler with money I'd made working every afternoon and weekend during high school. My family's money has never interested me. With it came strings. And unlike Pinocchio, I don't dance for anyone.

Until now, that is.

I want the restaurant. Caris can have everything else. She's earned it. But I've put in the blood, sweat, and tears for the bar. My bandaged toe is proof of that. So if I also have to give away a bit of my dignity by playing along with whatever my grandmother's latest scheme is, then I'll do it. "Do your worst, Evie," I mutter to myself, walking up the steps of her grand entryway.

As he always does, Bernard appears behind me. "Ms. Milsom, your grandmother is waiting for you on the lawn."

Wrapping my arms around the overdressed man, I smile. "Oh, Bernie, I've told you a thousand times. Call me Hailey. You used to change my diapers. Don't you think we're past the formalities?"

He shrugs me off and huffs. But his lips twitch slightly, as if he enjoys my banter. It must be so boring working here now that I've moved out.

My grandmother sits on the stone patio. She's surrounded by flowers and propped up by a pillow like a queen. Eveline Milsom is the empress of her manor and the head of this family, whether I like it or not. I drop a kiss onto the cheek she tips toward me and sit down opposite her. There are tea settings for four people. What in God's name does she have up her sleeve now?

"Bernie, you joining us for tea?" I tease.

He gives his head a shake and walks off.

"Must you go on like that, Hailey?" she trills, looking at me wearily.

I fluff up my shoulders in a little dance and raise my eyes in excitement. "Yes, Grandmama, I must." She hates when I call her that. God, I forgot how much I love annoying this woman.

Movement by the back door slider draws our attention. A woman walks out, and I'm rendered completely speechless. Her hair is a shade lighter than mine, as if she actually maintains her red hair, whereas I just let it be. However, despite that one difference and the Pollyanna outfit she's wearing, she's my doppelgänger. I jump up in fascination. "Holy shit, Grandmama. What kind of Freaky Friday act did you pull?"

The girl's eyes bulge as she stares at me. She looks at my grandmother and then back at me again. In what can only be described as sheer lunacy, I hold up my hand like I'm looking at a mirror and she's my reflection. I move it back and forth, and my anti-reflection mimics me, so I put the other one up. And dammit, she follows. God, this is fun. I move into the vogue routine, and that's where I lose her. "Aw, you were doing so well!" I cry, then look back to my scowling grandmother.

Where's Amelia when you need her? That girl would laugh

at me. I slip my phone out of my pocket to FaceTime her, but my grandmother's commanding voice stops me.

"Hailey, sit down."

I turn back to the odd vision before me and wink. "Don't worry, her bark's a lot worse than her bite."

The girl nods, but aside from that, she's silent. *Is she mute? I mean, that would explain the miming thing. And where did she come from? Is she a long-lost cousin? How freaking cool would that be?*

"Juliana, as you can see, this is Hailey. Hailey, this is your sister, Juliana."

I do one of those double takes like characters do in the movies and then point at my grandmother and laugh. "Oh, you're a funny one!"

The mute girl is gawking at me. No laughter. If anything, she looks concerned about my welfare.

With the way they're watching me, I let the laughter die, clear my throat, and cross my legs. "Okay, you're starting to freak me out. What's going on?"

"Precisely what I said was going on. Have you ever known me to make light of something so serious?" my grandmother asks. The veins in her face contract, and I find myself focusing on her hands instead. But they're equally veiny and do nothing to ease the tension sneaking its way through my shoulders.

The girl across from me, the one who practically mirrors my entire being, holds out her hand. "Jules Kingsley," she says in a soft voice. Unlike my fingers, hers are perfectly manicured. Because I run a business and am used to people sticking their hands in my face, my body takes over, and I shake the outstretched limb.

"Okay, Jules, what's your angle?" I ask, pulling back and crossing my arms. This girl can't just waltz in pretending to be family and fool a kind old lady into leaving her part of our inheritance.

Okay, no one would describe my grandmother as kind, nor is she likely to get swindled, but I've seen these things on Lifetime before. It's uncanny how similar we look, but I'm not buying what she's selling.

"My angle—" she starts, her brow furrowed.

But my grandmother holds up her hand, as if she's protecting sweet Juliana from an oncoming car. How motherly of her. "Hailey Mae Milsom, use your manners."

My manners? I'm pretty sure even Emily Post doesn't have an instruction manual for how to treat someone who's claiming to be your sister to scam your grandmother out of her millions. With my arms still folded and my body pushed back from the table, I relent. "Fine. When is your birthday?"

"August sixteenth."

I roll my eyes. Anyone could look that up.

"What's your father's name?"

The girl looks at my grandmother and then back to me before replying. "Thomas."

I shrug. "See, not my sister. My dad—"

Before I can finish the sentence, she replies, "Is Henry Milsom. He was married to Helene Milsom for eight years. They were high school sweethearts. They separated and agreed that my mother would take me, and our father would keep you and our older sister, Caris. Have I left anything out?" she asks my grandmother smugly.

My grandmother's lips are pressed in a line. She simply shakes her head. Then she digs around in the little pocket purse she carries at all times. It normally holds change and mints. It's odd how such a wealthy woman thinks tipping doormen with quarters is appropriate, but it works for her.

She slides a locket across the table and, with her chin, motions for me to open it. The gold locket has a rose engraved into it. It's worn, as if she's held it between her fingers for years. I slide it open, and sure enough, on the inside there is a picture with two identical babies.

Me. Times two. And I've never in my life seen it before. My throat goes dry.

"My dad wouldn't hide this from me," I whisper.

The girl raises her brow. "The same man who so easily gave up his child?"

My grandmother slams her fist on the table. "Enough. You are sisters, and I will not have you treating each other like this."

Eveline has spoken.

I swallow my anger. It's all too much to wrap my head around. I need Caris. She'll confirm that this isn't true. She was seven when our mother disappeared. I was six months old. We don't talk about her, but I can't imagine Caris would have hidden that I had a twin. This is insanity.

With a soft voice, the girl replies, "I'm very sorry. I was as shocked as you are when I found out. I can imagine how this must look. But I swear I don't want anything from you. Or you," she says, meeting my grandmother's eyes.

My grandmother shakes her head and covers her hand, showing her a kindness she's never shown me. Gentleness. Affection.

I lived in her house for twenty-five years and never got so much as a hug. But my long-lost twin sister comes back, and suddenly, she's rolling out the red carpet.

"Nonsense. You're my grandchild. You're a Milsom. You're entitled to the same things Hailey and Caris are entitled to."

I roll my eyes and settle deeper into the chair. There is no sense fighting this. Caris will handle it. She's the lawyer. She'll prove that this girl is nothing but a money-grubbing liar. I don't care if she looks like me. Or if there are two identical babies in that locket. My father would never hide this from me. We told each other everything. I can't...*just no*.

It's *not* possible.

"Listen, as interesting as this has been, I have to get back to the bar. Jules, it was nice meeting you. Grandma, I'll stop by later this week."

I stand, hoping to make a break for it before my grandmother can get her bearings, but the woman is always one step ahead of *everyone*. She slams her hand down on the table again, and I slink back into my chair.

"I understand this is a shock, Hailey, and we all know you don't handle change so well," she grumbles, "but this isn't only about you. I'm getting up in age…"

Oh, here we go. I tune out her five-minute rant and focus on my mirror image across the table. She's peering at me, looking just as perturbed as I feel. Finally, the saccharine charade is wearing off. Knowing that I'm going to have to live with whatever plan my grandmother has set in motion, I make a calculated decision.

"I'm sorry, Grandmama, you're right. This has all just taken me by surprise. I mean, Dad never mentioned Jules, nor did Caris. *Or you*, for that matter. But, of course, she's my sister. I'm sorry, Jules. Let's start fresh."

The girl narrows her eyes, but when my grandmother smiles at her, she slips back into the sweet girl again.

Yeah, I see the real you, missy. You're not fooling me.

"Of course. I know this is a shock," she replies, raising her brow at me.

She's got my number too. It's okay. I'm not trying to win her over. Just my grandmother.

"So, tell us Grandmama. What is it you'd like us to do?" Let's get to the point so I can get back to the bar and slam back enough shots to erase this day.

"As I was saying, I'm getting up there in age, and I would like to see my granddaughters enjoy their inheritance rather than waiting until I croak."

Jules's eyes fly wide, and she puts her hand over my grandmother's. "Oh, please don't talk like that. We just met. I've never even had a grandmother."

Internally, I roll my eyes. The girl deserves an academy award.

My grandmother smiles and then turns back to me. She won't be hearing the same sentiment from me. Not that I don't love my grandmother, but I've been waiting for her to tell me what this meeting is all about, and she's about to lay it out. She doesn't do false bouts of affection. Well, not with Caris and me. But Juliana seems to have opened up a different side to the old lady.

"All you have ever wanted was to run the restaurant, Hailey. And you've done a wonderful job managing it."

Color me shocked. My grandmother has never so much as said I had a capable bone in my body, let alone described any of my achievements as wonderful. "Uh, thank you," I stammer in surprise.

"And Caris, of course, has the land with the winery now, which she continues to grow."

I nod. Yeah, Caris took that piece of land and is building a gold mine. A winery, a hotel, the distillery, and the restaurant. It's beyond impressive and all because of her vision. To say I'm proud would be an understatement.

"And then there's my sweet Juliana. When your mother took you away, I opened Jules Ice Cream. It's part of a building downtown, and it will be yours."

I close my eyes to ignore the pain in my chest. Not because I want the building. Not because the money means anything to me. But because every Saturday morning, every summer, our father took us to Jules. And every damn time, he gazed wistfully at the sign.

He knew. I feel it in my bones.

I may not have a connection to the girl across from me, but my father did. And it breaks my heart that he never shared it with me. And he might not ever have the chance to.

"I-I didn't come here for your money," the girl stammers.

"Yeah, well, like she said, it's your right," I reply, accepting the truth of the statement. "Whether you want it or not, you're a Milsom, and with that comes rights and responsibilities. Welcome to the family," I say glumly.

She shakes her head. "I-I'm not even staying in town. I just came to meet you all. I have a life in California." She twists her fingers together, her eyes darting between my grandmother and me.

My grandmother stops her from twisting her fingers by holding her hand steady. "We only just met. You can't go back so soon."

"I-I don't know what my plan is," the girl says, chancing a look in my direction.

My grandmother looks at me too. Like they're waiting for me to beg her to stay. I just stare back. She's looking to the wrong person for validation.

"You'll stay here," my grandmother says again. "You, Caris, and Hailey. All my girls under one roof. It's what I want."

It's not intentional, I swear, but a loud screeching laugh tumbles out of me, and both women stare at me in alarm. "Sorry, but you can't be serious. You think Caris is going to move back into this house?" I laugh harder. Yeah, good luck with that. She'll lose her shit when she finds out about all of this. It would almost be worth agreeing to this ridiculous request just to watch my older sister have a mental and emotional breakdown daily dealing with my grandmother again. But the truth is, I would be right with her. I did twenty-five years. I served my sentence. It's time for my reward. The bar. I've earned it. The girl across from me, though? Not so much.

"Yes. It's my requirement. The two of you need time to get to know one another."

"I really don't know if I can stay. I'll have to talk to my mother."

I roll my eyes. So her mother—our mother—is still alive. "Does your mother know you're here?"

Her eyes flash with uncertainty, but it's quickly replaced by sympathy...*for me*. I don't need her pity. I'm sure I got the better end of the stick. My dad is awesome. And a woman who could leave her child behind...her daughters? Let's just say not knowing her doesn't hurt my feelings.

"I kind of told her I didn't want to speak to her and not to contact me. But I believe she knows I'm here," Jules says, looking down at her hands. It's so incredibly odd to see my hands but with creamy smooth skin and manicured nails. No wonder my grandmother is in love with her. She's the version of me she tried so hard to create. Like my alter ego or some crazy shit. Yeah, I can't live here with them. I'm not interested in all the comparisons that will inevitably be made. I need another plan. One that will get me the restaurant and my freedom.

"Grams, I have a suggestion. It seems like my sister and I could use some time alone..."

Jules wears a look of surprise, but I continue.

"If you intend on leaving her Jules Ice Cream, then she could probably use help fixing up the apartment above it so she'll have somewhere to live," I hedge.

My grandmother raises her eyes as if apprising my offer. I see her working the idea around in her mind, so I continue, not giving her time to find a flaw in my plan.

"The apartment needs work, but I think it could help us bond... working and living there...*together*."

The glint in my grandmother's eye lets me know I've nailed it. "You'd help Juliana with the apartment *and live there*?" she asks slowly, like she's really working this idea out. "And in return, I'd give you the bar now?" She knows my terms. Good, no need to sugarcoat it.

I nod.

Juliana's attention darts back and forth between my grandmother and me. My grandmother and I aren't *complete* opposites. The cold hard calculations are an inherited trait. Clearly, Jules does not have the same fortitude. I smirk. I've got this in the bag.

"While I appreciate the offer…*really*," she says, meeting my eyes with kindness. "I haven't made any decisions regarding staying here. This is all…*a lot*."

You're telling me.

I blow out a breath. "I need to get back to the bar. And I need time to get packed up. How about we meet at Jules Ice Cream tomorrow? I can pick up the necessary cleaning supplies and we can go from there." I offer her this modicum of a thread. If she wants to take me up on it, great. If not, I'll continue on with my life as I've been doing for the last twenty-eight years.

JULES
ICE CREAM
SUPER PREMIUM ICE CREAM
SUPER PREMIUM ICE CREAM

CHAPTER 7

JULES

The evening's events were certainly unexpected. Once Hailey left my grandmother's house, Caris appeared, and she was far less antagonistic. She wasn't exactly warm, but she didn't seem as surprised to see me.

"So you're the one Shawn kissed," she muses after our grandmother finally turns in for the night.

"Shawn?"

"By the docks?"

I stare at her for a moment, open-mouthed. After all that had happened today, I'd completely forgotten how it started. With the stranger pulling me into his arms and kissing the life out of me. How I managed to forget that moment is something I'll never understand. I'd never been kissed that way before. In fact, no one had ever stirred the kind of feelings he had with just the press of his lips against mine. The heat in my belly, the quickness of my heart rate. It literally stole the words out of my mouth and took my breath away.

Cheeks heating at the memory, I blink a few times and clear my throat. "Uh, yeah, that was me."

Caris blows out a breath. "He's a really nice guy. You should get to know him."

I shrug and smile sheepishly. "I'm a little overwhelmed with everything that's happened today. The last thing I have time for is a man."

"But you're staying, right?" she rushes out as if she really wants me here. It's surprising based on how cool and collected she's been until now.

I haven't given it much thought, but I do plan to stay. Even if my twin sister hates me and my grandmother is a bit controlling, I want to stick around to see what it's like to be part of this family. Especially when Caris is looking at me like she is right now. Like a concerned older sister. It's…comforting, if not a bit startling.

I twist my lips. "Honestly, I don't think Hailey wants me to stick around."

Caris huffs a laugh. "Hailey is used to doing whatever Hailey wants at any given moment. It will take her some time to get used to you." She reaches out and pats my knee. "But seriously, if she gives you a hard time, let me know. She can be difficult, but it comes from a good place." She chuckles. "*Mostly*."

I groan. What the heck have I signed up for?

Twelve hours later, I'm standing outside the ice cream shop waiting for my sister to meet me at our new home.

"Morning," I say cheerfully, holding out a cup of coffee to my twin.

It really is uncanny how much we look alike. Aside from the hair color and eye color, we're identical. Her hair is a touch more muted than mine, and while her eyes are brown, mine are green. Oh, and her choice of clothing. Does she always wear ripped jeans and T-shirts? She's in a white tee now, whereas I'm in a lavender top and slacks.

Hailey eyes the cup and takes it from me. "Uh, thanks, but it's lunchtime," she says, bringing the drink to her lips. When she closes her eyes and swallows, I can't help but smile. If there's one thing I do well, it's make a mean cup of coffee. Pastries too. It's sort of my unofficial *thing*. Something I discovered while working in a bakery between acting gigs. Until I got "laid off" by the man I was seeing, who apparently already had a wife.

I really *don't* have much of a life to go back to in Los Angeles.

Just another reason I'm so excited to get into this shop. I have an idea. It's something I can do on my own. Without my mother's help. But I won't know if it's even a possibility until I get my eyes on the space and see how Hailey and I get along.

"Well, hot damn, this coffee is delicious. You get it at Coffee Depot?"

I squint. "Huh?"

Hailey shakes her head. "The coffee shop. My friend Sara runs it. Did you get this from her?"

"Uh, no. I made it at..." God, I almost said home. As if her grandmother's house is my home. "At the estate." As soon as the words come out of my mouth, I want to smack myself in the face. First, I curtsy at my grandmother, and now I'm calling the house they grew up in an estate.

Hailey laughs. "That's good, Red."

"Red?"

"Yeah, like the hair. You must dye yours or something. Mine has never been that vibrant."

I shrug and twist a strand. "Uh, yeah. My mother and I have monthly salon appointments."

This time Hailey flinches like she's been slapped.

I just keep stepping in it.

She turns and motions to the door. "You got the key? Let's check out your new digs."

"Hailey, I'm—"

Before I can get the apology out of my mouth, Hailey holds her hand up to silence me. "It's fine. This is going to be awkward for a while. You love your mom, I love my dad, and neither of them loved us enough to figure things out. It's probably best if we just don't discuss it. I'm sure you have opinions about my father, and since he's my best friend…well, we just won't agree. So let's focus on this for now. If we're walking around on eggshells, we'll never win, and I don't do tip toeing well, as I'm sure you'll learn."

I nod, appreciating her honesty. I hand her the key. "How come it's not open?"

"Uh, we, um, had too much going on after the summer season to manage it." She pushes on the door. "You would really be doing us a solid by taking over."

I let that thought settle. I haven't made any decisions. And running an ice cream shop was never my dream.

"I left the cleaning supplies in the car. Let's see how upstairs looks. It's been a while since I've been up there. But if it's anything like my place above the bar…well, let's just say I hope you're good with a mop."

I groan. I can't say I've ever even used a mop. But I can't tell Hailey that my mother has always had a cleaning lady. It would just re-affirm her belief that I'm a princess who can't handle any of this. But I'm perfectly capable of cleaning up a bit. This will be fine. It will all be *fine*.

Hailey flicks on the lights and we study the room in silence. "Just as I remembered," she whispers so quietly I don't think the words were meant for me.

I scan the pink wallpaper and the big sign decorated with a multi-color triple-scoop cone that says *Jules Ice Cream*. The glass containers are empty, but the labels denoting each flavor remain.

Limoncello, chocolate, tiramisu, truffled caramel. Jeez, this is as fancy as the places out in California. Although I don't see any avocado ice cream. Thank God.

"Is there a room in the back?"

That's what I'm really wondering. Is there an area I could turn into a small kitchen? A place to bake. An ice cream shop is great, but in order to make this place profitable year-round, desserts and coffee would be ideal.

Hailey shrugs. "Not sure. Feel free to look." She's staring at a picture on the wall.

I follow her gaze, shocked to find a small photograph of my mother and a little girl standing next to a jolly-looking man. He's got the biggest smile on his face and his arm wrapped around my mother.

"Holy crap. That must be—"

"My father and Caris," she finishes for me.

In the photo, my mother is pregnant. With us. I turn to look at my sister, watching her while she studies the image intently. She reaches toward it and then pulls her hand back as if she's afraid to get burned.

"It's the only picture of her left," she admits. "When we were growing up, we would come in here, and Caris would stand here and stare at it. I wasn't old enough to understand, and when I finally was, I didn't care to ask. I just knew that our mother had left and that we didn't talk about it because it made Caris quiet."

I blow out a long breath and shake my head. This is a lot harder than I thought it would be. Or maybe it's exactly as hard as it should be. "I'm going to check out the back," I say finally, unsure of what to say and knowing Hailey doesn't want to hear it anyway.

She nods, still focused on the photograph.

Walking through the swinging door, I'm pleasantly surprised to find an open space in the back. The room holds a small stove, several freezers, a fridge, and a wooden countertop in the center. It's not perfect, but it will do.

My fingers tingle as I imagine the changes I could make. The food I could bake. *Could this really be an option?*

"Do you want to see upstairs?" Hailey asks, interrupting my thoughts.

"Sure."

I follow her up the steps. It's musty, and the walls are covered in at least an inch of dust. "When was the last time someone stayed here?"

Hailey shrugs. "No idea if anyone ever has."

At the top of the landing, she points to one of two doors. "This is the apartment you'll be in. There's another one over there," she gestures to the second door with a wave of her hand, "it's unoccupied. If you wanted, you could probably rent it out to make more cash."

I simply nod. Cleaning out one apartment and the shop downstairs will be more than enough for me to handle right now. Besides, I haven't even decided whether I'm staying.

The door creaks open to reveal a dark, dingy room. The only light in the place filters in through a window that's practically gray from dust. Hailey tries several switches, but none of them produces anything. I grab my phone and flick on the flashlight. That was a mistake. The cobwebs have their own cobwebs, and spiders must be swarming the place. I get the chills just thinking about the tiny creatures. "I, uh, I don't think we can stay here."

Hailey eyes me. "Afraid of a little work, Red?"

"You're telling me you'd rather sleep here than at your grandmother's? She can't be that bad."

Hailey laughs. "I lived with her for twenty-five years. You lasted a night. Believe me, you have no idea what you're talking about. And if this is what it takes to get my grandmother to finally hand me the keys to the bar, I'll make this place the nicest home you've ever lived in."

Doubtful. But I won't be the Debbie downer. "Okay, where should we start?"

"Uh, let me call Dane and have him look at the power situation. I have to get to the bar for a bit. You want to hang downstairs until he can get here and get the lights on? Then we can work on cleaning this place up."

"Sounds like a plan."

"I'll stop at my apartment and pick up some bedding, then see what we can do about getting furniture in here."

I laugh. God, I am a princess. I hadn't even thought about where we'd sleep. "Why don't I run to the store and grab stuff? I feel bad that you're doing everything."

"Suit yourself," she replies. "Do you…need a credit card or money?"

I shake my head. "I'm not here for a free ride, Hailey. I do have my own money, you know."

She looks me up and down, judging every inch of me. "Yeah, that's obvious. Okay, Red. I'll see you later, then."

She heads out, leaving me alone with my flashlight and the spiders.

CHAPTER 8

SHAWN

"**A**nd you're sure this is what you want to do?" Chief Reilly asks me as I sit across from him at his desk, never breaking eye contact.

I nod. "After the accident," I try hard not to wince at the mere mention of my career-ending injury, "I had no idea what I wanted to do with my life. Bartending was an easy distraction. Some friends needed a bartender, and I needed an escape. My best friend in Tahoe was a firefighter, though, and seeing the dedication he and his guys had to Tahoe, the things they did for our community, it had a purpose. This is what I'm looking for, sir. A purpose."

It's not easy being so forthcoming. I hate being vulnerable, but I really want this job.

The chief studies me for a moment. "And you're sure you don't want to coach the baseball team in town? This is a dangerous job with rough hours, and I know you don't need the money."

That's true. But being a firefighter isn't about the paycheck. It's about belonging. Being part of a team again. It's what I miss the most about baseball. My friends, the camaraderie. It's what I was hoping to find when I moved here. I loved my friends in Tahoe, but I wanted to be close to my family. Truth be told, I needed them. Living in my sister's basement at thirty-five was never the plan, but neither was losing my career at my peak. And after losing everything that I thought mattered to me, I needed time to lick my wounds and figure out my next steps. *These* are my next steps. I'm ready to move forward with my life and stop hiding.

"I want this job, sir," I assure him.

"There won't be any concessions. Guys get held for overtime, and I know you don't need it—"

I interrupt him. "Sir, respectfully, my bank account balance won't affect the job I'll do here. I'm 100 percent committed."

"And what about the bar?" he asks, referring to my job at Thames, where I bartend on the weekends with my best friends Amelia and Hailey. It's strange to think that I've only known them for a few months. But in that time, they've become a lifeline for me in this town.

Especially Hailey. I smile just thinking about our kiss. About our date tonight.

"I'll make it work," I reply. "I'll speak to Hailey and Caris. If they need me, I'll work around my shifts here, but my first responsibility will always be with the fire department."

He nods. "Good." He riffles through a stack of papers on his desk and leans back in his chair before standing and holding out his hand. "Congratulations, Shawn, Welcome to the Bristol Fire Department."

Outside the chief's office, Dane, the local electrician, and Mason, who owns a farm in town, are standing next to the fire truck.

"I was wondering if the rumor was true," Dane says with a grin, holding his hand out to me.

I don't hesitate to shake it while raising a brow in question. "What rumor?"

"That *Shawn Chase* was joining the fire department." The way he says my name, as if my first and last names are always necessary when talking about me, goes right up my spine. The Shawn Chase everyone expects is long gone. I'm just a regular guy—nothing special. But Dane wears a genuine smile, so I let go of the itch to correct him.

"So long as I pass the physical," I say, although I'm not too concerned about it.

I turn to shake Mason's outstretched hand. Both men have spent many a night at Thames with the other firefighters, so while I wouldn't say we're buddies, we're friendly.

"We'll have to celebrate. You free for a drink?" Dane asks.

I want to say yes. I've wanted friends, people who were mine alone and not just friends of my sister's, for a long time. Charlotte and Jack's friends are nice, but I can never be sure if they're just being kind to me because that's what people do in small towns or if they genuinely care.

But as much as I want to hang with these guys, I have a date. And I have to tell Caris and Hailey about my new job.

"Rain check?" I counter. "I have to get to the bar to let the girls know about the new job."

Dane nods. "All right, but we're holding you to it, Babe."

I squint my eyes, and Mason shakes his head. "Because of baseball," he mutters.

I pull on my neck and huff under my breath. Shaking the reputation is going to be harder than I thought. "Got it. See you guys around."

Even though I don't love the nickname, it's progress. New job, new friends…and hopefully a new girlfriend after tonight.

With a smile on my face and feeling lighter than I have in years, I head to Thames. I want to tell Amelia about everything before my date tonight.

I enter the restaurant through the kitchen, waving at Chef.

"Shawn, just the man I wanted to see. My wife loved the margaritas you sent home with me last week. Can you put together another batch for Saturday? It's our anniversary and I'm making dinner."

I slap his hand, and he pulls me in for a hug. "You got it, Chef," I reply. "I'll do ya one better though. I'll teach you how to make them so you don't have to wait on me next time."

He laughs. "You'll give me your special recipe?"

It's not that special. It's all about the liquor—I use ghost tequila, but I appreciate how much everyone raves about my margaritas. They've become my specialty here. "Anything for you, Chef. Is Amelia by the bar?"

He nods. "Think she and Hailey are doing some prep work. Go on in. You can teach me tomorrow when you're on shift."

"Sounds good, thanks," I say, excited and also nervous about seeing Hailey. My nerves go out the window, though, as soon as I step through the swinging kitchen door and into the restaurant, where I spot two of my favorite people.

Before last year, I probably would not have looked in Hailey's direction. She's loud, sarcastic, and too young for me. But her friendliness and flirtatious behavior helped me come out of my shell in this new town. And after watching my friend Ryan fall for his outgoing, feisty, best friend, I have to admit, maybe opposites attract. And after the earth-shattering kiss we shared, I certainly know the chemistry is there.

As I round the corner, I hear Hailey talking to Amelia. Before they spot me, I fall back against the wall and listen like a complete creep.

"You don't understand. This is epically bad. Completely ridiculous. It's like I'm living in the damn twilight zone. I have no interest in exploring this relationship and no idea how to say that without coming off like a complete bitch."

"You're not a bitch. Just be honest."

"How?" she screeches. "I don't want things to change. Is that too much to ask? I want my bar, my best friends, my life. I want it all to remain the same. And this changes *everything*."

I swallow hard and close my eyes. *The kiss.* My grand gesture. It changed everything, but it's not what she wants.

Fuck.

"Things don't have to change, Hailes. But maybe it's not the worst thing. I mean, aren't you curious?"

"No. Not at *all*. It's not something I ever considered or ever would have wanted. I'm happy with how things are. I don't *want* things to change."

So much for what Amelia and I thought when we were faking our relationship. Apparently, it meant nothing to Hailey. I slam my head against the wall.

Unfortunately, whether she wants things to change or not, we can't go back to how things were. I turn from the bar and walk out before either woman spots me.

"Where you going?" Caris asks, walking toward me, her blond bob barely moving.

I clear my throat and pull on my neck. In a matter of minutes, my good mood and lighter attitude are out the window. I should have known it was too good to be true. Next to nothing has gone my way since my career ended. One day, maybe I'll accept that kind of happy is nothing but a pipe dream for me.

"Uh, I actually need to talk to you. I applied for a position at the fire department, and the chief just told me I got the job." I look at my shoes, trying to muster even a hint of the excitement that coursed through me minutes ago.

"Ah, shoot, what are we going to do without you behind the bar? Practically half of our customers come to see the *Great Shawn Chase*,"

BRITTANÉE NICOLE

she says, emphasizing my name in just the way I hate.

I wince. There's nothing great about me. The guy everyone expects me to be, the one stadiums full of people used to chant for on a nightly basis, doesn't exist anymore.

"But I get it," she says when I don't bite into her teasing humor. "You certainly don't *need* to work, so if being a firefighter is what you want to do, you should do it."

Like me, Caris probably has more money than she needs, but she's one of the hardest working people I've ever met. Between her law firm, the winery, and now the distillery, she's a force to be reckoned with. And yet somehow, she still finds time to swing by the bar to check on her sister's only responsibility.

"I won't leave you high and dry. I can work until you find someone," I offer.

Caris shrugs. "No worries. There's always a line of college kids looking to get that lucrative bartending position. You sure you don't want to keep a shift or two? Firefighters only work like two days a week, right?"

I laugh. Caris may come off as judgmental, but she rarely means to be. "I don't exactly need the money."

She sighs. "Right. Baseball money," she says on a laugh. "Damn shame you never played for the Red Sox. We coulda used your pitching."

I shake my head. If I was so needed, then why did I lose my position? In all aspects of my life, I'm just short of what people are seeking. Anxiety squeezes my chest, making it hard to breathe. I need to get out of here. "Anyway, if you need me, let me know. If not, consider this my notice."

"Okay. Thanks. You already talked to Hailey, right?"

I pull on my neck again. "Uh, you think you could handle that?"

She narrows her eyes for a moment, but then clears her expression and nods. "Yeah, I'll take care of it. Oh, any chance you're looking

64

for a place to live? I'm sure you're ready to give Jack and Charlotte their space."

She couldn't be more right about that. It's the next thing on my list. New job, new place to live, and I was hoping to add *new girlfriend*. Oh well. Two out of three isn't bad. I blow out a breath. "Yeah, I'm looking for a place."

Caris smiles. "Perfect. If you don't mind doing some work, I've got quite a deal for you."

Keeping busy with a new project is exactly what I need. I hold out my hand to Caris. "Just tell me what you need me to do."

JULES
ICE CREAM
SUPER PREMIUM ICE CREAM
SUPER PREMIUM ICE CREAM

CHAPTER 9

JULES

"You're Hailey's twin, right?" The man with the tool belt and a smile asks, shaking his head and staring at me. "I gotta be honest. It's freaky."

I laugh. "Yeah, I felt the same way the first time I saw her. Thanks for coming over so quickly."

He wipes the dust off his jeans, and the dimple in his cheek dips deeper. God, he's good-looking. Like freakily good-looking. "I'm not sure you really want light. This place is scary."

I sigh. You could say that again.

"It just needs a good scrubbing." I keep it simple. I don't want anyone to think I'm complaining. As it is, I'm fighting an uphill battle.

"Hailey asked me and the guys to deliver a bed and couch, so I'll be back in a few hours. You sure you'll be okay cleaning by yourself?"

I search the space for the spiders that will no doubt be making an appearance. Little creepers will probably wait until Dane is gone and I'm by myself. *Oh, sugar.*

"I'll be fine. It'll be a good workout." I flex my arms, pretending I know what I'm doing.

"Right. Well, I'll let you get to it. The guys and I will be by later. Until then." He tips his hat in an old-fashioned goodbye and then walks out, leaving me staring at his rather impressive behind. I flutter my hand in front of my face. *What is wrong with me?*

My phone rings, and I jump as I continue cooling my face with my other hand. "Hi-ya, Amy!"

"Hey best friend. How is good old New England?"

I spin in a circle, taking in the room, and shudder. "Uh, great," I say, trying for excitement.

"Then why do you sound like you're about to have a tooth extraction?"

Never could fool her. I laugh uncomfortably. "It's just a lot. My sister…she's, well, my twin…she's difficult. But she's trying. *I think.* My older sister, Caris, is lovely. Aloof but kind. And my grandmother, she's a force. She gave me this building…" I circle the room again and roll my eyes. "And I'm going to stay here and open a bakery… and run the ice cream shop."

I hadn't consciously made a decision before speaking it aloud to my best friend, but I know it's true.

She screeches on the other end of the phone. "Oh my God! Then I need to come there. But shoot. I just got a part…ugh, I can't come until after Christmas—"

"You got a part?"

"It's nothing big. Just a side character. I barely have ten lines."

"That's not nothing, Amy. It's something. A *huge* something."

Her smile is evident in her voice. "It is kinda big, huh?"

"Yes! Congrats. When you come out here, we'll celebrate."

"At your bakery," Amy says proudly.

I bite my lip, remembering how much work I need to do. "Yes, at my bakery…All right, friend, I have to get this place cleaned up if I have any shot of sleeping here tonight."

"Oh! Yes! Okay, FaceTime me later and give me a tour once everything is set up?"

I cringe. If she sees this place, she'll be on the phone with my mom in an instant. They don't get along, but she'll be worried. And I can't exactly blame her. It's…scary. But it's nothing a little cleaning won't fix. I glance down at the blue carpet. At least I think it's blue. At one time, it was blue. I add that to my mental list of things to replace. "Okay. I'll try. Bye, love you!"

I hang up the phone and slide it onto a shelf in the kitchen so I can get back to cleaning. The kitchen is all wood, and there are old blue— once again, I think it's blue—curtains hanging from the ends of the cabinets, as if to create privacy between the living room and kitchen. It's hideous. No matter what color it is.

First things first, I grab the unsightly curtains and trash them. Already, I feel so much better. That is, of course, until the spider I knew had been hiding all along crawls out of the curtains and onto my hand as I'm dumping them in the barrel. Screaming and jumping around like a flipping lunatic, I try my best to remove the eight-legged critter from my body.

"Why?" I scream, flinging my hand, unable to shake loose the spider with the freakishly strong grip. "Why do you have so many legs? And those beady eyes? Why in holy water do you need so many legs? Jiminy Cricket!"

The door to the apartment swings open, and a man rushes in, shouting. "What's going on?" he asks, his attention darting around the room.

What good is he doing over there? "It's on my hand! Help!"

He steps close and looks down at me, then smacks my wrist quickly, smooshing the spider into my skin.

"What the—?" I stare at it—no doubt with my mouth agape—and then back up at him. The man from the docks. The man who kissed me. Dumbstruck, I state the obvious, "You just smacked me."

His lip curls. "I think what you mean to say is thank you. Jeez, Hailey, I've never seen you so worked up."

My brows pinch together. "You *smacked* me!"

"I saved you from the big bad spider you were screeching about. Seriously, you're afraid of a little daddy longlegs?" He shakes his head.

Confused by his appearance in my apartment, I ask, "What are you doing here?"

First the guy kisses me senseless on the docks, and now he shows up at my apartment and smacks me?

Okay, saves me from a spider, but still. Why does he keep appearing?

He pulls on the back of his neck. "I—uh. Caris told me about this place. Mentioned some projects that need to be done. You going to wash that bug off your hand now?"

I shudder, realizing the bug guts are still on my hand, and walk toward the kitchen. I stick my hand under the faucet and turn it on. It makes a jerking sound, and the water that sputters out is murky and brown. "Fudge! What is wrong with this place?" I shriek.

The guy laughs. "It's just rust. Let the faucet run for a few minutes. From the looks of it, the place hasn't been used in years," he says, perusing the room.

"Yeah, I think that's obvious. I told Dane I'd have it cleaned up before he gets the furniture here. Oh sweet baby kittens. How long do you think I have?"

He shrugs. "Do you want me to help?" He moves into the living room and kneels in front of my cleaning supplies.

"Ugh, no. I've got this."

He looks up at me with a frown. The water is finally running clear, so I avoid his inspection and turn my focus to the faucet, making sure nothing else jumps out to surprise me. Like a rat coming through the pipes or something. "Seriously, you can't even be alone with me for an hour? You'd rather clean this place up by yourself?" He stands up from where he was removing the cleaning supplies, wearing a scowl and clenching his fists. The way he glowers at me leaves me uncomfortable, and frankly, it's uncalled for.

"I, uh, just don't want to put anyone out. This is my project. *Please*. But I appreciate you, uh, saving me from the big nasty spider," I say with what I hope is a pacifying smile.

He takes a deep breath and runs a hand through his hair. He's got nice hair. And a lot of it. I'm pretty sure my hands explored it while he was kissing me. That's another reason he needs to remove himself from my apartment. Because now all I want to do is repeat that kiss. And I can't. I wipe my hand on the towel while he stares at me for a beat longer.

Finally he nods. "Okay. I'll see you later. Just holler if you see any more spiders," he says with a wink.

"Oh, you know I will," I reply before slamming my hand over my face and watching him walk out.

Is everyone in this town that good-looking? Or am I just that horny?

CHAPTER 10

SHAWN

What the hell is Hailey's problem? We've been friends for months. Sure, maybe I flirt too much, and the kiss obviously threw her for a loop, but I don't have a ton of friends in this town, and I counted her as one of them. But it looks like that one act may have cost me that friendship.

I walk into the apartment across the hall and hold my breath as the dank smell from inside hits me. When was the last time someone opened a window in here? I walk straight to the window and flip the lock, which is covered in dust, before sliding it open with a creak. I pull so hard my body jolts forward. "Damn, this place is old."

My eyes adjust to the dark room now that the light from outside is filtering in, and I'm thinking the light was a mistake. The room is empty, save for a square folding table and chairs. There's a well-worn rug covering the floor in the living room and beige linoleum in the kitchen. I turn the faucet on, allowing it to run like I'd instructed Hailey to do in the other apartment. The entire room practically heaves in a sigh as I do so, the space settling into a new visitor as much as I'm settling into my new apartment. "This is going to take some getting used to," I mutter under my breath, opening the Formica cabinets and finding them bare, except a pack of playing cards. I glance back over to the table and figure this might have been where Hailey's father met up with friends years ago. Not a bad spot for that, but certainly not a place anyone would want to live. Well, except for me.

Call me insane, but this space feels like promise. Like me, it's out of practice, but it's got good bones. I could make this a nice spot to live for a while. And the location can't be beat. It's got a great view of the bay and the restaurants and shops that line the street. Plus the fire station is within walking distance. Kids play baseball on the lawn in front of the water. I take another fortifying breath of fresh air and then head to the bedrooms and bathroom. I'm sure I'll need it.

An hour later, I'm standing outside the building, checking the foundation and making a list of things I need to get at the store.

"Why the hell do you look so stressed?" Dane asks as he pulls up in his red F-150. There's a couch in the back. That must be the furniture Hailey mentioned.

"Just having a weird day," I reply, rounding the back of his truck. "Here, I'll help you bring this up."

Dane hops out as Mason pulls up beside us with Colby in the passenger seat. He's a firefighter, too, and hits on Hailey almost daily when he comes in. He's not my favorite.

"Why's Hailey moving?" Mason asks as he hops out of the car.

Wait, Hailey's moving here? *I'm* moving here. What the hell is going on? Her apartment above the bar is far more convenient.

Mason shakes my hand in greeting, and Colby comes around to do the same.

"And why *here*?" Colby asks, grimacing at the building. Unlike the bar, which is located on the water, this is a block away. Sure, it's got a view, but there's nothing like being directly on the water. Being inside her current apartment is like standing on a boat. There is a view from every corner. Not that I've spent much time up there.

Dane lowers his tailgate and replies, "Didn't you hear? It's her twin, Jules. She's the one moving in." He motions up to the sign.

Jules Ice Cream. Jules...a twin...Hailey has a twin sister?

He continues, "Although Hailey *is* moving in with her. Not sure what the story is there. Oh, look, here's the princess now. Maybe she can fill us in."

I turn around to see Hailey heading toward us with a big smile on her face. She was nowhere near as friendly to me up in the apartment. I guess the rest of the firefighters are more up her alley. Or maybe none of them have accosted her with unwanted kisses.

"I can't believe you guys stole Shawn from me!" she says as she snakes her arm around my waist. I stare down at her tiny form in confusion. Less than an hour ago, she was shooing me out of her apartment and could barely look me in the eye, but now she's all touchy-feely? It's like she's a completely different person.

Mason smiles. "Oh, don't you worry, we'll definitely let your boy come visit. He'll just be doing it with us by his side. And hopefully he'll still get the bartender's discount."

Colby's dimple pops as he smirks down at Hailey. "Yeah, we better be getting free drinks as payment for our manual labor."

Hailey laughs at their antics, while I'm frozen in utter confusion.

With an arm still holding my waist, she turns up to me, lifts up on her tiptoes and drops a kiss on my cheek. "How about free kisses for everyone?" She beams and lets go of me before offering kisses to each of the guys.

Before she can plant one on Colby's cheek, he grabs her by the waist, hoists her up, spins her around, and then plants a kiss right on her lips. She laughs the entire time.

She's treating me just like she treats them, even after the kiss. As a friend. It's not romantic. Not between them and certainly not with me. I've been friendzoned, and I'll have to accept that. Even if the kiss we shared was hands down the best kiss of my life. Even if I've been reliving every moment of it in my head for the last twenty-four hours. It's better to have her as a friend than not at all.

"Where are we bringing this?" I ask, hoping to move things along. I may be okay with being friends, but that doesn't mean I want to sit and watch Colby fondle her. A man can only take so much.

"Right. Just upstairs. Let me run up and make sure Red is ready for us."

"Red?" I ask.

Hailey swallows and looks at her feet before making eye contact with me. "My twin. Sorry. It's going to take some getting used to. And wait until you see the two of us standing next to each other. It's some Freaky Friday shit, if I do say so myself."

Colby stares down at her with interest, one brow cocked. "Twins?"

She smacks him on the chest and he stumbles back.

"Ew, you sick bastard. Don't even start."

"So you look alike?" I ask, pulling on my neck and confused as hell by this entire day.

Hailey coughs out a laugh. "Yeah, if you can get past her hoity-toity clothes and stuck-up nose, I bet none of you could tell us apart."

I bark out a laugh. *Doubtful.*

We all stare as Hailey walks away. When I realize I'm not the only one staring at her ass, I turn around.

"So what's up with you and Hailey?" Colby asks.

I turn to the kid, who isn't quite as tall as me and certainly younger by a few years. At thirty-six, I'm old for a rookie, but not in comparison to most of the guys I'll be working with. Dane works as an electrician when he's not on duty and is the same age as me. He's also a single dad, so he seems a world older than me. Mason is probably around the same age. But Colby is twenty-six. He looks like he never leaves the gym, and he seems to get along with most of the guys. From what I'm told, he's constantly pulling pranks at the fire station.

"Nothing is going on with Hailey. We're just friends."

Colby smiles. "Awesome. So you wouldn't mind if I asked her out?"

I shrug even as I bite my tongue. "Not at all if she's interested. I'm not her keeper."

Dane mutters under his breath so only I can hear him, "But you sure wish you could be."

The window upstairs creaks open before I have a chance to respond, and Hailey leans out with a big smile. "Okay, boys. Come on up! We're ready for ya!"

I'm pretty sure we're all wearing matching idiotic grins. She's like a fucking shepherd herding cattle. And dammit, every single one of us will follow her commands.

It doesn't take long to get the couch up the steps. Colby screams "pivot" every few seconds, thinking he's being absolutely hysterical. And Mason looks like he might drop the couch down the steps just so it lands on Colby's foot. Dane and I bite back our laughter until we make it to the door, where Hailey stands with her hands on her hips and a smirk on her face. Behind her is a mirror image—minus the smile—who looks eerily similar to the woman I interacted with only an hour ago. In fact, she's wearing the same outfit that Hailey—not Hailey?—was wearing then.

Jules.

"Boys, this is my…uh, this is Jules. Red, these are the boys—Colby, Mason, Dane, and my best friend Shawn." She grins big at me.

My heart hammers in my chest. I meet her sister's eyes and hold her gaze. Or maybe it's her glare. Unlike her sister, she does not look enamored.

She looks heated. And nervous.

Then, as if she's remembered her manners, she sticks out her hand in a wave. "Hi, boys. Thank you so much for helping us."

Colby elbows me in the ribs. "Fuckin' twins," he mutters with the biggest smile.

Mine grows with him. What can I say? The attitude is contagious. And he's right. I'm staring at two of the most gorgeous redheads I've ever seen. One looks as uptight as they come, and the other is my best friend. And clearly not the woman I kissed. That's the reason I'm smiling. Because Hailey *does* have brown eyes, just like I thought. And her twin has the mossy green ones I got lost in on the docks.

Hailey didn't cringe over our kiss. She wasn't even there for it. And I'm not quite sure what to make of the fact that I shared the greatest kiss of my life with her sister.

Her *twin* sister.

JULES
ICE CREAM
SUPER PREMIUM ICE CREAM
SUPER PREMIUM ICE CREAM

CHAPTER II

JULES

While Hailey instructs the guys on where to put the couch, I work to put sheets on the bed. It's almost dark, and I've been through the ringer today. I seriously want to fall into bed and sleep until next week. When I finally finish what I'm doing, Hailey is the only one left in the kitchen.

"Did the guys leave?"

"Yeah. They had stuff to do. Don't worry. I thanked them for us both. Told them to stop by the bar for dinner and drinks." She grins.

"Ah, well, thanks," I say, awkwardness creeping into my tone now that we're alone in our living space for the first time. If she's uncomfortable, she doesn't show it.

"Do you want to come down to the bar for dinner? I can introduce you to some people…" she drifts off like she doesn't really want me to come, but maybe that's just my imagination. She's been nothing but helpful today. There's no reason for me to believe she doesn't want me here.

"If you don't mind, I'm just going to crash. But we, uh, only have one bed…"

Hailey shrugs. "That's okay. I'm not actually going to sleep here. You can keep a secret, right? We'll make sure my grandmother thinks I live here with ya. You can go about your life and do whatever it is you have planned for this place, and I can run my bar. Just like I planned."

I stare at her, dumbstruck, and for a moment, it looks like she's going to reconsider.

"You'll be okay, right?" she asks, sounding annoyed that she cares enough to ask.

Hmm. Will I be okay? I look around the apartment. It's cleaner than when I arrived, that's for sure. But I'm not entirely convinced I'm not sharing the space with a few spiders and a litter of rats.

I don't want to seem ungrateful though, or like I'm a spoiled princess, and I certainly don't want to force my sister to live with me. We can get to know one another some other way. Her secret is safe with me. "Yes, I'll be fine. Thanks for everything today."

"Yeah, sure. I mean, you did all the hard work. And the guys. Anyway, I'll see you tomorrow, I guess?"

"Right. Tomorrow." We awkwardly stare at each other for a moment longer. We should feel something, right? People say twins have a special bond. They finish each other's sentences, sense when the other one is sad, when they're in trouble or in pain. And yet, until recently, I didn't know she existed.

Is my twin receptor broken? Is hers? Shouldn't we be hugging? Or jumping for joy, in awe that we've found one another? I feel exactly nothing when I look at her. Perhaps even a slight irritation because she's so easy-going. And also because it's obvious she's been judging me since we met. Unfairly disliking me for my simple existence.

I'm a victim of our circumstance as much as she is. And I so badly want her to like me. To be best friends. To be *something* to one another.

If she feels any of those things, she gives nothing away. She finally offers a wave and walks out, leaving me alone in a new apartment, in a new town, to sit with my thoughts.

Or not really alone. Let's not forget—I've got the spiders to keep me company.

CHAPTER 12

SHAWN

I blow out a breath as I stare out at the deep navy ocean, which appears almost black and violent this late at night. I'm seeing none of it though. My mind keeps returning to mossy green eyes that sparked the moment I first looked into them yesterday. No matter how many times I turn the moment on the docks over in my head, I keep coming back to the same thought.

I didn't kiss Hailey—I kissed *her.*

The woman with eyes that remind me of Christmas morning. The girl whose face softened when she saw me—*as if she* really *saw me*—in a way that Hailey never has.

That's why I never made a move on Hailey before. She'd never given me *that* look.

I turn around and see Colby flirting with Hailey as she works the bar. She looks at me, and I smile before heading in their direction.

"It's fine," she's saying to Colby, tossing me a wink. "I'm just getting used to the idea that you've stolen my best employee."

I roll my eyes. "Please. Amelia is your favorite. Nice try though."

"She's not as pretty as you," she says, fluttering her lashes.

I laugh and make my way over to her. "Do you need my help? I can take drink orders if you want."

She smacks me with a towel and I dart out of the way. "No. You carried furniture up very steep steps and made it so my sister has a place to sleep. I can manage."

My chest tightens, and I lean my elbows on the bar to keep our conversation private. "I never knew you had a sister. Another one, I mean." I clear my throat, just the thought of Jules leaving my stomach in knots. "Where has she been all this time?"

Hailey laughs awkwardly and looks in the other direction. "I didn't know I had another sister either. *Surprise!*" she cheers with false bravado, pumping her fists in the air.

My stomach drops. "Wait, what?"

She sighs out a loud breath. "Apparently our parents pulled a *Parent Trap* and each took one of us when we were infants. I never met my mom and have no memory of a twin."

"You're kidding, right?"

"Does that sound like something I'd kid about?" she asks with a bit of a bite to her tone.

I glare at her.

"Okay, fine. I am the type to be dramatic and make stuff up, but this is real."

This time, I don't let her keep me at arm's length. I walk around the bar and pull her directly into my chest, hugging her tightly. "Damn, Hailes. How are you feeling about it all?"

She relaxes against me as she lets out another exasperated breath. Then she pulls back and leans against the cash register.

"Ya know, I don't even know how to feel. She's obviously my sister. We're like someone hit copy and paste. Only she's a prettier, more put-together version of me," she says with a dry laugh. It makes my fists squeeze, but before I can say anything, she continues. "I'm not insecure. It's just a fact. The girl is pretty. I can be categorized as cute, maybe even hot sometimes, but I'm not pretty. She's soft;

I'm hard. We're just…*not the same*. Which is fine. But having her around shines a light on all the things I'm not. Things that sometimes bothered me when I was a child. When people would compare me to Caris, but at least there were years separating us. Typically, our personalities and accomplishments were what people focused on, but we don't look all that much alike, so the comparison rarely moved into our physical attributes. If they did, Caris would win. Hands down, no question. She's put together. Tall and blond. A lawyer, a business owner. Hell, I'm sure she somehow knows how to shit pretty. But she's the standard for what I could be. With Jules, I'm afraid people will see her as the person I *should* be and pick apart my flaws when I'm judged next to her."

"Hailes," I say, as if it's a sentence in and of itself. "You are gorgeous. And an amazing friend. Funny. Loveable. Don't compare yourself to your sister. Either of them."

She nudges me with her elbow, and her lip tilts into a half-smile. "You have to say that because you're my best friend."

"I only tell the truth. Don't be so hard on yourself. And seriously, if you need help at the bar, I can make it work."

I hate that she's doing this all on her own. I hate that she feels this way. And I hate that I can't get her twin sister and our kiss out of my mind.

"I'm fine, I promise," Hailey says, completely unaware of where my thoughts have gone. "I've got to raise the next crop of young bartenders. I'm gonna close up and head out. You guys want one more round?"

"Nah," I say as I pull her to my chest again and squeeze. "I'm going to head out too. Want me to wait and walk you to your apartment?"

She shakes her head and then hesitates before adding, "You're a really good friend. You know that, Shawn? I don't have many guy friends and…well, I'm so glad I have you."

I can feel the air shift as I accept the reality of our situation. She *only* sees me as a friend, which is good because somehow in the last twenty-four hours, I've realized I feel the same. And once again, green eyes flit through my brain, reminding me of precisely why I feel that way.

"You'll always have me, Hailes. You sure you don't want me to walk you home?"

She waves me off and turns. "No, I'll be a while. Night, Shawn."

CHAPTER 13

SHAWN

"I think you missed a spot," someone calls. I arch my back and spot an old lady with white hair wearing a muumuu giving me a sly smile. "Down there." She points to the bottom of the fire truck and waggles her brow.

Behind me, Dane laughs. "Carmella," he says with faux sternness, "how many times do I have to tell you this isn't *Magic Mike*? And aren't you getting married soon?"

She shrugs, wearing a smirk. "Oh fiddlesticks. A girl can look, can't she?"

I have to hold back a laugh at her reference to herself as a girl. The woman is clearly in her seventies. But her devilish smile proves she's still got that young spirit. And I like it.

"Shawn." I hold out my hand to her in greeting.

She laughs as she takes it. "Oh, I know who you are, *Babe*."

Colby snickers beside me. "Because you played baseball," he reminds me, as if I don't understand the nickname.

I somehow manage to hold back an eye roll before turning back to the woman. "And you are?"

She steps in closer. "Carmella. You know, the Christmas festival committee is working on fundraising ideas. You boys in front of that fire truck with kittens seems like the perfect way to earn extra cash for this town's big ball. What do you say?"

I shake my head. Not a chance. "Sorry, ma'am, I'm new here. Wrong person to ask."

"Think the chief will agree?" she asks Dane.

He guffaws. "I highly doubt that. But he's inside. Feel free to chat with him."

Before she can provide us with another quip or shake of her hips, the station alarm sounds, making her jump.

"Sorry, Carmella, we gotta go!" Dane shouts.

Unlike her, none of us so much as flinch at the sudden noise. Instead, the blast sends a shot of adrenaline to my system. *Finally, my first call.*

I've been waxing this fire truck, playing cards, making dinner, and making friends for the past few weeks. And although I've enjoyed it, I'm pumped to finally do what I trained for.

We each run to the wall to grab our gear, then slip on our PPE—the personal protective equipment we wear—and run for the truck. No one talks as we wait to hear details of the call.

"Abandoned building on Wood Street. Fire is spreading quickly. Mason, Dane, you're on flank. Colby, Sam, Tim, you're on head. Shawn, go with Mason and Dane but make sure you listen to everything they say. No heroics. Let's make sure no one is inside, and then we soak it," the chief instructs.

No one hesitates when we pull up. I follow Dane around back while Mason talks to a neighbor, making sure there really is no one inside. The fire hasn't blown out any windows or caved the roof yet, so we still have time to control it.

It's the sound of a fucking meow that halts my movements. Dane and I look at each other, and I throw my head back in aggravation. Fucking cats. I push my head closer to the door and listen. The heat coming off the building almost burns my ear, but I hear the distinct sound again. *Meow.*

Dane shakes his head. "You've got to be fucking kidding me."

I put my mask on as I look to him for instructions on breaking down the door.

He shrugs and yells back to Mason, "Going in."

Then I slam my foot into the back door and jump back, prepared for the fire to come bursting out like in a movie.

Fortunately, all I see is smoke. The fire must be contained somewhere else.

From behind us, Mason confirms that no one is inside, but we continue in anyway. There may not be people in the building, but I can't walk away knowing an animal is trapped inside a burning building. There must be something on the books about this. Fireman and kittens—it's a thing.

Dane waves an arm, motioning for me to follow. We walk slowly, testing the ground as we go, never quite sure how sturdy the wood below is because the building is abandoned. These are all concerns we have to keep in mind, and fortunately, I paid attention during training. I took mental notes every time my best friend in Tahoe talked to me about his calls. I know what to do.

I scan our surroundings, but the smoke makes it difficult. Then I hear the noise again and spin. Sure enough, in the corner at the window, the cat is rubbing itself against the glass as it cries, its back arched and its fur standing on end. Poor thing is terrified. Huge men coming toward it wearing bulky PPE with helmets, face masks, and giant contraptions on their backs probably aren't any less scary, so I walk slowly and hold out my hand. The cat hisses, and before I can figure out my next move, Dane grabs the thing by its belly and motions for me to move out. The cat continues to hiss and scratch and bite at Dane, but his thick coat protects him, and he doesn't bat an eye.

It isn't until we get outside that we can finally speak.

"What the hell?" the chief says, storming in our direction.

Before we can respond, the cat jumps out of Dane's arms and hisses at us once more before running off.

Colby throws his head back and laughs. "Not even a thank you for risking your lives!"

I pull off my mask and suck in air, the cold fall day breathing new life into me.

"You didn't wait for Mason!" Chief yells again.

Mason shrinks a bit next to the chief. "They heard a cat and went in," he defends.

"Go help with the hoses. We'll talk about this when we get back," he barks.

Dane slaps me on the back as we run toward the truck, focused on putting out the fire. "Good job in there," he says with a smile.

My grin grows to match his. Despite being yelled at, that was the first time I've felt like I'm good at something in a while.

After my shift, I head to the winery to pick up the key to my new apartment. Caris finally got around to putting locks on the doors since it was never a residence before now. I've been meaning to get over there, but I wanted to tackle one new thing at a time and get settled in at work first. But it's time for me to get out of Jack and Charlotte's basement. Sleeping with their dog is getting old.

Before I spot Caris, I find Amelia's cousin Belle.

"Shawn!" she says with a smile as she flings her arms around me. "I heard you saved a cat today!"

I pull out of her hug and scratch my head. The fire was, like, three hours ago. How does she already know about the cat? And why is it newsworthy?

"Dane and I did." I chuckle. "He's the one who carried him out."

She smiles, flashing her red lips at me as her black hair swings behind her back. Belle is easily one of the hottest women I've ever seen. Long black hair, big blue eyes, and intense curves. She's also head over heels in love with her boyfriend Luca. I've gotten to know them both well through Charlotte and Jack.

"But you heard the cat's cries, right? And you kicked in the door as flames came flying back at you, then ran through a fire to find the poor animal and brought it to safety."

She sounds bizarrely excited about the whole exaggerated story.

"That isn't even remotely close to what happened," I object.

"Stop being so coy," a woman says from behind me. A woman whose voice I heard only hours ago. I spin around to find Carmella smiling at me. She's still wearing her red muumuu, and she's just as giddy as she was earlier. "I saw the whole thing, and it was enthralling," she says as she fans herself.

Belle wraps her arm around Carmella. "This is Luca's Nona," she explains.

Ah, that makes more sense.

"Excellent. I don't mean to be rude, ladies, but I'm looking for Caris. I'm supposed to pick up a key."

Carmella smiles. "Oh, she told me, dear. I have the key."

Belle spins toward Carmella. "Why do *you* have the key?"

"Mind your business." She shrugs, slipping it out of her pocket.

I hold out my palm, and she places it there, but before I can pull it back, she grips my hand tightly.

"Now listen, the water in the shower doesn't work, so she told me you should stay in the apartment across the hall until you get them up and running."

"But that's Hailey's sister's apartment," I point out in confusion.

"Yup. It's fine. There's an extra bedroom, and the girl doesn't know anyone. You'll make a wonderful friend, right, Shawn?"

I'm definitely not going to do that, but I'm too exhausted to argue with Carmella. After I get my stuff into the apartment, I'll head back to the station and shower there. I sigh. "Fine."

"She won't be there tonight because she flew home to get the rest of her things. She really wants to make a go of it here," Carmella offers.

"Jules?" I ask stupidly. Of course it's Jules. But I like to say her name, and just the thought of sharing the same space as her, of seeing her daily, sends my pulse skyrocketing. Clearly, I need sleep. The last time I saw the girl, she nearly bit my head off and glared at me the whole time.

"Yes," she says. "And Caris said not to stress about working on the other apartment right away. She knows the fire department will keep you busy."

I pocket the key and shrug. "I'll get it done. But if you don't mind, I'm going to pick up some stuff from Charlotte and Jack's. Thank you again."

Then I walk away, wondering what in the heck I just agreed to.

JULES
ICE CREAM
SUPER PREMIUM ICE CREAM
SUPER PREMIUM ICE CREAM

CHAPTER 14

JULES

I climb the steps of the bakery, a duffel over my shoulder and one of my suitcases hitting each step as I drag it and the way over fifty pounds of contents it contains up the stairs. The lady at the airport side-eyed me more than once, but I just offered to pay for the extra weight. I had no interest in pulling out my underwear or the baking supplies I refuse to part with while sitting on the airport floor.

Amy helped me pack up everything I owned under the cover of night while my mom was at an event. Maybe it was cowardly, and maybe it was childish, but I'm still mad at her, and I wanted to avoid her dramatics over my move.

I moved to Rhode Island.

I'm really doing this. I spent the last week at Amy's apartment. We had Thanksgiving dinner on her tiny fold-out table like true actresses, eating pizza, not turkey. But I did bake a pie, which we then ate straight from the container while it was still hot.

I tried to convince her that I could live with her. Part of me wants to stay in California. I don't need Rhode Island or my estranged family. But aside from Amy, there's nothing for me in Los Angeles, and she'll be insanely busy once filming starts. And in Rhode Island, there is possibility.

I just hope Hailey is more open to getting to know me than she was the last time I saw her.

I sigh as I reach the top step and press my head against the door, searching my purse for my keys. When I swing open the door, I call out to the spiders, "Honies, I'm home!"

Shockingly, no one greets me.

I take in the space, which, curiously, appears cleaner than I left it, and drop my duffel on the floor. Then I wander around, surveying the updates I most certainly had no hand in.

A new table and chairs in the kitchen, a paper towel holder, a toaster oven, and even a fancy coffee machine. Maybe Hailey moved in after all. The thought sends a jolt of excitement through me. *I knew this was a good idea.*

I walk to the bedroom opposite mine and knock. When no one answers, as expected, I turn the knob and find the room completely empty. Just like I left it.

A wave of sadness hits me. I don't know why I expected anything different. I just wish I didn't feel so alone. With a sigh, I turn around, ready to grab the rest of my stuff.

It takes me three trips up and down the stairs to get the other suitcases and four hours to unpack and organize. I'm starving by the time I'm done, and now is as good a time as any to go in search of Hailey. It sounds like she spends a lot of time at the restaurant, and since I need to eat, I might as well get this over with.

As soon as I step outside, I pull my jacket tighter around my chest. It seems that winter settled into New England while I was gone. Although I expected it to get colder, I wasn't exactly prepared for it. But it looks like the end of November signifies the end of warmth as well. Now I'll just wait impatiently—quite literally—for the first snow.

It only takes a few minutes to get to the docks where the restaurant sits, and when I walk in, my eyes work to adjust to the darker space. I spot Hailey almost immediately. She's leaning against the bar, attention fixed on her phone. When she looks up, her face flashes in what might be surprise at my arrival.

Disappointment rears its ugly head when she doesn't exactly jump to say hello right away. I didn't think my trip to California would bring about a personality transplant for her, but I won't lie and say that her ambivalence to my return doesn't sting. My skin heats as anger—and maybe embarrassment—floods my body.

Why doesn't she like me?

"How was your flight, Red?" she asks, completely oblivious to my current state.

I school my expression, refusing to give this person any more of myself than I already have. "Fine. How have things been here?" I ask, keeping the conversation light while I take a seat at the bar.

"Long. Be thankful you got the ice cream shop and not the bar. I'm down a bartender, and the college kids aren't going to cut it," she says as she reaches below the bar pulls out a menu for me.

"Do you need help?" I ask without thinking.

When her expression morphs into something akin to amusement and she gives me a once-over, as if she's assessing my worth, my cheeks warm.

"You ever bartend?"

"Uh, no…but it can't be that hard," I retort, squaring my shoulders. I don't like how this girl makes me feel. Inadequate, spoiled. Like my manicured nails and colored hair signify that I've never done a day's work. It's not my fault my mother raised me the way she did, and I'm no princess. I worked my way through high school, and I practically cleaned the entire apartment, spiders and all.

Hailey shrugs my comment away. "If you say so. Can you be at the bar tomorrow at three? I'll have Amelia show you the ropes. If you make it through the night and want to stick around, I could use help on the weekends."

The challenge in her voice and the doubt lacing her words fuels my fire. In all honesty, I have no interest in bartending, but I'm here to get to know my sisters. If this is the only way I can prove to Hailey that I'm worth her time, then it appears I'll be taking up bartending.

"Sounds good. I plan to work on the shop tonight anyway. The apartment looks better, thanks," I offer.

She shrugs but doesn't respond, her attention flitting around the bar like she's only half listening.

"Would you mind if I made some changes?"

"You heard my grandmother. It's yours. Do whatever you like. Now what can I get ya?" she changes the subject, treating me like nothing more than a customer, taking my pride and a little bit of my self-worth with her.

My chest squeezes in a way it never has. I'll need to grow a thicker skin when it comes to my twin. She's unflappable—my complete opposite. Strange how two people can literally share identical DNA and be so different.

CHAPTER 15

SHAWN

"How are the new living arrangements?" Dane asks, throwing a few cards my way. Our shift is almost over, and I can't wait to get home. The guys helped me move a couch into the new apartment, and Dane even got the lights and electricity working. It's sad that I consider that a win, but now I can see what I am working with. Even if it looks worse in the light.

I didn't bother moving my bed yet. There's just too much work to be done.

Caris asked me to take a look in Jules's apartment while she was gone so we could come up with a plan for what needed to be done in her place too. She's worried Jules won't stay, and to my complete surprise, she wasn't having it. She said she had gone shopping and would be there to clean up if I could help for a bit.

As soon as I saw what a disaster Jules's kitchen was, I decided to focus my energy there. I can live at the station for a bit, but this poor girl has nowhere else to go.

So instead of working on my place, I've been spending my time on hers.

I'd like to take all the cabinets out, sand them down, and paint them for her if I can find the time. A little paint would really brighten up the space and give it a clean feel. I could see her liking a nice white kitchen. With her attitude and the hoity-toity—as Hailey so aptly put it—way she dresses, she's probably used to nice things.

Not going to lie, I'm intrigued by the idea of living next door to her. Of seeing how she'll act when she comes back—whenever that might be. I get that packing up a life takes a bit of time.

Although I walked away from every single thing I owned in LA without looking back, I know most people wouldn't do the same.

"It's good so far. Want to come by tomorrow and help me sand some cabinets?" I ask with a waggle of my brows.

Dane laughs as he throws down another Ace. "Bring 'em by the shop and we can do it there. Jules mentioned wanting to do some work in the ice cream shop, so I don't want to make a mess there."

I groan at the cards he's laid out. "She did? When did you talk to her?"

A surprising burst of jealousy zings through me at this new information. She's not mine. Hell, I barely know the girl, but the idea of Dane *knowing* her drives me wild.

I'm so lost in my own jealousy that I don't catch Dane's response. "I'm sorry. What did you say?"

He laughs. "I said when we helped her move in. I chatted with her for a bit and came back to do some electrical work the next day. She asked about the wiring in the ice cream store. Sounds like she wants to put a kitchen in the back."

A kitchen? What would that mean for my living situation? I guess I'll have to wait to find out.

"Hey, Dane," the chief says from his office door, "you got a minute?"

Dane hops up. "Sure, Chief. What do you need?" he asks as he walks off without a glance in my direction.

"Shawn, join us. You were in the building too. Maybe you can be of some assistance."

I jump out of my seat just as quickly as Dane did, finding myself back in the chief's office for the first time since my interview. This time, I take the opportunity to look around a bit while I settle into the chair beside Dane.

No photographs of family. No wife, no kids. The chief is a long-time bachelor like us. Although his title garners the respect one would expect for an older man, he's only two years older than me.

"What can we do for you?" Dane asks, glancing at me and sporting a furrowed brow.

I shrug and look back at the chief. I'm clueless about why he'd want to talk about the fire we put out a couple of weeks ago.

"We got the report on the fire on Wood Street. Looks like it was intentionally set. I was hoping you guys could tell me if you saw anything strange. Anything that could clue us in to what happened."

"Intentional? In Bristol?" Dane's brows shoot to his hairline.

The chief nods. "You see anything?"

Dane and I look at one another. He's got a thoughtful look on his face that probably mirrors mine. I think back to that day. To the smoke. To the cat's cries. Someone intentionally set a fire...did they know there was a cat in the building? Fuck, that's messed up.

"No idea, Chief, I'm sorry," I reply honestly.

He nods. "What about you, Dane?"

My friend shakes his head. "No, but I'd like to go in and look around, see if I notice anything strange, if that's okay."

"I'll go with you," I offer. It looks like I won't be getting much sleep again tonight. Maybe I'll make it back to the apartment tomorrow.

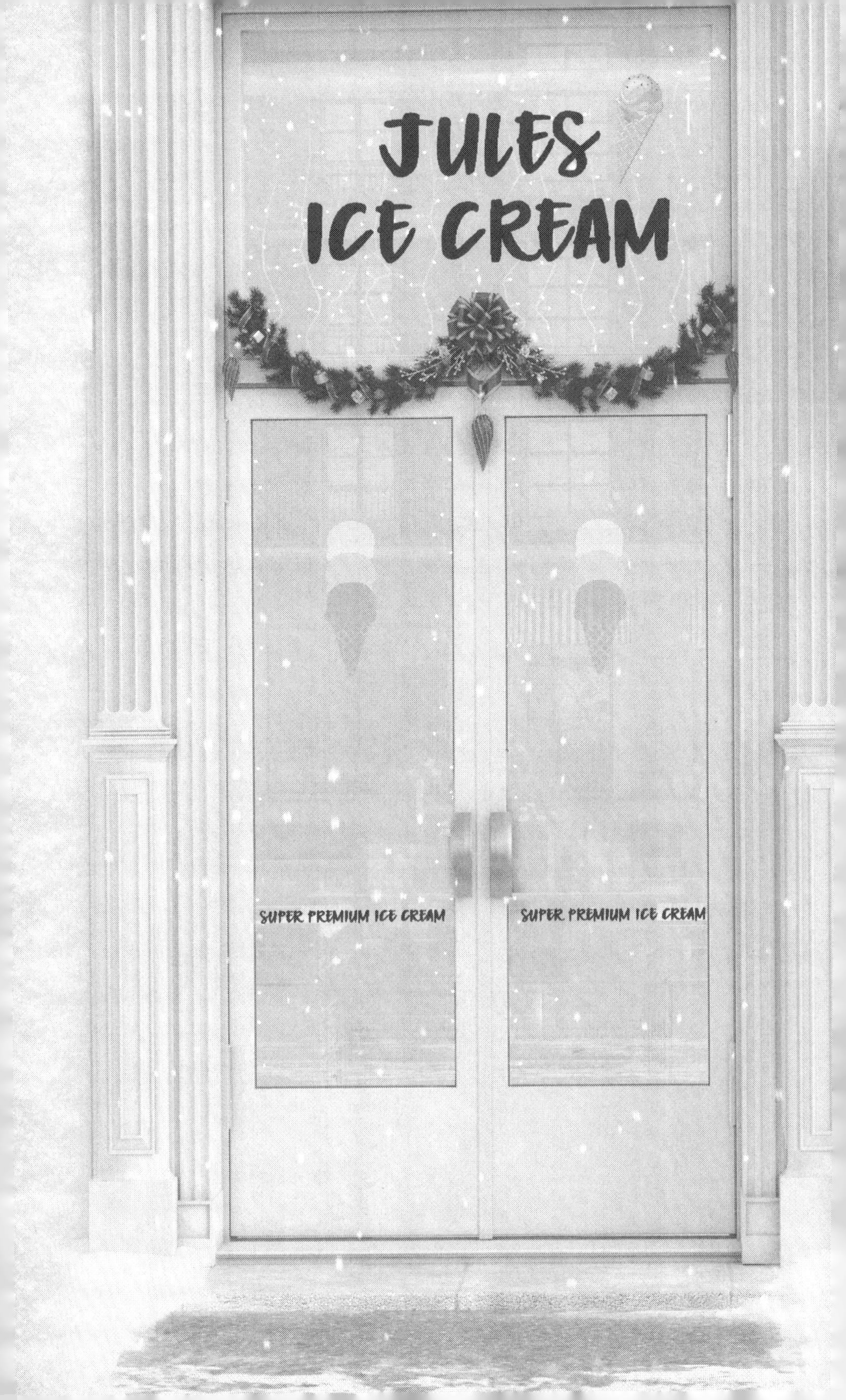

CHAPTER 16

JULES

I finish swiping mascara on my lashes and then paint my lips in a mauve lip-gloss before giving myself one more glance in the mirror.

Shockingly, I'm excited about my shift at Thames today. If I'm going to live here, I want to earn my keep. So bartending it is since I haven't figured out what I want to do about the ice cream shop.

As I head down the steps, I find myself smiling at the storefront. This place really is something. Even closed and all but abandoned, it's full of magic. It feels special. I'm so lost in my thoughts I don't register the person staring at me until I practically walk into him.

I hold my arms out to keep myself from falling into his wall of muscles and am met by his smirking mouth and eyes that glitter as if he's in on a private joke. The man from the dock. The perfect kiss.

"You okay?" he murmurs, wrapping a hand around my upper arm to steady me.

As soon as his fingers touch my skin, a warmth spreads across my chest, which means my cheeks probably match my hair color.

"Uh, yes—" I stammer, trying to find my bearings. What is it about this guy that makes me tongue tied? It's been weeks since that kiss, and I still taste him.

His grin grows. "Good. So you're the elusive sister I've heard so much about?"

"Am I?" I retort, confused.

"Unless you and Hailey have a triplet I haven't met," he replies, humor dancing in his eyes.

I'm so thrown off by the way he's looking at me, as if he's genuinely happy to see me, that I grapple with my own name. "Ah, yes. I'm Jules—" I point to the sign above the shop like it's explanation enough.

The hot guy simply nods. "Yes, I remember."

"And you're…?" I ask, trying to turn the focus from me. Last time we met, I didn't catch his name. I was too focused on not looking at him—or *any* of the hot men in my apartment—and on Hailey's obvious disdain for me.

"Shawn Chase," he replies and holds out his hand.

I gasp. "As in Shawn Chase of the Dodgers?"

His eyes flash. "Yeah, how did you—?"

I cut him off before he can finish. I am *starstruck*. "My stepdad is a huge baseball fan. *I* am a huge baseball fan. You had one hell of a curve ball."

I can't believe I didn't recognize him before now. I was so thrown by the kiss and then the spider…and I honestly never thought Shawn *Freaking* Chase would be living in this tiny town.

He looks away from me and flexes his arm uncomfortably, but then stops abruptly, like it's a bad habit he's caught himself doing, and grips his neck instead. "That's what they say."

That's when I remember the accident. His arm was never the same. My cheeks burn with shame. "I'm sorry…I—"

He holds up his hand. "No need to be embarrassed. Hell, I kissed you the first time we met. You've got *nothing* on that humiliation."

I laugh awkwardly. "I was wondering if you remembered."

He grins, and it does something to my insides. Twisting them in knots and sending liquid heat rushing through my veins. There's just something about a grown man and a grin.

"I don't usually make a habit out of kissing strangers, so…" His eyes meet mine, still full of mirth.

An unbidden smile pulls at my lips. "No? Figured famous baseball players kissed strangers all the time."

"*Former* baseball players," he says with a wince, "and if we could keep that under wraps, that'd be good."

"The kiss?"

He laughs. "No. Although I suppose I should apologize for that."

I look down at my shoes now, afraid my interest in this conversation is written all over my face.

His voice takes on a teasing lilt. "*But* if I remember correctly, you *did* kiss me back."

My heart pounds. He's not wrong.

Before I can reply, the bell over the door jingles. Shawn looks away, his face brightening at the stranger stepping inside.

"I've been looking all over for you," a woman says to him. She waves at me as if we know one another, and on instinct I wave back.

Shawn shrugs and smiles at the pretty brunette. "Well, you found me."

"We're going to be late. You ready?"

Shawn turns back to me, his eyes skating over my frame. He looks pained. This must be his girlfriend. Or maybe just a date. Either way, he's not free to chat.

"Have a good night, Shawn. Your secret is safe with me," I whisper as he walks by.

He winks, and his fingers graze against my skin, lighting each inch on fire. It's too bad he's unavailable, because for once I wouldn't mind dancing within the flames.

|||

CHAPTER 17

SHAWN

"What was that all about?" Charlotte asks with a raised brow and clear judgment.

Under my breath, I mutter, "Maybe the mix-up I was looking for."

Charlotte, the eternal romantic, pulls on my arm before I can cross the street toward Independence Park. "Your what?"

I shake my head. *What am I doing*? Opening up to Charlotte about the kiss with Hailey's sister would guarantee it became the hottest new gossip in town, and it would spread like wildfire. She'd tell Jack because they have no secrets. He'd tell his sister, Amelia, and suddenly, everyone would know.

I'm not sure what to make of my thoughts on Jules just yet. I thought I liked Hailey, but those feelings pale in comparison to the desire and the longing and the flat-out fixation coursing through me since I shared that kiss with Jules. And damn if my interest isn't piqued. She's finally back. And now she's living right across the hall.

"*That* is Hailey's twin sister."

Charlotte's eyes narrow, and she almost trips while walking and thinking at the same time. My little sister is a bit of a klutz, and adding this confusion doesn't help. I grab her arm to steady her and move us across the street quickly.

"Oh! I didn't know Hailey had a twin."

"Neither did she," I quip.

And neither did I, but I'm beginning to think it was a really good surprise.

Before she has time to ask another question, my future brother-in-law interrupts us. "Hey, I heard a strange rumor," he says, scratching the back of his head and eyeing me joins us on the sidewalk.

I hold up my hands in defense. "I swear to God I never touched your sister."

He punches me in the arm—my bad arm—and I wince.

"Okay, okay. I did touch her, but it was all in good fun, and I did it to help her. Don't give me that look."

Jack laughs. Amelia and Nate are officially back together, but I can't help teasing everyone about our fake dating.

"No, that is *not* the rumor I heard. Although I have no idea how anyone fell for that little show you put on."

Charlotte grimaces. "Ugh, it was gross hearing her talk about you like that."

I grin obnoxiously, making sure to kick one side of my mouth a little higher so my dimple pops. "What? Women can't get enough of your handsome brother. You know that."

She shudders, Jack laughs, and I shrug.

"What rumor are we talking about?"

"The apartment you rented from Caris isn't actually livable," he says, eyeing me nervously.

"It's not?" my sister practically screeches.

I roll my eyes at her dramatics. "Calm down."

"It's just…" She hesitates, dancing around what she's really concerned about—I know my sister too well. She's worried I'll move back in with her and Jack. Which is totally understandable. They're getting married and they deserve this time together.

As much as I'd like to goad her, I put her out of her misery. "Don't worry. I'm not moving back in."

Charlotte looks at Jack and then back to me before blowing out a breath. "You know we loved having you live with us."

I roll my eyes as laughter shakes my body. "Please. I see how you look at your fiancé. I'm *not* moving back in."

Jack shakes with laughter and smacks my sister's ass, much to my chagrin. "Sassy, here, can't get enough of me."

"Ridiculous," my sister says with a roll of her eyes. "And that's not what I was getting at. It's just that ever since…well, the accident…"

I watch her dance around the topic again, and I hate everything about it. Losing my career, everything I worked for my entire life, has been hard to move through. Not to be overly dramatic, but it's like losing a limb, and yet the arm that doesn't quite do what it was paid millions for remains attached to my shoulder, a constant reminder of the life I lost.

The half-truth slips from my lips far too easily. "I promise the apartment is fine. It's got a bed, heat, and electricity. What more do I need?"

A couch can be considered a bed, right?

"You don't have to leave the house on my account," Jack says with genuine concern.

Charlotte glares at him, then turns that look on me. "Yes, you do."

I laugh and put a hand over my heart. "Wow. Way to make a brother feel wanted."

Charlotte smiles. "You need this. You've been…*stuck*, for lack of a better word, for the past year. This is good for you." She turns to her fiancé and elbows him. "The guy has plenty of money. He could buy any place he wants. I'm not being a jerk by forcing him out, I promise."

She's right. I played professional ball for more than fifteen years, and I made a shitload of money. Slumming it in their basement wasn't necessary, but it was where I needed to be to get my head on straight. Charlotte is right though. I've gotten too content with not moving forward. If I don't take this leap, I'll be the weird uncle who still lives with them in ten years.

"Okay, now that we've settled that, can we get a move on? I haven't slept in days and I'm starving."

JULES
ICE CREAM
SUPER PREMIUM ICE CREAM
SUPER PREMIUM ICE CREAM

CHAPTER 18

JULES

The fire roaring in the fireplace on the back wall, the one closest to the water, warms the bar. Behind it is a gorgeous view of the bay. No wonder Hailey likes this place so much. It's incredible. A blonde stands behind the bar, her attention focused on a man sitting opposite her with a lazy grin on his face and tattoos climbing his arms. I search the restaurant for Hailey, but when I don't spot her, I resign myself to interrupting these two.

The man spots me first. His eyes light up, and he reaches out and pulls me in for a hug. I lean away, confused and thrown by his forwardness.

"Jeez, Hailey. What's wrong?" he mutters.

The blonde on the other side of the bar interrupts quickly. "That's not Hailey, Pearson. Let the poor girl go. This is her sister."

The woman gives me a smile as she holds out her hand. "Amelia Pearson. You must be Juliana."

I take her hand and nod. "You can call me Jules. I was supposed to meet Hailey here. Is she around?" I ask, looking again for my missing twin.

The man next to me coughs out a laugh. "Holy shit. You guys are identical!"

Amelia eyes me, her gaze trailing my body and reeking of judgment. "They're similar but not identical," she says quietly. "Hailey had to run an errand. She asked me to train you. Is that okay?"

I can only imagine what Hailey has told this Amelia person about me. She doesn't give off a friendly vibe, and I'm not exactly thrilled that Hailey dumped me on one of her employees. "Uh, sure," I stammer.

The man next to me reaches across the bar and grabs Amelia by both hips. He pulls her toward him until his lips are flush against hers, then murmurs something into her mouth. At that, she bites down on his lip. My toes curl into themselves. I don't think I've ever witnessed something so hot in my entire life. And we're in public. Holy hell, is it scorching in here. And it's not just the fire.

My mind briefly flits to the baseball player who kissed the hell out of me. He probably possesses a woman like that. Hell, I can only imagine what we looked like when we kissed.

A groan and a deep laugh come from behind me. "Can you not go after my sister like that in public?"

I spin around to find a tall blond God standing feet away from me. He has a hand covering his eyes. Beside him is the hot baseball player. He's wearing a huge grin on his face. "Now you know how I feel when you're all over Charlotte."

The brunette I saw in the shop with Shawn elbows him in the ribs. "Shut it, you!"

Shawn winks at me and walks to the bar. "Hey, Nate. Ames, you need any help behind the bar?"

Amelia points to me. "I've got help. Have you met our newest bartender, Jules?"

Shawn swivels and faces me, his eyes dancing. "Oh yeah? Congrats."

I shrug and stare idiotically. I can't keep up with all the people. I'm an introvert, and without Amy to handle the social interactions for me, I've reverted back to the shy, silent girl who prefers to go unnoticed. What was I thinking when I offered to work here? This is my worst nightmare.

Amelia waves. "Come on, Jules, I'll get you set up back here. Shawn, pick whatever table you want. I'll send a server over." Then she turns back to the man she was just making out with and points at him. "I'll see you at home, Pearson."

He shakes his head. "Nah, I'm gonna stay and catch up with my brothers." He throws his arms around Shawn and his blond God-like friend and pulls them toward a table.

Brothers? Is everyone in this town related?

I'm startled when a warm hand squeezes my arm. I turn to meet the eyes of the woman I saw at the store. The one who left with Shawn a little while ago.

"I'm Charlotte. Welcome to Bristol. That was my fiancé, Jack, and Shawn is my brother."

Oh, her brother.

I try to contain the smile this brings to my face, but I fail completely. I shouldn't be excited that she's not Shawn's girlfriend. After my last dating disaster, I do *not* need to get mixed up with a baseball player. Former or not. He has heartbreak written all over that gorgeous face of his.

"I'm Jules," I reply.

Charlotte beams. "*Oh, I know*. I've heard *all* about you."

Uncomfortable with her tone, I shrug. Probably from Hailey. Maybe Charlotte is another friend she's been complaining to about me.

In a low whisper, she says, "From my brother," like we're in on a secret. She motions toward their table with her chin, and when I turn, I find Shawn staring directly at me. His eyes meet mine, and when he smiles, the warmth of it radiates through me, all the way to my toes. "Ames, go easy on her," Charlotte sings before squeezing my shoulder again and making her way to her table.

I pull my attention from them quickly. Charlotte had to warn

Amelia, so that means this girl doesn't dawdle, and I don't want to give her another reason to dislike me.

"What can I do?" I ask as I come around the bar and stare at all the gadgets and bottles. I've certainly witnessed plenty of servers working the soda squirter things, but I haven't the faintest idea how.

"You ever work in a bar?" she asks.

I shake my head, and Amelia tosses me a lemon. Thankfully, I catch it with ease.

"You're on chopping duty then. We'll train between customers. But if it gets busy, just do what I say, and we should be fine."

The next few hours are busy—like can't stop to think, let alone take a drink of water busy—but that doesn't keep me from noticing the eyes tracking my every move. And it's not Amelia, who likely wants to kill me. She asked me to get a soda for a customer during an exceptionally busy rush, and I inadvertently shot the man in the face with the squirt gun.

In my defense, I tried to do it myself, and when I couldn't get it to work, the guy scoffed at me like I was an idiot. He told me to show it to him, so I did, and then I miraculously hit the right button, resulting in orange fizz spraying all over his round, smug face.

I tried really hard to school my expression, but when I heard Shawn's deep chuckle and he offered me a mock bow from across the room, the smile broke free.

"How's your first day going?" Charlotte asks as she comes to say goodbye to Amelia, who is currently shooting daggers at me.

I shrug sheepishly. "Safe to say my second day will have to be better."

Shawn's hand on my shoulder surprises me. "I'm gonna give you a hand," he says softly in my ear. "Don't stress. Ames has a lot on her plate, and you're doing great."

Amelia looks pointedly at Shawn's hand on my shoulder, and I grimace, shrugging out of his embrace. I don't need a man to come to my rescue. And I don't want Amelia telling Hailey that I can't hack it. Hailey already thinks I'm a princess who can't get her hands dirty. The last thing I want to do is prove her right.

"I'm fine, thanks," I mutter, trying to avoid his gaze. He makes me nervous. He also makes me want things I can't have. Like him.

He regards me for a few seconds before shrugging. "Suit yourself. Ames, I'll be with the guys if you need me," he says, avoiding me completely before he disappears.

"He's a really freaking good guy. Don't screw with him," she says in a low voice. "He was just trying to be nice."

I hold up my hands in retreat. "I'm going to run to the bathroom." I rush off, not waiting to see her reaction. No matter what I do tonight, it's wrong.

And not for nothing. Where the heck is my twin sister?

JULES
ICE CREAM
SUPER PREMIUM ICE CREAM
SUPER PREMIUM ICE CREAM

CHAPTER 19

JULES

When I'm stressed, I bake. It's the only thing that can quiet my incessant thoughts. After my disaster of a shift at the bar, I rushed to Walgreens, popping in just before it closed, and bought one—okay, more than one—of every baking ingredient I could find. Anything that would pair well with sugar.

I *need* the sugar.

Now sugar and powder coat every surface of my kitchen. I bite into the warm, gooey brownie and sigh. The chocolate explodes in my mouth as I lean back and stare at my mess.

My ex hated the mess I'd make in his kitchen. Jared kept the space immaculate. He cleaned every bowl as he went. He'd use a bowl for mixing and stick it in the sink to soak while he moved to the next step.

Not me.

Whereas Jared used the same bowl over and over again, I'd have fifteen of them littering his kitchen. It drove him nuts.

But one of the reasons he could be so neat was that he knew every recipe by heart. He knew what step to take next to make the french torte that sold out daily. He had every ingredient laid out precisely how he liked for each pie. And he had clear instructions for everyone to follow to ensure everything was just as he liked.

Not me.

I would take over the kitchen while he slept. Or at least I thought he was sleeping. Apparently, he was going home to his wife.

"Don't go there," I remind myself before taking another bite.

I didn't go to culinary school. I have no training outside of what Jared taught me and my own experimenting. But when I was in his kitchen, in the dead of the night, I could spend hours creating desserts.

I never wrote down a recipe. Never followed one either. I just...*created*.

The downside of that, of course, is that when I discovered something delicious—something Jared wanted to sell in the bakery because it was so good—I couldn't recreate it. Just a pinch off one ingredient, and the entire thing would be different.

I study my reflection in the old oven, doing my best to redirect my thoughts. Powder dots my nose, and I swipe at it, hoping the memory of my scoundrel of an ex-boyfriend and ex-boss will disappear along with the fine dust adorning my face. None of that matters anymore. My only focus should be on figuring out how to make a go here.

I take another bite of brownie and slide to the floor. Perfectly sculpted donuts sit warming inside the oven at my back, which I've turned off. I can't even think of taking a bite of one. I'm stuffed. And exhausted.

My phone rings, and I jump at the sound. I scoop the phone out of my pocket and accept Amy's FaceTime request. I try swiping the remaining powder from my face, but since the white substance lines both sides of my hands, I only spread it farther onto my forehead.

"Hey, bestie!" Amy sings into the phone.

I don't have the energy to do anything but stare at her.

Her smile drops. "Oh my goodness. It must be a stage-five disaster if you look like that. What happened?"

I breathe in deeply to keep the tears from streaming down my face. I don't want her to know how bad it is here. How utterly alone I am. She thinks Hailey is living with me. She thinks I've got a job I'm excited about. Neither of those things is true. I'm failing at everything…

The tears start.

I blow out a breath.

"Just miss home." I give her a half-truth. I curl my knees up to my chest and try to muster a smile. "What are you up to?"

"Nuh-uh," she says, shaking her head. "Tell me the truth. Do I have to come and kick some twin ass?"

I laugh at the thought of it. Hailey would take Amy down in a second. Amy may be taller, but she's got nothing on my sister's attitude. I'm pretty sure her stare could cut a person in half. And I can't even figure out how to work a damn soda gun.

I'm a disaster.

"I'm just not good at this," I admit. "And I miss you," I say again. Because I really freaking do. "Do me a favor. Let's not focus on me. Tell me about the part you just got."

CHAPTER 20

SHAWN

"You know, boys, if you washed the trucks with no shirts on, we could probably raise enough money for a new station," Carmella says in a deep bedroom voice that makes me shudder and leaves me shrinking inside my pants.

I nod at the woman. She's wearing an orange muumuu today. It has a pumpkin on it. I bet she'll switch this one out for one with Christmas trees tomorrow.

"I'll mention it to the chief," I tell her.

She smiles and waves goodbye as she and the other ladies who walk miles around town continue on their jaunt.

"Probie, make lunch," Colby hollers as I finish shining the last speck he found on the red fire truck. Behind me, Dane chuckles.

I curse under my breath. Don't get me wrong, I know how to be low man on the totem pole. I played in the summer leagues and the minor leagues. I got scooped up after one season in the minors, so although I've done my fair share of bullshit while being the rookie of the team, being treated like shit is not exactly something I'm used to. And the only reason Colby is riding my ass is because before I started here, he was the probie. But I doubt Dane or Mason rode his ass this hard.

Dane claps my shoulder and says in a low voice, "If you get us tickets to a Sox game, I'll tell Colby that Hailey agreed to a date if he wears nothing but suspenders while washing the truck."

I put a fist to my mouth to hide the laughter that image conjures and shake my head. "Oh yeah. I'll get you season tickets if you can make that happen."

Mason whistles under his breath. "Mr. Big Shot, here, making promises."

I flinch. I have to be careful when I offer shit like that. I'm surrounded by hard-working blue-collar guys. They're firefighters, plumbers, and electricians, and as much as I like to pretend I'm one of them, our bank accounts disagree. I don't *have* to work; they do.

I give a shame-filled shrug, and Dane grabs me by the shoulders, pulling me back from the spiral of self-loathing I was diving headfirst into. "Don't let him get to ya. He's a grumpy shit all the time."

From the rig, Mason growls, "I can hear you."

"That was intentional," Dane quips, leading me into the station and toward the kitchen. "Do you miss the bar yet?"

I laugh as I run my hand over my face. "Nah, I was there last night. Honestly, I'm sure I'll be helping out for a few more weeks. Hailey and Amelia have their hands full."

"Especially since Amelia is back with her ex. You were hitting that, weren't you?"

I laugh uncomfortably. Amelia is my friend. And my sister's future sister-in-law. Although I'm used to men talking about women that way, I'm not okay with it when it comes to family. "We're just friends. And yes, she's back with her husband. Thank God. I'm pretty sure they would have set fire to a few structures if they hadn't worked their shit out."

He reaches into the fridge and pulls out cold cuts, then points to the bread in the corner. I grab it, and we get to work on assembling sandwiches. While I love to grill, the weather has turned, and I'm not offering to stand outside for any of them.

Colby and Mason saunter in, and a few other guys join them, settling down at the table and chatting. "Hey, Shawn," Colby says loudly, drawing my attention to the table and quieting everyone around him. "What's the word on Hailey and her twin sister?"

I swear this guy is looking to get hit.

Turning slowly, I school my expression. "Not sure what you mean. I honestly don't know her sister that well, and Hailey is fine."

Colby laughs and rubs his hands together. "Yeah, she is."

I clench my jaw. *He's twenty-six. He's only twenty-six. Cut him some slack.*

"Word on the street is the sister is working at the bar now too. You gonna hit that?"

Tilting my head back to roll the stress from my neck, I ignore him. It's the only way I can avoid a confrontation because we're getting dangerously close to one. Why am I so protective of her though? I barely know the girl, and every time I run into her, she's got a chip on her shoulder. I shake my head. "Doubtful."

Dane smacks me on the back, probably sensing my unease. "Come on, let's eat."

"You think this is a good idea?" Dane asks in a grumble as we walk into the bar together.

"We don't have much choice. I wasn't going to let *him*," I say, motioning to Colby in front of us, "give the girls a hard time."

As we were getting off our shift, Colby suggested drinks at Thames. Yes, I'm aware that most of the firefighters end up here on a regular basis. I've worked here long enough and been privy to their shenanigans, but tonight it felt like he was out to prove something, and I sensed that Hailey would need me. Okay, maybe she wouldn't need me. The girl can handle herself, but I'm not so sure about her sister. And I can't help but feel protective of Jules, although I have no idea why.

I want to pull her into my chest. I want to hold her hand. Okay, maybe I do know where this feeling is coming from. I want to kiss her again.

We settle at the bar, and Amelia looks up with a smile. "Two nights in a row, Shawn. Some may think you're really starting to miss me." She winks as she puts napkins in front of us and waits for our drink orders.

"Nah. Just wanted to see how your newest employee is doing." I motion to Jules. She's in the corner, wiping sweat off her forehead, looking completely and utterly out of place.

Amelia shudders. "I have no idea how she's going to make it through the holidays. The Christmas festival starts next week, and this place is going to be a mob scene. And God forbid she's still here by summer."

A laugh escapes my mouth before I can stop it, and Jules shoots me a look. *Shit.*

"What'll you have?" Amelia asks.

A lecherous grin breaks out on Colby's face. "I'll have a double… of whatever she's serving," he says, motioning to Jules.

Another freaking twin joke. The guy is unbearable.

"Oh, I'm sorry. She's not on the menu, fuckface," Amelia snaps, turning to face Colby full-on and blocking his view of Jules. And just like that, I know Jules has a new friend. Amelia doesn't like many people. She keeps to herself and her family, but she is fiercely protective and doesn't take anyone's bullshit.

Colby's retort is cut off by a loud hissing noise at the other end of the bar. We all turn toward the sound, finding Jules hunched over and trying to tap the keg. Before I can open my mouth to warn her of what's about to happen, her hand slips, and the keg sprays her and every surface around her. She shrieks and lets go of the tube, and the pressure from the keg sends the foam flying out. The pipe whips around in the air like one of those inflatable guys at a car dealership and sprays Jules in the face. Her screeching is only overpowered by Amelia's growling and Colby's laughter.

"Yes! Wet T-shirt contest!" he cheers.

I jump up and slide over the bar. I pull Jules out of the spray, and with my arm behind my back, I grab the hose and point it in Colby's direction. Amelia is definitely going to kill me because I'm sure I'm soaking half the bar, but it's totally worth it. Especially when I hear him screeching like a boy going through puberty.

I fold it in half like I would an outdoor hose, confident I've made my point with Colby, and put my hand on Jules's hip. "You okay?" I ask quietly in her ear.

Amelia somehow manages to keep her cool and grabs the tap from me, patting me on my shoulder. "Take her in the back and get her cleaned up."

I push Jules forward. It's like she's on autopilot. Her body is tense, and she barely registers my touch. She just follows my instructions with a whimper. It's only when I get her into the kitchen that I notice she's shaking in what I'm sure are sobs. The staff working in the kitchen look up, each one eyeing us critically, but I shake my head sternly so they know to leave it alone. I push Jules into a utility closet and grab the string for the single light above. When she doesn't turn around to face me, I place my hand on her shoulder and whisper, "It happens to the best of us. It's okay."

A bark of laughter escapes through her sob. "Okay? Okay?" she shouts, spinning around and revealing her red, splotchy cheeks. "How is anything okay? I just destroyed my sister's bar! The sister who has no interest in getting to know me, who was supposed to move in with me but barely spends a moment of time with me…the sister who can't be bothered to train me. And for some unknown reason, I'm the idiot trying my damnedest to prove to her that I can work in a bar. But surprise, surprise, she was right, I can't—"

She's near hysterics, so I do the only thing I can think of to stop her rant. I angle in and press my mouth against hers in a searing kiss. At first, she doesn't react, and I wonder if maybe I've made an epic mistake. I pull back and inspect her face for a reaction.

She stares at me, silent, and then bites her lip.

"I'm sorry. You were spiraling and I didn't know—"

This time, I don't get to finish my sentence. She throws her arms around my neck and pulls my mouth to hers, sucking on my bottom lip and forcing a groan from my throat. I push her back against the racks, knocking paper towels to the floor. But I ignore the mess we're making, instead grabbing below her ass and picking her up so her legs are wrapped around me.

Like the first time, the kiss is incredible. Out of this world. She tastes salty, like tears and beer, but also, somehow, like everything I've ever wanted. Hope and passion and desire. Her tiny legs squeeze tighter around my waist, pulling me as close as she can get, practically riding my now obvious erection.

"You okay in there?" Amelia asks with a knock.

Jules pulls her lips from my mouth and looks away, dropping her arms and trying desperately to push me off her.

I refuse to let her go.

"Yup, we'll be right out," I call, straining to hide the desire in my voice. Then I tilt in so we're forehead to forehead and stare at her until she finally meets my eyes. "You okay?" I whisper.

She shakes her head against mine. "No," she breathes.

I let out a sigh and lower her slowly to the floor. "You're gonna be all right," I say again. "You're safe with me."

She focuses those green eyes on me, as if she's just realizing I'm the one in here with her. She places her palm against my chest and looks down at the floor. "Thank you," she says quietly.

"Go on home." I motion to the door. "I'll help Amelia."

She shakes her head. "But Hailey—"

"Isn't here," I offer. "Listen, I don't know what's going on between the two of you, but give her time. She'll come around. Go home and get some rest. You can try again tomorrow."

She drops her head in resignation and moves past me. Once she's out the door, I put my palm on the shelves and lean into them, trying to find my bearings.

What the hell just happened? It's like every time I'm around that girl, I can't keep my hands to myself. No, forget that—I can't keep my *lips* to myself.

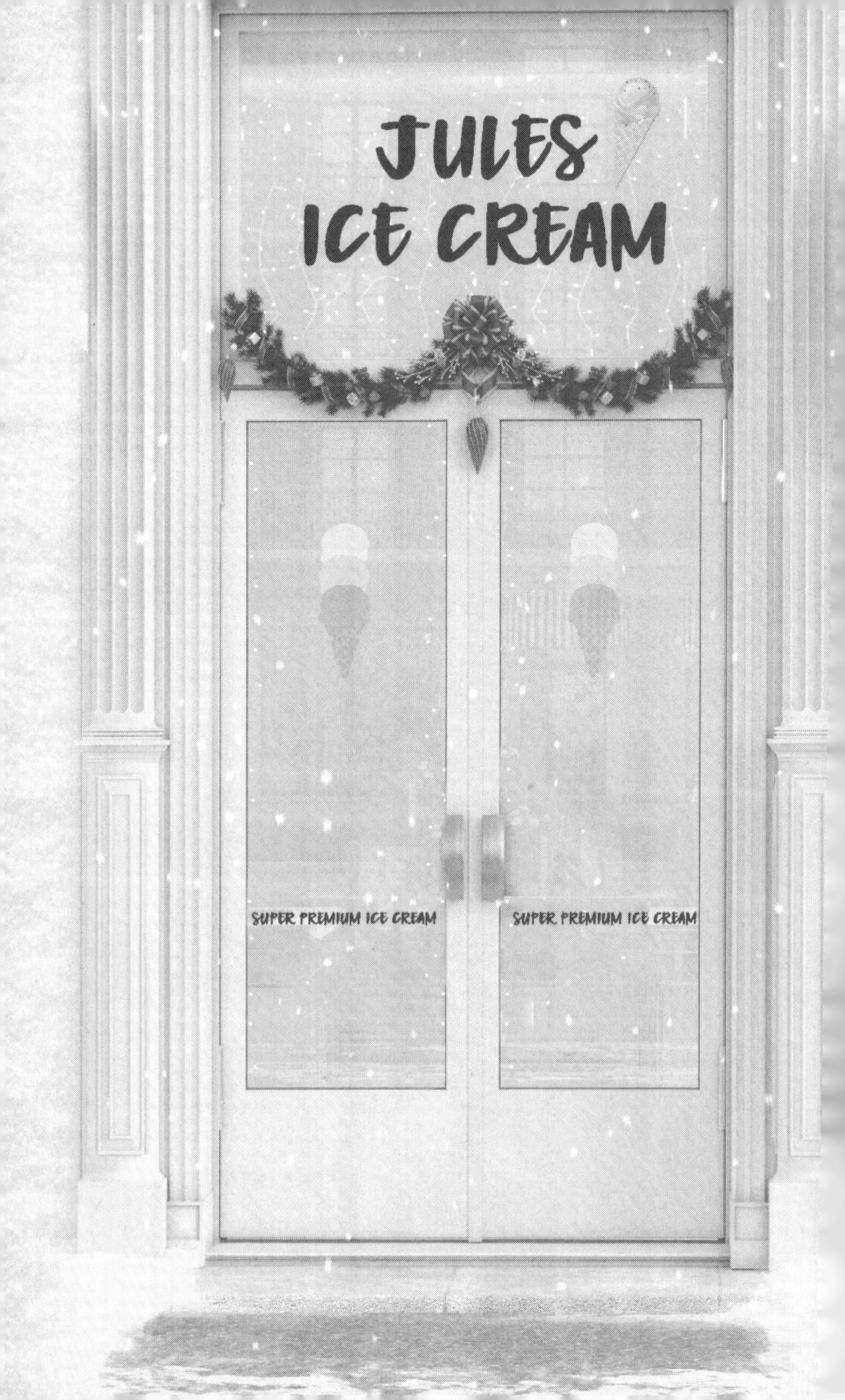
JULES
ICE CREAM
SUPER PREMIUM ICE CREAM
SUPER PREMIUM ICE CREAM

CHAPTER 21

JULES

"You really don't get it," I say into the phone, which I have set on the bathroom counter while I strip out of my beer-soaked clothes. "I'm coming home. This is pointless. I've tried so hard to get to know my sisters. Caris is nice but busy. And Hailey? Don't even get me started on Hailey. She's definitely avoiding me. Which is impressive, considering we're supposed to be living together and I work at her bar."

I'm bent over, slipping a sock off, when I spot the ring of dirt around the back of the toilet. My stomach rolls. "This place isn't even sanitary." I touch my fingers to the shower curtain I purchased, the only new thing in this bathroom, and stare at the pink walls of the shower, which have turned a dingy shade of mauve from wear and tear. I shudder. "You wouldn't believe it unless you were here."

Amy laughs on the other end of the phone. "Babe, I'm trying to be supportive here, but you sound just a little—"

"Don't you dare!" I screech, the tears bubbling and my throat clogging on a sob. "You seriously have no idea how bad it is."

"Prissy. You sound prissy. Like me. Which is fine, because I totally am, but you aren't. You're easy-going, Jules. You're the girl who goes along with everything, gets along with everyone—"

I interrupt her. "That's because I don't *talk* to anyone. I stand by your side and let you do the talking. I can't treat people one way or another because I'm normally silent. But I have to talk here. Because *you're* not here."

She hums into the phone. "Yes, that is a problem. Honestly, Jules, I can't get there for another few weeks, but I could fly out for the holidays. We can have our very own snowy Christmas."

I grumble, "I don't even know if it snows here."

"But you love hot chocolate and Christmas lights. We could walk around the cobblestone streets, hand in hand, looking at all the decorated houses. It has to be better than southern California at Christmas."

I hum as I step into the shower. She could be right. I do love Christmas. Even if I've never experienced a traditional one. I've always wanted that. And honestly, when I first found out I had sisters and they lived in New England, I imagined this scenario where I'd come here and we'd bond, have sleepovers, drink hot chocolate. And yeah, wear matching Christmas pajamas. Okay, I sound like a five-year-old…or a stay-at-home mom. But honestly, it's what I've always dreamed of. Christmastime for an only child is lonely. Especially with a mother like mine.

The hot water beats down on my body, erasing the beer and the tears, but Shawn's taste is branded on my lips. I don't know what came over me, but when he kissed me, when he stopped my world from spiraling by taking all the control from me, I finally felt grounded. When his fingers dug into my thighs and he pushed himself against me, and I felt *him*, every solid, illicit inch of him, my entire body buzzed.

"So what do you say?" Amy says from outside the shower, pulling me from my thoughts.

"*Fine*." I drawl, my voice echoing against the bathroom walls.

"Thatta girl!" she calls. "Okay, I'll talk to you soon. Love you, bye!"

She's gone before I can reply, and I'm back to scrubbing my hands over my body and through my hair. Amy's right. I can do this. I just need to adjust my expectations. So what if Hailey wants nothing to do with me? I'll get to know my other family members instead. I'm done sucking up to her. Everything I do from here on out is for me.

Just as a sense of self-satisfaction brings a smile to my face, eight little legs appear before my eyes, doing a little twirl right above my head, and I scream bloody freaking murder.

CHAPTER 22

SHAWN

I've just slipped off my shoes and set down my keys on the kitchen counter when I hear a bloodcurdling scream. Without thought, I run across the hall and throw the door open to Jules's unlocked apartment in search of the imminent disaster waiting for me.

Standing in the middle of the living room, dripping wet and stark naked, is Jules. I know I shouldn't stare, but god, I can't help but rove over every inch of her, drink in every curve, admire the way her skin glistens from the shower.

"What the heck, Shawn? Stop staring at me!" she screams as she holds one hand over her boobs and the other over her most private parts.

My eyes dart up to her face and my cheeks heat. Shit, that was wrong. "Is everything okay?" I pant out, willing myself to focus on her face.

"Jiminy Cricket, turn around!" she shrills.

Immediately, I swivel in the other direction but continue my inquisition. "You were screaming. Is someone here?"

I hear her bouncing and look over my shoulder just in time to see her reach for an oven mitt to cover herself. Fighting back a smile, I press my lips together and walk to the bathroom. "I'm just grabbing a towel for you," I say before she accuses me of trying to get near her.

The shower is still running, and the bathroom is filled with steam. I turn the nozzle, grab a white towel from the rack, and hold my hands over my eyes as I walk back out.

She grabs the towel from my hand. "Thanks," she says softly.

I peek at her between my fingers and watch as she fastens the towel over her breasts. They're covered, but they're pushed up and still glistening. My mouth waters.

This is not my proudest moment.

"You can go," she says with more force this time.

Finally, my mind starts working again. "I'm sorry, but you were screaming. What happened?"

She sighs heavily and looks at the ground. "There was a spider."

I turn my head to the side and throw a hand over my mouth to fight back the laugh bubbling up.

She catches it anyway. "Would you want to be naked in the shower with eight legs crawling up to you in there?" she shouts, flinging an arm toward the bathroom. This girl sure can scream. I'd prefer if it was my name.

Fuck, now I'm hard.

Okay, maybe I was hard like five minutes ago when I saw her naked for the first time.

"Do you want me to kill it?" I ask, staring down at her lips now.

She pulls the bottom one between her teeth, and I have to stifle a groan.

"Would you mind? I'm going to put on some clothes."

I shoot her a smirk. "Would I mind you putting on clothes? Yes."

Her cheeks turn pink, and she rolls her eyes before looking away.

"I'll take care of your spider, Red."

She darts a look at me, her eyes dilating. But I don't stick around to see what her latest issue is. The girl yo-yos between shy and feisty in seconds, and I'd rather not get slapped.

I do a thorough search of the shower but don't find a spider anywhere. Maybe her eyes were playing tricks on her. I take a moment to steady myself in the bathroom, staring at my reflection, silently telling myself to get my shit together, then I walk back out.

In the living room, Jules is fully clothed. Practically every inch of her body is covered. She's even got her hoodie pulled over her head and cinched tight. "Did you take care of it?"

"It's all set," I lie. I feel like a bit of a jerk, but admitting that I didn't find a spider will either make *her* think that *I* think she's crazy—which will probably result in anger—or she'll never get back in the shower again because she doesn't believe me. Neither of those seems like a good option.

When she beams at me, I'm thrilled with my lie. "Thank you so much." She sighs. "God, you must think I'm a disaster. Every time I run into you, I'm like a damsel in distress."

I shrug. "I don't mind being your knight."

She laughs and looks toward the door. Right, that's my cue. "Well, if you need anything, I'll be across the hall," I say, pointing to the door.

Her eyes jump up to meet mine. "You're what?"

I laugh uncomfortably and study the floorboards beneath me. "Uh, when you left for California, I moved in across the hall. I'm doing some work on the building, and Caris said I could stay there." I rub my neck and chance a glance at her. Shit. This is news to her. "Caris didn't tell you?"

Jules shakes her head. "No, I haven't seen her since I got back. That place was a disaster when I checked it out. You must have worked a miracle to be sleeping there."

I laugh. "Yeah, it's still a bit of a disaster. And the plumbing in the shower doesn't work. So be happy the spiders are your biggest worry."

Her eyes go wide. "You don't have a working shower?"

I shrug. "It's fine. I take them at the station or at my sister's."

She stares at me for a moment and then walks out the door without saying another word. I follow her, curious as to what she's doing. As soon as she gets to my apartment door, she glances back at me. "May I?"

I nod. "Be my guest."

She walks in and looks around, and I take the opportunity to observe her. Something about her calms me, even when she's freaking out or freezing up. She's finally let the hoodie slip from her head, and it's fallen off her shoulder, exposing creamy white skin I have the urge to press soft kisses against. Her wet hair hangs limply in a lopsided ponytail, drops of water falling onto her neck and sliding down the very shoulder my eyes are trained on. When she turns back to me, her cheeks are pink and her eyes wild.

"You're sleeping on a couch?" she asks, pointing at the pillow and comforter folded neatly at one end.

I smirk. "It's not so bad. I have a pretty girl for a neighbor and this beautiful view of the bay," I say, pointing toward the window.

She rolls her eyes and bites on her bottom lip, then paces the apartment. "This is crazy," she mutters under her breath. "He can't sleep in an apartment with no plumbing…and on a couch. This is nuts." She turns back to me and shakes her head, still murmuring angrily. She's cute like this, all worked up but too nervous to actually voice her concerns.

"You got something to say over there, Red?" I tease, propping myself up against the wall, my arms folded over my chest, completely at ease watching this ball of nervous energy work through her concerns.

She looks up at me, almost like she's surprised to find me here, and then she shakes her head again. "And he's too good-looking for his own good. Standing there like that all calm while I'm unraveling before his very eyes. Can you not?" she finally says.

"Oh, are you talking to me now?" I tease.

She narrows her eyes.

"What am I doing wrong now, sweetheart?" The word rolls off my tongue so easily, making me realize how badly I wish she were *my* sweetheart.

"Oh, forget it." She sighs. "You can't stay here."

"I can't?" I ask, amusement dancing in my eyes.

"No." She shakes her head resolutely. "I'll text Hailey and see if you can stay in her room."

"She, uh." Once again, I grab the back of my neck, trying to figure out the right way to tell her that Hailey has no intention of staying in that apartment with her. "Doesn't she have her own place?"

To say I could actually see her deflate would be an understatement. All light leaves her eyes, and her face falls, like she's as sad as a forgotten puppy. The urge to pull her into my arms and crush her against my chest is strong, but I hold back, waiting for her to take the lead.

"Oh yeah. I guess she does," she replies softly, looking away from me. She takes a deep breath, straightens her shoulders, and lifts her chin. "You can stay in her room then. Until you get this place up and running, I mean."

"You sure that's okay with you?" I ask. The idea is more appealing by the second. Living with her. Getting to see her every day. Hopefully wet and coming out of the shower again. "I'm a neat freak and I make an awesome omelet," I offer, shrugging a shoulder. "And I sleep at the fire station a couple nights a week. I can head there now if you're uncomfortable."

She shakes her head. "That's not necessary. Honestly, I doubt I'll be staying long."

My good mood deflates. I barely know her, and yet every time I see her, I want to learn more. I try to keep the disappointment out of my voice when I respond. "That's too bad. I'll have the guys help me move some of the stuff over tomorrow, but only if you're sure. They were going to help me bring my bed here in the morning."

She nods. "That works. I'll get you a key."

"Oh, Caris already gave me one," I say, and her eyes dart to mine in confusion. "Because I was going to do some work on your apartment too," I clarify, and she seems to relax. "I'll be fine on the couch tonight," I promise.

She bites her lip but nods again. "Okay, well, I'll let you get some sleep then."

I push off the door and open it for her as she walks by me. I need to get away from her before I try to change her mind with my lips… and I don't mean with words.

Just as I'm shutting the door, I hear her squeak out, "Thanks again, Shawn."

I give her a half-smile. It isn't until I lean against the solid wood that I finally take a breath. I scrub my hands over my face in frustration. I know two things. I really like that girl, and I really want her to stay.

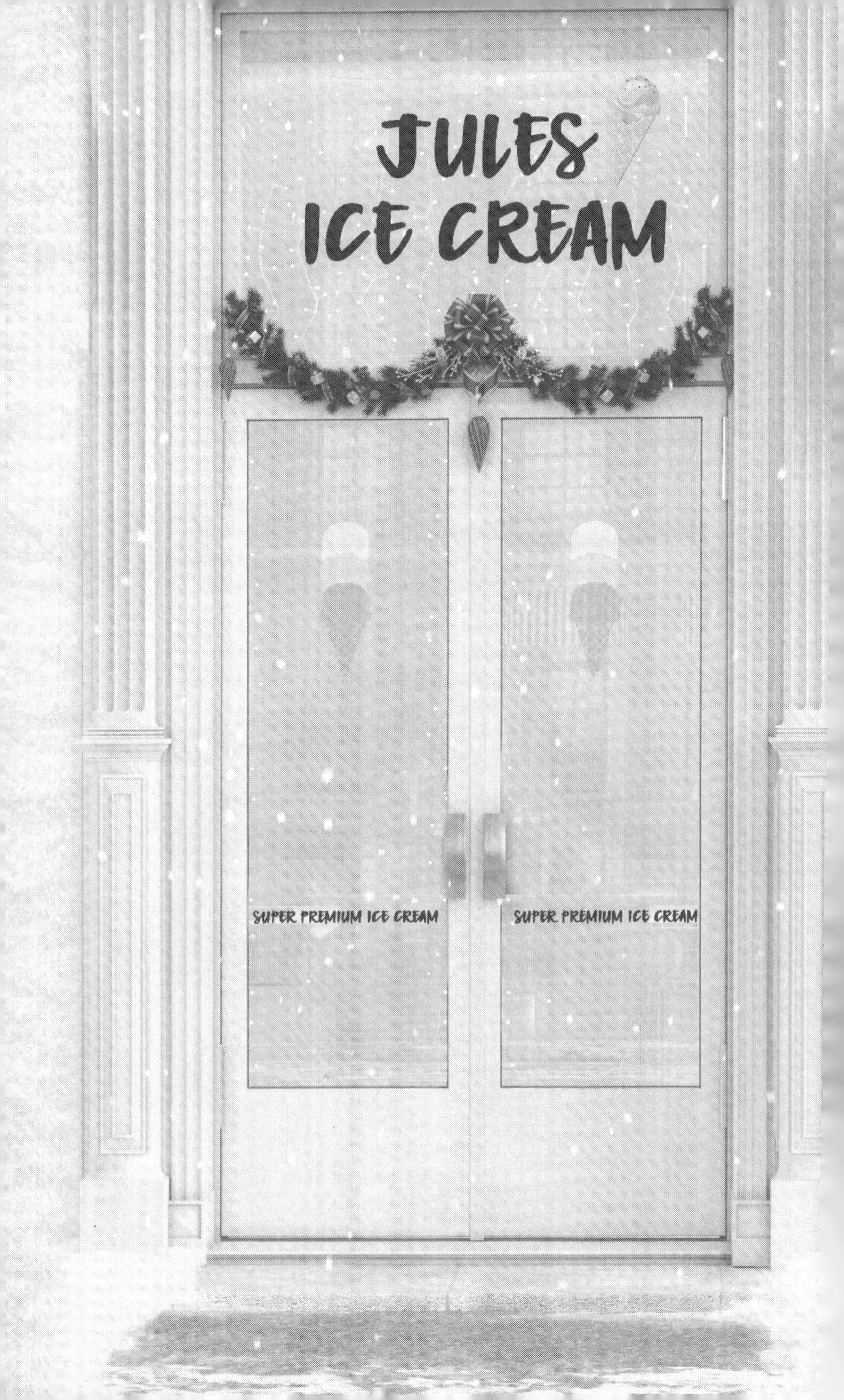

CHAPTER 23

JULES

I'm pretty sure I've reached the epitome of low.

Looking around the small bar hidden on the side of the bowling alley, I know I have.

The truth is I need to drink. Like I need a drink more than anything right now, and I'm not even much of a drinker. But after the last few days—screw that. After the last two months—I need a drink.

First, I find out my boyfriend, who is also my boss, has a wife, which leads to being without a boyfriend as well as a job. Then I find out that my father didn't want me. And let's not forget my mother's betrayal. I discovered that I have two sisters I never knew existed. Then I meet them, and my own twin wants nothing to do with me. Oh yeah, and I practically destroyed my sister's bar yesterday.

Yep, I need a drink. And since I'm hiding from my sister, along with everyone else in that Hallmark town, I'm drinking at the bowling alley. It's not even a real bowling alley. They call it duckpin bowling. The pins are miniature, as are the balls. It's actually pretty interesting to watch, but that could be because I'm three margaritas in. They aren't even good margaritas.

"Oh, who are you kidding, Jules? You have no idea what a good margarita is."

Yes, I'm talking to myself. I have no one else to talk to. Amy will fly out if she knows how miserable I am, and I don't want to ruin her shot at the part she's working on.

"Want me to make you a margarita, Red?"

The hair on the back of my neck stands at attention, as do my freaking nipples, the second Shawn's warm breath tickles my ear.

I groan loudly and slump across the bar.

"You're going to give me a complex if you keep reacting to me this way," he says on a soft chuckle. His mouth is still too close, even though he's several feet away. It's like he's branded me.

I groan again. "Can't a girl hit rock bottom in peace?"

Taking my groan as an invitation, I guess, he laughs and sits on the stool next to me. "Tell me what's bothering you. Maybe I can help."

I lift my head, only for a moment, to raise a brow in a *really, buddy?* signal. He just smirks. What it must be like to have that kind of confidence.

Another aggravated sigh leaves my mouth, but I give in. "Let's see. Where shall we start? I moved across the country for a family that still doesn't want much to do with me. I practically destroyed my sister's bar. I have no friends—"

He cuts me off before I can add, *and my boyfriend was married and fired me.*

"I can be your friend." He smirks again and crosses his arms, giving me a perfect view of what can only be described as arm porn. Is that a thing? Maybe it's the margaritas talking, but I'm pretty sure this man could star in his very own film. I'd pay to watch it.

I scoff, finally taking my eyes off his biceps. "You're only saying that because you've seen me naked."

This time he graces me with a real smile. His eyes crinkle, and happiness radiates off him. This is the first time I've seen him actually happy. He's been sexy, he's been domineering, he's been flirty. But *this* smile? It makes my heart ache. If being his friend means I get to see that smile daily, it would be like medication. A little dose might actually get me through each dreadful day.

"Now I'm not saying that you being naked wasn't a definite perk of our 'friendship'"—he uses air quotes—"but that isn't the reason I want to be your friend."

"It's the kissing, isn't it?" I tease, perking up a little at the banter. But just a smidgen. I mean, it's hard to be depressed when Shawn Freaking Chase, former baseball player and the hottest man I've ever seen, is smiling at me the way he is right now.

I avoided him all day. Left my apartment at the crack of dawn so I wasn't there when he officially moved in. I've been to every store in Bristol, sat in a coffee shop for hours reading a book on my phone, and then I came here to this bowling alley bar, figuring I'd be safe. But no, here he is in all his glory.

His cheeks practically split as his smile gets bigger. "The kissing definitely didn't hurt." He shakes his head, grinning, and looks away from me for a moment.

I immediately feel colder. Like his attention creates physical warmth.

Wanting to bask in his heat again, I say, "So if it's not the nakedness, and it's not the kissing, why do you want to be my friend?"

He turns back to me, his eyes going soft. "Because I could use one too."

The admission is full of vulnerability. And that's when I see it. The reason I haven't seen him smile like this until now. He's got baggage too. He's going through something. And although I could definitely use a friend, knowing he needs one—that I could actually help him— makes the decision a no-brainer.

I lift myself up from my slumped over position and smile. "I can be your friend."

Shawn's grin returns and my heart skips. "Great. Now. You mentioned margaritas. That one not doing it for ya?"

I look behind me to where the bartender stands. He's working through a line of bowlers right now. The bar is just a tiny room with three stools hidden behind the arcade area. It really is a pathetic place to choose for a drink.

"Yeah, it leaves something to be desired. What are you doing here, by the way?"

He motions behind him. "Bowling with the guys from the fire department."

My cheeks heat. "Shoot. You're here with friends, and I'm monopolizing your time with my groaning about my miserable life."

"Stop. We just established that you're my friend too. I came in here to get a pitcher of beer while the guys got the lane set up." He looks at me for a second and then adds, "Would you want to join us for a few games?"

"No…I wouldn't want to impose."

Shawn jumps up and pulls out my stool, with me on it, and turns my legs so I'm facing him. "Come on, Red. We're friends now, and friends bowl. So giddy up."

I can't help but laugh. "Did you just summon me like a horse?"

He shrugs. "Did it work?"

I smile. "Yeah, okay. But I'm buying the beer."

"Yeah, you owe the guys for moving your stuff. That's a good way to make friends," he teases.

I shoot him a look. "Seemed to have worked to your advantage since you're living there too now."

Shawn winks and lifts me off the stool as I squeal. "Right, we're more than friends. Come on, Roomie. We've got asses to kick."

"How are you settling in?" Dane asks as Shawn walks up to the lane to take his shot. My eyes are laser focused on his very fine behind

in those jeans. His butt should have its own zip code. It's a perfect bubble. I never knew that was my thing, but I'm learning that all things Shawn turn me on. Which is dangerous. Impossible. He's now my roommate, and I'm pretty convinced he's a player.

The winks, the flirting, the *kiss*. That man has heartbreak written all over him, and I've had enough of that.

I tear my eyes away and shrug in answer to Dane's question. He chuckles low. "Yeah, he's pretty dreamy."

"What? No…I just…" I can't form a coherent objection. The heat in my cheeks, which undoubtedly means they're bright red, gives away my embarrassment.

"It's okay. Your secret's safe with me." He gives me a genuine smile.

I really like Dane. He was so kind to me when he helped with the electricity and moving me in. But I barely got to say thank you or get to know him at all. Maybe it's time to change that. He's easy to talk to, and I could use another friend.

"So what about you? Any girlfriends?"

Dane shakes his head. "Nah, my wife and I recently separated. My focus is on my sons. Besides," he says in a clear attempt to change the serious turn of this conversation, "I know every girl in this town. Unlike Shawn, I wasn't lucky enough to meet the new girl first."

Pushing against his shoulder, I laugh. "Stop it. He and I are just friends."

"She's right," Shawn says, surprising me as he walks up. "Although I'd prefer if you'd take the 'just' out of it. Kinda giving me a complex."

My eyes drop to his lips as he speaks. I can't help it.

Dane chuckles and mutters "bullshit" next to me. Hopefully quietly enough that no one caught it but me.

"Where's Hailey?" Colby asks from the table next to me, where he's filling a cup from the pitcher of beer.

I wince, unable to hide my disappointment. "Not sure. She doesn't live with me anymore. Apparently, this big oaf does." I point to Shawn.

His grin is so big his dimple pops. "You'll be happy about that when you have a new kitchen and someone to kill all the spiders." His eyes light up as he speaks, obviously thinking back to last night.

I look away from them all and focus on sipping my beer to hide the blush threatening to creep up my neck *again*.

Colby turns to Shawn. "You know where Hailey is tonight?"

"She's working. And she wants nothing to do with you."

This gets even Mason to laugh. He's always so quiet. When it's not his turn, he sits in the corner, watching people, wearing a look of indifference on his face and a flannel shirt over his chest. It's like his uniform. I've never seen him in anything else.

"Thought you weren't interested in her?" Colby says defiantly to Shawn. This has me looking up. *Is he interested in Hailey?*

Shawn shakes his head. "I'm not. We're just friends. But you are definitely *not* her type."

Hmm. Just friends. Jealousy courses through me. *Shawn and Hailey are friends…what kind of friends? Kissing friends?*

Fortunately, Colby is as interested as me. "So you've never hit that?"

Shawn's jaw clenches. Yeah, I wouldn't have put it that way and I retort, "Please. She's my sister. Have a little respect."

Four pairs of wide eyes turn in my direction. Even I'm a little surprised by my outburst. And I'm annoyed that I said it because I wanted to hear Shawn's answer.

Mason stands up and steps between Colby and Shawn, then leans down to grab his beer. "Can we just fucking bowl and stop acting like a bunch of pussies?"

I close my eyes in appreciation, even if the only words Mason muttered tonight are those. He turns to me and rasps out an apology. "Sorry for the language."

I smile up at him. "No worries. I agree. Can we just freaking bowl?"

Yeah, I'm not really good at the cursing thing.

I stand and grab a ball, hyped up from the entire conversation. I strut up to the lane like a boss, swinging my hips, knowing all eyes are on me. As soon as the ball swings back and I release it, I tilt my body, willing the ball to follow my eye line.

It slows as it gets close—that's the key to duckpin bowling I learned in my time watching from the bar. You don't want to hit them as hard as you can. And if you hit them just right—bang, all ten pins fall down. Before I can jump up in excitement, Shawn's bellowing cheer reverberates in my ears and he lifts me over his head like I'm a trophy. He spins me around, and I make eye contact with Dane, who's giving me a look that says *just friends, my ass.* Colby is pouting because he has yet to get a strike, and Mason's lips are tilted just a fraction. He nods to me in congratulations. But Shawn? You'd think he hit the pins for how excited he is.

"Put me down," I say, laughing as he slides me down the front of his body, too slowly to be appropriate, if I'm being honest. My body heats as I feel the ripple of muscles below his shirt and we come face to face, nose to nose. He's still holding my hips and keeping me in place so my feet can't reach the ground.

"Hi," he says, staring into my eyes, his voice low and sexy.

"Hi, roomie," I whisper back, nearly breathless.

"That was a nice shot, Red."

I can't help but focus on his lips, and I lick my own at the sight, completely lost to his breath against mine and the pounding of my heart. Or maybe that's his. That's how close we are, so I genuinely don't know.

"Your turn, *Babe,*" Dane crows, interrupting a moment that shouldn't have occurred.

"Babe?" I tilt my head in question.

Shawn rolls his eyes and finally drops me the final few inches to the ground.

Under his breath, he mutters, "Everyone's a comedian."

"Like the baseball player," Colby explains the obvious.

I press my lips together to hide my laugh. Poor Shawn. I know his career ended on a bad note, but he honestly deserves the nickname. He was one hell of a baseball player.

He catches my smile, and his dimple pops with a grin. "Oh, you like that, Red?"

I nod, giddy. "I told you. I have a thing for baseball."

He leans down to grab his ball, and I home in on his bubble butt again. Yeah, he is one heck of a babe. "Feel free to use the nickname then, Red. I'll be your babe any day of the week." He winks before he walks to the lane and slams the ball far too hard, knocking down only two pins.

I laugh along while the guys tease him. Honestly, it's turning out to be one heck of a night.

An hour later, we're sitting in Bristol House of Pizza, still smiling.

"I can't believe you've eaten three slices of pizza!" Shawn teases from across the booth.

Dane snuck in beside me before Shawn could, and I swear I saw him shoot Dane a look. Colby and Shawn sit on the other side, and Mason sits in a chair on the end. I can't imagine him ever sliding into the booth. He puts off a vibe that says he probably doesn't like getting *that* close to other humans.

"Are you trying to give me a complex?" I joke, pretending to be affronted.

Shawn shakes his head. "No, I'm impressed. Just don't know

where you put it."

Dane laughs beside me. "He's totally checking you out now."

I shove my elbow into Dane's side. "He is not."

"I *so* am," Shawn says with a raise of his eyebrow. "And I'm trying to figure out how you look that good if you eat like that."

"If you must know, I enjoy Zumba." I look down at my plate so the guys don't see the way my lip wobbles. I miss Zumba. I miss going to Zumba with Amy. I miss Amy. Tonight was a good distraction, but that's all it was. I'm no closer to figuring out what the hell I'm doing here.

"Oh, we've got Zumba here," Colby offers.

I feel Shawn's eyes on me, but I don't dare look at him. If I do, I know the tears will fall. God, I'm an emotional basket case. Who cries over Zumba?

"Yeah, the guys and I love Zumba," Shawn says.

I can't help it. I look at him in shock.

Dane shifts next to me. "We do?" he asks.

"Yeah," Shawn says, his gaze holding mine. "It's good for the core muscles. Chief makes us go."

He's lying, but it's adorable that he's trying to cheer me up. "Oh yeah? Now that's something I'd pay to see."

Colby shrugs. "I love Zumba. Hot girls in yoga pants. Sign me up."

"When's the next class?" Shawn says.

Colby already has his phone out. "Thursday," he replies, an excited glint in his eye. "You think you could convince Hailey to go?" he asks me.

I shrug. "She doesn't seem like the type."

Dane quips, "And you're saying we are?"

I huff a laugh.

Mason grumbles, "I'm not."

I bite my lip to keep from cackling at the mental picture of

Mason at Zumba I've dreamed up. Would the growly man sweat it out in his flannel shirt? I bet he wears it to the gym. Before I can stop myself, I envision him swinging his hips to salsa music, and the laughter breaks free.

I think everyone knows why I'm laughing. Well, everyone but Mason, but he doesn't seem interested in our hysterics.

"So, Zumba. Thursday night at six. We on, Red?" Shawn asks.

"Oh, we are so on," I reply, my mood lifted exponentially.

CHAPTER 24

SHAWN

"I can't believe you got us roped into going to Zumba," Dane grumbles as he ties the laces on his sneakers.

Mason mumbles next to him, but I'm pretty sure it's a growl rather than actual words.

Colby bounces beside me. "Guys, this is going to be awesome. Did you not hear me? Spandex. Hot girls!"

Chuckling, I simply enjoy the show. I've only worked with these guys for a few weeks, but I'm finally settling in. Finding a rhythm. Just like I did when I played ball. It feels fucking good. "I don't want to hear a word out of any of you. You heard Jules. She needs something that reminds her of home."

Dane shakes his head.

"What?" I ask, annoyed that he's being so difficult. "I thought you liked Jules."

Dane lets out a low laugh. "Oh, I like her, all right. But none of us likes her as much as you."

I fold my arms across my chest. "What are you getting at? I'm trying to be nice. I know what it's like to be new in town. To feel like your life is falling apart."

Dane nods and stands up. He claps me on the back, pulling me closer. "You're doing a great thing. And we're all gonna show up and smile. Show the girl a good time. Give her a reason to stay. But let's be honest about why we're doing it."

I shrug him off. "Because she's a nice girl."

He laughs. "No. We're doing it because you like her, and you asked us to."

Colby bounces and shakes his head. "Yeah, not me. I'm doing it because of the spandex."

Mason throws a sock at Colby, nailing him in the face. "Can you fucking knock it off with the damn spandex?"

We freeze, and every one of us gapes at him for a moment.

Then he turns to me and grumbles, "We're doing it because you fucking like her."

Surprised by Mason's outburst, and, quite frankly, that he spoke at all, I grab on to the first thing that comes to mind. "Wait, you guys *like me*?"

Mason rolls his eyes and practically growls as he walks away.

I take off after him, light on my toes because I'm finally one of the guys. And it feels really fucking good. Even if they're hitting a little too close to home. Even if I can't act on my attraction. Not only because Jules is my roommate, but also because she's Hailey's sister. It's too complicated.

Dane catches up to me and gives me a look. "I know what you're doing."

"No idea what you're talking about." I'm not even sure what I'm doing most of the time.

"*Babe*, you fucking light up when you look at the girl. Seriously, you expect me to believe that when you're alone in the apartment with her, you aren't figuring out six different ways to kiss her?"

Actually, I'm trying my hardest *not* to kiss her. It's like a full-time job finding reasons to not be in the apartment alone with her because all I want to do is press her against the door and feel her body under my fingers. But I don't tell Dane that I've worked three extra shifts just to stay busy this week. Instead, I reply, "I really hate that nickname. And no. I'm just being friendly."

We walk down the street toward the rec center where Colby has directed us. Jules is standing outside, waiting. Her red hair is high on her head and her cheeks are rosy—probably because it's December in New England and she's from California—but to top it all off, she's wearing the damn spandex Colby has been going on about. Now I understand his obsession.

I've seen the girl naked. I've relived the memory of her body more than I'd like to admit, and yet, right now, staring at the skintight black fabric molded to her body, I have an entirely new obsession.

And more importantly, I know I'm screwed when she looks up at me and smiles, her face lighting up as her eyes meet mine. That smile has me even more enamored than the pants.

Beside me, Dane puts a voice to my thoughts. "Friendly, my ass."

JULES
ICE CREAM
SUPER PREMIUM ICE CREAM
SUPER PREMIUM ICE CREAM

CHAPTER 25

JULES

The vision of Shawn and his firefighter besties prancing around the rec center is permanently branded on my brain. Watching them pretend they actually go to Zumba on the regular—or that they've ever been involved in a group fitness class that wasn't related to their fire training—was adorable.

I expected Shawn to be embarrassed by how ridiculous he looked. Mason certainly was. Colby had the moves down pat, though, while Dane grunted in aggravation as he halfheartedly followed the steps. But Shawn smiled as he fell over. He laughed as he spun out too far during one move of Katy Perry's "Firework." And he charmed the hell out of the older ladies when he bumped into them so that rather than glaring at him like they would anyone else, they simply batted their eyes and grabbed for his muscles, giving him firm squeezes and big smiles. "Oh, it's okay, officer," one lady had said.

"He's not an officer," I grumbled under my breath.

But I guess I wasn't quiet enough because Shawn shot me a wink when he saw my scowl, leaving me blushing profusely.

When we cross the threshold of our apartment *together*, he's still sporting quite the cocky grin, like he knows what I'm thinking—how gorgeous he looks when he smiles—and I awkwardly bolt toward my room to avoid doing anything stupid. Like kissing him again, since that seems to be all I do when I'm around him.

But as I sit in my bedroom, twisting my hands, letting my anxiety get the best of me, I know I can't hide from Shawn forever. Clearly, I'm attracted to him. That doesn't mean I have to act on it. I've made it through twenty-eight years of not acting on every impulse, and I refuse to let Shawn Freaking Chase be the one thing I can't resist.

I've made up my mind, but my heart and body haven't quite caught up, so I peek out my door and scan the living area. When I see the coast is clear, I walk to the kitchen, head held high, smile plastered on my face. See? I can do this. Just going to the kitchen to make dinner. Nothing to be anxious about.

No—*oh sugar*. My very naked roommate walks out of the bathroom with a towel slung low around his hips, water cascading down his chest like a damn waterfall.

And tattoos. Beautiful black ink swirls over his chest.

My knees go weak. I never knew tattoos were a *thing* for me. Especially the way they're glistening right now.

Did the man not consider drying off? It's almost like this was intentional.

I raise my brows and force my eyes to follow—I will not gawk at my hot ex-baseball player roommate.

He stops just outside the door. He's wearing a look of anticipation, with one side of his mouth kicked up in a half-grin. Almost like he's waiting for a response. Crap. Was he talking to me?

"Hmm?"

"Take a picture. It'll last longer." He flashes me another grin and then puts his hands on his hips and poses. "Or do you think I look better with my arms crossed and leaning against the door? I've been told I have one sexy scowl," he teases.

I roll my eyes and leave him standing by the bathroom.

Men.

"What? My sense of humor not as good as my abs?" he calls as he follows me into the kitchen. Seriously, he needs to work on boundaries.

I shake my head, keeping my focus averted. "I'm making dinner. Are you hungry?"

He takes another step into the kitchen, holding his towel at his hip, *still dripping,* and leans over my shoulder to look at what I've laid out on the counter. The smell of his body wash leaves me salivating.

"Hmm, taco meat…how can I help?" he asks as he remains far too close for comfort.

"You can start with getting dressed, *roomie,*" I say, pushing past him and making my way back to the fridge.

Shawn's laughter fills the room. "Am I making you uncomfortable, Red?"

I have a love/hate relationship with that nickname.

"Shawn, you promised," I whine, spinning around and facing him.

His brows knit together. "Promised what?"

"To be my *friend,*" I remind him.

Shawn's face immediately flashes with regret. "Shit, Jules, I'm sorry. I really *am* making you uncomfortable." He lifts an arm, probably to grab at the back of his neck—a move I notice he does when he's worried or stressed. Only this causes his towel to slip. I let out a loud hiss at the sight. It's like that moment before two cars collide, when you know it's going to happen and there's nothing you can do to stop it. The sound is involuntary, but Shawn's eyes dart up to mine, and he grabs the towel before it dips too low. He backs away slowly, one hand up in retreat and one hanging on tight to the terry cloth. "I'm really sorry."

I sigh, feeling bad about making *him* feel bad. *Stupid, stupid, Jules.* He was just being friendly, joking around, and I had to make it weird.

"It's fine," I call after him, but he's already dipped into the bedroom, and I'm left to hit my head against the fridge, feeling completely ridiculous.

Ten minutes later, while I'm still berating myself and cutting up the onions and peppers, Shawn creeps out of his room. He stays on the other side of the kitchen as he watches me.

"Do you, uh, want some help?" he offers.

I spin around to respond, the knife in my hand. He throws his hands up again, his eyes going wide.

I roll my eyes at the sight I must make, like I'm protecting myself from his advances. I set the knife on the counter and wipe my hands with a towel, then take a deep breath and turn around. "I'm sorry," I say softly.

When I look up to meet his eyes, the lines around them are creased in confusion. "Why are you sorry?"

"You were just joking around, and I made it weird…and I made you uncomfortable."

Shawn moves a few steps closer, and suddenly, the air feels thicker. "You didn't make me uncomfortable, Red. You established your boundaries. I'm sorry I crossed them." He reaches out a few inches but stops himself and firmly sets his hand on the counter, like he's trying hard not to touch me.

I rub my fingers together and take a deep breath to slow my heart rate. "Seriously. It's fine. I'm just…" I falter. How do I explain what's going through my head? "This is awkward, no?"

Shawn shrugs. "Why?"

I sigh, digging deep for the courage to admit the truth. I think it's time we deal with the elephant in the room. "Because we kissed."

"Twice," he says with a smile, almost as if he can't *not* smile when thinking about it.

I blush. The heat burning my cheeks is so hot they've got to be as red as my hair.

"Yes, twice. Isn't that weird for you?"

Shawn relaxes into the question, as if he's been waiting for it. As if the idea of kissing me is one he's rolled over in his head just as much as I have.

"I quite enjoyed it, actually," he teases, inadvertently licking his lips. *Or was that on purpose? Is he a player, or is he unaware of the effect he has?*

As if he senses my spiraling, he reaches out, letting his fingers dance across my elbow. My body tingles at that innocuous touch. He might as well have splayed his hand against my thigh for the way my body reacts to him. Liquid heat pools in my belly.

"I won't do it again," he promises.

"Kiss me?" I squeak. Losing the possibility of pressing my lips against his again or tangling my tongue with his or relishing the way those fingers trail through my hair as he pulls me closer, to get one more inch, a better angle, more of me, practically deflates my entire being.

He closes his eyes for a beat and exhales, then studies me. "Not if you don't want me to. Not if you'll leave and go back to California to avoid me. I'll stay in my room and be a perfect gentleman, I promise."

I nibble at my bottom lip, mulling over what's really bothering me. It's been niggling in my head for a while, the question I haven't even dared to ask myself until now. Why this man, who sets my skin on fire, makes me dizzy and calls me Red. *Why* did he kiss me? That day changed my life. It pushed me to move to this town, to come up with this crazy idea to open a bakery, and now I'm *living* with him.

Based on his perpetually calm and collected demeanor, it would appear our kiss was nothing more than a blip on his heart monitor. No effect whatsoever. Making it so easy for him to live with me, interact with me, flirt with me, *touch me,* while I'm over here unraveling at the seams.

"Why did you kiss me?"

"In the storage closet?" he asks.

We both know that's not what I'm referring to.

I shake my head.

Shawn sighs. "Can we discuss it over margaritas?"

A pang of disappointment makes my chest grow tight. Part of me hoped it'd be an easy answer. That he saw me and just couldn't *not* kiss me. But clearly, there's a lot more to it than that. And it requires tequila.

Oof.

But I manage a tiny smile. "Sure, I'll put the peppers and meat on while you make the margaritas?"

He nods, a firm dip of his chin, his smile tight.

We stand beside one another in silence as he works on the drinks and I prepare the food. It isn't until we're sitting across from one another and he's handing me a glass and offering a toast, that we break the silence.

"So…?" I ask awkwardly.

Shawn takes a healthy sip of his drink and then sets it down.

I can't stand the trepidation in his expression. "We don't have to——"

But as I speak, so does he. "I thought you were Hailey."

Our voices get jumbled together, but I'm pretty sure I heard him correctly.

"Uh, you can go," he offers.

I shake my head. "No, clearly yours is…did you say you thought I was Hailey?"

He scrubs a hand over his face, then focuses on me. "Yes."

My stomach bottoms out, but I manage to fake a coughing laugh. "Wow, that's just…" I take a deep breath, working to move past the humiliation. *He kissed me because he thought I was my twin sister. The twin sister who hates me. Excellent.* "That's great." I plaster on a fake smile.

The lines on Shawn's forehead crease in bewilderment. "It is?"

I reach for my drink and take a fortifying sip. "Yes, it's great. Now we can be normal. No more of this crazy sexual tension. It's just—you like my sister. That's what this was all about." Of course he does. She's fun, successful, interesting. Everything I'm not. "Ah, gosh, I feel so much better."

"You do?" he says, still with a confused lilt to his voice.

"Oh, yes. This is good." *It's soul crushing.* "Can you pass the cheese?" I point to the cheddar next to him.

He absentmindedly picks it up and hands it to me as I start the process of putting together the perfect taco.

First I layer the cheese, then comes the meat—that way the cheese can melt a bit—then the lettuce and another layer of cheese followed by a healthy dose of sour cream and guacamole. I feel Shawn's eyes on me the entire time, but I take a big bite before he can ask me if I'm okay.

Because I'm totally fine. Even if the voice in my head sounds a bit like Ross from *Friends*, I swear, I am *fine*.

"Eat while it's hot," I say between bites, ensuring that our conversation is paused while he makes his food. I just need, like, two minutes to wrap my mind around this, and then I'll be fine.

Because clearly it's fine.

Okay, I'm a freaking lying liar, and I'm spiraling, but no one needs to know that, so I'll just keep chewing, and it will be…

Yeah, even I can't say the word again. This is so not fine.

CHAPTER 26

SHAWN

ules has gone completely silent as she eats, and she sips her margarita in an exaggerated manner every time I look up, as if to say, *oh, look, I'm still occupied and can't communicate with you.*

It's making my knee jump and my chest hurt. But that's not the worst of it. The worst is how when she isn't chewing or drinking, she's rubbing her damn fingers together, which is a tell of hers. Over the last few days, I've noticed her doing it when she's anxious. And I made her feel that way. *Fuck.*

Unable to stand another moment of her anxiety, I reach across the table and rest my hand on top of hers, stopping the incessant rubbing she's doing with her thumb. Her gaze shoots to mine, but she ducks her head again quickly. It's obvious she doesn't want to discuss it anymore, so I squeeze her hand and smile. "This is really good. Thank you."

She sighs in relief. "Thanks. My dad—er, my step—no, *my dad* is a big fan of tacos. We'd make them together every Tuesday night when I was growing up."

I relax when her voice goes soft and take a sip of my drink before asking, "Are you close with your dad?"

Her face goes pink. "I am. Was. Am." She sighs again. "My mother divorced him when I was in high school. He's remarried, but he's still in my life, and he is always so supportive," she says on a quick breath. "But obviously their divorce changed things. And now it's the holidays, and I'm here…trying to reconnect with my *real* dad. Is that even the right terminology?" she asks as her face pinches in disgust. "Like somehow the man who raised me isn't my *real* dad?"

"No. The man who raised you is your real dad. This guy…he can be something to you as well, if you want him to be, but that doesn't change who your father has been your whole life."

She gives me a watery smile. "That is…well, perfect."

"I get it," I admit. "I was also raised by my non-biological father. And he's amazing. The greatest dad in the world."

"Really?" She looks at me with genuine interest and compassion in her eyes.

"Yup. My father taught me how to play baseball. He sat with me in the hospital after my accident…" My arm cramps at the mention of it, and I massage the phantom pain. My limbs are fine, despite my inability to throw a baseball the way I once could. But that loss feels as big as…I shake off the trajectory of my thoughts. "Your father is the person who was there for all those moments. And he'll be there when you go back."

My stomach clenches at that realization. She's likely only here through the holidays. "What is your plan, by the way? While you're here?"

With this, her face brightens. "Actually…I haven't talked it over with my grandmother yet, but I kind of want to see if I can turn the ice cream shop into a bakery as well."

Hope blossoms inside me. She's thinking of setting down roots. "Oh yeah? You're a baker?"

Her demure smile greets me again. "I mean…I don't know. I

A VERY MERRY MARGARITA MIX-UP

never went to school for it or anything, but my friends and family always liked my treats. Well, my dad and my best friend Amy…Jared and my mom never did."

"Who's Jared?" The question is out of my mouth before I've thought it through.

"My ex," she says sheepishly. "He was also my boss, and, turns out, he had a wife." She drops her eyes and rubs her fingers together again.

I drag a hand through my hair. "Wow, we really don't know each other that well, huh?"

She laughs. "We did get thrown into this living together thing pretty randomly."

I tilt my head. "I'm really okay with staying at the fire station if you'd feel more comfortable. Or I can get another apartment. It's not a big deal."

She shakes her head. "Honestly…?"

I nod. "Yes, I only want your honesty."

"It's nice having you here. I feel…*safer.*"

"Because I can protect you from the spiders?" I tease.

She smiles. "Yeah. And it's nice to have a friend."

My stomach flips at the mention of that specific F-word again. It's the last thing I want, but it's all she's interested in.

I fold my arms across my chest. "So, as your friend, how can I help make your bakery dream come true?"

She shakes her head. "Oh, you don't need—I didn't mean…" Once again, she's scrubbing her thumb hard.

I squeeze her hand. "It's okay. I'm offering. So tell me, what's your plan?"

She relaxes. "I need to get an industrial stove, which is expensive," she says, "so I'll start out by making a few things here. If you don't mind, that is…" she scrunches up her nose like she's worried I won't agree.

I shake my head. This girl. She's too nice for her own good. "As long as you let me taste test," I offer.

She beams. "Oh, that would be amazing! Then I would know whether I'm any good."

"I actually have a better idea." I grin, cooking up a plan mentally. "The town has a big Christmas festival. What if we got you up and running over the next week, spread the word about your plans, and set up a booth at the festival so people in town could sample your desserts?"

Her eyes are like saucers as she replies, "A Christmas festival?" Her tone is dreamy, like I've promised her a trip to Hawaii or proposed marriage.

"I take it you're a fan of Christmas festivals?" I chuckle.

"What's there not to be a fan of? Happy families strolling down the street with hot chocolate, snow-covered streets, streetlamps straight out of a Dickens novel, scarves, a horse-drawn carriage… *oh*, reindeer!" she exclaims.

I laugh. Her excitement is adorable. "Hang on there, Red. I'm not sure about snow, but we can make the rest happen."

She shakes her head, grinning. "I know it sounds dumb, but I had this idea in my head that when I met Hailey and Caris, I'd finally have that perfect New England Christmas. In California, my mom sets up a beautiful Christmas tree. And my dad would always spoil me and watch Christmas movies, but I was an only child. I had no one to share those memories with, ya know? And I just…I've never had a white Christmas, never wore matching Christmas pajamas with anyone…" She looks down, pushing her hair back shyly. "I sound ridiculous, don't I?"

"You don't. Not at all. Even though my sister was a pain when we were kids, and her enthusiasm over just about everything drove me crazy, I look back now and smile. I had her by my side. And you're right. It does make for some great memories."

Charlotte can be a bit much, but she has the biggest heart.

"She was really nice when I met her."

"She'd love to hang out with you. In fact, I think she's planning to stop by and see if you want to get together."

Jules bites the inside of her cheek and looks down again. "She doesn't have to do that."

I've had just about enough of this girl's distorted view of herself and her irrational concerns about being a burden.

"Outta that head, Red. She'd love to hang out with you. It's what she does. She loves friendship…and girls…and *love*." I laugh at the last word, because really, the minute she finds out I'm living with Jules and that I'm working so hard to spend time with her, Charlotte will be mentally writing our love story, and far quicker than I have. And let's be honest, I've already got a million plot lines cooked up. But I've got to slow myself down because that *isn't* what this girl needs right now.

Jules smiles. "Okay."

"How 'bout I clean up, and you whip us up some dessert? I want to test your baking skills before I get you a booth at the Christmas festival."

She laughs. "Oh, you think I'm faking my abilities?"

I smile. "Yeah, sweetheart, let's go with that."

JULES
ICE CREAM
SUPER PREMIUM ICE CREAM
SUPER PREMIUM ICE CREAM

CHAPTER 27

JULES

Once I got over the shock of Shawn's admission about his feelings for Hailey, we had a pretty great night. He helped me make chocolate chip cookies for the guys at the station, and we each had one—straight out of the oven with vanilla ice cream on top—before we mumbled our good nights and retired to our separate bedrooms.

Sure, I tossed and turned a bit, reliving our kiss—both kisses, actually—but eventually sleep took over, and today, I feel like a new person. Shawn is my friend—*my roommate*—and he's going to help me make friends with the locals and turn this ice cream shop into a bakery.

As I step into the shower, dreams of donuts and cream puffs filter through my brain. If Shawn can finagle a booth for me at the Christmas festival, what should I serve? What will people fall in love with? I need a dessert that will make them want to come to my bakery.

Just as I'm flipping through the recipe Rolodex I've got stored in my brain, eight little legs come into view. Or very long legs, actually. I let out a bloodcurdling scream as I stare at the monster before me.

It's just a small spider. It can't hurt you.

But also, it's a freaking spider and I'm naked in the shower and it could totally fall on me and live in my hair forever.

I breathe in deeply, making sure not to take my eyes off the creature perched on the ceiling. I swear it's looking down at me in judgment. Today is a new day. If I want to run a business and live on my own, I need to learn how to live among the spiders of the world.

Or something like that.

None of my silent pep talks are working, so I try it out loud instead.

"Okay, Charlotte, you and I are gonna have a little chat." Yes, I'm naming the spider Charlotte. It seems friendlier, and also, it's the only thing I could come up with on the fly. "You are going to stay there," I say, pointing at it as I use my other hand to cover my chest, like the spider has an interest in seeing my boobs, "and I will stay here. I'll shower very quickly, and then I'll leave you to it. So just, uh, stay in your corner and we'll both get out of here alive."

I swear the damn thing nods at me. Now that we've come to an agreement, I squirt shampoo into my hand and quickly run it through my hair while I continue covering my most sensitive body parts with my other arm, never taking my eyes off the spider.

I take what can be categorized as the fastest shower in history and then slink behind the shower curtain, not daring to move it for fear the spider will get spooked and fly at me, and then I grab a towel. I don't reach in to turn the shower off until the towel is covering my hair, which a spider could easily live in, and then I run out of the bathroom, screeching like a banshee until I hit my bedroom door. I fling it closed, hop onto my bed, and pant, out of breath but safe from the spider. Even then, I pat myself down, making sure I didn't bring any runaways with me.

It isn't until a good five minutes later that I burst out laughing at my own insanity.

Thank God Shawn is already at the fire station and didn't witness my complete insanity.

An hour later, I make my way downstairs to measure the kitchen of the ice cream shop. The setup isn't perfect, but if Shawn helps, we can make this a functioning bakery kitchen.

I'm so focused on the layout I don't hear the telltale sound of the bell ringing above the shop door or the echo of footsteps getting closer to the kitchen until I'm spinning around, holding my chest, and blowing out a surprised, "Oh, Jeez," at the sight of my twin sister.

"Sorry, I didn't mean to scare ya," Hailey says easily, tilting her hip into the counter and staring at me. She eyes the tape measure in my hand. "What're you doing?"

My anxiety flares at the way she scowls at the tape measure, as if I have no right to be here. "Just measuring. Caris said this place is mine," I remind her.

Hailey shrugs. "Yeah, I know that. I mean, what are you doing with the tape measure?"

"Thinking about putting in an oven," I admit, biting my lip as I gauge her reaction.

"Okay," Hailey says slowly. "Sorry I missed you at the bar the other night. Dad had a bad night."

I twist my lips at the mention of our father. I still haven't had the guts to ask where he is. Why he isn't around. Does he even know I'm here?

"What's wrong with him?" I garner the courage to ask.

Hailey looks away quickly as she walks around the kitchen, taking in the space. "He had a stroke…" she admits quietly, then her eyes jump to mine. "But don't go spreading that around town. He doesn't want anyone to know. What have you been up to lately anyway?"

I shake my head, even though she can't see me, at the sheer amount of information packed into that statement. "Is he okay?"

She lets out an aggravated sigh. "He will be. But no…he's not. He's alive, but he's in a rehab facility. And he's not the type to just sit. It's been miserable for him."

I bite my lip, ruminating on how I should feel about this. Should I be sad? Concerned? The twisting in my gut tells me I care. Even if *he* didn't care enough to fight for me. To keep us all together. And I care about how it's obviously affecting Hailey. But before I can say anything else, she changes the subject. "So what have you been up to?"

"Um, just getting settled. Working at the bar. I got a little distracted yesterday with Shawn and the guys at Zumba."

Hailey spins and all but pins me to the wall with her eyes. "*What?*"

"Zumba. We went to the Y. He said the guys at the fire station go regularly. Chief makes them or something." I'm rambling now, but I can't help it. I'm nervous. I don't know why I'm explaining this to my sister, but I feel like I have to justify the time I'm spending with Shawn.

Hailey tilts her head at this information and laughs. "Yeah, no. What?"

I realize I've tilted my head, too, and to an outside observer, we're probably mirror images. To test out my theory, I cock my head in the opposite direction, but she doesn't move hers. Well, that's disappointing. If she had twin radar or whatever it is, she'd have mirrored my actions. She'd find my humor funny. She'd smile or maybe just *like* me.

But instead, we're strangers who look identical but know nothing about one another and she, quite frankly, looks at me like I'm an alien.

"Did you come to see him?" I ask. Small talk with her is useless, so I might as well get to the point.

"Who?"

"Shawn," I say with a tired sigh.

"Why would I come *here* to see Shawn?"

"Because he lives here," I say, and tentatively add, "with me."

"He lives here with you?"

Okay, I couldn't get the girl to mirror my face, but my words seem to be on point. "Yes," I say firmly.

"I don't get it." Her cheeks grow red, and her voice raises an octave. "Since when do you two even *know* each other?"

"Since we became roommates," I say, tipping my chin up and crossing my arms. I have no idea why I'm so worked up. Or why I feel the need to fight with my twin sister over a man I know is into her, but her attitude is making my blood boil.

"This is like the chicken or the egg conversation," Hailey mutters to herself. "I've got to go." She offers me a small wave and turns. The bell above the door jingles as she leaves, and then the place is silent.

I slump against the wall. *What the heck was that about?*

And what the heck is wrong with me? I've wanted a relationship with her since the moment I found out about her, and now, when I'm finally given the chance to talk to her, I practically fight with her over a boy.

A boy who, by the way, only kissed me because he *thought* I was Hailey.

A boy my sister obviously likes.

Oh.

Oh.

My sister likes him.

And he's my friend.

That's how I'll get on my sister's good side. I'm going to set her up with Shawn!

CHAPTER 28

SHAWN

"You want me to allow your girlfriend to use the ovens?" Chief asks with a skeptical arch of his brow.

"*Friend*. She's my roommate, *not* my girlfriend," I explain, pointing to the oversized kitchen we barely use. "It's the neighborly thing to do," I admonish.

The chief laughs. "Right, *friend*. Hey, Dane, come here a sec," the chief bellows, and all the guys look up from where they are eating lunch at the table.

Dane puts down his spoon and joins us near the oversized oven.

"I heard from Mrs. Pearlman that you were at Zumba the other day. That so?"

Dane grumbles. "Yeah, this one over here made us go."

I sigh. This is going to be more difficult than I thought.

"Why you have my guys going to Zumba, Chase?" Chief asks.

"It's a good workout," I reply evenly.

Behind us, Colby laughs. "It's a great spot to meet women, Chief. You should come next time."

The chief eyes him, and his laughter stops. "Was Chase's roommate there?" Chief asks Dane.

My buddy looks at me but barely hesitates before growling

another yes.

Chief smiles like I've just stepped in shit. "As I was saying, you want your girlfriend to use our stoves."

I roll my neck band decide to let him spin this however he wants. I just want to have stoves lined up for Jules before I ask the Christmas Committee about a booth for her. "Yeah, Chief. That all right?"

He nods. "So long as Dane supervises, it's fine with me."

Dane's brows practically touch his hairline at that. Shit. I'm going to owe him big.

"Yes, sir," Dane grumbles again. He shoots me a glare before looking for the chief to dismiss him.

"In fact," the chief says, a twinkle in his eye, "I think you all should help Chase's girlfriend feel at home. Since you've already accompanied her to Zumba, why don't you help her in the kitchen too?"

The entire table groans except for Colby, who shouts, "Yes! I love the Christmas festival."

I cringe and shoot an apologetic look at the crew. This is *not* going to help me fit in.

My phone buzzes in my pocket as I take a seat next to an annoyed Mason. When I take it out, I see Hailey's name with the incoming text.

Hailey: Hey, you around to grab dinner tonight?

Me: Can't. I'm working. Everything okay?

It's not odd for Hailey to text me, but she's been so busy with work and visiting her father that she's rarely around anymore.

Hailey: Yeah, I just miss you. Heard you moved in with my sister.

I twist my lips at this information. I wonder who she heard it from. Also, I'm pleasantly surprised to see she's calling Jules her sister. Maybe they have a shot after all.

Me: Miss you too, Hailes. How 'bout I come by the restaurant after my shift ends tomorrow?

Hailey: Sounds good.

Hailey: You just going to breeze past the fact that you're living with Red?

I laugh out loud and just shrug when Mason glowers at me.

Me: Nah. We'll talk tomorrow. You should give her a chance. I think you have a lot more in common than you think.

Her only reply is **Yup.**

The next part of my plan is approaching the Christmas committee. And quite frankly, they're scarier than the chief.

Lucille and Mitzy despise each other, and yet they're on every committee together. I honestly don't know how the rest of the members stand being around them for extended periods of time. It usually only takes a few minutes in their presence to lose my mind. But today I'm not going to let them get to me.

I'm Shawn fucking Chase, for goodness' sake—I can handle a few cougars.

"Why are you mouthing that you're Shawn fucking Chase?" Dane says as he saunters up to me, wearing a smirk.

Fucker.

"Doesn't Lucille love you?" I ask as we walk into the Coffee Depot, where the ladies meet every afternoon to gossip while they watch people pick up their children from school. Maybe they aren't *actually* gossiping, but it sure looks like it with the way they huddle close and sip their matchas.

"No," Dane says, shaking his head. "No, no, no. Don't even think about it," he warns as I push him up to their table.

Lucille's lips turn up in a Cheshire grin at the sight of him. "Oh, hello, boys. Dane, we've missed you at church this week."

Dane grumbles an excuse about being busy with his boys' basketball league and shoots me a look.

I return the glare. He needs to work his charm.

"Oh, Shawn, don't you look at my Dane like that. We all know why you're here, so get to it."

Shit. I grab the back of my neck. "You do?"

The women all look at each other, clucking their tongues as they do.

Lucille laughs. "Of course we do. We know *everything*," she says with a scary grin. A woman in her fifties should not be that scary. I swear she could take down the mob.

I stand tall and clear my throat. *I'm Shawn Fucking Chase*, I remind myself again.

"I'd like to volunteer to help at the Christmas festival," I say with my signature smirk.

All four women stare at me dubiously. When the silence gets unbearable, I panic. Like I said, they could take down the mob.

"And so would Dane," I add, throwing my arm around him.

"Oh no I wouldn't," he mutters.

Lucille just shoots him a look that shuts him up. "And why would we let you help?" the redheaded cougar asks, eyeing me suspiciously.

I scoff. "*Let* me? Aren't you looking for volunteers? Carmella told us you needed help," I throw in, knowing the lady in the muumuu is the true mastermind, even if these women like to pretend they're in charge.

"Why don't you tell us what you really want?" one of the other women interjects.

I turn my gaze to her and try my best smoldering stare, but she doesn't even bat an eye at me.

I'm starting to get a complex.

I think I've lost my ability to smolder.

"Fine. I need a booth at the Christmas festival for baked goods, and I need you to let Jules Milsom and me volunteer for all the events."

I put all my cards on the table and wait.

The four of them look at one another, communicating silently, and then Lucy speaks. "If the fire department does a calendar this year to raise funds for the Christmas ball."

Dane huffs.

I shoot him a withering stare but turn back to the ladies and nod. "Sounds great."

"I'm not done," Lucy replies.

Arms folded across my chest, I start to sweat. "Okay, what else do you want?"

"You boys all help us set up and take down the festival booths."

I nod with a roll of my eyes. "Yes. That's why we're here. We're *trying* to help you. Why are you making this so difficult?"

She tuts at me. "We already have a full set of volunteers. I don't need your help. You need mine. And you're asking us to do a favor for someone we don't know. Hailey isn't too keen on the new girl, and you're asking a lot if you want us to cross Hailey," she retorts.

I sigh. "Hailey will be fine."

"Says the man who's going after her sister after being obsessed with Hailey for months," she clucks, eyeing me shrewdly.

"What do you want?" I manage to grit out. I'll do anything to end this conversation and get Jules the booth. Although I don't want them to know that. Jules needs this. She needs the town to rally around her arrival, to support her new business, to welcome her into the Bristol family. It's the only way she'll stay here, and I really want her to stay. One would think the women who go on about holiday cheer and town pride would be better at exuding it.

Lucille smiles, knowing she has me. "The calendar, the setup and takedown of the booths, and an auction—dates for the Fourth of July

Ball with all the single firefighters—and you've got yourself a deal."

I throw my head back and silently curse at the sky. The guys are going to kill me.

Dane eyes me like I've lost my mind when I hold out my hand to shake on it. "You've got yourself a deal. But not a word of this to Jules. I don't want her to know *anything* other than that you ladies are dying to have her at the festival because you tried *these* cookies and were raving about them. Got me?" I threaten, plopping down the Tupperware container filled with the best chocolate chip cookies I've ever had.

Lucille reaches in, as do her sidekicks, and they each take a bite. One moans, and the other holds back a smile.

Lucille looks up at me innocently. "You should have led with the cookies. These are divine. Can't wait to stop by the new bakery," she says with a wave. "See you at the Christmas festival meeting on Friday," she coos. "And make sure the guys are all there!"

Dane elbows me in the side on our way to the door. "The guys are going to kill you."

I think of Jules's smile last night when I told her about the booth. It's totally worth it. Then I think of the next thing she wished. Time to move to the next step of my plan.

"What are the chances of getting a few reindeer for this festival?" I ask Dane.

JULES
ICE CREAM
SUPER PREMIUM ICE CREAM
SUPER PREMIUM ICE CREAM

CHAPTER 29

JULES

As I walk down Hope Street, admiring the Christmas decorations adorning every lamp post and shop window, I can't help but hum "Have Yourself a Merry Little Christmas." It's like I stepped into a Charles Dickens play, and I'm warmed from the inside out. Even if it is a ripe thirty-five degrees. The Christmas spirit is in full swing in downtown Bristol, and I finally feel like I'm settling into my new little town.

One woman with bright red hair and a swing to her hips smiles knowingly at me and croons, "Good Afternoon, Jules."

I smile in shock. How does she know who I am?

Beside her, a woman gives me a little wave, and I don't make it more than ten feet before another offers a greeting and tells me how excited she is to try my baked goods.

It's like I'm Belle in *Beauty and the Beast*, and all the townspeople are welcoming me. I may just break out in song. Shawn must have delivered cookies to the residents like he said he would.

I hang a left down state street and am met by more friendly waves and acknowledgments. Greg at the Bristol House of Pizza (I only know his name because it's on his shirt), and Sydney from Clink—an adorable gift shop with locally made items. Two policemen wink at me and holler, "Thanks for the cookies," as I practically stumble into Thames for my evening shift.

The fire in the corner roars to life, and for once, I don't walk into the bar with anxiety. It's all because of Shawn. I try not to smile at the thought, but it's pretty impossible when he clearly went to all this trouble just so I would feel welcomed by the town.

In the corner, Amelia is leaning across the bar and pressing a quick kiss to Nate's lips, but when she tries to pull away from the guitarist, he snakes his hand into her hair and holds her in place, deepening their kiss. The electricity that spikes between them is palpable, even from across the bar. The way he dominates her while he simultaneously falls at her feet, pulling back and giving her a lazy smile, takes my breath away. That is one besotted man. God, what it must feel like to be the recipient of that kind of devotion, to be the reason for the desire that's written all over his face.

I must be staring because Amelia's got her head cocked and her hands on her hips when I finally register that she's calling my name. "*Hello*, stop being so creepy and grab the orders from the back and bring them to table eight," she says with a narrowing of her eyes.

"Sorry," I mutter and suddenly find myself rubbing my thumb, trying to settle my nerves again.

"It's not Jules's fault your husband practically puts on a porno when he kisses you in public," Hailey teases—shockingly. Is she… defending me?

Nate chuckles at that. "What can I say?" he teases. "My girl is irresistible."

Hailey sticks her finger down her throat in his direction. "Try resisting her anyway. We've got a business to run. Hey, Red," she says, throwing a head nod in my direction, "try not spraying down my bar tonight, okay?"

So much for the friendly sister.

194

I squeeze my finger tighter and laugh it off. In the kitchen, I find three platters, which I balance precariously on my tray.

Before I can walk into the dining room, the chef looks up over the oven and gives me a knowing smile. "The cookies," he says slyly. "You'll have to make some for our cookie ice cream dessert."

My nervousness from only moments earlier once again melts, and I smile. "Oh, thanks. Jeez, Shawn really made it around town, didn't he?"

Chef beams. "He's a good one, that guy. Don't hurt him."

I laugh off his suggestion. "Oh, we're just friends. He's—" I stop myself before I tell him about Shawn's crush on Hailey. The same one that pulverizes my spirits a little more every time I remember it. But then I shake off the melancholy. Shawn wants Hailey. And being with Shawn would make even the crankiest of women glow, so obviously my sister will be happy, and happy people don't hate their siblings. This is a *good* thing.

I mean, according to Elle Woods, right?

"Yes, he's a great guy," I finally say, dipping my head and leaving it at that.

As soon as I've delivered the food, I head back to the bar. Hailey and Amelia are laughing together, and I can't help the pinch of jealousy I experience at the scene. It's not that I don't like Amelia. She can be a bit abrasive, and she's not my biggest fan, but in the end, she had my back last week when everything went haywire with the keg. I've observed her interact with a handful of our regulars, and it's clear she's a loyal friend. But I wish my sister was laughing with me. That she was even *open* to laughing with me. But when I walk up, she quiets and focuses on work again.

"I'll be right back," I say, moving quickly toward the storage closet in the kitchen—a.k.a., my new favorite hiding place. As soon as I shut the door, I let my entire body shudder and then force my muscles to relax. "It shouldn't be this hard," I mutter to myself. And my happiness shouldn't be so wrapped up in whether one person likes me. Even if she happens to be my sister. But as I rub that familiar spot on my thumb, the one that's worn smooth because of my constant attention, I know I won't feel whole so long as things are strained between us.

And in truth, I wonder if I've ever felt whole at all.

The bar is about to be hit by the dinner rush, and I have no excuse to hide any longer, so I make my way back out and look for my sister. It's time we talk. Not seriously, not yet. My ego couldn't handle Hailey's direct honesty right now. Just, you know, I'll instigate some small talk and try to hold my own. But as I round the bar and search for her, I find only Amelia. She's got a smirk on her face, and she's watching the commotion in the dining room.

Nate leans across the bar and points to where she's looking. I turn, taking in the scene in slow motion. Hailey wears a big smile and leans in close to her companion at a table near the back. Her auburn hair, which is a few shades darker than mine, is draped seductively against one of the broad shoulders I dream about. She presses herself closer to Shawn and then drops her head back and laughs at something he says. His entire face lights up as he watches her.

I bite my lip to stop from saying anything. Not that anything appropriate for the situation would come out of my mouth. *Stop flirting with the guy I like*. Ridiculous. *He was mine first*. Incorrect.

Just as I'm about to turn away, Shawn focuses on me, and our gazes meet across the bar. The look sets my body on fire. Where he was smiling at Hailey, he's burning me. His eyes don't warm, they turn molten. This isn't in my head. It's written clearly in the intensity of his stare. It's been two days since we've seen each other. Since we retreated to our rooms the other night. And the way he's looking at me right now suggests that he's been thinking about me as much as

I've thought about him. But then Hailey says something to him, and he looks away, taking all the heat of that interaction with him. Like a cloud passing over the sun without warning.

"They're just friends," Amelia says softly, pressing her body close to mine.

"Hmm?" I ask, playing dumb.

She hip checks me and gives me a forlorn smile, then slowly repeats herself. "*Just*. Friends."

I shrug, doing my best to act unaffected. "Oh, well, I mean, whatever they want."

She laughs. "He's one of the good ones."

Why does everyone keep implying that I'm going to hurt the guy? One, I barely know him, and two, he's not interested in me. He likes my sister. *Clearly.* When I sneak another glance in their direction, they're lost in conversation again. It's like the moment we shared was a figment of my imagination. Just like our kiss.

The night goes by quickly. Despite how my traitorous eyes continually wander back to where Shawn and Hailey sit, I'm busy with customers seeking warmth from the cold. Nate strums his guitar, entertaining everyone with country Christmas music—mostly classics, with a few originals thrown in. Amelia even joins in to sing with him. The entire bar is drawn to their orbit, whereas my universe exists two tables over. When Hailey finally stands up and hugs Shawn goodbye, my entire body slumps with relief. Finally, he's leaving, and I won't be tormented by their date.

Shawn doesn't disappear though. Instead, he makes his way to the bar, his smile tired but warm. "You seem to be getting the hang of this," he remarks, settling himself on the stool.

I wipe the space in front of him and put a napkin on the bar. "I haven't taken down any kegs tonight, so that's progress, right?" I joke.

His chocolate brown eyes brighten at my lightheartedness, but they're surrounded by circles. He's clearly exhausted from working his twenty-four-hour shift. "Ya miss me at the apartment?"

"Oh, Charlotte and I were just fine. But we'll be happy to have your company tonight."

His eyebrow shoots up. "My sister came over?"

I laugh at the coincidence and shake my head. "Oh no…the spider. Charlotte."

Shawn just stares at me.

"She was in the shower again…" I say, as if that explains my insanity.

"Charlotte, the spider." He grins. "You named the spider?" he says with a teasing lilt to his voice.

He reaches out and puts his hand on mine. It's only then that I realize I've been wiping the spot on the bar since he came over. Apparently, another nervous tick of mine. The warmth of his hand leaves me momentarily breathless. I fixate on his big hands. They're calloused and swallow mine completely. I shouldn't, but I can't help but imagine how they'd feel gripping other parts of my body. Kneading at my skin, running through my hair, pressing between my thighs.

"Jules," he says, bringing me back to the present. "The spider?"

I shake my head. "Oh yeah. Spider. Yup. Charlotte. Ya know, *Charlotte's Web*? Makes her less scary."

It might be my imagination, but his entire face brightens every time I speak. "Right. *Charlotte's Web*. All right, then. I'll go pay Charlotte a visit. I could use a shower and some sleep. Do you want me to wait so I can walk you home?"

A glance at my watch confirms that I still have another hour until my shift is over, and he's looking more tired by the second. Shaking my head, I finally pull my hand from below his. "No. You go get some rest. I'll see you in the morning."

Shawn doesn't move right away. His focus remains on me for another moment, and then he knocks on the bar and stands up. But before he can walk off, I remember my interactions with the citizens of Bristol today.

"Oh, Shawn," I call after him.

He looks up at me with a brow quirked.

"Thanks for delivering the cookies to everyone. It was…well, it was really nice to be welcomed by so many people, and that's all because of you."

Shawn's right cheek lifts as his lazy smile grows. "Nah, it's because your cookies are so good." He winks. "And you're welcome."

I bite my lip to keep myself from saying anything else.

JULES
ICE CREAM

SUPER PREMIUM ICE CREAM   SUPER PREMIUM ICE CREAM

CHAPTER 30

JULES

As I reach the ice cream shop, I study the sign like I always do. Jules. It's a small connection between me and the father I don't know. The one I'm too scared to visit. It's silly that I'd come all the way here, across the country to live on my own, only to avoid one of the people I returned for.

But emotions don't always make sense. Why is it easier to fight for an ounce of Hailey's attention than it is to confront a man who let me go so many years ago? Will he wonder why I even came? Or be angry I'm here?

But the sign. It's the one thing he kept of me. And if what Hailey said was true, the picture of my mother—with us both in her belly—that hangs inside the door must be proof that he thought of me. Maybe even held some affection for me. He never changed the name. He could have renamed it, dedicated it to the daughters he raised, but he didn't.

The bell over the shop door announces my arrival. Hopefully it didn't disturb Shawn. I scurry up the steps as quietly as I can, twisting my hands, nerves growing in the pit of my stomach. I untangle my fingers long enough to open the door and peer into the apartment.

Gray sweatpants cover Shawn's legs, which are sprawled across the couch. The light on the table softly illuminates his face and the book he holds. His lids are heavy, but his eyes spark to life when he spots me. "Hey, Red," he rasps, his voice as tired as he appears. "How was the rest of your night?" He folds the book closed over his hand and grants me his full attention.

Surprised he's awake, and reading no less, I find myself at a complete loss for words.

His lips quirk up on one side, and he watches me, almost as if my presence brings him joy.

"I-it was good," I stutter before looking down and slipping off my shoes. I can feel Shawn's gaze remain on me as I remove my jacket and slip into the kitchen to get a glass of water. I turn toward him awkwardly, because I don't know if I should sit here or go into my bedroom so he can be alone. After a moment of indecision, I finally look toward his book. "Whatchya reading?"

Shawn studies me for another moment, his eyes never quite giving away what he's thinking, and holds it up to me. "*Tangled in Tinsel.*"

I repeat the words obtusely. "*Tangled in Tinsel*?"

An easy smile takes over his face, like the way I parroted his words back to him was endearing. "Come 'ere, Red," he says, tapping the spot next to him on the couch. And next to him would be an exaggeration because he's taking up the entirety of the couch, so even sitting on the edge would put me so close it would be impossible not to touch.

I stare at him and squeeze my finger as I do. Can I handle being that close? I can't have him, and the proximity seems like pure torture.

"Red," he says in a more demanding tone, one that leaves no thinking to be had, and I go to him, moving quickly at his command. "Good girl," he says when I perch on the edge. He slips his arm against my hip and pulls me so I'm falling back and into his arms, leaving me with no alternative but to turn my body and hold on to him.

202

I tip my head back and watch him, waiting for his next move, the air growing heavier as time stands still under his stare.

And then his smooth voice starts up again. "My friend's girlfriend writes romance novels," he clears his throat, "and I read them all, so she suggested I read her friends' books too. This one is by Elyse Kelly."

I have to hold back a laugh when he shows me the cover. A hot man with a bare chest and donning a Santa hat is literally tangled with lights. "What's it about?" I ask, barely hiding a smile.

If Shawn is embarrassed, it doesn't show. Just like at the damn Zumba class, Shawn fits in everywhere he goes. Even with a naked man in his hand, he wears a confident smile. "Two friends who meet at Christmastime. They decide to explore their clear attraction for one another and find out they share the same kink."

My eyes bulge. Did Shawn just say kink? Shawn Chase, freaking baseball extraordinaire, who is currently holding me with one arm and holding a naked man book in the other, just said *kink*.

Yup. He definitely did. And why does that word turn me on? Is that a kink in itself? Just hearing about one.

"Wh-what kind of kink?" I sputter softly.

Shawn chuckles and pulls a piece of hair away from my face as he looks down at me. His face is aglow in lamplight, the sight ramping up my heart rate to an insane speed. "Your cheeks are turning the color of your hair, Red. Is this making you uncomfortable?" he asks, and for the first time tonight, even though he smiles, a hint of uncertainty surfaces, and his eyebrows pull together in concern.

I shake my head and let out a breathy "no."

His smile warms, and he blows out a hot breath. "Good."

"So, what's their kink?" I ask, garnering a little more confidence.

"Shibari." The word rolls off his tongue.

I stare at his mouth, as if those amazing lips are hiding secrets I'm dying to know.

"Shi—shi what?"

"Shibari," he says again with a breathy laugh. "It's the art of tying one another up."

My eyes are probably huge right now. "Oh," I say quietly, looking away and knotting my hands together. Is that what he likes? Being tied up? That's…*different*.

"I take it you've never heard of it," he supplies.

I look back at him shyly and shake my head.

"That's okay. Do you want me to read to you a little so you can learn about it?"

The way he offers, with no judgment whatsoever, like he'd be okay whether I said yes *or* no, leaves me feeling brave, so I nod.

"Should I start at the beginning?" he asks, opening the book to the first page.

"Sure."

For the next hour, Shawn's voice delivers a story that has me alternately smiling, clenching my thighs together, and blushing tremendously. The entire time, his other hand rubs softly against my arm, comforting me and lulling me into an almost comatose state. Until they take out the rope.

I couldn't fall asleep, even if I hadn't slept for days, when Shawn's deep voice tells me how beautiful Quinn looks as Mason wraps her in rope. My breath grows uneven, and I find myself biting my lip in anticipation, waiting for him to get to the sex. But just as Mason says he wants to taste her, Shawn looks down at me with a yawn and shuts the book. "Finish tomorrow, Red?"

I practically growl against his chest, and he laughs softly into my hair. "You can't do that to me," I whine and push against him, which only makes him laugh harder.

"So greedy now that you got a little taste, huh?"

I press into him, embarrassed.

"Go get some sleep, Red. I'll see you in the morning."

"Tease," I say, shaking my head before pushing myself up and walking toward the bedroom door.

Before I get inside, though, I think I hear him mutter under his breath, "You have no idea."

CHAPTER 31

SHAWN

Despite being exhausted, I lie in bed, wide awake, for a long time. There wasn't a chance in hell I could have kept reading with the sounds Jules was making as she inadvertently rubbed her leg against mine. I had three seconds to get away before my want for her became so evident it would poke her in the damn eye.

Fuck, my flirting made her uncomfortable the other day, and then I went ahead and read her a damn sexy nighttime story.

I blow out a breath and stare down at my erection. We are not doing this tonight. She's in the next room. *It's wrong.*

Especially when the thought of tying her up is playing on repeat in my head.

It's clear as day that she wouldn't be into it. She's too quiet, too reserved, too proper. Although she could certainly benefit from being tied up. For me, it's a therapeutic thing. During baseball season, I would use the ropes to de-stress since I rarely ever had flings in season. They took too much energy and time away from baseball.

Just the image of Jules in a stitch corset design, the ropes lifting her breasts, the way her soft skin would look against the deep red fabric, has my dick begging me to give in. And the whimpers she'd make as I tightened them or pressed soft kisses against her skin as I tied her—

I scrub a hand against my head. *Stop thinking about her like that.* I've never even thought about Hailey like this, and Hailey would probably enjoy it more. But seeing her tonight just reiterated the differences between the two of them. I don't see Jules when I look at Hailey and vice versa. They may be similar in appearance, but that's where the likeness ends. In every other way, they're strikingly different. Where Hailey is sarcastic in demeanor and tone, Jules is soft and light.

Hailey always has me laughing, but Jules sets my skin burning, and when she looks at me, as if she wants me to take control, I feel like the strongest man in the room. Like I'd move heaven and earth just to calm the constant war of emotions I see battled on her face every day.

Tying Jules up would free her. It would also unleash me.

But as I lie in bed knowing I'll never make that move, the noise I hear through the wall surprises me more than even her reaction to our evening's read-aloud. Music plays low, but it doesn't hide the faint buzz and a soft whimper. Like a fucking creep, I strain forward so I can listen.

The sound of Jules's soft cries as she chases her pleasure is easily the hottest thing I've ever heard.

If she can do it, so can I.

I slip my hand below the waistband of my sweats and pull out my straining, dripping cock, and then I grip myself firmly, closing my eyes and listening to her soft moans of pleasure. It doesn't take much to imagine the way she's lying naked in her bed, one hand twisting her nipple while the other slides her vibrator in and out of her tight pussy. How her hand probably travels down to play with her clit, circling as she gets close to the edge, then pulling back because she wants to prolong it. I think she'd like me taking her to the edge and back repeatedly, leaving her crying out and begging for release.

I pump harder, and the image of her is accompanied by the high-pitched sound of my name like a battle cry, one she couldn't hold back because her orgasm has taken her by surprise, the strength forcing my name from her lips, and I come all over my stomach with hers on mine.

JULES
ICE CREAM
SUPER PREMIUM ICE CREAM
SUPER PREMIUM ICE CREAM

CHAPTER 32

JULES

Pat the dough, sugar, flip it around, sprinkle again, roll it out, and repeat.

My focus is split between the donuts I'm shaping and the recipe card I'm filling out to document my steps. If I'm going to open a bakery, I can't just wing every recipe like I used to. It's great for making a batch here and there for friends or family, but if I want to operate a business, I'll need help, which means that employees will need to know how to make my creations. And, even more essential, I'll have to recreate each recipe over and over so my customers know what to expect. Adding even a dash of lemon or a sprinkle of vanilla into a recipe can completely change the flavor. I wouldn't necessarily say one is better than the last or, God forbid, worse, but when I find what I like, I want to know I can do it again.

But today's recipe isn't new. It's a tried-and-true blueberry lemon donut that Amy always raved about. I'm making two batches. One for Shawn to say thank you for all of his help lately, and another to bring to my grandmother's house. I'm having lunch with her today before I finally meet my father.

It's a big day.

Huge.

And if I wasn't having such a big, huge, monumental day, maybe I'd have time to freak out about how I sat on the couch with Shawn last night while he read me a naughty book. And how I then went to bed and pleasured myself to the thoughts of him doing the things the characters did.

But I don't have time to think about any of that.

And he was clearly not as affected as I was by the events of the previous evening because he walked out of the shower a few minutes ago humming "It's Beginning to Look a Lot Like Christmas" and being his normal jolly old self.

Meanwhile I'm over here spiraling. But I'm not, because I'm totally focusing on these donuts and whether I'm supposed to put the lemon in before or after the blueberries because I never freaking write it down.

Sprinkle the lemon, then swirl in the blueberry?

Yes, that's it.

"Whatchya making?" Shawn says, leaning over my shoulder.

And because I've been so in my head, I scream before turning toward him and pushing him backward. "Jeez, could you walk a little louder? For a big man, you're *very* good at sneaking around."

Shawn laughs like I haven't just lost my mind and presses me against the counter so he can get closer to the goods.

The food. *Not me.*

"Looks good. When will it be ready?"

His just-out-of-the-shower scent washes over me, but it's his closeness that makes me dizzy. Of its own volition, my body presses closer to his. I grab the counter and turn to keep myself from wrapping my arms around his neck.

This is bad. Reading that book was bad. Thinking about him while I did certain things…*oh so bad.* Now it's all I can think about.

Can he tell? Does he know what I did?

"Relax," Shawn says, confirming my inner rantings. He pulls my hands apart and squeezes where my thumb was just pressing into my skin. "Do you want me to give you space?" he asks softly, staring down at me like he really can see the inner workings of my brain.

I shake my head nominally, my mouth opening as I stare up at him. Probably involuntarily, he licks his lips, and then he pushes a strand of my hair back, sending goosebumps scattering across my skin.

"Good girl," he whispers.

Another shiver goes through my body, his praise at my relaxation making me think I can fight this anxiety as long as he's near. Or maybe I don't want to banish it completely. That way he'll have a reason to touch me again.

"Now tell me what you're making, Red," he says smoothly.

I give myself one more second to relax into his touch, and then I push off and lift the platter to show him. "Lemon blueberry donuts. I'm making some for you to take to the station and some to bring to my grandmother's."

Shawn stares at me for a few moments and shakes his head, a small smile on his lips. "Don't ever change, Red. You are one of a kind."

Butterflies take flight in my stomach and dance around lightly. I've never experienced such kindness, such genuine affirmation, from anyone. I'm at a complete loss for words. "Thank you," I finally say softly before turning back. "Would you like to help me roll them out?"

Shawn's eyes light up. "You gonna show me how to do this? How about I stand behind you, and you can use my hands however you need?"

Just the idea of him standing behind me reminds me of that scene in *Ghost*, and instantly, I'm imagining what he's going to be using those hands for…and how I *need* him to use them.

My laugh comes out breathy. I roll my eyes when all I really want to do is beg him to press me against the counter and show me how good he really is with his hands. "You're such a player," I tease, trying to remind myself that is exactly what he is.

Shawn waggles his brows. "Why do you say that?"

I poke him in the stomach. "Because you got game."

Shawn grabs my arm and spins me around so my back is to his front and he dips his chin so it's on my shoulder. As he speaks, his breath tickles my ear. "Use me, Red."

Forget butterflies. There's a damn inferno blazing in my stomach now. I gulp down my nervousness and try to talk him through it. Baking is the one thing I know how to do. I could make these donuts in my sleep. "First let's get a little powder on your hands," I say, pressing the sugary substance into his fingers.

He twines his fingers with mine so our movements are one, making my breath go shallow.

"Now what?" he murmurs into my neck, his lips whispering softly against my skin.

"Now we roll," I reply, almost breathless, reaching into the dough, his hand still pressed to mine, and grabbing a clump. I set it on the sugar-dusted counter and maneuver it into the shape of a donut. The entire time, Shawn's heart beats against my back, his body heat warms my skin, and his cheek is pressed to mine. Strong fingers work with mine to create the miniature pastries I hope he'll love. I'm surrounded by him and submersed in this moment. I've never felt so connected to another person, and yet we're fully clothed. There is an intimacy coursing between us every time we're together.

Too soon, the donuts are rolled out and we inspect our creation. "We did good," I say slowly, not quite ready to let him go. He makes no move to back away. His fingers remain wrapped around mine. Finally, I clear my throat. "We should get cleaned up."

Shawn nods against my shoulder. "Right." Then he pulls his sticky fingers from mine and walks to the sink. He flips it on with his elbow and nods for me to go first. I scurry over and wash my hands quickly and then give him the opportunity to do the same.

"I'll just fry these up, and then you can take some whenever you want to go."

Shawn nods, but his silent attention remains on me for several beats before he blurts out, "Come out with me tonight?"

"Huh?"

"My sister asked me to come over for dinner. Her fiancé, Jack, will be there, and Amelia and Nate probably. And possibly Charlotte's best friend Steph and her husband."

My anxiety flares at just the thought of being in a room with so many people I barely know.

As if he can read me like a book, he steps up close to me and pushes my hair back from my face. He leaves his hand there, just holding my head. "Please come. I won't leave you alone at any time, but it would be good for you to meet more people."

I stare up into his chocolate eyes. I trust him more than I've trusted almost anyone. There is a calmness and a kindness to him that isn't easily replicated or faked. This man is the real deal, and for some reason, he's offering to be my friend. And he wants to help me with my business, with my sister. He's helping me settle into a town I thought wouldn't welcome me and introducing me to his friends.

"Thank you," I whisper.

The right side of his mouth lifts in a smirk. "You'll come?"

I nod. "Yeah, I'll come."

For a moment, we're frozen there, looking at one another, and I wonder if he'll kiss me. I *hope* that he'll kiss me. But then he nods and pushes himself away, pulling his hand from my face. "I have to get stuff ready. You sure you don't need my help with anything else?" Shawn asks, although I think we both know I didn't need his help rolling the donuts—I just enjoyed it.

Swallowing down my embarrassment over the lack of a kiss—and that I wanted it so freaking bad I almost went up on my tiptoes and took it myself—I nod and give him a big smile. "All good here."

And then he's gone.

JULES
ICE CREAM
SUPER PREMIUM ICE CREAM
SUPER PREMIUM ICE CREAM

CHAPTER 33

JULES

I arrive at my grandmother's at twelve thirty as instructed with my donuts in a carrier and wearing a simple caramel-colored sweater dress, black knee-high boots, and a smile. Bernard greets me at the door and gives me a once-over before nodding in approval and taking the donuts from my hand. "Mrs. Milsom is expecting you. She's planned lunch in the solarium."

Also known as a sunroom to us normal folk. I laugh to myself. Unlike the last time I was here, the house is fully decorated for Christmas. It's a bit over the top, with white angels in every corner and silver and gold garland.

Shawn wouldn't decorate like this. There'd be red and green, maybe even some tinsel, which I'm sure would drive my grandmother crazy, and perhaps popcorn around the tree. Just the idea of it leaves me smiling. Will Shawn want to put up a tree? I've never had a real one—my mother always said she was allergic. I really hope Shawn and I can go to the tree farm and cut one down. That just feels *so* Christmas.

I roll my eyes at my foolishness almost immediately. We aren't dating. Why would he want to cut down a tree with me and decorate like we're a couple? I sigh as my fingers begin to work themselves over one another.

"Juliana, you look absolutely beautiful," my grandmother says as I come into view. The solarium is bright from the afternoon sun, and the bay sparkles in the distance. I'm sure this room is magical on snowy days. It probably feels like being outside, minus the cold. I hope I get to experience it.

I grab the hem of my skirt and shift to curtsy again but catch myself before I do this time. *Oh sugar! What is wrong with me?*

Brittle hands pull me in for a hug, and I find myself wrapping my arms around her small frame. She smells like peppermint and lavender. A strange combination, for sure. "Thank you for having me."

"Of course," she says smoothly. "Let's sit. I want to hear all about how your time in Bristol has been."

Over the next hour, I fill my grandmother in on my life, leaving out the fact that Shawn is living with me because she's still under the impression that Hailey and I live together, and I don't intend to give my sister another reason to hate me. I tell her about working at the bar, to which she gives a surprised smile and says that she hopes Hailey is going easy on me. After a while, I finally work up the nerve to share my idea about the bakery. This is the subject I've been most nervous about broaching. Although she said it was my building and I can do what I please, it's still legally hers, and I'm asking to make some very big changes.

"That's a lofty idea," she says after I explain in probably too much detail. I'm so nervous I can't help but babble. For a moment, she studies me, almost as if weighing my worth. I hope she likes what she sees.

Fiddling with my fingers, I wait for her to continue. When I catch sight of Bernard giving me a gentle nod from the corner of the dining room, I supply, "I brought some donuts. Would you like to try one?"

Her eyes light up. "I love donuts."

I was *not* expecting such excitement from my prim and proper grandmother, but I'm certainly happy to hear it. Bernard disappears and returns a few minutes later with the donuts plated beautifully, along with a tray of various choices for tea.

"Oh, this looks so good!" I gush, and redness tinges his ears. The blues and yellow of the donut swirl together, and I can't help but warm at the memory of how they got that way. After I fried them, I drizzled them in a lemon glaze, and my mouth waters, just dying to taste one.

I hope this tastes like the batch I made a few months ago.

I *think* I got the recipe right, but with Shawn breathing down my neck, quite literally, it's anyone's guess.

My grandmother waits for Bernard to put a donut on her plate, and then she holds it up to me and we cheers our baked goods. It's absolutely the cutest thing I've ever seen. Little old lady everyone thinks is so scary cheersing me with my donut.

Slowly, she brings it to her mouth and takes a bite. Her eyes flutter shut, and she hums to herself. After she swallows, she beams at me. "Juliana, that was the most delicious donut I've ever had. It practically melted in my mouth."

My smile can't be contained. "Really?" I ask nervously.

She takes another bite and then sets what's left on her plate. "Now tell me what we need to do to turn that shop into the best bakery in town!"

CHAPTER 34

SHAWN

"I don't understand how your interest in a girl got us all roped into taking off our shirts for the cougars of Bristol," Mason says in quite possibly the longest sentence he's ever spoken.

Before I can respond, Hailey leans across the bar, her eyebrows waggling in excitement. "Shawn Chase interested in a girl! Who's the lucky lady?"

I slam my elbow into Colby's chest as he takes a deep breath like he's about to blurt out her name. "No one." I give her my signature grin. "Since when do you listen to these bozos?"

Mason gives a harrumph that would rival Eeyore and takes a sip of his beer. Dane chuckles into his drink beside him, and Colby eyes me like he can't decide if he'd rather sock me in the face or blurt out my secret.

Hailey is nothing if not a dog with a bone when she wants something. "Colby, if you tell me, I'll give you free beer all night."

Colby slaps me on the back, and to my surprise, says, "Nah, I think my friend Shawn here is going to treat me to a nice Johnny Walker Black, right, *Babe*?"

I grind my molars and nod to Hailey. She rolls her eyes and points a finger in my direction. "I'll figure it out sooner or later. You can't hide from me, ya know?"

As she's walking away, Mason mutters, "You only hid your crush on her for months. I think you're safe."

Once again, Dane laughs into his beer, and I just shake my head. *Why am I working so hard to make these guys like me?*

"What did Chief say when you mentioned the calendar?" Dane asks.

"He knows it's for a good cause," I reply. "He's fine."

Mason grumbles, "Did you tell him he's gotta be in it?"

Colby laughs. "No way! Chief? That'll be the day."

Dane pipes in. "He's not much older than me, and he's better looking than you."

From behind the bar, Hailey quips, "Yeah, he is. Pretty sure Chief Williams will kill anyone who looks at him though."

It's no secret that the chief of police and our chief are best friends who also happen to kind of hate each other. It's fun to watch. Kara wants nothing to do with him, so she says, but that doesn't keep her from practically arresting every woman who goes near him.

"Stop listening in on our conversations," I say, shooting Hailey a look of feigned annoyance.

She laughs. "I'm going to find out who your crush is one way or another. You might as well tell me."

"I'm not sixteen. I don't have a crush."

"That's true. You're an old man compared to me," she says.

Dane laughs, almost choking on his beer.

"I really don't know why I come here," I say in mock irritation and stand.

Hailey swats at me and grabs my shirt, pulling me in close. "Because you love me. Now sit back down and I'll stop bugging you. I'm sure you'll tell me when you're good and ready."

I huff and drop into my seat. "Right. Hey, Jules mentioned she was going to see your dad today. How's he doing?"

Hailey's entire demeanor stiffens. "She what?"

Whoops. Guess Jules didn't mention it to Hailey. If they've talked at all about anything. "She's having lunch with your grandmother and then going to visit your dad. I think she's going with Caris."

I check my phone. The guys and I came in for a late lunch since none of us were working today. Jules is probably already on her way to the hospital. I hope she's okay. It's weird how I have this urge to reach out to her. To text her. To want to be by her side when she meets her father. She doesn't need me there. We've only just met. And yet…I shake my head. I'm getting ahead of myself. Like always, I'm overthinking everything.

Hailey's eyes narrow and she bites her lip. "Of course she is."

"What's that supposed to mean?" I say, irritation seeping into my tone.

At this point, all the guys have stopped talking and everyone is focused on us. This is not the way to have this conversation. Not that it's my conversation to have. Hailey and Jules need to work this out between themselves. Hailey can be the most loyal, fun-loving friend, but it can be hard to break through her tough exterior. I just don't know why she's being that way with Jules. Everything about Jules is soft and kind, so Hailey's fangs make no sense. Her sister isn't any more at fault than she is for the way their parents handled things. Jules was just as much a victim to their dumb plan as Hailey.

"Forget it," I say quietly. "We can talk about this later."

"There's nothing *to* talk about. I'm not sure what my sister has been saying to you, but I've barely had a conversation with her. I haven't *done* anything to her."

This time, it's not false bravado when I stand up. Placing my palm flat on the bar, I look her dead in the eye. "Hailes, you know I love you, but you are missing out *because* you won't talk to her. *That's* the point." I nod to the guys and walk out.

JULES
ICE CREAM
SUPER PREMIUM ICE CREAM
SUPER PREMIUM ICE CREAM

CHAPTER 35

JULES

He's just another person. A human being I happen to share blood and half my DNA with, but also just a person. There is no need to make this a bigger deal than it is. I wring my hands together, repeating these facts to myself while I wait for Caris to arrive. She needs to get here before I lose my nerve.

"Hailes, I didn't realize you were coming in today," a man says with an accent I can't place, offering me a kind smile.

I shake my head. "Not Hailes," I mutter.

His blue eyes, which are an absurd contrast to his dark skin, light up. "Oh, you must be Juliana." He offers me his hand. "I'm Dr. Steele. Maddox Steele." When I still look at him like he has two heads, he explains further. "I'm a friend of Caris's. And I'm your father's doctor. Well, one of them."

"Oh, it's nice to meet you." I take the hand he's offered. Although the man in that room is not my father, I remind myself. As Dr. Steele knows quite well if he's friendly enough with Hailey to use her nickname. "I'm supposed to meet Caris here," I offer.

He nods and smiles, shaking his head in wonder. "You really are remarkably similar to Hailey…and yet so different."

I dip my chin as my eyes do a sort of awkward bulge. He's *really* staring. "Yup…well we're twins *so*…" I twist my fingers anxiously.

His smile remains plastered on his face. "Do you want me to take you in?" he asks, pointing back to my father's room.

I shake my head sharply. "Oh, God no," I say before I can stop myself. And as soon as I do, I know I can't go in there, *period*. I want to meet him. I really do. But not right now. Not this way. I need someone. I need Amy or…Shawn.

Gosh, how did he become such a comfort to me so quickly? Only a week ago, I was nervous when we were in the same room, and now he's like my comfort blanket.

That thought sends me spiraling down an entirely different, ridiculous path. What am I doing getting attached to a baseball player? He's just being kind to me, and I'm wrapping my tentacles around him like I need him to breathe. I need to get out of here. I need fresh air.

"Are you okay?" the doctor asks, placing his large hand on my shoulder. I jump at the connection. "You look like you're having a panic attack," he observes.

Yup, you don't need a medical degree to see that I'm spiraling. *Good job, Doc.*

I nod and breathe in and out slowly. "I just…I need to go," I say, then spin on my heel and walk toward the door without stopping.

CHAPTER 36

SHAWN

I've just removed the last cabinet face when the door to our apartment swings open.

"Oh!" Jules says, as if she's surprised to find me in our apartment. "I, uh, I'll be…" she points to the door and spins toward it.

I can tell by her demeanor and her insane ramblings that she's not okay, so I jump off the counter, drop my tools, and push toward her. I grab her shoulder before she can make it past her door and turn her to face me. "Hey, Red. You okay?"

She lets out a shocked screeching peep but avoids looking at me.

"Jules," I say, softer this time, holding both her arms at her sides and waiting for her to look at me. When she doesn't, I dip lower so I'm eye level with her. Her breathing is erratic, and she's holding herself so tight she might crack. "What happened?"

Tears fill her eyes. "Kiss me, please," she says softly, almost begging.

I shake my head. "Not because I don't want to, sweetheart, but because that's not what you need right now."

"You don't even know me," she yells, but it's a half-attempt at anger.

Knowing only one other way to calm her, I pull her close to my chest. "I got you," I say and squeeze her tight.

Her body continues to shake with sobs so violent they vibrate through my chest.

"I got you," I whisper again. I hold her until her sobs subside and she stills in my arms, and then I lift her up and carry her to the couch.

She avoids my gaze, embarrassment marring her blotchy, tear-streaked face. Her heavy sighs and attempts at deep breathing to get herself under control break my heart. I push her against my chest and cradle her until her breaths match mine.

"Thank-thank you," she stutters softly. She covers her face with her hands and mumbles, "I'm so embarrassed."

I don't force her to look at me. Instead, I speak quietly and allow her to keep her head down. "It's okay. Seriously, I have anxiety. I totally understand how you're feeling right now. And I'm here for you…"

"But why?" she asks, finally looking up at me in bewilderment. "Why are you here for me? Your best friend hates me. You barely know me. And yet you keep showing up for me…*why*?"

"Because I care about you, Red." I wipe the tears from her cheeks with my thumbs, unable to stop myself from touching her, even after the tears are no longer a problem. I stroke her cheek repeatedly, soothing us both. "And for the record, Hailey doesn't hate you. She's just—" I pause, at a loss for why Hailey is being so hard on her sister. "Give her time," I finally say, knowing I have nothing else to offer and truly believing that if Hailey gave her sister a chance, she'd fall for her just like I have.

Maybe not *exactly* like I have, since I'm clearly still falling. It's a perpetual state I don't think will ever end.

"I went to the hospital…" she says as she stares into the distance. "To meet my father."

I stroke her back to let her know I'm listening, but I don't interrupt.

"And I couldn't do it. I couldn't go in there. And I realized…" she takes a deep hiccupping breath before she looks back up at me. "I really wanted Amy there."

I nod. That makes sense.

"But she can't be there…because she's in California," she explains, as if I don't know this already.

"And then I realized if I couldn't have her—" Her eyes meet mine. They hold so much loss, so much uncertainty, but also… hope. "I realized if I couldn't have her, I wanted you. Which is crazy," she says, shaking her head, like the idea that I would be there for her is insane.

This time, I don't allow her to look away. I use two fingers to tip her chin up so she's forced to look me in the eye. "It's not crazy. You've got me. I'm right here."

"But you barely know me."

I smile. "I know enough to know that I like you a lot."

"You do?"

My laughter shakes us both. "What's not to like? You're ridiculously likable."

"I am?" she says in almost astonishment.

I nod, stroking her cheek again. "You have this way about you. Jeez, Jules, you don't even see it, but everyone is enamored with you when they meet you. And the fact that you don't curse, but you still try to—like, who says jiminy crickets? Who names the spider in the shower? Or bakes for the entire fire department? You are one in a million, and I'm honored that when you're struggling, you trust me to be there for you."

She blinks at me in wonder, and it takes everything in me not to kiss her. "Spiders are less scary with names," she whispers.

I can't help but bark out a laugh. "Yes, sweetheart. Yes, they are." I press my forehead to hers and smile.

"Thank you," she says softly.

"Always." I squeeze her hip and look into her eyes. "You always have me."

She breathes out, as if exhaling all the pent-up stress she's been carrying, and then she looks at me again. "What did you do to the cabinets?"

We both break out into laughter, and I hug her closely. "I'll fix them, I promise. You still want to come with me tonight?"

Jules's green eyes meet mine and she blows out a breath. "Can I get cleaned up first?"

I motion to myself. I'm covered in dust from sanding down the cabinets. "I need a shower, so you've got plenty of time."

"Say hi to Charlotte for me," she teases with a smile as she wiggles out of my hold.

I laugh, pulling her back and hugging her again. Then, before I do anything stupid—like drag her into the shower with me—I shoot her a wink and slide her off my lap.

JULES
ICE CREAM
SUPER PREMIUM ICE CREAM
SUPER PREMIUM ICE CREAM

CHAPTER 37

JULES

You're ridiculously likable. I cycle through our conversation at least ten more times while I scrub my face free of makeup and try to make myself presentable.

"Spiders are less scary with names."

"Yes, sweetheart. Yes, they are."

He called me sweetheart. Shawn Chase called me *sweetheart*. And he held me like I *was* his sweetheart. Suddenly all the anxiety I've been drowning in about my family has flown out the window, and now I'm nervous about seeing Shawn's family again. I want them to like me. No, I *need* them to like me. Mostly because they matter to Shawn, but also because I really need friends.

If I've learned anything over the last few hours, it's that.

Shawn *can't* be the only person I know in this town.

But yeah, if I'm being honest, I mostly care because they're his people. And sweet baby kittens, I think I really like him.

As we walk out of the building and Shawn turns around to lock up, I take a moment to inhale the cool winter air. Christmas is right around the corner, and hopefully I'll get to experience my first snow soon.

Shawn takes my hand and twines our fingers together before he leads me toward his truck. "Is it far?" I ask as he opens the passenger door and waits for me to hop in.

"Nah, just a quick five minutes down the road," he says, leaning over me and snapping my seat belt across my lap. It's adorable and comforting, and before he can move away to close the door, I grab his hand and kiss him quickly on the cheek.

"Thanks for tonight."

Shawn gives me a lazy grin. "Anytime."

As he shuts the door, I kick my legs out in front of me in excitement and shimmy my shoulders. Maybe I even squeal a little. I almost hide the sound, but Shawn must hear when he opens his door because he shoots me a smirk. "You okay there, Red?"

I fold my lips in and nod. "Fine," I squeak.

He laughs and turns the key in the ignition. "Tell me about lunch with your grandmother."

I smile. That actually went well. I fill him in on how she said she'd help me with the bakery, and then I get lost in telling him about my plans. I talk excitedly for at least fifteen minutes while Shawn smiles genuinely and asks questions before I realize that we've been parked in front of a house for a while. "Uh—is this your sister's house?" I cringe at how oblivious I've been.

Shawn nods. "Yup. You ready to go in, Red?"

I punch him in the shoulder when I spot people staring at us through the window. "Why didn't you tell me we were here?"

Shawn shrugs, that lazy smile of his tattooed on his face. "Because I like listening to you."

"But your family is waiting for us," I say, pointing toward the window full of people.

Shawn doesn't even spare them a glance. "Let them wait. I like seeing you smile, and you should see the way it takes over your face when you talk about the bakery." He shakes his head in wonder.

I'm left almost speechless. "I—what?" I fumble when I finally find my voice.

Shawn grins casually, like he didn't just set my world spinning again. "Come on, Red. You ready to meet your new best friends?"

Although everyone was staring at me curiously—or, more accurately, at the way Shawn was holding my hand as he made introductions—for once, I wasn't anxious. Something about him always calms me.

It also didn't hurt that his sister tripped and spilled her drink on her friend Steph when she introduced us. That took some of the attention off me.

"Sassy, when you going to learn you can't do two things at once?" her fiancé Jack says as he pulls her onto his lap.

"You're just going to leave me to clean up this mess?" Steph asks, shooting daggers in their direction.

Charlotte giggles. "*Please*. If I try to help, we both know you'll end up wearing our dinners. Just get Pat to help you," Charlotte says with a smile, pointing to the man behind Steph, who's already holding a towel.

"I've got it," a tall woman with long black hair and the most gorgeous blue eyes I've ever seen says. She grabs the towel from him and blots Steph's shirt. "I'm Belle, by the way," she says as she looks back at me. Holy cannoli, this woman is drop-dead gorgeous. And don't even get me started on her curves.

"Jules," I mutter.

Shawn squeezes my hand and pulls me closer. "You okay?"

I nod. It's a lot, but I'm miraculously not intimidated by any of these women.

"Oh, fancy seeing you here," a voice says from behind us.

When Shawn and I turn, Amelia and Nate are walking in. He's got his hand gripping her side tightly. I'm drawn to the way he possesses her. Like he's nervous she could disappear if he doesn't hold on for dear life. As if she knows he needs reassurance, she offers him a smile I've never seen on her face. She lights up just for him.

"Oh fiddlesticks," an older woman says as she walks out of the kitchen. "Earl, can you grab the club soda?"

I smile. *Fiddlesticks*. That's my kind of woman. She and Belle study the red wine stain on Steph's blouse.

Charlotte pats the spot next to her and Jack on the couch. "Come chat. They'll be busy for a while," she says with a smile. Like Shawn, she sets me at ease.

"I'll get us drinks. Will you be okay here?" Shawn offers quietly.

Charlotte laughs. "I'm not going to murder her. She'll be fine. Let the girl breathe, Shawn."

He smirks at her. "I mean, you could trip into her with a knife. We've got to be prepared."

Both Jack and I laugh, and Charlotte's hand flies up to her mouth in mock offense.

"I'll be fine. *Go*," I say, nodding toward the kitchen so he knows he can leave me for five minutes. As Shawn gives me one last glance, I sit down next to his sister.

"How is living with my brother?" Charlotte asks. Jack pulls her against his chest, but she smacks him away and rights herself without breaking eye contact with me.

I stare down at the rock on her finger. It's absolutely gorgeous. Rose gold and a big diamond. When she looks up at him, she blushes, and he kisses her quickly before sliding her off him.

"I'll give you two a chance to chat. Better check on Shawn."

"Thanks, Mav," she says softly.

"Mav?" I question.

Charlotte blushes again. "Oh, he was in the Air Force, so I like to tease him."

My jaw drops to the floor. "Like a pilot?"

Charlotte's brown eyes, which are identical to her brothers, light up. "Yes. I fell backward when he told me. Like, literally fell backward at the airport and hit my head on the dirty floor."

I laugh at the mental picture she creates. It seems exactly like something she would do. She's so down to earth and normal and, well, clumsy.

"Anyway, less about me and more about you. *So you and my brother…*" she says with a wicked glint in her eye.

"Are just friends," I offer.

She laughs. "Maybe that's what you want, but not him."

I shake my head, even though I want her to be right. "No, he likes my sister…we, just…we're roommates, and we go to Zumba together, and he's really into Christmas stuff, so he's signed me up for all of these things so I can get to know people in town—"

She shakes her head, her mouth morphing into an *O*. "My brother at Zumba?"

I shrug. "Yeah, he said the guys at the fire station go for strength training."

She gives me a knowing look. "Did he now? Interesting. Very interesting."

Timed perfectly, Shawn and Jack return with drinks. Shawn sits next to me and hands me a red drink with what appears to be a sugar rim. I raise my eyes to him in question.

"Christmas Margarita," he mumbles.

"You make it yourself?" I tease.

He shrugs. "I know you like margaritas…so yeah."

Charlotte looks on knowingly. "Margaritas, Zumba…what else do you guys have in common?"

One of Shawn's eyebrows arches perfectly in his sister's direction. "Hmm?" he replies, as if he didn't hear her.

"I didn't know you went to Zumba. That's so interesting. I'd love to join you guys. When do you normally go, *Shawn*?"

Jack squeezes her hip. "Pretty sure we'd have to put you in bubble wrap, Sass. Don't tease your brother."

I laugh at the easy banter the three share, reveling for a moment in the way they include me in their conversation.

Amelia steps into the room, drink in hand, and squeezes Jack's shoulder. "What are we teasing Shawn about?"

Jack looks up at his sister with a smirk. "Don't you think you've put the guy through enough? You already made him fake date you to get this clown back." He points to Nate, who stands with a knowing smirk behind them both. "You all need to let the poor man be."

Amelia laughs and holds up her hands. "Hey, he didn't do it for purely selfless reasons. He wanted Hailey just as much as I *didn't* want Nate."

Every head in the room swivels in her direction, and Shawn mutters under his breath. "Jeez, Ames, really?"

As if the cellular network gods are smiling down on me, my phone buzzes in my pocket then, giving me an excuse to avoid this conversation.

"Shit, sorry," she says, flashing him a look of apology. She looks to me, and to where Shawn is gripping my hip possessively. Even I hadn't noticed he was doing it because it's become a habit of his lately.

"'Scuse me," I say to the room full of people staring at me and pull out of Shawn's grip. A flicker of disappointment crosses his face, but I point to the phone where Amy's name is flashing. "I have to take this."

Shawn looks me in the eye, ignoring everyone else. "Hailey and I are *just* friends."

Looking at my lap, I manage to whisper, "So are we."

Before I can make sense of the hurt etched on his face, I hop up and rush outside, where I find a small deck. It's cold, but I'd take frigid temperatures over the heat in that room any day.

CHAPTER 38

SHAWN

I blow out a breath and watch Jules disappear outside. "I should go after her," I say, bracing myself on the armrest of the couch.

Charlotte holds her hand out to me. "Give her a minute and then go. It's a lot."

Amelia sits next to me with apologetic eyes. "I'm so sorry, Shawn. I didn't realize you had…" She trails off.

"Feelings for her? Yeah, I was trying to play it cool," I admit.

Maybe a little too cool. *Does she really think we're just friends*? How come no one ever looks at me like I could be their everything? I scan the room, eyeing each of my friends and family members. It's like everyone has found their soulmate, their best friend, their *person*…and I'm always the side character. The friend, the brother, the bartender, but never worth a starring role.

As if she can hear my thoughts, my sister puts her hand over mine. "It's just a lot for her, and the situation is tricky. You *did* have feelings for her sister. The one she's trying so hard to get to know."

Amelia scoffs. "Yeah, and Hailey isn't making it easy."

"Why is that?" I ask honestly, because for the life of me, I can't figure it out. And I want to. I want to help Jules feel comfortable here. I want her to have the family, the business, the community she so desperately craves. Then maybe she'll be open to other things as well.

Amelia shrugs. "You know Hailey," she says, like that explains everything. Then she meets my eye. "I'm really sorry. I didn't realize you'd moved on from Hailey to Jules."

I slump back into the couch. "It's not like that. *At all.* My crush on Hailey ended before I developed feelings for Jules. She's just…Hailey is my friend. I realized that a few weeks ago. She sees me that way, too, and she's never given me this *feeling* that I get around Jules."

"Which is?" my sister asks softly.

"Like my heart just walked out of the room," I reply, staring at the door.

Jack chimes in. "I know that feeling."

My sister looks back at him and melts into his arms.

"Me too," Nate echoes.

Amelia's eyes raise to his, and she offers him the kind of smile she reserves for him alone.

"What do I do?" I ask desperately. Amelia's right. This is a strange situation. Yes, I was once attracted to Hailey, but I never acted on it. Those lukewarm feelings are long gone and have been replaced by this burning need for Jules. A need I've never had for another woman.

Luca, Belle's boyfriend, leans forward in his chair. I hadn't even realized he was watching. He's a private investigator and blends in well when he wants to, I guess. "You asking how to make a girl swoon?"

Belle rolls her eyes as she settles herself onto her boyfriend's lap. "So cocky. You think you can give advice on this, Green Eyes?"

He squeezes her around her waist, and she laughs before snuggling into his arms. "I won over my enemy, didn't I?" he teases. "Find out what she likes and do those things. Tease her, flirt with her, make yourself so visible in her life that there's no way she won't realize you're *it* for her."

Every person in the room nods in agreement, and I consider my plan.

From the kitchen, Carmella shakes her hips. "And if that fails, tie her up and make her listen to you."

Everyone laughs at the joke, but she's got my wheels turning now. I can't help but smile at the idea. I know exactly what my girl needs. And that's exactly what she will become. *My girl.*

JULES
ICE CREAM
SUPER PREMIUM ICE CREAM
SUPER PREMIUM ICE CREAM

CHAPTER 39

JULES

Things were awkward after Amelia's comment about Shawn and Hailey last night, but Shawn didn't let me stay outside alone for long. He joined me on the deck but was smart enough not to bring it up. What is there to talk about anyway? At one point, he had a crush on my sister, and now he apparently doesn't. Is that weird? Kind of. Is it a deal breaker? I don't even know what kind of deal it would be breaking. We're *just friends*.

And, apparently, I'm a liar because not long after all of this happened, Shawn's hand was back in mine. I laughed along with his friends, joked around, and joined in on the games they played for the rest of the night.

Jack set up beer pong on the deck. We played with red beer because it was *festive*. Luca and Belle beat everybody until Earl and Carmella stepped up, and then they kicked all of our butts. Honestly it was a really good night, despite the few awkward minutes early on.

When I wake up the next morning, the apartment is empty, but I find a note from Shawn on the kitchen counter next to a brewing pot of coffee.

Red,

I had fun last night. I have to run a few errands. Meet me at town hall at 3 p.m. for a Christmas committee meeting.

Shawn

I hold up the note and laugh. *A Christmas committee meeting? Is that even a thing?*

And then, because it sounds like a Christmas committee meeting would be the perfect place for me to bring a few sweet treats, I get to work making cookies and donuts in hopes of winning over some townies.

The red brick building downtown is unassuming, and as I struggle to open the door with the dessert container in my hand, I'm interrupted with a quiet, "I've got it." I turn around to find Mason in yet another flannel shirt.

I freeze and give him a once-over. He doesn't seem like the type to be involved with the Christmas committee. "Thank you," I say, then I unstick my feet from the sidewalk and step into the building.

"You brought treats?" he says with a slow smile, surveying the container.

"I'm trying to make friends, remember?" I tease.

Right then, Shawn turns and spots us, and his mouth splits in a blinding smile. My steps falter when I realize that reaction is for me.

Mason grumbles beside me, "You don't need to bake for their affection."

I turn to him in surprise. He's a man of few words, and that seems like more than just making conversation. In fact, I've discovered he rarely speaks unless he has something important to say, which makes his comment more meaningful. "Thanks, Mason," I say, really meeting his gaze to show him how much I appreciate his sentiment.

He shrugs. "That doesn't mean I don't want one of those donuts."

I laugh. "You can have first dibs."

When I look back up, Shawn is in front of us. He smirks before holding out his hand to take the container. "We're going to have to up our Zumba classes if you keep baking for us, Red."

I lift my shoulders and smile. "You said you loved Zumba. We could go after—"

Mason nudges me with his shoulder. "'Member how I just said you didn't need to bake for affection? Finish that sentence and I'll change my tune." He shakes his head and steps away, mumbling, "I'm going to grab a coffee so I can stay awake for this. Babe, you owe me." He shoots Shawn a look, and for once Shawn doesn't wince at the nickname.

I giggle and decide to try out the nickname myself. "Yeah, *Babe*. You owe me too. I thought we were going to read the rest of the story last night, but you fell asleep." I stick out my bottom lip in a fake pout.

Shawn shakes his head and grins. "All in due time, Red. All in due time."

"What do we have here?" A woman with fiery red hair asks, sidling up next to Shawn and wrapping her hand around his bicep.

I have an overwhelming urge to growl *mine*. It's insane. I'm pretty sure I've never growled in my life, and he is most definitely *not* mine.

"Lucy, this is Jules. She's the one I told you about. She's new in town, and she's the new owner of Jules Ice Cream. She's moving forward with her plan to open the bakery and was kind enough to bring some of her treats for everyone today."

My heart pitter patters in my chest at the way Shawn so proudly focuses on me as he speaks.

Lucy looks me up at down, and I somehow manage to hold myself upright under her gaze. It's not unlike how the women in California would judge me at the country club. I've got this. Boobs out, smile plastered to my face, and hand extended in greeting. "It's so nice to meet you, Lucy."

She raises her eyebrows, like she's got my number, but she takes my hand. "Shawn, I only count three firefighters. You promised me the entire department."

I eye Shawn. *What's she talking about?*

Shawn slips his arm around Lucy's shoulders and pushes them in the direction of the table where other pastries are laid out with coffee. "Someone has to be at the station in case a call comes in. Don't worry. Our deal still stands."

Deal?

The sound of clapping across the room steals the attention of everyone nearby, and I turn my focus to the woman in the front with the white hair and big smile.

Carmella.

Finally, my muscles relax. This woman is a riot. She's in her seventies and is wearing another ridiculous muumuu that should be relegated to the *only wear at home* section of her closet. But here she is, heading the Christmas committee meeting in the bright red monstrosity.

I adore her.

"Okay, my Christmas elves. We have a lot to get done in the next hour. Everyone take a seat."

Shawn shoots me a grin, and excitement buzzes through my body. I'm not sure if it's his smile or because I'm actually here, but my pulse just skyrocketed.

A small-town Christmas committee. It's like I've walked onto a Hallmark movie set, and yet it's real life.

Shawn sets my desserts on the table and grabs a cookie for himself before sliding his hand into mine and leading me to the open seats next to Mason. I spot Colby and Dane in the back. Dane nods in my direction, giving me a friendly smile, while Colby gives me a flirtatious wave. I laugh when Shawn's grip on my hand tightens.

So possessive.

Carmella begins before I can put too much thought into it though. "The festival starts next Saturday. The fire department has graciously offered to put up the booths this week, so for those of you with booths, please make sure you schedule a time for them to help you."

From the front row, Lucy interjects. "I found someone who will lend us a reindeer. Shawn, do you think you could go with me to pick him up in New Hampshire?"

I practically choke on my saliva. She wants Shawn to drive with her to get a reindeer? That's the worst pickup line I've ever heard.

Carmella shakes her head. "Oh, fiddlesticks, Lucy. I already signed you up to help the seniors crochet mittens and hats to sell at the festival this weekend. Looks like Shawn will have to go with someone else. I'm sure Jules wouldn't mind. Right, darling?" She winks in my direction.

All eyes in the room dart to us, and I shrink under their scrutiny. "Um…"

Shawn squeezes my hand. The hand that is still waffled with his, like I belong to him. My breath catches in my throat as I stare down at the connection. What exactly are we doing?

"We've got it," he says. "Just give me the information, and we'll make it work."

Carmella claps her hands in excitement. "Oh good."

Shawn takes a sip of his coffee and nods at her.

"And Shawn," she continues, "don't forget to bring the rope."

The coffee sputters out of his mouth, and Mason's shoulders shake in silent laughter beside me.

The rope?

JULES
ICE CREAM

SUPER PREMIUM ICE CREAM   SUPER PREMIUM ICE CREAM

CHAPTER 40

JULES

The guys invite me to dinner—they're having pizza down at the station—but I've got another shift at the bar, so I have to decline.

I'm nervous. Hailey is working tonight too. This will be the first time we work together without Amelia as a buffer.

Walking down Hope Street, though, I don't focus on those nerves. Instead, I watch as the store fronts transform their windows into beautiful Christmas displays. Next week during the festival, everyone who comes will vote on their favorite Christmas display. I'm not exactly sure what the winner receives, if anything.

Bragging rights, maybe?

The amount of money being spent on the gorgeous decorations can't be worth that alone.

But maybe it's just another way this town shows their spirit, because as I watch people decorate, I don't see neighbors competing. I see Greg at Bristol House of Pizza hanging lights on Fran's Yoga studio, and Sarah from Hair, Heart, and Soul painting a Christmas scene on little Ms. Emerson's Sunset Café.

People smile at one another while they work together to beautify downtown, and I find myself smiling, too, as I hum Christmas tunes and stroll slowly to work.

When I enter Thames, Hailey is behind the bar talking to a customer and wearing a big smile on her face. I breathe in deeply, hoping tonight goes well.

"Hi, Hailey," I say, slipping off my jacket. I fold it up and stash it behind the bar, waiting to see what kind of response I'll get from my twin.

She raises her head in my direction and gives me a tentative smile. "Hey, Red. Just me and you tonight. You up for the crowd?" She makes her way over to where I'm slipping my apron around my waist.

"Hope so," I offer.

That's usually the extent of our conversations, so I'm surprised when she continues talking. "How's the apartment?"

"Shawn did a good job cleaning it up while I was gone, so it's not too bad." I laugh. "Well, aside from Charlotte."

Hailey's eyebrow shoots up. "Charlotte moved in too?"

I laugh. "Oh, no. Not *that* Charlotte. The spider in the shower. I named her Charlotte."

Hailey shakes her head. "You are very strange."

This just makes me laugh harder. Although a bit uncomfortably. "That I am," I admit.

"Speaking of Charlotte, I heard you went to her place last night. How was it?"

I feel like I should tread lightly here. Is she annoyed that I spent time with her friends? "It was good…"

"Heard Carmella beat all of you in pong," she chuckles and rolls her eyes. "That old lady cracks me up."

The tension in my back relaxes and I let my shoulders drop. "She really is something. And you should have seen her at the Christmas meeting earlier. Does she always wear muumuus?"

Hailey tosses her head back in laughter. "You'd think she'd only wear them in summer. Or you know, not out of the house, but yes," she says, trying to catch her breath. "She really does wear them daily."

For a moment, Hailey and I stare at one another. The laughter has left us both smiling, and it feels…normal. Then she turns away. She grabs a rag and goes to work wiping down the bar. Taking the hint, I check that the fruit is prepped and ready, but she surprises me when she continues to talk.

"So you're helping out with the Christmas festival?"

"Yup. Shawn said they needed more help, and I don't really have much going on at the moment," I admit.

"You've been spending a lot of time with Shawn…" Hailey says, pinning me with a look.

I scan the bar, hoping someone will need a drink, anything, so I have a minute to figure out how much I want to admit to her. Shawn says he's not interested in her, but is she interested in him?

If she is, I need to put some distance between myself and Shawn. Even though I keep saying we're just friends—*and we are*—my feelings toward him right now definitely don't fall into the "just friends" category.

"I think he's just being nice to me since I don't really know anyone."

Hailey winces. "I'm sorry. I should have been the one introducing you to people."

Her response and the ease with which she brings it up floors me. I don't even know what to make of it, so I just stare at her.

She sighs. "Listen, Shawn may have pointed out that I've been… *unkind*…for no reason. You didn't put us in this position any more than I did." She takes another deep breath. "Could we start over?"

I bite the inside of my lip and rub my fingers together but force myself to turn and meet her tentative gaze. "I'd really like that."

"Great, so how 'bout you get to work on chopping those limes, and I'll teach you how to make Shawn's favorite drink? I think we both owe him a margarita for putting up with our crazy."

Unable to help myself, I ask, "Can I ask you a question?"

She looks up at me. "Shoot."

"Do you like Shawn?"

She cocks her head to the side, and her eyebrows furrow in question, but she doesn't respond.

"I mean, *like*, like Shawn."

"We're not in elementary school, Red. Spell it out for me."

"Are you interested in being more than friends with him?"

Hailey laughs and throws her rag onto the bar. "Oh God, no!" She laughs harder. "Shawn's like…he's like a brother to me."

My entire body relaxes, but Hailey scrutinizes me for a moment more. "Wait…you and Shawn…*you're* the one?"

My cheeks go hot. "I'm the one what?"

She shakes her head. "Never mind. Chop those limes, Red. We've got a fireman to make happy."

As "All I want for Christmas" by Mariah Carey plays over the speakers and the fire roars in the corner, I can't help but think that all I've wanted for Christmas suddenly seems a heck of a lot closer.

CHAPTER 41

SHAWN

While I was bummed Jules couldn't join us for pizza tonight, it gave us time to work on the next part of my plan for giving her the best Christmas she's ever had.

"There is no way this tree is going to fit in your apartment," Mason grumbles, gripping the nine-footer from the bottom while I pull it up the steps, leaving a trail of pine needles in our wake.

"Can we decorate it too?" Colby says from upstairs, where he's opening the apartment door with my keys.

I grunt and pull it up the final step, shooting him a look. "No. That's the best part. Jules gets to decorate it."

Colby's face falls. "Well, can we at least stay and help?"

This time it's Mason who scowls. "You don't decorate a tree the night you get it. You have to let the branches settle."

While Mason doesn't say much, this is his business—trees— so he's passionate about it. And damn, am I happy this is his thing because Christmas trees were in low supply this year. Most local stores only had five footers. That wouldn't do. Jules needs the perfect evergreen. Wide and tall, with hearty branches that won't sag when we hang the heavy ornaments I splurged on.

I had no idea what colors she'd want, so I might have bought several options. Is she a Christmas plaid girl, or does she prefer red and green? Colorful lights or white lights?

The variety of options at the home improvement store was overwhelming, and I want her to have whatever she always envisioned. Angel on top? Got it. Prefer a star? Handled.

I may be in over my head here.

Dane sets up the stand we purchased while Mason and I balance the tree and Colby goes below it to the base.

"Little to the left," Dane says, and we shift the tree. He stands back and appraises it. "No, to the back," he says. We shift it again. "Like to the window," he says with a smile, and I glare at him as we once again reset it. "No, closer to the wall," he says slower, and his smile grows.

I finally catch on to where this is going and bark out a laugh, jostling the tree a little in the process.

Below the tree, Colby huffs. "Seriously, I'm pretty sure I'm going to have bugs in my hair. Can you guys set this right already?"

Dane starts in again, "To the sweat drip down my—"

I sing "balls" and let go of the tree, which is now perfectly set, while Dane and I break out in the Lil Jon's song.

Mason rolls his eyes and Colby huffs out a few curses from below the tree. "You guys owe me a beer," he mutters. He sits up on his knees and watches Dane and me make fools of ourselves as we dance around the room like rappers.

I nod toward the fridge. "Help yourself." Then I grab the vacuum and get to work cleaning up the pine needles before Jules gets home.

Once the trail of evidence from the door downstairs has been erased, the guys and I settle at the kitchen table and apprise our handiwork.

"Looks pretty good," Dane says, his beer bottle tipped to his lips.

He's right. We placed the tree in front of the window, and it looks great. I just hope Jules likes the surprise.

"Are the two of you going to get the reindeer tomorrow?" Dane asks, spreading himself comfortably in the chair.

"Sunday," I reply. "Tomorrow we'll decorate the tree."

"You've certainly got a lot of plans with this girl," Mason grumbles beside me, shooting me a look.

I don't even deny it. I really do. "I just want her to feel comfortable here."

Dane laughs. "Yeah, you aren't doing it because of that."

Colby grins. "It's because you want to get in her—"

Mason punches him in the arm before he can finish his sentence. "Careful there."

I watch Colby and take a long swig of my beer. He has the decency to look sorry.

The door swings open, and Jules comes to a stop when she sees us sitting at the table. She's wearing a black tweed jacket and a black beanie with a puff on the top that makes me smile. *She* makes me smile.

"Hey, Red. Come have a beer with us." I wave her over.

Jules regards us for a moment, lip caught between her teeth, and tentatively steps into the apartment before sliding her jacket and hat off. Her hair is messy, making me wonder what she'd look like waking up next to me. I *need* to experience that.

"Hey, guys," she says softly, looking each one of us in the eye as she smiles. "I'll let you have your guy time," she says. She turns like she's going to head toward her bedroom to hide out but freezes when she finally spots the tree by the window. "What in the candy cane is that doing here?"

Mason chokes on his beer, and I grin at her latest attempt at a curse.

"Like it?" I ask. I stand and follow her toward the tree. She tugs lightly on one of the branches, her chest rising and falling as she takes a series of deep breaths.

She turns to me, her eyes alight with pure joy. "Love it," she murmurs before throwing her arms around my waist and hugging me tightly. I wrap her up and soak in this feeling. Reveling in all the good that is Jules. A man like me doesn't deserve someone so bright, but I'm taking her anyway.

From the kitchen, Colby whines, "Uh, I'm the one who sat under that tree and made it stand for you. Don't I get one of those hugs?"

Jules squeezes me one more time before moving quickly to the kitchen and hugging each one of the guys. I feel her loss immediately. Dane winks at me when she hugs him and he pulls her onto his lap.

I have to bite my lip to keep from growling. Fucker. Instead, I walk to the fridge and grab a beer for Jules and then settle back in my seat while the guys pepper her with questions about her day. As I flick the cap off, I study how she's perched on Dane's lap. When she turns her attention my way, I curl my finger, summoning her to me.

She smiles and moves to the chair beside me, but I grab her waist and pull her onto my lap, inhaling her red hair as I do. She smells like fire from the bar and the remnants of her shampoo. And sugar. She always smells like sugar. Must be all the baking she does.

Jules giggles. "Your breathing is tickling me," she says, trying to slide off my lap and into her own chair again, but I hold her tight.

"Wanna do some more reading tonight, Red?" I whisper into her ear.

I think it's unintentional, but just the mention of our books leaves Jules wriggling against me, and not in the way she was when she was trying to escape. Suddenly I *need* the guys out of our apartment. She doesn't reply to my comment, but when she leans her head against mine, I take it as a good sign.

"All right, guys, Jules had a long day. Let's let her get some rest." It takes everything in me not to just tell my friends to get lost.

Dane gives me a knowing smirk, but they all stand up.

Colby looks to the guys. "Night cap at Thames?"

Dane laughs. "You realize you have *no* shot with Hailey, right?"

Colby makes a face. "Oh, I'll wear her down. Just you wait."

They continue to fight as they get their jackets, and Jules follows them to the door to thank them again for the tree.

The entire time, I remain seated, watching her. Needing time alone. But I don't miss the last thing she says before they leave. "Come over tomorrow night to help us decorate the tree? I'll make dinner and dessert to say thank you."

I close my eyes in irritation. I wanted to decorate the tree alone. I hoped tomorrow night would be the perfect night to tell her how I feel, but seeing how excited she looks at the mention of cooking for everyone has me getting up and agreeing. "Yeah, I'll make the margaritas and Red will make dinner. You bozos can hang the lights."

Dane eyes me in surprise. He knows me well enough to understand my hesitation, but I nod encouragingly. He takes the hint. "Just let us know if we can bring anything."

"Or anyone," Colby says as he waggles his eyebrows. "Like maybe you could invite Hailey."

She's quiet for a moment but then replies, "I'll ask what she's doing."

Now *that* is a turn of events I didn't expect. A very pleasant one at that.

I shut the light off in the kitchen and walk toward the living room. Jules closes the door, then she turns to me, and for a moment we watch each other in silence. The moonlight from the window pours through, lighting up her face, and I'm utterly mesmerized by every inch of her.

She's why men write sonnets. Why poets strive to find the perfect words. The way she makes me feel with just a glance can't be described using the alphabet. It's chest squeezing, heart pounding, and happy.

We speak at the same time. "I'll grab the bo—" I say as she

stumbles, "If you're too tired—"

We both laugh when we realize we're speaking over one another.

"I'm not too tired," I offer. "Why don't you go get in some comfy clothes, and I'll grab the book? Wanna come to my room to read?"

Her eyes go wide. "Like in your bed?"

I laugh. "We could sit on the floor if that's more comfortable for you, but I figured we could spread out a bit more than we can on the couch."

She nods like that makes perfect sense. "Oh, yeah, sure. Okay. I'll be there in a few."

While we both have tasks to complete, neither one of us moves. We continue to regard each other, the electric current between us pulling tighter. I'm officially ready to let the sparks fly.

"Go get changed, Red," I murmur.

Her eyes raise in challenge. "Yes, sir."

Well, fuck me. This night just got more interesting.

JULES
ICE CREAM
SUPER PREMIUM ICE CREAM
SUPER PREMIUM ICE CREAM

CHAPTER 42

JULES

What am I doing? What am I doing? What am I doing?

The words play on repeat in my head while I rifle through my drawers, looking for something to wear. This feels like a turning point for us. Like whatever I put on under my sweats matters.

As in, Shawn Chase is going to see my underwear.

And if that wasn't stressful enough—newsflash it is!—I'm pretty sure Shawn isn't into vanilla. And I don't mean the ingredient.

Shawn reads dirty books. I enjoy reading dirty books with Shawn. And he was a baseball player. Like the kind of baseball player who was in the news weekly, not just because he was amazing at what he did, but because he looks like he does, carries himself with a smile, and is a genuinely good guy. And women took notice. *Lots of women.* He wasn't a reported player or anything, but I imagine many of the women he escorted to events also ended the night with him.

I'm not a virgin, but I don't have a lot of experience. And with the few partners I have had, the sex has always been vanilla. I'm a vanilla girl. But when Shawn read to me the other night, the way his fingers were delicately scraping across my skin while he spoke of ropes and ties and spanking in that deep, husky voice…I can't lie. I was intrigued.

But am I up for the challenge? What if he's *too* into it? What if he finds me boring?

My insecurities are exhausting. The voice in my head constantly reminds me that I'm not enough. About what could go wrong. What I lack.

Without thinking, I dial Amy. It's eleven p.m. here, so it's eight in Los Angeles. I don't expect her to pick up. She's probably out with friends, so I'm pleasantly surprised when she does. "Baby *girl*, how are you?" she says in a drawl that makes it clear she's been drinking.

It is Friday night. If I were in LA, we'd probably be at Blue right now. We'd be dancing and working off the stress of the week. Maybe that's what I need. I've yet to see an actual club in Bristol, though, so I should probably make time for another Zumba session. Without Shawn and the boys. I need to let loose, and I definitely can't when they're around.

Even if Shawn totally does and probably wouldn't judge me at all. A warmth settles within me. He might even enjoy it.

"Um, hello. Do you not have service?" Amy croons, the noise level behind her quieting a little. When I hear the flush of a toilet, I know she's made it into a bathroom.

"Sorry. Yes, I'm here…I just got…"

Amy interrupts me. "Distracted by your brain. Yeah, I know how you work. So talk to me. What's going on?"

God, I miss her.

I blow out a breath. "I'm just…spiraling a bit," I whisper. Admitting things to Amy will be pointless if Shawn can hear me. "I only have a few minutes. I told Shawn I'd get changed, and then we're hanging out…and I'm freaking out about what to wear."

Amy laughs. "*Oh.* That kind of hanging out, huh?" I can practically hear her rubbing her hands together.

"I'm not really sure, to be honest. We're going to read a book together."

"Uh, what?" Amy spits out. "God, you are so—" she stops herself, but I know what she's going to say.

"Vanilla," I finish for her.

She laughs. "Well, yeah. You live with one of the hottest baseball players LA has ever seen, and you're going to spend your evening reading a book with him?"

Whispering, I say, "An s-e-x book."

All I hear is muffled distant music on the other end of the line.

"You there?" I panic.

She laughs. "Uh, yeah. Just wrapping my brain around it all. You can't even say the word, but you're about to read about it *with Shawn Chase.*"

"Could you *please* stop referring to him like that? I do not need the reminder of how out of my league he is."

I stare down at my clothes again. This is ridiculous. I've already wasted a good ten minutes with this conversation. Shawn's probably going to fall asleep.

"Okay, if you aren't going to be helpful, I'm gonna hang up," I mumble.

"Black boy shorts under sweats, no bra."

"What?"

"That's what you should wear. You've got cheekies, right? They don't scream *I thought I was gonna get some*, if you do in fact, *get some*. And the no bra…well, if you're reading about s-e-x, as you put it, he'll be able to tell when you get excited, and that will definitely get him excited."

"Okay, I gotta go. I'll call you tomorrow."

Amy shrieks on the other end of the phone. "Ah, have fun, my girl!"

As soon as the phone clicks, I stare down at the underwear I've laid out on my bed.

"No bra," I mumble to myself.

JULES
ICE CREAM
SUPER PREMIUM ICE CREAM
SUPER PREMIUM ICE CREAM

CHAPTER 43

JULES

In a long-sleeve LA Dodgers shirt, loose-fitting black sweats, and the *cheekies*, as Amy refers to them, I beeline for the bathroom to wash my face, brush my teeth, and throw my hair up into a loose ponytail.

Makeup free, all freckles and comfy, I pause in front of Shawn's door before knocking.

"Come in," he says, his voice somehow deeper and more gravelly.

When I open the door, he's sitting on the bed, book in hand. He's wearing a pair of gray sweats that mold to his muscular legs, with no shirt. I'll repeat that. *No shirt.*

And man, does he know how to not wear a shirt.

I'm so focused on the sinewy muscles, the light smattering of hair, the taut shoulders and strong arms and his tattoos that Shawn has to clear his throat to get my attention. When he does, my eyes snap to his and I find myself smiling because he's like Clark freaking Kent. Black glasses frame his chocolate eyes, the sight of which sends me melting into a puddle.

Superman is my weakness.

Let's be honest. Shawn Chase is my weakness.

Involuntarily, a whimper leaves my throat. I point at him. "Wha-

what are you doing with those?"

Forget the lack of a shirt. Wearing glasses like that is a surefire way to get in my pants. Quick.

"These?" he asks, almost shocked by my reaction. Has no woman ever reacted to him in glasses before? Because that's the real travesty here.

I breathe deeply and look away. I need to find my bearings. But the surroundings don't help my cause. Candles flicker on both sides of his bed, giving his face an almost ethereal glow.

He leans against a dark wood frame and pats the spot next to him on the bed. His sheets are red and white flannel, and his comforter is a heavy red down. I do my best impression of someone with grace, attempting to slide onto the bed delicately, but before I can sit, Shawn clears his throat again. "What are *you* wearing?"

I bite my lip and look down, double-checking. I can barely remember my name while he's got those glasses on and with all those muscles on display. I tug on my shirt with my thumb and forefinger and ask, "This?"

Or can he tell I'm not wearing a bra? Does that make him uncomfortable? Oh, sugar!

"Turn around," he says in that strong voice of his that leaves no room for questioning.

Like a car model, I spin slowly, confused.

"Eighteen," Shawn says softly, tracing the number on the back of my shirt. Oh. *Oh*!

This is embarrassing. I'm wearing Shawn Freaking Chase's name on my back. I'm wearing his *number*. He probably thinks I'm like a stalker or something. This is—

"That is the fucking hottest thing I've ever seen, Red. Get in this bed."

Um, all right, then.

"Since when do you wear glasses?" I finally gain the courage to ask.

Shawn smirks. "You like them?"

Um, yeah.

"They're glasses. What's not to like? Or like. Or anything. They help you see. *Do* they help you see? Could you not see before?"

Palm meet face. *Jules, shut up*!

"You're awfully adorable when you get worked up, Red," Shawn says, gripping my hip and pulling me so close we're touching. His hip, my hip, my back against his bare chest, and his strong arm wrapped around me, holding me in place.

"I'm not worked up," I argue. But I totally am. My words come out breathy and my body is rigid, fighting the urge to melt against him.

He chuckles. "Whatever you say. Want me to read, or are you going to sit here all flustered the whole time?"

I glance at him out of the corner of my eye. I can't help but bite my lip at the sight of his black glasses sliding forward a bit. *Why is that so hot*? "Do you need glasses, or are these part of a costume you put on to lure unsuspecting women into your bed?"

Shawn full-out laughs. "You are quickly becoming my favorite person." With a smile, he continues like he didn't just leave my chin on the floor. "I normally wear contacts, but my eyes were bothering me, so figured I'd wear glasses to read. That okay?"

I manage to squeak out an *uh-huh* and drop the subject. If I don't look at him, I'll be fine. Sure, I can feel his muscles through my shirt, and his warmth is wrapped around me like a cocoon. And don't even get me started on that smell. Why do men always smell so good? He smells like a new car, and I'm embarrassed to say I really want to take him for a ride.

What is wrong with me?

"Where were we?" he asks, thumbing through the pages of the

paperback. "Oh, right. Quinn just found out that Mason likes to tie women up."

"And he found out she likes it too," I say quietly, and I can't keep my attention from moving back to his face.

For a moment, he just looks at me, and I wonder what he's thinking. My entire body is buzzing. My thighs clench together tightly, and I'm all but salivating at the idea of pressing my body against his and just going for it. But, of course, I don't. I turn away again, and after a long moment, he takes a deep breath and reads.

At the sound of Shawn's voice, I can't help but twist my fingers nervously. A vision of Shawn standing in front of me with a rope, wrapping it around my waist, under my breasts, across my back, all while whispering the words he's saying now, about how delicious I taste, how he can't wait to thrust inside me…I squeeze my legs tighter, and my breath comes out shallow.

Shawn stops, studying me, his glasses slipping farther down the bridge of his nose. When his eyes meet mine, they flare with heat.

"Are you nervous, Jules?" Shawn asks, watching my ever-moving fingers.

I swallow slowly and shake my head, willing my hands to stay still. He doesn't turn back to the book though. His focus remains trained on me, and I can't help it. I start to shake.

Shawn closes the book and I let out a little whimper.

He sinks down lower so we're facing one another. "Jules," he murmurs, my name like a feather against my skin as his breath fans across my face. "Has anyone ever tied you up?"

I study him. His words feel blurry, like I must have misheard him. There is no way he's thinking about tying me up.

When I don't respond, Shawn pulls his thumb against my lip, pressing down on it softly. "You're so beautiful, Red."

A shiver runs down my spine. All I can do is blink up at him.

278

"Thank you," I somehow manage.

His smile turns lazy. "It's hard to focus on the book when you're sitting in my bed wearing my name on your back. You realize that, right?"

I melt a little more, my body boneless while he continues to move his thumb back and forth across my lip, making it difficult to form a coherent thought, let alone utter one. "Sorry?" I offer, almost as a question.

Shawn laughs. "Let's go to bed, Red. We have a long day tomorrow."

His words are like cold water, dousing the raging fire within me. I expected him to kiss me. To maybe talk more about this tying me up thing. Did my nonresponse leave him thinking I'm not interested in it? *Am I interested in it*? I've never even thought about being tied up before. And now I'm bound so tightly in my own nerves and *want* and *need* that I think I really, really do want him to tie me up.

If that's what he's into. Obviously.

Summoning a smidgen of courage, I reply, "What if I don't want to go to bed?"

Shawn's eyes flare again, and he pulls my chin between his fingers, moving so we're only a whisper apart. "Go to bed, Red," he says gruffly before pressing a kiss against my forehead and turning onto his back. He slides his glasses off and gets comfortable, clearly dismissing me.

I huff. Between Amy calling me vanilla and Shawn's dismissal, I'm irritated. I may not curse, and maybe I haven't tried many things in the bedroom, but I'm not a complete novice. Why did he invite me in here with candles, no shirt, a sexy book, and those damn glasses if he wasn't going to make a move? Did my lack of experience with being tied up disqualify me?

While part of me wants to strip down and show him what I'm capable of, the other part of me, the girl one who lives in her head, who fiddles with her fingers, and whose heart rushes a million miles per minute when he's near, chooses to listen to his command. He told me to go to bed. So that's what I'll do.

"Night Shawn," I say, granting his wish.

CHAPTER 44

SHAWN

I've never wanted a woman more in my life. I had to get her out of my room though. What was I thinking asking her if she's ever been tied up? The answer to that is so obviously no. If she had been, if she knew what it felt like to have the rope dig into her skin—to feel the pressure that comes when it wraps so tightly your body can finally relax—she wouldn't be the bundle of nerves she always is. If she had a clue about the kind of therapy it could provide her—not sexually, but for her mind—she'd have rope beneath her bed like I do.

And if she'd ever been tied up by someone else, if a man had wrapped her soft skin, branded her, and teased her with the cotton or the jute, she'd have confidence in her sex appeal.

Just the image of her with the red rope I purchased today makes me hard as a rock.

But tonight wasn't the night. I needed to leave her curious. Interested. Yearning for me to tie her up. She needs to be so wound up with need that she can let go of her insecurities about asking for it.

And hopefully that's how she'll be this weekend. This weekend, Jules and I are going to New Hampshire. There will be one bed, no distractions, and Jules. And if I have my way, she won't be able to say she's never been tied up again.

JULES
ICE CREAM

SUPER PREMIUM ICE CREAM   SUPER PREMIUM ICE CREAM

CHAPTER 45

JULES

Shawn is gone before I wake up, but he's left another note next to the coffeepot. I'm getting way too used to these notes. He's definitely a grade-A roommate.

But is that all he is? It feels like things are pushing past that, but after last night, I'm getting mixed signals. I refuse to spend my morning stressing over it though. I have other things on my mind.

Before I get the chance to chicken out again, I head to the hospital to see my father. It's time.

For the second time in as many days, I stand outside his room. But this time, I watch how Hailey sits beside his bed, asleep, with her body draped across his legs.

My interloping is interrupted by a man's voice. I jump and spin around, finding Dr. Steele—Maddox—smiling at me.

"Decided to give it another go?" he asks with kindness in his eyes.

I shrug in indecision. "Possibly," I admit.

He nods. "You can go in. Hailey should be heading out shortly anyway. She won't sleep much longer."

"How long has she been here?" I ask, curious to know more about my twin and her relationship with our father.

"Since last night."

My eyes bulge. Last night?

Maddox shakes his head, a half-smile playing on his face. "I keep telling her she's going to run herself ragged. She's in the bar until late at night, and then she sneaks in here and sleeps until the morning nurses kick her out."

"How often?"

Maddox studies me before answering, and he holds his neck as he does. Like he's not sure he should give me this information.

"Most nights."

I suck in a breath.

"She wasn't avoiding you, per se," he says, expressing my exact sentiment. "But Joel was her best friend…is," he corrects himself. "Joel is her best friend. You've never met a bigger daddy's girl."

The warm smile he has is focused on my sister. He clearly has strong feelings for her. I wonder if she knows.

"Come on, I'll take you in there. It's time to rip off the Band-Aid."

And, maybe because he's a doctor, I listen to him.

Following him inside is like walking into a space I have no business being in, but my feet keep moving until I'm standing only a foot from my father's hospital bed. He opens his eyes when Maddox clears his throat, and he focuses his attention on me almost instantaneously. His breath halts, his eyes grow wide, and then a smile pulls at the left side of his face. The right stays frozen in place.

"Jules," he whispers, but his mouth barely moves, so it comes out garbled and quiet.

Maddox sticks a straw to his lips, and I watch him sip, but a little water dribbles down his face. Maddox dabs it with a napkin before I can react, but my father's green eyes remain on me. My eyes. It's uncanny and so strange.

"Hi," I whisper and give a stupid wave.

At the commotion, Hailey stirs, and I prepare myself for her coldness. The tension between us may have eased the last time I saw her, but I wouldn't be surprised if this is too much for her. She's just waking up, and I'm standing here, hovering, having a moment with my long-lost father.

Her eyes flutter open, and she looks up at her father first. "Hey, Daddy. You okay?" she asks softly, already pushing herself up.

Maddox rests a hand on her shoulder. "He's fine," he murmurs.

She turns to him, her cheeks going rosy at his attention. *Interesting.*

"Why don't we grab a coffee?" he suggests

That's when she spots me, standing here like a freaking mute reflection of her. Her brows jump, but when Maddox grabs her hand, she visibly relaxes. "Hey, Jules." She sighs. "I'll be back, Daddy." She turns to her father and presses a kiss to his forehead.

Half his face smiles, and my heart cracks.

"Meet me in the cafeteria after," Hailey says when she passes me, and in the most shocking of twists, she reaches out and squeezes my hand. "Go easy on him, okay?"

I nod, confounded.

My father tries to adjust himself but struggles. One half of his body cooperates, but the other doesn't get the memo. Without thought, I move closer. "Here, let me." I offer him a hand and help him sit up.

He sighs in frustration. "My body," he grunts, embarrassment evident.

"It's okay," I soothe, the fight for indifference a losing one. What happened twenty-seven years ago when my parents separated somehow doesn't matter right now.

"No," he shakes his head, although it sort of just jerks to one side. After breathing in deeply, he tries again, "I'm so glad you're here."

A tear slips down my cheek. I try to swipe it away quickly, but he sees it. "Me too," I say, voice shaky.

"Your mother—" he starts, but I put my hand over his. It's surprisingly soft but also cold. Is that because of the stroke?

"If you don't mind," I interrupt, "I'd like to just…can we not talk about my mother? *Please*," I beg.

He offers a half nod, then shocks me with his next words. "How 'bout you tell me about the bakery?"

"How—" I start.

"*My* mother," he replies.

Ah. That makes sense. And then, because I have no idea what else to do, I start talking.

After leaving my father's room with a promise to return later in the week, I head to the cafeteria to find Hailey. I spot her huddled with Maddox in the corner at a table, their shoulders close. He's smiling at something she's saying. His entire face lights up when he's watching her. It's really freaking adorable and way too intimate.

Do I interrupt? Leave them be?

At war with myself, I don't see Carmella's white hair, or her green muumuu with the red Christmas ornaments displayed on it, until she's standing directly in front of me, waving her hand in my face. "Hello, dear. Are you all right?"

She doesn't look at me though. She follows my line of sight and smiles. "Oh, those two. They still haven't realized what the rest of the world can see plain as day. Am I right?" she tuts.

I have to laugh. This woman really has no filter. "I wouldn't know. This is the first time I've seen them together," I admit.

She titters. "Well, it only takes a few seconds to see it. Kind of like how our Shawn looks at you."

I fumble for words and take a step back. From this conversation, this woman…my feelings. "Oh, we're—"

She stops me with a hand on my wrist, halting my retreat and the way my fingers twist around each other incessantly. "Don't even try it. The man is obsessed. But that's not why I'm here. I want to talk to you about the Christmas ball."

I perk up at that, despite my interest in her previous statement. *The man is obsessed.* I'll be rolling that around in my head for a few days. And what makes her think he has any interest in me. But right now, I need to focus on the mention of a Christmas ball. "What about it?" I ask.

She looks down for a moment, hesitating. "You see," she says, bringing her head back up, her brow furrowed in genuine concern, "the person who normally handles our baked goods is in the hospital. It's why I'm here, actually. Visiting her." She fidgets and looks away quickly.

"Oh no. I'm so sorry to hear that. Will she be okay?"

"Er, yes. She's…it's just a bout of diarrhea."

I blow out an involuntary breath through my nose. "She's in the hospital because of…diarrhea?" I whisper the last word. We're in a cafeteria, after all, even if it's located in a hospital and most of the people here are wearing scrubs or white coats. The doctors and nurses probably have strong stomachs, but I bet they would prefer to *not* think about a topic like this while they're eating their breakfast.

Carmella's eye twitches, and she nods. "Yes, a very bad bout." She clears her throat. "*Anyway*," she sings, moving the conversation along, "she was supposed to start baking today for the Christmas ball next week. She makes everything, and now we don't have a baker. We don't want to get everyone else sick, right? It could be contagious."

"Oh, of course," I agree, although I don't know why she's telling *me* all of this.

"I ran into Shawn, and he thought maybe you would be interested in baking for the ball."

I shake my head. "No, I mean, I'm not set up to cater something that size." Maybe one day, but I don't even have a working commercial kitchen.

She smiles. "Oh, but the fire department is going to help. Shawn already offered. Dane is at your shop installing the oven your grandmother ordered. Shawn and the boys are cleaning the kitchen and getting everything set up for you."

I suck in a breath.

He's what? Why? What is happening right now?

In shock and at a loss for what to do or say, I glance at my watch nervously. It's eleven already, and I was planning to make meatballs and lasagna for the guys tonight. I have to get going or it'll be midnight before dinner is ready. "I'll—er—I'll talk to Shawn," I relent. I need to go, but I don't have an answer for her.

As I back away, Carmella smiles. "Okay, dear. I'll put together the list of desserts we need and the numbers. Just let me know how much you charge, and I'll get you a check!" She waves at me again.

I give her a crazed smile. "Sure, okay…um, thanks!" And then, since I'm not paying attention, I back straight into my sister.

She lets out a harrumph when I smack into her chest. "Whoa, there Red. You okay?" she asks.

I turn to her, my face flaming with embarrassment. "Sorry, I, uh—"

"It's okay," she interrupts, "You aren't the first person to run from Carmella, and you most certainly won't be the last. The woman can be relentless. She's a firecracker, for sure," Hailey chortles.

I'm thrown off by her friendly demeanor. This is the second time in as many days that she hasn't been terrible. My bewilderment at the interaction leaves me doing something crazy.

"Do you have plans tonight?" I ask.

Hailey tilts her head like she's surprised by my random change in topic. I'm surprised, too, so I don't blame her.

"It's just that Shawn and I are decorating our tree, and the guys from the station are coming over to help. I'm making dinner, and you totally don't have to come, but if you wanted to, it could be fun. And I don't know...actually, I've never decorated a real tree, but I'm excited, and Shawn seems excited, and I know how close you two are—"

Hailey holds up her hand to stop my rambling. "Breathe, Red." She snorts.

I obey, sucking in a lungful of air before letting it out. Then I turn the color of a tomato, I'm sure. "Sorry."

She laughs. "It's fine. And although it sounds fun," she lets me down easy, "I have to work tonight."

"Right. Of course," I say, holding up my hands to keep myself from crying. Why do I feel like crying? What is *wrong* with me?

Hailey places her hand on my arm, and that show of affection almost makes me burst into tears. "Seriously, Red. Thank you for the invite. I'd come if I didn't have to work." Her voice is soft, sincere, and she gives me a contrite smile. "Enjoy decorating though. Is it really your first time?"

I bite my lip. "Uh, yeah. My mother—" I stop short when Hailey winces. *Why do I keep doing this*? "We never decorated," I finish.

"That's crazy. My dad—" she winces again, then goes on. "*Our* dad always made Christmas the biggest deal ever. With the holidays coming up, it's really sinking in that this year will be different. So if I've been difficult—"

I stop her. "This is hard for everyone. Let's just...we'll try, okay?" I offer.

She nods. "Have fun tonight." I smile and turn to leave as Hailey adds, "Seriously, Jules. Thanks for the invite."

JULES
ICE CREAM
SUPER PREMIUM ICE CREAM
SUPER PREMIUM ICE CREAM

CHAPTER 46

JULES

When I get home from the hospital, Shawn is nowhere to be found. But there are several hot firefighters in the shop's kitchen. Including Dane, who, as Carmella mentioned, is hooking up the absolutely gorgeous oven my grandmother and I ordered only the day before. Silently I stand in the doorway, taking in this vision I had for myself that somehow Shawn, my grandmother, and this wonderful town are bringing to life.

"What the…" I whisper as I walk into the room and run my hand against the new butcher block sitting on an island in the center of the room. The wood is smooth below my fingertips. I can't wait to dust it with flour and start on a batch of sugary creations.

Dane looks up and smiles at me from his position on the floor. "Hey, Jules. Uh, Shawn just…" he falters for a moment, but when I break out in a big smile, the tension in his face eases. "He got called into the station. He really wanted to be here when you saw the surprise, though, so can you, uh, act surprised later?"

I laugh. And also, my mind goes a million miles per minute. Shawn wanted to surprise me. Shawn did *all this* for *me*. *Why?*

"It looks amazing in here. And yeah, I can act surprised. Thank you guys so much for all of this. I promise unlimited baked goods and coffee for the rest of your lives."

The guys in the room perk up and cheer, and Dane shoots them a look. "That's not necessary, Jules. Everyone in this room is happy to support you and excited to stop in for your donuts when you're up and running."

My face warms as I relax. These guys have a way of making me feel like I'm one of them. Like I belong. *Here.*

"Thank you," I say again, quieter now.

"You're welcome." Dane grins. "Now go upstairs and don't come back down until Shawn comes to get you. I've heard you've got a dinner to start on anyway. Whatchya making?"

"Meatballs and lasagna work?" I offer to more cheers.

Dane laughs. "There's your answer."

I shake my head in wonder at the kitchen transformation. Then I head upstairs and dial my grandmother, starting on my long list of thank yous. Although I'm most interested in thanking a certain tall baseball player. And I can think of a few ways to show my appreciation.

Hours later, the door to our apartment swings open, and in walks my favorite person. "Honey, I'm home," he sings like the loon he is.

"In the kitchen," I holler. I pull the lasagna out of the oven and hit the door with my hip before placing the steaming dish on the towel-covered counter.

Shawn takes in long lungfuls of the Italian scent and groans. "Jeez, I would have gotten a roomie years ago if I knew this was a perk." Leaning over my shoulder, he ogles the food while I lean back against his chest, unable to help myself. He's just so freaking perfect.

"I heard an interesting rumor today," I start, ready to tease the man before he has the chance to bring me downstairs for the surprise.

"Hmm?" he says, nuzzling my neck, making me lose all thought.

I push myself away from him and spin so he can't quiet me with his touch.

For the record, it was a bad idea. Because now I'm faced with his hopeful eyes. They're melting like fudge on top of a chocolate Sundae and have just a glint of mischief in them, like he knows what I'm going to say and he's already figured out how to talk himself out of my scorn.

"I ran into Carmella today," I chastise.

Shawn can't hold back his smirk. "Oh yeah? How is the crazy lady doing?"

I bite back my smile. "She seems to think I'm going to bake for everyone in town for the Christmas ball. Do you know where she would get that crazy idea?"

Shawn's smirk turns into a full-on grin as he crosses his arms and regards me. "Yup. Pretty sure it was me."

I guffaw. "Shawn Chase! Have you no shame?"

He throws his head back with a laugh. "Not really, to be honest. Not when it comes to you," he adds with a waggle of his brows. "And don't start on the whole you can't do it, or that you don't want to do it. You and I both know this is a great opportunity. The people of this town are tough to crack, but once you're on the inside, they're loyal to a fault. And they want *you* on the inside. This is huge, Red. *Huge!*"

"But how will I bake for that many people? *With this stove?*" I point to it and shriek. As if on cue, it creaks. Look at that, even the oven is playing along with my plan to give Shawn the surprise he wanted.

"Well, Red, maybe you should let me get to my surprise before you bite my head off." He narrows his eyes at me in reprimand, and I feign indifference. Gosh, Amy would be so proud of my acting skills.

Shawn grabs my hand and practically pulls me like a rag doll out of our apartment and down the stairs. I protest mildly, but my acting is no match for the golden-retriever level excitement Shawn Chase emits. The man is giddy. He flings open the kitchen door and points inside like he's Vanna White. "Your kitchen, milady," he proclaims.

My hand flies to my mouth, and this time, my reaction is not calculated. Because as amazing as it was this afternoon, the room is even more striking now. Above the stove top against the wall is a sign that says "Jules." There are pink and teal baking dishes and bowls piled high, cake stands, and cupcake trays. You name it, the kitchen is stocked with it.

"This is—" I'm speechless. There are no words to express my gratitude, my awe for what he's done for me.

I turn to Shawn, my face hot, an onslaught of tears threatening to spill over.

He shakes his head and pulls me against him. "No, please don't cry, Red. Did I overstep? Oh damn. If you want—"

I press my fingers against his lips and shake my head, unable to speak but refusing to let him apologize. "You did all this for me?" I croak.

He nods, for once looking the tiniest bit bashful. "Well, I had some help."

I laugh as tears pour down my face. "It's...*why*? Why did you do this?"

Shawn shrugs. "Because I could. And because you deserve it."

I shake my head, so confused. "You...this...it's *everything*."

Shawn brings a hand to my cheek and swipes away my tears, gazing at me with such affection it makes the air whoosh from my lungs. "No, Jules. You're everything," he whispers. He moves closer, his eyes searching mine, his lips only a whisper away.

As I pop onto my tiptoes to close the distance, to finally feel his lips against mine again, the jangle of the bell above the front door sounds and voices filter through the building. Shawn and I stare at one another while a battle rages in his eyes.

Will he kiss me? Do I want him to?

I see the decision written in his chagrinned expression. He presses his thumb against my bottom lip and pulls at it, then leans in and kisses the side of my mouth, the place where my smile forms.

"Absolutely everything," he whispers before stepping back.

A shiver runs down my arms as the guys enter, their loud voices and excitement drowned out by the beat of my racing heart and the rush of blood in my ears.

"Aw, we missed the surprise!" Colby shouts.

Dane rolls his eyes, and I laugh through my tears. Mason, of course, stands stoically, feet wide and arms crossed, but even his lips lift a little when he looks at me.

I nod at him and give a shaky "thank you guys so much," working to steady myself.

"And in case you didn't know, these clowns will be our helpers while we bake this week. You just tell us what to do, and we'll get it done for you. Right, guys?" Shawn says, mock glaring at his friends.

It's absolutely adorable how much he always wants to help, and it's even sweeter how his friends agree. He may be doing this for me—which I appreciate more than I could possibly express in words—but these guys are showing up because of him. And that means something to Shawn since he's been trying to find his place at the fire station.

"Come here, Red," Colby says, arms out wide. "Group hug!"

A low growl rumbles in Shawn's throat, and his arm finds its way around my waist, effectively keeping me from moving toward Colby, but I grab his forearm and push forward anyway, throwing my arms out. Dane and Colby accept the group hug with enthusiasm, but I have to grab Mason's plaid shirt to get him in on it as well.

When Dane crows, "Come on, Babe. Don't want to miss out on hugging your girl," I finally feel Shawn behind me, begrudgingly wrapping his arms around all of us.

In a group hug, smooshed between some of the biggest men I've ever seen, I feel more loved than I ever have before. It's not lost on me that I've been labeled *Shawn's girl*, but in this moment, I feel very much like I'm theirs as well. These guys have become my friends too.

"All right, I'm starving," Mason grumbles, pulling away first.

I laugh and swipe the back of my hand against my cheeks, removing the waterworks that managed an encore because of the man sandwich I just found myself in. Then I lead them up the stairs to the food.

With "Rocking Around the Christmas Tree" playing, full stomachs all around, and Shawn's special Christmas margaritas in hand, we swarm the tree. Dane and Shawn handle the lights while Colby and I sort through the ornaments. Mason is, of course, sitting on the couch, watching all of us with a glint of amusement in his eye.

"You could help, you know," Dane teases.

"I provided the tree. Raised it from a seed. I'm all set right here," he says. He takes another sip of his margarita and winces. "Why don't you guys have beer?" he grumbles.

Shawn laughs. "Because, as Amelia says, beer takes no thought, and as a retired bartender, I want to keep up my skills."

I smile at their verbal jabs and hum along to the music.

"Colored lights or white ones, Red?" Shawn asks, holding up the two options.

I take in the ornaments spread out around me, feeling particularly partial to the burlap and buffalo plaid set. "White," I say with a smile, pushing the ornaments I like toward the tree. "Can we use the colored ones down in the shop?"

Shawn winks at me. "Whatever milady wants, milady gets," he teases, turning back to string the lights.

Everything feels easy with these guys. They treat me like I've always been a member of their little pack.

Dane takes a sip of his margarita, which is next to me on the floor, and motions up to Shawn. "How are things going?" he asks in a low voice.

I shrug. "Everything's been perfect. You guys are all incredible."

He shakes his head. "You know that's not what I mean."

I do. But I don't know where Shawn and I stand. I know where I *want* to stand. Beside him at all times, holding hands, hopefully close enough to kiss again. When he's around, things feel easy.

"It's all good," I say again. "You guys really don't mind helping out with baking duty this week?"

Dane winks. "For you? Anything."

I look up and catch Shawn watching us with a smile on his face. I think that's what I like most about him. He's not overbearing. He's just happy to see me happy.

Until now, there's never been a time in my life where I had that.

The song shifts to a slow version of "Happy Christmas" by John Lennon and Yoko Ono, and suddenly, Shawn is pulling me up and pressing me against his chest. He spins me around the room, singing loudly.

I find myself laughing, surprised yet again by this man. He can sing. He can dance. What can't he do?

Colby attempts to pull Mason up, and Mason growls, but Dane laughs and takes Colby's outstretched hand. They exaggerate their movements as they dance circles around us.

With my head against Shawn's chest, I smile at the scene around me. "Thank you," I say, unable to stop myself from gazing up at him.

He looks at me with genuine affection. "For what?"

"You made my first experience with decorating a real Christmas tree perfect."

Shawn brings my hand to his chest and continues to sway. "Good, Red. I plan on making every one of your Christmas wishes come true."

CHAPTER 47

SHAWN

Nine hours later, we're in my Ford F-150, headed northbound, on our way to New Hampshire. Jules came out of her room this morning wearing a green sweater that falls off her shoulder every five minutes in a ridiculously mesmerizing manner. And I'm not sure if she's wearing a strapless bra or no bra, but the mystery is making me batty and keeping me far too distracted from traffic, which is where my full focus should be.

We have to-go cups of coffee, donuts that Jules made yesterday—which I've almost polished off already—and our overnight bags.

"Any requests?" I ask, pointing to the radio. Christmas tunes are playing on at least two stations, and although that would be my go-to choice for a ride to pick up a reindeer, I'm not sure where her head's at this morning.

"Oh, can I hook up my phone?" she asks with a glint of something akin to excitement in her eye. There might be a hint of nervousness in her expression too as she waits for my response.

I motion for her to take control. "All yours, sweetheart."

She smiles and plugs in her phone. I turn back to the road, although my eyes keep wandering back to her. She taps on her phone for a few more seconds before a voice comes over the speaker.

"This is Audible," the man says in a commanding way.

A book. Interesting. *What exactly is sweet little Jules up to?*

I raise my brow in her direction, and she shrugs, but I can practically feel her squirming.

When the man announces the title, I once again shoot a glance in Jules's direction. Tessa, the friend who sends me romance-reader care packages, writes spicy books, so I've read quite a few. *The Salacious Players' Club* is a series by Sara Cate and is all over book discussions because it toes the line. But she didn't pick just any of the books from that series. She picked the one where a husband "shares" his wife with his best friend.

Fifteen minutes in, Jules's cheeks are flaming and she's wringing her hands. I manage to remain silent, but when the first chapter involves three people, she finally screeches and taps frantically at her phone. "Oh fudge. How do I make it stop?"

Trying to hold back my laughter, I glance in her direction. "You weren't enjoying that?"

She hits my arm. "Shawn! Seriously, help me!"

She squeaks again—it's the most adorable thing—so I grab her phone from her and unplug it, thus ending her humiliation. I hand back her phone and keep my eyes on the road, knowing she's about to jump out of the car. But out of the corner of my eye, I can see her cradling her face.

"Jules, please don't be embarrassed," I say, grabbing her hand so she can't hide behind it.

She turns toward the window. "Ugh. I'm so sorry."

"Why are you sorry? If those are the kind of books you like, I'm game," I tease.

"Stop it."

"It's good. I've read the others in the series. Just hadn't gotten to that one yet," I admit.

"You have?" she asks, surprise evident in her tone.

I shrug as I maneuver around another car, and we take off in the left lane. Finally the traffic is moving and I can focus on the conversation. "Yup. So what made you pick *this* one?" I ask, honestly curious.

She sighs but doesn't turn away from the window. At least she's got a great view of the mountains we're driving through. "I was looking for books with Shibari in them." She pauses and finally angles her body toward me. "That's what we were reading about…that's what you're into, right?"

I squeeze her hand. "Kind of. Although probably not how you're thinking," I say honestly. But before we get to me, I want to know her thoughts on the subject. Why she's looking into things I might like. And why she's wearing crimson on her cheeks right now. "Is it something that interests you?"

Jules bites her lip. "I know I'm probably not like the women you're used to…I'm…*vanilla*." She says it like it's a bad thing.

I pull her hand to my mouth and kiss her knuckles. "Look at me, Red."

She turns those gorgeous green orbs on me, giving me all her attention.

"You can ask me anything you want. I'm an open book. But please, Jules, don't think that what you are—who you are—isn't exactly what I want. You don't have to read the books I read or do things you think will make you less…vanilla to make me happy. I just like being around *you*. Hear me?"

She hums her assent, and I'm pretty sure she tries to pull her hand back, but I press it against my leg and don't let go.

"So ask me anything. What do you want to know?" I shoot her a glance, then focus on the road in front of me again, waiting for her to summon the courage to ask the questions floating around her mind.

"Have you ever tied someone up?" she asks in almost a whisper.

I smile. "Not in the way you're thinking."

She heaves out a heavy sigh. "What does that mean?"

"When I played baseball, I would get horrible anxiety when I had a bad game. Like couldn't get out of my own head. Spiraling. Exactly what you don't want to battle as a pitcher in the major league."

Jules is quiet beside me. Not many people know about my debilitating anxiety. For years, I hid it well. But it flared with a vengeance when my biological father tried to come back into the picture when I went pro. Balancing a professional career while agonizing about my real father, who was only interested in me because of my success as a baseball player, not because who I was on my own, became too much.

I was never enough on my own. For anyone.

"I had no idea," Jules confesses.

I shake my head. "I didn't want anyone to know. But we had a trainer…she spotted it. And since I wanted to combat it naturally if I could…" I sigh. "I'm not embarrassed by my anxiety. Millions of people struggle with it. But as a baseball player with unlimited funds and an amazing, perfect life—from the outside, at least—I felt like a failure. Admitting that, with all I had, with no logical reason to complain, I still didn't feel like I was enough. Like, how dare I struggle when I had everything at my disposal?"

Jules moves closer, pressing against the center console between us, and grasps my hand, which is still pressing her other one against my thigh. "You can't stop how you're feeling. And your feelings aren't any less valid because you have money or a good career."

I nod, comforted by her understanding and by the feel of her warm hands enveloping mine. It's why I was drawn to her. I saw it immediately. She's an empath, and I knew she would understand. But more than that, when I'm around her, my mind stops racing. I can't explain it any more than I can explain that while I'm tied up, my brain stops. My breathing evens. With Jules's hands around me, I feel the same calmness. The same relief. And I've *never* had that before.

"I know that. But at the time…it was hard to get a handle on it. And then I was introduced to ropes."

She sucks in a breath.

"It's not a sexual thing for me, not always. I practice it by myself… and I'd like to share it with you because I get the feeling you could use it too."

"So you…you don't want to tie me up because you like me like *that*?" she asks, trying to hide the disappointment clearly written all over her face.

My voice is deeper when I reply. "Oh, I want to tie you up for a lot of reasons, Jules…if you'll let me."

She's quiet for a few seconds, and I worry I've scared her. Then she murmurs, "I think I'd like that."

JULES
ICE CREAM
SUPER PREMIUM ICE CREAM
SUPER PREMIUM ICE CREAM

CHAPTER 48

JULES

The rest of the ride was heated, but Shawn didn't push for more information. He turned Christmas music on, and after a few minutes, we were both singing along with Mariah Carey at the top of our lungs. I swear the man has more personality in his pinky than I do in my entire body. He's so full of life and fun that it's hard to imagine that he struggles with the same loud mind and out-of-control thoughts as me.

But I know how easy it is to cover up an overactive mind. Or a mean one. To smile through the fear and push down the anxiety.

But today I'm not doing that. Being with Shawn left me focused on the present. Not the what-ifs, not the concerns about my family in California or the spiraling uncertainty about my new family here. Everything falls to the background when my hand is in Shawn's, when he's smiling or singing, when his chocolate brown eyes offer lightness to my sometimes dim world.

"You ready to meet Santa?" Shawn asks as we walk into Santa's Village with stupid, goofy smiles on our faces.

"I still don't understand how I never knew this place existed. Like there are real reindeer here, Shawn! Real reindeer!" I can't shake my excitement. We each have a cup of hot chocolate in our hands as we watch young children feed the reindeer carrot after carrot after carrot.

Shawn laughs. "You knew we were coming to pick up a reindeer for the festival. Did ya think I made it up to get you alone for the night?"

I shrug and give him a teasing grin. "Maybe. I mean, it seems more likely than the existence of real reindeer."

Shawn puts an arm around my waist and picks me up, almost like a football, then flings me around. "My hot chocolate!" I shriek as it falls out of my hands and empties onto the ground. He grabs my hips and forces me to wrap my legs around him. Our faces are so close that his warm chocolaty breath mixes with mine.

"I'll buy you four more, Red."

I laugh and put my palms on his cheeks, staring at him in amazement. Every moment with him is better than the last. "You're crazy. You know that?"

He smiles, drawing my attention to his lips. God, I want to kiss him again.

"Come on, let's go sit on Santa's lap and make sure he knows what we want for Christmas."

Like a lunatic, he follows the signs directing visitors to Santa, still carrying me, but I can't convince myself to feel even a hint of embarrassment.

Yes, people are staring. Yes, we're making a scene. But I'm happy and Shawn's smiling. And that's all that matters right now.

I have to literally fold my lips in to keep from bursting out in laughter at the sight of Shawn sitting on Santa's lap. Because yes, of course the six-foot-three baseball player who's wearing dark jeans and snow boots thought it was imperative that he sit on St. Nick's lap like Buddy the Elf. He's ridiculous. And I'm obsessed.

"Come here, Red. It's your turn." He motions for me, but he doesn't get up. And Santa, the good sport that he is, just smiles and gives a jolly laugh that makes me wonder if he is, in fact, the *real* Santa. Because if there are real reindeer here like Shawn promised, then maybe we took a left turn into the North Pole.

Or he's a well-paid actor who doesn't want to break character in front of the children, even if he has a two-hundred-and-twenty-pound man child on his lap.

But I like the first option better.

I wave my hand, trying to dislodge him. "You're going to break Santa," I whisper-shout.

Santa gives another jolly laugh when Shawn finally stands up. He lifts me up and sets me on the man's lap, much to my embarrassment. "Shawn…you can't just go around picking people up!"

He winks at me. "I'm a fireman. It's what I do."

I roll my eyes and turn my attention to Santa. "Sorry, sir…Santa… um, Mr. Santa?"

His belly shakes with laughter, and for a moment, I'm brought back to my childhood, sitting on Santa's lap in an outdoor mall in Los Angeles, begging him to bring me a sister.

The memory jolts me. I haven't thought about it in years. My friend's mom was pregnant, and I was jealous that she was going to be a big sister. I wouldn't shut up about how I wanted my mom to have another baby. I remember climbing onto Santa's lap and begging for a baby sister. Santa looked at me a bit nervously before glancing in my mother's direction and confirming that she was not, in fact, with child.

My mother smiled through her embarrassment, but I knew better than to believe the faux cheer on her face. As soon as we got in the car, she berated me for embarrassing her and told me one child was more than enough.

I never mentioned wanting a sibling again.

"And what would you like…" Santa begins, pulling me from the memory. He's wearing a nervous smile and studying me, like maybe I've been staring at him for longer than I realized.

"Jules," Shawn offers.

"Jules," Santa mimics. "Yes, Jules. I've heard you've been a very good girl. What is it you want for Christmas?"

Without thought, I give the same answer I did all those years ago. "Sisters. I want a relationship with my sisters." And then, catching myself and the wistful way I've said it, I add, "Matching Christmas pajamas for me and my sisters…that's what I want."

Santa nods, and I blow out a breath, but when I turn, Shawn is watching me. I'm not sure what the intense look in his eyes means. I just know I need fresh air and his hand in mine.

I slip off Santa's lap and walk straight into Shawn's open arms. He drops a kiss on my forehead and pulls me to his side, an arm draped over my shoulders as we turn.

"I like Christmas pajamas as much as the next guy," Shawn whispers, "but personally, I hope you brought my shirt to sleep in tonight, Red."

I guffaw so loud he has to pull me into his chest to stifle the sound. He always knows the perfect thing to say.

"Thank you," I manage when I've finally gotten myself under control.

Shawn just smirks and continues moving. "So tell me, Jules, if you had to pick between Chinese or pizza for dinner, what would you choose?"

CHAPTER 49

SHAWN

Walking down Candy Cane Lane with an apple cider donut in one hand and Jules's hand in the other, I'm pretty sure I've died and landed in North Pole heaven. There isn't a place on earth I'd rather be.

"Have you always loved Christmas?" Jules asks as I offer her a bite of my donut. I have a bag of them stuffed under my arm, so she could have her own, but I'm enjoying feeding her immensely. The way her tongue darts out to lick the excess sugar off her lips, though, *that* has me thinking about tonight.

I've taken things slow, not wanting to pressure Jules. Especially while she's working so hard to fit in, to fix things with her sisters, to figure out her business. I don't want to be just another distraction or ask too much of her when she's already got so much on her plate. I want more than that.

And truthfully, I think I can be more. For once, I might be enough for someone. With my experience with anxiety, I feel like I can help her. And I want to be that person for her so badly. To support her, hold her when she needs it, cheer for her when I can. Even if it turns out that she's not ready for anything else.

"Yes, Christmas in my house always lasted the entire season.

My dad would pack us into the car and my mom would make hot chocolates to go. We'd listen to Christmas music, and Charlotte and I would stare in amazement at the lights as we passed. We'd chop down our own Christmas tree and decorate with the neighbors. And then on Christmas Eve, my mom would give us each a present to open. It was always pajamas"—I pause when I realize my mistake, remembering Jules's face when she talked about all she wanted for Christmas, but she just nudges me with her shoulder and smiles, so I continue—"and then we'd all wear our pajamas to bed and wake up at the crack of dawn to open more presents than necessary," I finish quietly.

Jules closes her eyes and hums. "Sounds magical."

"I know you have a few things on your list for the perfect Christmas, and I've already made the reindeer one come true...so tell me, Jules, what other Christmas traditions have you missed out on?"

She beams at me, and as Gwen Stefani's "You Make It Feel Like Christmas" plays over the speakers, I hold my hand out to her. When she takes it, I spin her before pulling her into my arms and dancing goofily. She smiles her gorgeous, addictive smile, and shivers skate across her skin under my fingers.

"Let's see. There's a lot I haven't done..." she giggles when I eye her, "as far as Christmas goes," she reprimands.

I laugh. "Okay, Red, lay it on me. What types of things do I need to plan over the next few weeks to make this the best Christmas ever?"

She leans against my chest and sighs. "Just keep being you. You're more than enough."

My heart hammers in my chest as I soak up her words. She'll never know just how much they mean to me. Then, on another giggle, she retorts, "But if you happen to see mistletoe, I've never been under one of those."

Peering around, I pull her along, then spin us until we're below the greenery she's requested. We're in a Christmas village, so this is an easy request to fulfill. There are gigantic mistletoe decorations every five feet. I tip my chin up and smirk. She laughs before hiding her face in my chest.

"Don't get shy on me now, Red."

Jules pulls back a fraction, her lashes fluttering open as her emerald irises sparkle and her lips part. I can't help it. I take her in, soaking up this moment. We've kissed before, but when we did, I didn't know her like I do now. I'm doing it knowing exactly who she is and what she needs. This time, it's only about us, not about her anxiety, not about my mix-up…this kiss is *all* us.

Lowering my head so we're a breath apart, I whisper, "I have a feeling this is going to be my best Christmas yet."

And then, as she smiles back, my lips meet hers in a grin. The sweetness doesn't last though. As soon as her lips are against mine, my body takes over. My hands move to her hair, cradling her so I can get better access. She wraps her arms around my neck and digs her fingers into my hair, pulling me closer, our tongues tangling, eliciting a soft whimper from her and pulling a groan from deep in my chest.

Someone clears their throat nearby, angling to get by us, so I move us off the sidewalk, but I don't let her go. She tastes like cinnamon, chocolate, and sugar, and I cannot get enough. But even if she didn't taste like a bakery, I'd be hard-pressed to give her up.

She's the first to pull back, her eyes wide and her fingers touching her lips in what appears to be shock. "What was—wow—you—do they like, teach you how to kiss the life out of a woman at baseball camp too?"

"Breathe, Red," I say, chuckling at the disaster that is Jules.

Her eyes search mine. They're still sparkling, but there is a hint of fear there, and maybe a little apprehension. Like she's looking for reassurance from me. I squeeze her arm and do my best to arrange my features in a way that tells her everything I'm not quite sure how to say.

It's never been like this with anyone else. I'm crazy about you.

JULES
ICE CREAM
SUPER PREMIUM ICE CREAM
SUPER PREMIUM ICE CREAM

CHAPTER 50

JULES

I am *squirming*. We have to get through dinner before we get to whatever is going to happen tonight. Will he tie me up? To relieve my anxiety? Just to teach me how to use it in the future? Or, and this is what I really want it to be, will he tie me up and finally *touch* me? Because after that kiss, I *need* him to touch me.

Carmella apparently made our hotel arrangements, and I'm pleasantly surprised when we pull up in front of a gorgeous yellow hotel with a view of snow-capped mountains in the background. Snowy hills roll across the land as far as the eye can see, and a horse and carriage wait out front.

"What is this place?" I whisper as a smile skates across my face and I slip my hand into Shawn's. He's always holding it out to me. I've never been with a man who wanted to hold hands. Who enjoyed such a simple touch the way he does—like the innocent connection gives him comfort. Who craved it as much as I did.

But with Shawn, there's no questioning it. He doesn't give me a moment to wonder, and he doesn't let my mind run rampant with insecurity. With a hand held out, he knits our fingers together and smiles at me as he does it. He's always making sure I know I'm wanted. It's surprising and sweet *and* makes me want to jump his bones.

"The committee only booked one room—but I'm happy to arrange for another if you're not comfortable," Shawn says while we wait at the check-in counter.

I bite my lip, but I don't hesitate. "I'm comfortable."

Shawn studies me. "You sure, Red?" he asks, pushing my hair back out of my face, both his hands fanning across my head. I feel so cherished, so protected, so special under his touch.

"Positive," I reply.

He angles forward and presses his lips gently against mine. "Good. I promise you're safe with me," he says, pulling back and watching me reverently.

I smile. "I know."

After a long day of traveling and exploring Santa's Village, Shawn and I order Chinese and eat it in the lobby. There are multiple fireplaces, floor-to-ceiling windows looking out at the white mountains, and cozy chairs and tables positioned throughout with chess and checkers games set up between them. We decide on a game of checkers because I've never played chess, and we eat straight from the containers while he regales me with stories of his baseball career.

"I know what happened to end your career," I hedge, almost uncomfortable bringing it up, but for once Shawn doesn't wince at the mention of it, "but how did you end up working in a bar? And then as a firefighter?"

Shawn wipes his hands and leans back in his chair, taking a sip of his red wine before answering. "I had a friend out in Tahoe—she was the one who taught me Shibari."

I sit a little taller at that. "Did you two date?"

Shawn shakes his head. "No, it was never like that. She was just…

she was someone I could talk to. A friend I could rely on when things went south. She'd recently been through some tough things, and she and a group of friends purchased a bar in Tahoe—the Silver Lining."

I hum. "Sounds magical."

Shawn laughs and shakes his head. "You joke, but it kind of was."

"Really?"

He leans forward, as if he's letting me in on a big secret. "They had this thing...there were dollar bills all over the walls. People would write down their wishes. The things they wanted most. It kind of made people take a minute and look at their lives. Really ask themselves what they were missing."

Interesting. If I were there, I'd probably wish for exactly what I'm getting out of this entire trip to Bristol. I've been pushing myself outside my comfort zone and forcing myself to question what I really want from life.

Shawn eyes me. "You're thinking about what your wish would be, aren't you, Red?"

I smile. He knows me so well already. "Go on, I want to hear about yours first."

"I spent the months I was there bartending. Brooding, angry that I'd lost everything, that my team had given up on me so quickly." He clears his throat and dips his head before focusing on me again, his expression serious. "That I just wasn't enough," he admits, defeat in his eyes.

"How'd you get past that?" I ask honestly, because I haven't seen the person he's describing. The man before me is confident, goofy, cocky sometimes, sweet most of the time, and overall has a positive attitude. The man he claims to have been is so far removed from the man in front of me.

"Honestly," he pulls on his neck, "I'm not sure I did. I just..." He blows out a breath. "I met you, and I know this sounds like a cheesy line, but Jules, until you, I was treading water. I could put on a smile. I could hang with the guys. But inside, I was struggling. My mind moved a million miles per minute. My pulse would skyrocket at the mention of my career or when someone called me Babe—it *hurt* to just be."

Without thinking, I stand up and crawl into Shawn's lap, my hands in his hair, my fingers kneading his scalp while I wait for him to continue. "But now?" I ask.

"Now…" he says, looking down and blowing out a breath before raising his eyes to mine again. "Now I feel like I fit somewhere. *With you.* Is that crazy?" he asks, vulnerability lacing his every word.

I shrug. "If it's crazy, then I guess we both belong in the asylum because I feel the same way. You quiet my mind in a way no one ever has. In a way nothing ever has. I feel…" I struggle to put it into words, but I try because it's important that he knows. "You feel like home."

A slow smile spreads across Shawn's face, then. He pulls my body close to his and brings his lips to mine. "Let's go to bed, Red."

"Not to sleep though, right?" I tease.

Shawn laughs gruffly. "Couldn't sleep if I tried." And then his lips meet mine again in a rough kiss.

JULES
ICE CREAM
SUPER PREMIUM ICE CREAM
SUPER PREMIUM ICE CREAM

CHAPTER 51

JULES

We race to the elevator, hands twined tightly, smiles painted on our faces. If I wasn't so giddy, I might care that our mission is obvious to everyone we pass. Shawn pulls me through the lobby, his long legs eating up the distance, but I struggle to keep up. He stops abruptly and grabs my waist, hoisting me into his arms and over his shoulder in a fireman hold as my giggles draw even more attention.

Children wearing Christmas pajamas turn in our direction, and I wave to their mother from my upside-down position. Fortunately, she lets out a laugh as well.

When we finally make it to the elevator, Shawn lowers me so I slide down his chest and gazes at me adoringly while we wait for the door to open. I turn away from him, afraid I might maul him—or fall head over heels in love—if I keep looking into his beautiful stormy brown eyes. Either option seems likely at this point. And surprisingly, I'm not scared of the possibilities.

Shawn makes me feel safe. He makes me believe that everything that has gone wrong in my life has actually gone right. Because every disappointment, every fear, every mistake, has led me to this moment, to this man. And to what I believe will be so much more than just one night.

"I can't wait to see how beautiful you look tied up, Red," he murmurs into my ear, pressing his hips against my back and lifting my hair to trail soft kisses along my neck. His warm breath sends a shiver across my skin, but his words are what leave me shuddering in anticipation. "Your soft freckled skin bound with my rope...*fuck*," he growls, getting both of us too worked up for our current location.

A whimper sneaks past my throat, and then the elevator door opens. Shawn guides me inside and hits the button for our floor, then the close door button so no one else can join us. He spins me so my chest is against the elevator wall and presses more kisses down my neck.

"Tell me, Red, how do you like it? Slow? Rough?"

The combination of small kisses along with the hardness of him rocking against me and his words is all-encompassing. He's on my lips, on the tips of my fingers, burrowed beneath my skin and straight to my heart.

"I have a feeling you'll be nothing like I've ever experienced," I admit. "I couldn't give you direction if I tried."

He twines the fingers on one hand with mine and spins me again so I'm facing him, but he takes my other hand, too, and holds them both above my head as he leans down so we're face to face. "You want me to take control, Red? You want me to quiet that mind of yours?" He brushes his nose along my jawline, making me breathless. "Make it so the only thing you remember is that from here on out, you're mine?" he murmurs in my ear before nipping at my earlobe.

My knees wobble, and I press into him, giving him all my weight. "Yes," I answer breathlessly. "Please," I beg.

Shawn continues to pepper hot, soft kisses against my neck, down to my shoulder, to where my sweater keeps falling. "This right here. You've been driving me crazy with this, Jules," he says, pulling the sweater farther down my shoulder. "I've been dying to know what's

328

under it though," he admits.

I lean my head back so he can continue to kiss my neck. "Guess you'll have to wait and see," I tease.

He pauses his kisses for a moment and looks at me. "Will you show me? Will you undress for me while I get out the rope?"

I squeeze my eyes closed, already wondering if I'll be able to deliver what he's looking for. I remember Jared's words, his disappointment at how I didn't always perform precisely how he wanted…

"Outta your head, beautiful. I won't ask you to do anything that makes you uncomfortable."

His reprimand reminds me that this is Shawn. He's my friend. He cares about me. I open my eyes and look up at his concerned face.

"I got you, okay?" he says softly.

I press my lips together and nod. Because he does. I know he'll take care of me.

The elevator dings our arrival, and he squeezes my hand as he guides me toward our room.

There is a fireplace in the corner of our bedroom, and Shawn points to it when we walk in. "I'm going to get a fire started. Relax for a few, okay?" He leans down and kisses me softly, making me practically purr in pleasure.

When he pulls away, he smiles and shakes his head. "In case I forget to say it later, thank you."

I quirk a confused brow. "Thank you?"

"For trusting me. For letting me in. For being you." His eyes light up in wonder. "I don't know what I did to deserve any of it, but I just want you to know I don't take it for granted, Jules."

I bite the inside of my lip. I'm at a complete loss for words, so I stupidly utter, "Okay."

A smooth laugh passes Shawn's lips.

Before he walks away, I grab his arm and squeeze. "Do we need a safe word?"

He laughs. "A what?"

"Ya know, in case things get"—I bite my lip as I look down and whisper—"painful."

Shawn grasps my chin between his thumb and forefinger and rubs softly as he scrutinizes me in amusement. "Red, I'd never hurt you. Everything I'll do is for your pleasure. If things get too tight or too much, all you have to do is tell me."

My stomach sinks in embarrassment. "Right."

As if he can feel my disappointment, he smiles, his thumb still rubbing my chin softly. "Unless you want a safe word?"

I bite my lip to keep from smiling too big. I *really* want a safe word. It's so not me, and I love that. I nod.

"Okay, Red. What should it be?"

I tap my finger against my cheek while I think. "How about Prancer?"

Shawn's laughter fills the room. "You want your safe word to be one of Santa's reindeer?"

I try to bite back my smile again, but I embrace my crazy. "Yup," I say, popping the *P*.

He shakes his head. "Favorite person," he says with a wink, then he heads to the fireplace, and my head grows five times its original size.

Unsure of what to do while I wait, I make a beeline for the bathroom to brush my teeth and assess myself in the mirror. My cheeks are flushed and my lips are swollen from our elevator make-out session.

"Okay, Jules, you got this," I say to my reflection. "No, you don't," I laugh. "You *so* don't."

Outta your head, Shawn's voice reminds me, and I smile at myself in the mirror. I'm safe with him. I look at my fingers, which I've been rubbing together nervously, and I shimmy my shoulders in a burst of courage. I could go out there and tell him I want to cuddle, and he would do it without complaint. He's not going to force anything. And I want this. I want it so badly that I can think of nothing other than having Shawn's hands all over me. The images I've conjured of him tying me up play on repeat in my head.

"You've got this," I say to myself again, more confidently this time. And even if I don't, *Shawn's* got me.

When I open the bathroom door, I find a shirtless Shawn with his hands on his hips, focused on his suitcase. The sound the zipper makes as he pulls it mixes with the crackling fire. My breath hitches when he pulls out a crimson red rope and inspects it with a faint smile on his face. He turns like he can feel the power of my gaze on him, and the flames of the fire dance in his eyes. "You ready, beautiful?"

I swallow and nod.

"Do you trust me?" he asks, his face open to any answer.

"One hundred percent."

His eyes flare and he sits down on the settee in front of the fire. "Let me see that gorgeous skin, Red."

My chest rises and falls as I work up the courage to slip my jeans down my hips. I'm pretty sure it's not seductive or perfect, but Shawn never looks away. His rapt attention remains fixed on my body while I slip my sweater over my head and reveal the matching black set Amy reminded me to wear.

"So beautiful," Shawn murmurs. "Now crawl to me."

CHAPTER 52

SHAWN

Everything fades away as I take in the sight of Jules. My mind, my heart, my damn pulse. Even the fire stops crackling for a moment as Jules submits and drops to the floor.

In that moment, something else takes over. Resolve. She's mine and I'm hers. It's that simple.

There are no outside concerns. No lost baseball career, no exes, no disappointing fathers or mothers. No siblings who don't meet expectations. No careers that have gone sideways. There is nothing but creamy skin and emerald eyes. Smooth limbs and freckles. Perfect curves and a seductive smile. Jules quiets my mind, relaxes my heart, and impels my body to take control.

"Such a good girl," I praise.

Her chest expands in confidence. Her legs elongate, and she arches her back, pushing her ass higher and preening at my words. Her movement is slow. She's just as relaxed in her submission as I am in my control. I rub the rope between my fingers as she comes to a stop at my feet. "On your knees, Red."

She rises up and shakes out her hair. She has no idea how sensual she is. How her every movement is soft and makes me want to reach out and protect her from the world. The innocence, the purity. It's almost too much because I know in a few moments I'm going to be the one to steal it from her. But I also know it's what she needs. She needs that release. She needs the confidence that will come once she's bound and on her knees. Once she's stripped of all her thoughts, and her *want* is in control.

I scrape my knuckles against her cheek, and she leans into my touch.

"Was that okay?" she asks softly, her lashes fluttering as she seeks my approval.

I can't help myself anymore. I pull her into my lap and cradle her. "It was perfect." I hold the rope up to her chest, appreciating the contrast of the crimson against her milky skin. "You can touch it, sweetheart. It's cotton. I wanted to use a really soft one for your first time."

Dainty fingers brush against the rope, and I hold my breath in anticipation of her response.

"It's beautiful," she whispers.

I lean down and kiss her cheek, then the corner of her mouth, her forehead, her nose.

Her breaths get quicker with each passing second and with every brush of my lips. And then, when she can't take it anymore, she wraps her arms around my neck and looks at me with only the tiniest hesitation. "Is this okay?"

"You can touch me however and whenever you want, hear me?"

Her teeth dig into her bottom lip and she nods. "Then I guess I have some exploring to do."

She arches up and bites my bottom lip, raking her teeth across it as she pulls back. I groan at the pressure. At her teasing. At the sight of her coming into her own. It's only been a few minutes, and already she's getting comfortable.

"May I?" I ask, splaying my hands around her ribcage, indicating that I want to lift her.

She nods. "You can touch me however and whenever you want… *hear me?*" she mimics in a teasing voice.

I laugh as I slip the rope into my back pocket and pull her against me. I stand from the couch and carry her to the bed, where I lay her down and take a moment to survey her. "Take off your bra," I say. My breath gets caught in my throat while I watch her maneuver to unclip the back. She slides the black strapless off easily and throws it into the corner of the room.

I hiss as I stare at her perfect breasts. Her pink nipples harden, and I lick my lips in anticipation.

Reaching behind me, I pull out the rope and smack it lightly against my other hand. Jules jumps a bit at the sound of it hitting my skin. But the reaction isn't one of fear. Instead, her eyes dilate and she bites her lip, her attention fixed on the rope. I have to wonder, then, if she'd be into something a bit more…like a soft whip. I've never dabbled in any of that. I've never even tied a woman up for pleasure. I've only ever used it for therapy. But right now, with her, I'm imagining all sorts of ways I could use my previous training.

"Remember your safe word, Red," I tease.

Any nervousness melts away as she settles into the bed. "I think we'll be okay," she mutters, looking away from me, trying to hide her gorgeous smile.

"Say it for me anyway."

She hits me at maximum wattage this time. "Prancer, Dancer, Donner, and Blitzen."

"Oh, getting cocky now, Red? I got news for you—I'm going to make you feel so good it'll be hard to think, let alone sing about Santa's reindeer."

Her eyes flare, and I take the opportunity to run the rope against her chest, enjoying the way her skin prickles at my touch and the way she inhales sharply as she watches the movement.

As her nipples pebble, I can't help myself. I kneel on the bed, tilt forward, and suck one into my mouth before pulling away and blowing across the now wet bud.

"*Oh,*" she whimpers, rolling her hips just a little.

"Perfect." I use the lift to my advantage and slip the rope under her back and pull it out the other side. "So perfect," I murmur. "I'm going to make this loose, Jules," I say, meeting her eyes. "But if anything feels like too much, just let me know."

"I know my safe word," she replies with confidence.

I shake my head though. "Safe words are for when absolutely necessary, and like I said, you'll never have to use it, sweetheart. Just tell me if it's too tight or if you're uncomfortable and we'll adjust or stop, okay?" I wait for her consent, and when she breathes deeply and nods, I smile. "Words, Red. I need your words."

"Yes, sir," she replies to my absolute fucking delight.

"It's like you were made for this," I say with pride as I begin the task of wrapping her in rope. I want to teach her the process. I want her to know how to do this so she can use it, too, but for tonight, I just want to lose myself in my work. I want her to relax, and I want to make her feel.

My hands brush against her as I work, and every time she inhales or whimpers or sighs, my cock grows. It's painfully hard in my jeans, but seeing Jules in the diamond design is all I want. It isn't until I've tied the last knot that my muscles completely relax. "Exquisite," I say, taking in the way her beautiful body is twisted in crimson rope. The design against her skin and the way her lips are parted as she stares at me make me insane.

"Can I see it?" she asks, looking down her body.

I nod and offer her my hand. Her palm is soft and warm and steady when I lift her and guide her to the floor-length mirror by the bureau. I stand behind her and watch as she studies the way the rope loops around her waist, how it tightens under her breasts and holds them up before it moves across her chest and swoops down to her back. With my knuckle, I rub softly across her skin, following the trail of the rope. She shivers at my touch and leans back against me.

"Do you see how beautiful you are? How perfect my girl is?" I ask, waiting for her eyes to lock on mine in the mirror. "Now I want you to watch me make you come. Can you do that for me, Red? Can you stand there and look pretty while I fuck you with my tongue?"

She bites her lip again before nodding.

Knowing she won't last long on her feet, I slide the settee from where it sits near the fireplace, positioning it perfectly in front of the mirror. "Lay down for me, but keep your eyes on the mirror," I say as she settles onto the seat, lying back and turning her head as requested. I pull it so it's directly in front of the mirror, and then I kneel in front of her. With one hand on her breast, I twist her nipple between my fingers while my other lifts one of her legs onto my shoulder. Rubbing my mouth against her smooth skin, I kiss up her thigh until I reach her panties. I nip at her sensitive skin through the black lace, and she bucks against me.

"Shawn," she cries out as my tongue darts under the lace, pushing it to the side. After just a taste of her, I know I'm a goner. I need more. I don't think I'll ever get enough. With both hands, I pull down her underwear and toss them in the corner near her bra. Jules laughs, but before she can catch her breath, I pull her body to the edge of the seat, placing both of her legs on my shoulders, and press soft kisses against her lips. Sucking, licking, and teasing her as she cries out over and over again until she starts to shake. I look to the side, filling with pride when her green eyes meet mine in the mirror.

"Such a good fucking girl," I mutter as I kiss her. "You listen so well." Then, as a reward, I suck on her clit until it throbs in my mouth and she comes apart in my arms.

As she lies there, completely spent, her legs weak, I place one down, kissing her thigh as I ease it off my shoulder, then repeat the process with the other. "Where you going?" she asks softly, leaning up and looking down at me.

"I'm going to set you on the bed and untie you."

But as I put an arm around her to scoop her up, she stops me. "Wait, what about you?"

"What about me?"

"Don't you want to…" She looks down at the obvious bulge in my pants.

I shake my head and smile. "That was a lot for you, Red. I don't want to push too much on you tonight. There's plenty of time for that."

She props herself up on her elbows. "But aren't you—"

I stop her. "I'm perfect, Jules. I told you. Tying you up is as much for me as it is for you. It was perfect." And it was. I don't need the release right now because I'm relaxed. The noise, the anxiety—it's all gone when I'm with her.

"Untie me if you want," she says softly, "but please…I need to feel you inside me. I need it more than I think I've ever needed anything." Her face is flushed, but her eyes are still alight with desire.

"Do you want me to untie you, Red?"

She considers me for a moment and shakes her head.

I bring my lips to hers and kiss her softly. "Then let's see what else these ropes are good for," I say before lifting her up and carrying her to the bed. Gently, I drop her against the pillows and watch her as I unzip my pants. From my pocket, I grab a condom. I rip it open with my teeth and toss the wrapper before lowering my boxers.

Her eyes heat as she stares at my erection.

"Are you sure, Jules?" I ask, gripping my cock, thrusting just enough to satisfy the ache, while her eyes track my every movement.

"It's beautiful," she says.

I can't help but laugh at the sincerity in her voice. "Why, thank you, Red. That's just about the best reaction I've ever gotten."

She rolls her eyes and swats at me. "Always teasing me," she says with a smile. "Forget what these ropes can do. Come here and show me what that can do."

"Do the honors," I say, handing her the condom.

She lifts onto her knees and braces one hand on my shoulder while sliding the other across my shaft and pushing the condom to the hilt. I press her back so she falls onto the bed and kneel next to her as she opens her legs wide for me.

"Such a good girl," I say and rub my thumb against her clit, staring down at how wet she is for me. I slip one finger in, preparing her as I slowly swirl my thumb. Right before her eyes close in ecstasy, I press the tip of my cock against her. Her eyes fly open, and she lets out a low moan.

"I need your lips," I say, then I crash my mouth into hers, kissing her while I slide inside.

She gasps against my mouth as I fill her completely. Propped up on one arm, I watch her while not completely crushing her. And for a few seconds, we look into each other's eyes, moving slowly. I listen to her little whimpers as I go, learning, memorizing, exploring.

"You're perfect, Shawn. You feel…" She sighs as I push back in again. "You feel like you were made for me."

I close my eyes at her words. At the emotion they evoke. At the way I feel the sentiment in my soul. It's true. This girl was made for me, and after years of feeling like something was missing, I feel irrevocably complete. I've finally found my person.

"Want to see what these ropes can do, Red?" I say, pulling her up by them, being careful to support her back so they don't pull too hard.

She smiles. "You don't have to be so careful with me. I won't break."

I place my forehead against hers. "You sure?"

She hits me with a naughty wink. "I know the reindeer's name. Don't worry. *Now teach me.*"

Fuck. My cock springs inside her, making her giggle. I slide out of her and flip her around. "Ass up, Red."

I pull on the ropes, lifting her to exactly where I want, and then, just as she's getting settled against the pillow, I slam into her.

I slide in and out repeatedly, holding the ropes with one hand and pulling her closer so I can slip my other hand around her waist and rub her clit. Then I run circles while I move my cock in and out of her until she tightens, her body pulsing around me and pulling my orgasm from me as she screams.

"Can't tell you how gorgeous you look tied up and taking my cock, Red." I don't stop. I want to pull every ounce of pleasure from her.

She pulses around me, her cries the greatest thing I've ever heard. The sight of her squeezing me as she's tied up like a fucking Christmas present is easily the most incredible sight I've ever seen.

The moments between that and when she's lying in my arms and I'm rubbing circles on her back are a complete blur. I'm not sure if I blacked out or saw stars. I just know that when we're finally lying together, completely spent and satisfied, I've never been happier.

"Wow," she mutters. "That was just…"

"I know."

She looks up at me, her green eyes growing watery. "That was a lot."

Rubbing my knuckles against her cheek in awe, I smile. "It was everything, Red. It was absolutely everything."

JULES
ICE CREAM
SUPER PREMIUM ICE CREAM
SUPER PREMIUM ICE CREAM

CHAPTER 53

JULES

If being tied up and pleasured by Shawn was a kind of decadence I've never known, then being cuddled and worshiped by him as he unties the ropes and kisses each indentation on my skin is ecstasy. The soft murmured words of praise—"You did so good, pretty girl"—mixed with those same lips scraping softly against my skin in reverence leaves me reeling.

Pulling me under the covers, Shawn settles me against his chest. He runs his hands through my hair in an almost hypnotic way.

"I'm exhausted, but I don't want this night to end," I admit through a yawn before nuzzling into him.

He pulls my chin up so I'm looking into his warm chocolate eyes. "Nothing is ending. I've never been as sure of anything in my life as I am that you belong in my arms."

This man.

I close my eyes and relish in the pure joy I feel at his words. "You are something special, Shawn Chase."

"Just trying to live up to what you deserve, pretty girl. Now rest. We've got a Christmas festival to get through and a bakery to get up and running."

I shake my head in amazement, then almost immediately drift off to sleep in what surely must already be a dream.

It's sometime before sunrise when one of our phones rings, and although I ignore it, I feel Shawn shift to pick it up. "What's up, Dane?" he asks sleepily.

"Another one?" he asks. "Where?" After a moment he says, "No, we're still in New Hampshire…Okay, I'll call you when we get on the road in the morning…" He lets out a low laugh and glances down at me. When he sees that I'm awake, he presses a kiss against my forehead. "Yeah, I'll tell her…Bye, Dane," he says in an annoyed tone, although he's still smiling. His eyes are alight with secrets that make me impatient for daylight.

"Everything okay?" I murmur.

Shawn smiles ruefully. "Fire," he rasps. "Nothing for you to worry about though."

"Should we head back?" I say, propping myself up on an elbow.

Shawn laughs and pulls me back down. "Jules, we're four hours from home. And we still have a reindeer to corral. Safe to say we won't make it back before the fire is out."

Twisting my lips to hide my smile, I look away. "So we really are picking up a reindeer?"

"You think I used it as a ruse to get you alone in a hotel room, Red?"

I laugh. "I wouldn't put it past Carmella."

He chuckles too. "Me neither. But no, we really are getting a reindeer for the festival."

I sigh. "Is it weird how excited I am about the festival?"

Shawn shakes his head and stares down at me, his fingers running circles on my arm. "No. Now get some rest, sweetheart."

The reindeer farm is expecting us at eight, so unfortunately, Shawn and I don't have time to linger in bed. But if I thought the reindeer at Santa's Village were special, these make me believe we really have stepped into the North Pole.

The trees tower so high they blend in with the white and gray sky. Snow drips down each branch, as if suspended in time. The ground is painted white for miles on end. A weathered wooden sign with evergreen paint indented into it stands tall as we journey down the long driveway.

"How did you find this place?" I ask in wonder, staring at the big, beautiful sign.

"All Mason." Shawn laughs. "His family has a Christmas tree farm. Maybe there's like a club for Christmas farms where they get this information."

I burst out laughing. "You're telling me that grumpy Mason is the one who found this magical place? And that you think he actually, like, attends conventions or something to meet other Christmas farm people?"

Shawn barks out a laugh. "Yeah, now that you say it like that, it sounds ridiculous. Okay, Red. Let's get our reindeer and get out of here."

"What does he eat?" I ask, rubbing his soft nose. Can reindeer be household pets? Because this one is freaking adorable, and I'm pretty sure I *need* to keep him.

"I've left some feed in his pen for you to take, and like horses, he enjoys sugar cubes and carrots," the man says, patting our reindeer on the head. "Other than that, lots of greens. And this guy loves apples."

"What's your name, big fella?" I ask, smoothing the fur along his jaw.

"Prancer," the farmer says.

Shawn and I just about fall over laughing. The man gives us an odd look, and Shawn shakes his head. "She's got a thing for Prancer. He's her favorite of all Santa's reindeer."

I press my lips together to contain my laughter and nod. "Yup… really love Prancer."

Oh, Sweet baby kittens. It's going to be quite a week.

With *Prancer* secured in his pen on a trailer attached to Shawn's truck, we drive in the slow lane, taking our time on the way back to Bristol. Bing Crosby croons some of my favorite Christmas songs, and Shawn holds my hand while he turns to me and sings loudly. I'm so happy, my cheeks hurt from all my smiling.

But each passing mile is accompanied by a slight surge of anxiety. What's it going to be like when we get back? When we're in front of people? We had these perfect twenty-four hours, and everything has changed. I feel like I'm his.

And he told me I am.

But men and women have different ideas about what that means. At least, any man I've ever been with has. For Jared, it meant I did everything he said, worked beside him, planned a future with him, fell for him, all while he was married to someone else. A fact I didn't know until she walked into the bakery and introduced herself as his wife.

Shawn isn't Jared, I remind myself.

Even twenty-four hours into whatever we are, I know this will be nothing like my last relationship.

"Outta your head, Red," Shawn says with a mischievous glint in his eye. "Or else I'm going to have to figure out a way to get you to shout Prancer."

I laugh. "Thought I wouldn't ever need my safe word," I volley back.

Shawn smirks. "So true, babe. So true. But seriously, what's on your mind? Talk to me."

I settle back in my seat and fiddle with the seat belt.

Shawn doesn't give me the opportunity to twiddle my fingers for too long though. He grabs my hand with his free one and twines our fingers. "Talk to me."

I roll my eyes as I fall back against the seat. "Fine, ya big bully," I tease. "I'm just kind of wondering what exactly we're doing."

His ridiculous smile makes me giddy. "Well, pretty sure we're listening to Christmas music and saving Christmas in Bristol by delivering sweet Prancer so all the children can wear the same cheesy grin you did when you first saw him."

I huff. "You're impossible."

"Impossibly good-looking? I'm aware." He winks before turning his attention back to the road, finally giving me the space I need to say what we both know I mean.

With my eyes on the snow-covered evergreens, I offer, "I just mean…are we telling people what happened between us?"

When I gather the courage to look at Shawn, he's wearing a serious expression—brow furrowed and a frown marring his handsome face. "No, Red. We aren't going to tell them I tied you up…"

My stomach sinks. Maybe I got it all wrong…

But then he squeezes my hand and smiles. "Pretty sure I told you the first time I kissed you. I don't kiss and tell. But am I going to be shouting from the rooftops that you're my girlfriend and I'm your boyfriend? Yeah, we're telling people that." The pride on his face is unmistakable.

"Your girlfriend?" I ask.

"Yeah, Red. You're mine. I'm yours. That's kinda how this works. Any problem with that?"

I bite my lip as I look out the window and mutter, "Nope. That's fine."

Shawn's laughter makes my insides dance.

JULES
ICE CREAM
SUPER PREMIUM ICE CREAM
SUPER PREMIUM ICE CREAM

CHAPTER 54

JULES

"Thanks for letting us leave Prancer here," Shawn says, patting our favorite reindeer on the head.

Mason rolls his eyes. "Prancer?"

Shawn and I exchange a look and a secret smile.

"I didn't name him," Shawn says lightly. "Everything go okay with the fire this morning?" he transitions.

Mason runs his hand across his beard and looks out into the field of trees that looks like a backdrop of a darn Christmas movie. There are Christmas lights surrounding the entire plot of land, and every few trees are lit up. It must be a pain to set up, but it's absolutely spectacular. It's so contradictory to Mason's personality. It's grumpy, broody man meets Christmas farm owner.

Odd.

"I don't know who keeps starting these fires, but I'm sure it's not random," Mason admits.

Shawn shakes his head and blows out a breath. "I was thinking the same thing. That's three buildings in the span of a month. I mean, what are the odds of that being a coincidence?"

Mason grumbles, "Not fucking high when we have had a total of five fires a year for the last few years." He then looks at me sheepishly.

"Sorry for the language."

Shawn grins at me. "That's okay. Our Jules here is a lot tougher than we give her credit for."

I roll my eyes.

"You're both ridiculous. So what makes you think the fires are intentional, aside from the fact that there have been so many?"

"They're almost too perfect. Too controlled. And yet we can't find the source. Granted, we probably need to call in an investigator to really take a look. Chief was on the phone with some guys he knows in Boston. They're going to call around and find someone who can come down."

Shawn perks up. "My best friend in Tahoe is a fire investigator. Maybe I can run it by him."

Mason shrugs. "Couldn't hurt."

"All right, man. I'm going to get this one home so we can shower. Remember, you guys need to be at the bakery at eight a.m. sharp tomorrow."

Mason glares at me like I was the one giving orders. I hold up my hands. "Hey, you guys volunteered."

Mason grumbles, "Right."

I lean up and press a kiss against his cheek. "Thanks."

He slumps a little in relaxation, his cheeks pinking at my touch. "See you tomorrow, Red," he grumbles.

"Bye, Mr. Christmas," I tease and then pat Prancer on the nose before taking Shawn's outstretched hand.

CHAPTER 55

SHAWN

The lights in the bakery sparkle as we approach. We stopped for lunch after our trip to Mason's farm to drop off our reindeer.

Our reindeer.

I'm already obsessed. Already making plans. Already calling things ours.

The last time I had someone, it all crashed into a fiery disaster. My career ended, my car went up in flames, and the relationship was over before it even got off the ground.

No one knew what really happened that night. The reason I was on that road. Driving around to clear my head.

The media went on and on about how I saved the boy. How I'd seen the accident happen. How lucky he was that I found them.

And all those things are true. I'm thankful I was there. I'm happy that an eight-year-old didn't die that day. But when I reached into the car to pull that boy out and my arm got stuck and I saw the lights of the truck coming toward us, I won't lie and say that I didn't wonder what the hell I was doing. The boy got out. I pulled him out before the truck barreled into his vehicle, careening it into my car and causing everything to burst into flames. But my arm got stuck. And the tug and the pull and the panic led to a crack and a break…and my entire world ended.

And I was driving, working through the bomb my girlfriend had dropped on me. How she wasn't sure about us. It was safe to say the end of my career made her sure. She was suddenly positive that she didn't want a future with me.

I wasn't enough.

I was never enough.

Until now.

With Jules, I can be enough. *I will be enough.* I'll make every one of her dreams come true. I'll give her the Christmas she always wanted, the bakery she dreamed about, the friends and family she craved, and more love than she could hope for.

"Hey, babe," she says, dragging me from my thoughts as we walk into the bakery, a dreamy smile on her face. "Ah, it's good to be home." She breathes in and spins.

My heart literally somersaults at the joy radiating from her. "Wanna make me a dessert?" I say with a smile, knowing she's itching to get back into the kitchen. She's barely had a chance to use it since we installed the new oven.

"Really?" Her eyes light up and she slips off her jacket.

I laugh. "Yeah, I'll take our stuff upstairs and then meet you in the kitchen."

"You're going to help me?" she asks, the excitement making her practically glow.

"Yeah, Red, I'm going to help you." I drop a kiss on her forehead as I pass her on the way up to our apartment.

Ours.

There's that word again.

It only takes a few minutes to get settled. When I hang up Jules's jacket, I find her phone in the pocket, so I put it on my charger before heading back down to my girl.

A VERY MERRY MARGARITA MIX-UP

I find her in the kitchen, flour spread out on the butcher block, dough beside her, and "Baby It's Cold Outside" playing on the radio. I knew she'd love the speakers Dane had installed. She peeks at me over her shoulder, the bridge of her nose already dusted with flour. I push closer, spinning her so she's looking up at me, and wipe the powder from her face with my thumbs.

"Hey, you," she whispers, her green eyes soft and warm and watching.

"Hi, sweetheart," I murmur, mesmerized by this moment. There's magic in the way she looks at me.

She wraps her arms around my neck, likely getting flour all over my clothes. I couldn't care less. Nothing feels better than Jules's touch. Her arms around me. Her mouth against mine.

She bites that pouty lower lip, never breaking her gaze.

"Don't do that, sweetheart."

She tilts her head. "Do what?" she asks, confusion marring her tone.

"Bite that lip. Unless you want me to throw you over my shoulder and tie you to my bed, *don't* bite that lip."

Just the image I've painted has my cock twitching.

She smiles. "Doesn't sound like an awful way to spend the night."

I spin her around before I lose control, and she gasps when I press my erection into her back. Running my hands down her arms, I drag my nails slowly against her soft skin until my hands cover hers. With my mouth to her ear, I speak in a low voice. "What are we baking?"

She shivers beneath me, her voice coming out breathy as she says, "I was thinking fudge."

I hum against her neck. "Can we melt some of it down so I can lick it off your body?"

She whimpers and nods against my shoulder.

Her movements are like silk as she pulls out the cocoa and mixes it with vanilla and other ingredients I don't recognize. We work hand in hand. Literally. Me refusing to leave her body except when she's grabbing bowls or tools or whatever item she needs to prepare the fudge. She uses my hands, and we laugh as we work. I can't help the impulses to randomly pull her from a task to kiss her, spin her, dance with her around the room as Michael Bublé sings. I drizzle chocolate syrup down her skin when she isn't looking and lick up her neck, making her moan and then giggle as our lips meet again.

Every moment we have is special, fun, light. Because they're spent together, and we're made for this. We're made for each other. When she finally wraps the fudge in plastic wrap and plops it into the fridge, I'm on her, pressing her body back against the cold metal, dying to be inside her.

I scrape my teeth against her jaw as my hands dip below her shirt, caressing her smooth skin. "I need you," I say between kisses.

She slips her tongue between my lips, and it's the only agreement I need. I lift her up and carry her out of the kitchen, promising to help clean up down here after we've made a proper mess upstairs. When we reach the top step, I drop her to her feet and slap her ass. "Go into your room and get your toy."

Her eyes go wide with surprise and she lets out a cute yelp. "My toy?"

I level her with a stare. "Red, I heard you…"

Her cheeks turn rosy and the flush expands to her chest. She's so fucking adorable. "Heard me?" She cringes, clearly embarrassed.

I don't give her time to sink into that feeling though. "Get the toy and meet me in my room."

She nods as I push her into our apartment.

But before she can get too far, I add, "And don't worry about your underwear, Red. You won't be wearing anything for long."

She bites her lip on a smile as she leaves, and I hurry into my room to get set up. Tonight I plan to take Jules to the edge and back. Multiple times.

JULES
ICE CREAM
SUPER PREMIUM ICE CREAM
SUPER PREMIUM ICE CREAM

CHAPTER 56

JULES

Molten lava courses through my body as I rush around my room like a lunatic.

"Go into your room and get your toy…I heard you… Don't worry about underwear…" Shawn's words echo in my head on repeat. They're burned into my brain and making it hard for me to breathe.

I reach into my drawer and grab my pink vibrator, wincing in embarrassment. I can't believe I'm actually listening to him. This is completely crazy.

My reflection looks back at me in the mirror, my cheeks a bright pink and the smile on my face huge.

Shawn makes me so unbelievably happy. I pinch the skin on my arm and yelp. "Yup, this isn't a dream."

He said no underwear, but I'm already wearing them. Does that mean I take them off? What do I put over them? It's almost more stressful now that he's given those instructions.

Outta your head, Red.

I bite my lip and smile, remembering his words. Everything that man says is perfect. And he wants me.

With his instructions in mind, I slip off my jeans and grab his

T-shirt again. I change quickly and head out the door. At the last minute, I realize I forgot my pink friend, and I grab it before rushing to Shawn's room, as if someone is going to catch me heading to his room to do naughty things.

The tree sparkles in the living room, and I smile to myself. This man has gone out of his way for me so many times over the last few weeks. The tree is only one example. I step to his door and knock.

"Come in, sweetheart," he says.

When I step inside, Shawn is lighting a candle beside his bed, wearing those damn glasses again, and the room smells like warm apple pie. He raises his eyes, taking in my outfit, his eyes traveling slowly from my feet to my hips, catching for a moment on the shirt and then finally smiling as he looks me in the eye. It's the slow, sexy grin he's perfected, probably after years of practice.

"Fuck, you're beautiful," he says as he blows out a breath and winces when the match burns in his hand. "And a fucking hazard," he says with a laugh, then blows out the flame for good and tosses the match into the trash.

I bite my lip and stare at him. He's changed into nothing but gray sweats, and his chest glows in the candlelight. His body is molded like a sculpture, his abs contracting with each shallow breath. My eyes catch on the ink on his chest that I've yet to ask about. It's just another layer of this man that I'm dying to understand.

"Come here," he says in his low gravel that makes my insides liquefy, his commanding tone leaving me clenching and excited.

I don't hesitate. I shuffle straight toward him and look up at him, waiting for his next command. He reaches out and touches the hand that's gripping the vibrator, making my cheeks go hot. "You listened. You'll be rewarded for that, sweetheart."

A whimper escapes as I lick my lips in anticipation. He wraps his hand around the toy and meets my gaze. "May I?"

A VERY MERRY MARGARITA MIX-UP

I nod. I have no idea what he wants, but I'll say yes to just about anything right now.

He takes the vibrator from my hand and trails it up my thigh, pushing my shirt up just enough that he exposes my bare skin. We both hiss at the same time, and his eyes darken. "No panties. Just like I asked."

"*Commanded,*" I reply in a breathy pant.

His eyes dance. "You like when I tell you what to do, don't you, Red?"

I nod eagerly.

He rubs the vibrator across my breast, making me moan. "No bra either?" he says in surprise. "*Fuck.*" He switches it on and rolls it over my nipples, and my head falls back. Between his bare, inked chest, the black glasses, and the way he's looking at me, I could probably come without much effort. Add in the vibrations, and I'm just about toast. And he hasn't even touched me.

"Shawn, please," I beg. I'm not even sure what I'm begging for.

"Patience, honey. I'm going to get you there, but we're going to take this slow."

I whimper again. I need him to touch me. I need him inside me. The wait is driving me wild. Shawn presses closer and drops the vibrator on the bed, then with both hands, he slides my shirt up over my head and tosses it to the floor. His fingers brush delicately down the length of my torso, and then he grips my hips and holds me in place. I look up at him, waiting for his next move. He licks his lips and then licks mine.

Sweet cinnamon buns, that is *hot.*

"You taste like sugar," he murmurs before licking my lips again. I open my mouth, and he kisses me slowly. He wraps his arms around me, and I can't help but let loose a groan. The warmth of his body, the feel of his straining erection, and his tongue are all too much and yet not enough.

"Get on the bed," he says in that commanding voice again, pushing me back until my legs hit the mattress and I stumble back like he wants me to. He rubs his thumb over his bottom lip and regards me, but raw hunger in his gaze. "This is going to be so much fun," he says, grabbing something off the table beside his bed. It's a knotted black rope. Four bundles of them. Fascinated, I watch him walk to the edge of the bed and look up at me with a smirk. He places the rope down and pulls on the footboard. It pops open and exposes a round hook drilled into the base.

"What is that?" I ask, popping onto my knees to get a better look.

He grabs one of the ropes and loops it through the hook. "What does it look like?" he teases.

It looks like a freaking fantasy. My thighs clench in anticipation. Is he going to tie me to his bed?

He smiles like he can hear my thoughts, and then he grabs another one of the ropes and loops it through the hook on the opposite side of the bed.

Holy Christmas trees. He's going to tie my entire body to this bed, isn't he?

"Uh—are you planning on using that on me?" I ask nervously.

Shawn pauses and looks up at me. His glasses fall slightly forward, and arousal pools between my legs. "Only if you'll let me. I may give you commands, Jules, but you're always in control." He pauses and then says it again. "*Always.*"

I nod and then reply honestly. "I was just asking. I, um," I hesitate.

Shawn waits patiently. "You can say anything to me."

I take a deep breath. "I *want* you to use them on me."

Shawn smiles, and I feel it all the way to my toes. His eyes alone warm me from a distance, but his smiles? They make my skin burn.

"Good," he replies. "Because I really want to fucking tie you up and play with your pretty pussy all night."

Oh, sweet Crackerjacks.

Whatever my face is doing leaves him smiling again, and I practically melt into the bed.

Shawn walks toward me. No, he prowls, his movements slow and deliberate until he's standing beside me, his knees hitting the bed as he leans down and pushes me back onto his pillow and brings his mouth to mine. His glasses fall forward again, so he pulls them off and tosses them onto the bed.

I whimper. "I love your glasses."

He smirks. "They were getting in the way, Red. And nothing will stop me from kissing you." He presses his lips to mine, and we kiss for what feels like hours. His legs straddling my hips. His hands in my hair. His tongue everywhere.

He pulls back, leaving me panting. "You're a distraction," he says softly.

"Sorry." I grin.

He chuckles. "No, you're not."

I shake my head and I stare up at him, a stupid grin on my face. "You're right. I'm not sorry at all."

He kneels above me and reaches for the headboard, flipping another compartment open and exposing more hooks.

"I'm a really big fan of this bed," I say with a sigh.

Shawn looks down at me and grins. "I'm a really big fan of you naked and tied to my bed, Red."

I laugh. "You don't say."

He leans back to grab the ropes and prepares them like he did the ones at the foot of the bed. My entire body tingles in excitement and my thighs clench. I know I'm completely soaked. Shawn returns his attention to me and holds out his hand. "I'll keep it loose, I promise," he says affectionately, taking my wrist. He brings it to his lips and kisses it gently.

"I trust you," I say, my eyes locked with his.

"Good," he murmurs before taking the rope and wrapping it around my wrist. He ties it loosely while I watch in awe. I don't know why I like this so much, but I love the attention he gives me when he ties me up. He repeats the kiss on the inside of my right wrist and ties that one as well. My arms are spread open for him, and he takes the opportunity to kiss me gently, and then he drags his teeth down my jaw, and my legs squirm beneath him.

"Oh Shawn, it's all so much," I pant.

He licks my neck, then bites the same spot and licks again. "You taste like sugar. Always. I can't get enough."

My back arches into him, and he takes one of my nipples into his mouth, licking and then biting down softly, causing me to cry out.

He moves down my body, licking at my stomach and biting at my pubic bone, my hips bucking in excitement.

"Look at these pretty pink lips. You have the most gorgeous pussy, Red. Is it wet for me?"

His dirty words leave me dripping. What is this? What is happening? And why do I freaking love it?

"Yes," I reply, embarrassed by just how wet I am.

"Such a good girl, Jules. Too good. I think I'm going to enjoy bringing you to the edge, sweetheart." He slides his fingers between my lips and groans. "You're fucking soaked."

When he dips his tongue between my lips, I cry out in ecstasy. "Oh, yes. Right there," I say, pushing against his mouth, all inhibitions out the window. I need his mouth on my clit more than I need anything else.

He chuckles against my bare skin, sending a chill coursing through my body. "Not yet, Jules. Not yet."

The whine that leaves my mouth is borderline offensive. "Please,"

I beg.

He doesn't give in though. Shawn continues his trek down my body, dragging his tongue down my legs, kissing between my thighs, until he reaches my ankle, where once again, he presses soft kisses before tying my left foot down. I lift my head to watch as he does the same thing with the right one, and then I lean back with a groan. My entire body is exposed right now. My legs are spread wide, and Shawn is still dressed in his sweats, sitting up on his knees, staring at me.

"I've never seen anything more beautiful than you spread out for me on my bed. You're a vision. Fucking perfection."

I shiver at his words.

He stares for a few more beats, and then he reaches across me to grab for the vibrator. The scent of him—winter and burned wood—leaves me moaning. I shift slightly, trying to reach for him the only way I know how.

He chuckles as he leans close. "You need me, baby?"

"Yes."

He kisses me softly, his tongue parting my lips. And then I hear the telltale sign of the vibrator, and I jolt as he runs it across my nipple, kissing me through it. He alternates between both breasts, and I'm practically panting into his mouth. The vibrator drags down my stomach, and I drop my head back, so ready to finally be touched. He rolls it across my clit, making me scream in pleasure, but then he pulls it away and goes back to kissing me.

Why won't he just put it in?

My wrists strain as I writhe beneath him when he rolls the vibrator against my clit again, this time dragging the tip between my lips and pressing inside just barely.

My mouth falls open, and I cry out again while Shawn stares at me, his honey eyes melting. "That's it, baby. Tell me how good it feels. Tell me how badly you want this to be my cock instead."

I moan and press my hips against him, trying hard to rub against his erection. But he pulls back and laughs.

"Look what you're doing to my sweats," he teases, showing me the wet spot on his pants.

I groan in embarrassment and turn my head to the side since I can't cover my face. But Shawn grabs my chin and forces me to look at him. "You think I don't love knowing you're so wet because of me? That you made this mess because of what I'm doing?" he asks, pointing to the wet spot on his pants again. He loops his thumbs into the sweats and drags them down his hips, taking his boxers with them and revealing his hard length, glossy and straining toward me. "I'm literally leaking just staring at you, Red." He thrusts once into his palm.

I quiver and lick my lips, dying for a taste.

"Oh, you want this?" he says, holding himself.

"Yes, please," I pant, licking my lips again.

His eyes dance as he crawls up my body until he's hovering above my face. I stick my tongue out to lick at him, and he hisses. "Fuck, Red. So greedy for it." He takes himself in his hand, and I open my mouth, waiting. Since I'm tied up, my movements are limited, but when he finally slides himself in and grips the headboard, he takes control. "You okay?" he asks softly.

I nod as tears roll down my face. He's so big, and I'm so turned on my body begs for release. When he finally pushes in and out of my mouth, my core flutters, making me groan around him.

"Oh fuck, Red. That feels so good," he murmurs, sliding in and out again. I start to gag, and he pulls back. His fingers swipe at the tears falling from my eyes. "Am I being too rough?"

I shake my head. "No, I just need…" I hesitate.

"What do you need, baby?"

A VERY MERRY MARGARITA MIX-UP

I whine. "I need to come. Please, Shawn. Let me come."

Shawn scoots down my body and presses his lips to mine, our breath mingling as he says, "Okay, baby. I'll let you come."

"Oh, thank God," I pant as he moves lower, biting my nipples before settling himself between my legs.

The buzz of the vibrator sounds again, and he plunges it inside me at the same moment that his lips find my clit. He circles his tongue, sucks, and circles again. All while moving the vibrator in and out at a punishing speed. It doesn't take long before I'm cresting through my orgasm, the intensity of it taking me by storm. He replaces the vibrator with his fingers and moans when I come all over his fingers and his tongue. "Yes, baby. Fuck, your pussy is clutching my fingers so tight. I can't wait for it to strangle my cock. Are you ready for that?" he asks.

"Yes, please. Now, Shawn. I need you now."

He sits up and grabs for a condom in the bedside table and rips it open with his teeth. Then I watch as he slides it over his wet head. Carefully he leans over me, his arms straining to hold him up, and pushes inside me. I stare down at the way his cock moves in and out, his abs contracting as he works himself over me.

He continues whispering dirty words in my ear, kissing up my chin, licking at my mouth. I can do nothing but take it all. Every pounding strike. I don't expect to come again. He's not touching my clit. I can't move my hands to help, and I've already had an orgasm that beats all previous ones. But suddenly I feel the inside of my body flutter and heat pool between my legs. He's hitting my g-spot, and I can't control the scream that leaves my body when he shudders inside me. We come at the same time, Shawn pumping until my body has gone completely limp.

And then he kisses me softly before rolling off me. I'm still in a complete fog when he unties my ankles and kisses up my leg. Then

369

he climbs over me and undoes my hands. I flex my fingers, trying to get used to my ability to move, while Shawn wraps me in his arms and holds me tightly.

"Fuck, baby. You did so good," he murmurs and drops a kiss to my head, holding me tight. I've never felt so cherished in my life.

I snuggle into him, completely spent, and fall asleep in his arms.

JULES
ICE CREAM
SUPER PREMIUM ICE CREAM
SUPER PREMIUM ICE CREAM

CHAPTER 57

JULES

Groggy and sore from our long, incredible night, I wake to Shawn pressing soft kisses against my cheek. "Baby. Baby, wake up," he whispers with urgency.

My eyes fly open at the gravity of his tone. I'm disoriented at first, confused about where I am. When I see his concerned face, I wipe the sleep from my eyes and sit up. "What's wrong?"

Shawn grabs my hand and looks at me apologetically. "I'm sorry, Jules. We just got called out. There's a fire," he says, remorse tingeing his every word.

"It's okay."

"No, sweetheart. The baking." He looks absolutely distraught. "We won't be able to help."

I give him a sad smile. He does so much for me, and he's obviously torn. I'll freak out about everything I have to do later. Right now, he needs to focus. "I'm fine. Go put out fires and save the world."

Shawn sighs heavily. "I hate this," he mutters before brushing a kiss against my lips.

I look up at him and smile. "Stay safe, okay? I'll be *fine*," I remind him.

He looks at me longingly, like he wants to crawl back into bed with me, but he stands up and heads to the door. "I'll stay up all night with you and bake, Red. I promise."

"Go," I reprimand. "I'll be fine."

I was, in fact, not fine. About five minutes after Shawn left our apartment, I got myself out of bed and realized just how completely screwed I was. I had two hundred cupcakes to make, twelve dozen cookies, two hundred cannolis, and twelve pies. And let's not forget the cake in the shape of Prancer that Carmella thought was the *cutest idea ever*. A cake made to look like a reindeer. And not like a sheet cake. No, she wanted one that could stand.

"Gah!" I scream as I stumble to the kitchen and turn on the coffee pot. Next on the list is a shower. It may be four in the morning, but with all the extra baking on my plate, I'll need every minute I can get.

After stripping my clothes off, I step under the scalding spray and nod to Charlotte. I think even she's surprised to see me so early because she scurries into the corner, thus making my shower more tolerable since I don't have to dance in my tiny corner and rush through each task in hopes she doesn't use her silk to repel down and hang out on my naked body.

Once I'm showered and dressed in one of Shawn's flannel shirts over a pair of black leggings and a black tank top, I take my coffee to the couch and create my lists. If I have any hope of getting this baking done, I'll need to be organized and efficient. Which means I need all of my recipes written out. A tall order for me, but one I'm dedicated to.

Blowing out a breath, I strategize, working through scenarios for a way I can get everything done on my own. But no matter how many times I turn it over in my brain, there's just no way to avoid pulling all-nighters all week. Even if the guys had been around today, the timeline would have been tight.

"Well, no time like the present," I declare, standing and readying myself to head down to the bakery. Fortunately, Shawn had all the ingredients I needed delivered while we were in New Hampshire, and they're sitting in the beautiful fridge that was here when I took over the ice cream shop. It took a little time and some elbow grease, but now it looks sparkling new.

The blaring of my phone startles me, and my coffee goes sloshing all over my tank top. "Oh, hell's bells!" I screech as I frantically hit the buttons on the side of my phone. It's only four a.m. I don't have neighbors to wake, but in the still of the early morning, the noise is *so bleeping loud.*

"Hello," I grumble into the phone without looking at the screen.

"*Babe,*" a voice drawls on the other end. "I *miss* you!"

I throw my head back and silently curse at the ceiling. Really, God? This is how you want to do me this morning? I mean, I get it. I haven't exactly been an angel this week—being tied up and all—but in general, I'm not a bad person. And Shawn is the only man I've ever let tie me up. And he's a really good guy. Like really good. Not like this…this…Gah, I can't even find a term for him without cursing.

"Jared, are you drunk?" I ask with a sigh.

"Come home, babe. Please. I miss you so much."

I pull the phone away from my ear and sneer at it. He misses me? Is this guy serious? Where the hell is his *wife*?

The laugh that escapes my lips is almost maniacal.

"Jules?" he asks, confused.

Because I have absolutely nothing to say to this idiot, I hang up and head to my bedroom to change out of my coffee-stained clothes.

I flick on the Christmas lights the guys hung in the kitchen—just the sight makes me grin and sends a rush of serotonin through my system—and pull up Spotify on my phone. Shawn's friend from

Tahoe, the one who writes spicy books, has playlists to go with all her books, and I find myself bopping around to the playlist for her most recent Christmas novel, smiling as I belt out Taylor Swift's version of "Last Christmas."

My hands move on autopilot as I sprinkle flour onto the butcher block and then lay out my first batch of dough. Hips swinging, lips singing, and fingers kneading, I make my way through batch after batch with a smile on my face. It may take me days to do this, and my fingers may be ready to fall off by the ball on Friday, but I've never felt so at home in a space. Shawn and the guys took care of every minute detail, including things I never knew I needed.

At eight a.m., I start to panic. I've only made it through prepping the dough. The panic surges like a tidal wave when the bell above the front door jingles. I slap my hands against my apron, ready to shout that we're not open. I'd originally thought I could handle serving donuts and coffee this week while the guys and I worked on desserts. But I now know that was a bad idea and really hope whoever is out there can spread the word that Jules is not, in fact, ready for customers, despite my insane goal to be.

But as I round the corner into the bakery, I find Carmella and Belle deep in conversation and stripping off their winter jackets, hats, and mittens.

"Um, hello," I say, startling them both. Despite being in my store, they seem surprised to see *me*.

"Oh, fiddlesticks, Jules! Announce yourself next time rather than stalking in like a baby kitten and giving an old lady a heart attack!" Carmella reprimands, holding her hand to her chest and leaning on Belle for support.

Belle rolls her eyes over the white-haired drama queen. "Happy baking day!" Belle cheers. "Your little helper elves are here. Although this one may be more trouble than she's worth," she teases, pointing at Carmella.

I squint in confusion. "Baking day?"

She doesn't have time to answer before the door opens again and Charlotte and Amelia barrel in. Without greeting anyone, Amelia waves at me and says, "Please tell me you have hot chocolate. If I can't have coffee because of this baby, then I need chocolate to be up this early on my day off."

"Baby?" I whisper in shock.

They ignore me and continue the conversation. "Of course she has chocolate. This is a bakery!"

I freeze, bewildered. Why are all these women in my bakery at eight a.m. on a Monday morning? "What baby? What's going on?"

Amelia sighs. "I'm pregnant. Get with the program. You really don't have hot chocolate?"

I smile and my head. "Congratulations. Of course I do. Head into the kitchen and sit down. I'll melt some chocolate and get started."

Belle's eyes go wide. "You're going to make hot cocoa using *real* chocolate?"

I laugh again. "Um, yes."

"Oh, we are so going to be best friends," she says. Then she stalks toward me and throws an arm over my shoulder, pushing me toward the kitchen.

I glance back, finding a beaming Charlotte following us with Carmella and Amelia right behind her.

When we enter the kitchen, Carrie Underwood is singing "Have Yourself a Merry Little Christmas," and I can't help it. My eyes start to water. What is happening right now? Why are these women here? And why am I weeping as I warm chocolate?

The women *ooh* and *ahh* over the beautiful new kitchen, the pink and teal pans, the Christmas lights, the sign Shawn custom ordered for me. All of it makes it hard for me to breathe. Finally getting my bearings, I turn around and gape at them. "*What* is going on?"

Charlotte smiles. "Shawn called."

She says it like it's an explanation in itself. And I suppose it is. *That man…*

The kitchen door swings open again, and this time, I'm met by the two women I've wanted most in the world. The breath whooshes out of my lungs. "What—" I stutter.

Caris is all business. Without hesitation, she says hello and wraps me in a firm, almost warm hug, while Hailey hangs back and chats with Amelia, only offering me a small wave.

"Put us to work. What can we do?" Belle asks as she opens the fridge and checks out the ingredients.

"I—uh—" I fumble for a moment, unsure where to start. Then I remember my list. The recipes I put on paper. For once, I'm not just winging it. "Over there," I say, pointing to my notebook. "The recipes are all in there."

Carmella smiles. "Okay, how about you do what you need to do, and I'll take out a recipe for each of us to start? You just walk around and supervise. Make sure everyone is doing what they need. We got this, Juliana."

My mother is the only one who calls me Juliana, and although I don't exactly miss her since I'm mad at her, I also kind of do. I've ignored her phone calls for weeks, and just hearing the name only she uses creates a small pang in my chest. Gosh, if I don't get these emotions under control, I'll need to add tears to the ingredient list of every one of these pastries.

I suck in a big breath and offer everyone a shaky smile. "Thank you so much."

Charlotte puts a hand on my forearm. "It's what friends are for."

My eyes drift to Hailey as she adds, "*And sisters.* Now put us to work."

JULES
ICE CREAM

SUPER PREMIUM ICE CREAM   SUPER PREMIUM ICE CREAM

CHAPTER 58

JULES

The ladies didn't just show up for me that day. They showed up after work every evening all week, and along with the guys, we would bake into the night. Some nights, Carmella would bring bruschetta, and we'd throw back shots of limoncello—it was apparently imported from Italy, and Belle smiled big when it was first brought out.

Other nights, Hailey would drop off burgers and fries from the bar. She couldn't always stay because someone needed to keep the place open, but she'd show up during the day instead, and we'd actually get some time alone. We also stopped by the hospital to see our father almost every morning. And even though we couldn't stay long, I was slowly getting to know them both. I still didn't know what happened between him and my mother all those years ago, but right now, I wasn't going to ask. Focusing on the past wasn't going to bring me closure.

The girls had joined the guys and me for Zumba a few times over the week as well. It was a good break from all the cooking, and Charlotte got a kick out of teasing Shawn, while Colby enjoyed staring at everyone in their spandex.

Unfortunately for him, that also included Carmella. She brought a group of older ladies with her. One even had pink hair, and she kept teasing Belle about how Spinning with Seniors was on a road trip. The joke went over my head, but apparently Belle originally met Carmella when she accidentally moved into a fifty-five and up community, and she used to do spin classes in the mornings with them. Now that she's living with Luca, they miss her classes. Zumba seems like a happy medium. Colby was less than thrilled though.

And things with Shawn? They just kept getting better. Whenever we don't wake up together, he leaves me little notes by the coffeepot. This morning, he left mistletoe on top of the note.

Hang this somewhere in the bakery, Red. I want a reason to kiss you every day.

XOXO, Shawn

I immediately texted him. **Thanks for the coffee and the mistletoe. You know you never need a reason to kiss me though. These lips are yours.** I followed it up with a kissing emoji.

My phone lit up with his quick response. **Good answer, baby. But the mistletoe reminded me of you, and I wanted you to know that I'm always thinking about kissing you.**

I then spent the morning baking mistletoe cookies and delivered them to the station for the guys. Shawn was beaming, and he might have even snuck me into the bunk room for a few minutes and kissed me senseless. And then he dropped to his knees and kissed me on my other lips until I was grabbing his hair and begging him for release.

He does love when I beg.

I was nervous that things would be awkward when Hailey found out we were dating—that maybe she really did have feelings for him and it would cause problems. But to my surprise, all she did was turn to him and say, "Hurt my sister and you're dead to me."

I'd been so touched that I burst out laughing when she looked at me and quipped, "Hurt my gem of a best friend and we're going to have a problem." Her face was so serious I actually believed her.

But things with Shawn are just *too good*. And it all feels right. Especially right now.

He's got me tied tight to the hooks on his bed while he drips wax onto my naked body. I hiss when the hot wax makes contact with my skin, but Shawn's lips follow the trail with kisses, making me buck my hips, waiting for him to finally give me what I really want. "So needy tonight, Red," he murmurs, sinking down between my legs.

As he tilts the candle and the steaming wax hits my most sensitive area, I whimper. "Please, Shawn. I need your lips." I feel his smile against my skin and groan again. "Please," I beg.

"Tell me where you want them," he teases, his mouth brushing against my skin but never going quite where I need him.

"I need them down there," I try.

He shakes his head, his scruff rasping against my thigh. "*Tell me where you want me, Red. Use your words. I want you to be dirty for me.*"

I huff and stare up at the ceiling of his bedroom. "I don't say that word."

"What word?" he murmurs softly, rubbing his nose against my skin and looking up at me with those mischievous brown eyes of his.

"I know what you're trying to get me to say, but I don't say that word."

He chuckles and sets the candle on the nightstand. "So if I told you I wanted to kiss your pretty little—"

"Don't say it," I cut him off.

He closes his eyes and shakes his head, grinning. "Don't say it because you don't want me to? Or because you like the sound of it too much and realize you are *so* much dirtier than you thought?" He nibbles the sensitive skin at the inside of my thigh, and his eyes dance in a challenge.

"Prancer," I whisper.

Shawn climbs on top of me, caging me in with his arms. "You're not supposed to use the safe word like that, Red."

"I can use the safe word however I choose, and I'm choosing to use it now. Prancer, Prancer, Prancer," I say on a laugh.

Shawn's eyes light up, and he laughs along with me. Then he presses a kiss to my mouth. When he pulls away with a big stupid grin on his face, he grumbles, "God, I love you."

His eyes practically double in size then, and I'm sure mine do too. I suck in a breath, waiting for him to qualify it. "I mean," he grabs at the back of his neck, "God, I love how funny you are. You make me so happy, Jules."

I swallow and examine him, taking in his expression. I know he misspoke, but now the thoughts running through my brain are all, *I love him, I love him, I love him.* Sweet kittens being held by a fireman, I love him!

"Jules," he says, watching me, his eyes softening.

"Untie me, please," I beg, needing my arms free.

Shawn sighs and gets to work unhooking both my arms and my legs. My mind whirs, and I can't focus on the way he gently loosens the ropes and kisses each mark on my body. It isn't until I'm completely free that I find my words.

"Shawn," I say. I grab at his hand when he's finished with the last tie on my ankle. "You make me so happy too."

His smile is instant, his calm demeanor falling into place as his lips turn up and his eyes lighten. I give him a matching grin. I think we both know what the other is really thinking—how we both feel—but I'm not quite ready to say it just yet.

"I do?" he asks softly, almost nervously, pushing my hair off my face.

I lift my hand and rub my fingers softly against his cheek, enamored by him. "Yes. You've made me so unbelievably happy,

Shawn. I never…I never thought I could have all this. A new life, the bakery, family, friends…my sisters. I dreamed I'd have every one of them, but not even I could have dreamed you up. And you're the reason all of this is happening. The reason my life feels so right. You're my person, Shawn."

He crashes his lips to mine, then sinks down between my legs, our bodies pushing together without hesitation. As soon as he shifts and presses inside me, I groan in relief.

"I'm so crazy about you, Jules. I'd do anything for you," he promises.

Unlike before, when sex was focused on the pleasure or on the spice, tonight, it's just about love.

JULES
ICE CREAM
SUPER PREMIUM ICE CREAM
SUPER PREMIUM ICE CREAM

CHAPTER 59

JULES

As I walk into Linden Place, I'm blown away by the gorgeous flowers on not only the tables but snaking up the walls. Poinsettia and ivy are woven in a beautiful design, with golds and Christmas lights flittering between the leaves and blooms. I can't help but stop and stare, in awe of the gorgeous design.

"Amelia does a beautiful job, doesn't she?" Shawn whispers in my ear as he squeezes my hand.

"Amelia did this?" I ask, surprised. I had no idea she had this kind of talent.

Shawn nods. "She owns Pearson's Flower Shop with her mother-in-law. She's the event designer, and she's taken over the shop now that Karen has retired."

I suck in a breath. "It's absolutely beautiful."

"Let's go make sure all your desserts are set in the kitchen," he offers, knowing I'd want to be sure. He talked me into attending the ball as a guest since caterers had been hired to handle the food setup. I'd begrudgingly agreed, even though I wasn't sure I could relax. Of course Shawn, being the man he is, knows that if I see that everything is set up properly, I'll finally be able to relax and enjoy the night. I smile at him as he leads me to the table where the desserts are plated.

"What did you do?" I ask, staring down at the stack of business cards in front of a tray of cupcakes. They're printed with a girl holding a cake in front of her face so all you see is red hair. Across the top of the cake is "Jules Bakery," followed by the address, phone number and a website address. I don't even have a website!

Shawn smirks. "Merry Christmas, sweetheart."

I smack him. "Seriously Shawn, what is this?"

He pulls out his phone and slips it to me. The website pulled up in the browser with the image from the business cards emblazoned across the screen. The site is barebones, but it does have a few pictures of a whole slew of us baking in the kitchen this week, and even some pictures of the finished desserts.

"How?" I whisper. "How did you do this when you were busy helping me? Busy fighting fires?" I shake my head in amazement, holding back tears.

Shawn presses his hand gently against my cheek and looks down at me with love. "I told you I'd do anything for you, Red. Just let me."

I sigh out a contented breath and pop up on my toes to kiss him. When we pull apart, I lick my lips, savoring the taste of this sweet man like he's one of my desserts come to life.

Behind me, someone clears their throat, and Shawn and I both turn.

My grandmother eyes us both with interest. "Hello, Jules," she says with a smile.

I take a step away from Shawn and wrap her in a hug. "I didn't realize you were coming. I'm so glad you're here though. Now you can see the pastries I made with the new oven. Thank you again." I hold my arm out toward the dessert table like I'm on a game show.

She eyes them appraisingly. "I can't wait to taste them. And who is this young man?"

I look to Shawn and decide to be completely honest. "This is my boyfriend and roommate, Shawn Chase."

"It's so nice to meet you, ma'am," Shawn says, extending his hand to my grandmother.

She takes it. I'm sure her manners wouldn't allow her to ignore the formality, but I can tell by her raised eyebrow that she's not happy. "I thought Hailey was your roommate," she says skeptically.

I turn to Shawn, unsure of how to respond. I thought by now she knew Hailey wasn't living with me.

Once again, I just go for the truth. "No, just Shawn and me. We have separate rooms though," I add. Not that I've been sleeping in mine. Even when Shawn has to spend the night at the firehouse, I sleep in his bed. There's something comforting about his smell, his sheets, him.

He wraps his arm around my waist, knowing, as always, just what to do. "Make sure you save me a dance, Mrs. Milsom," Shawn says. "I'm going to get this one to our table so she actually eats before she starts stressing about the desserts again."

I think we both know that's not what I'm stressing about anymore, but my grandmother just nods.

"Can't wait to try them. And Shawn," she says as he starts to lead me away. "Make sure you come for Sunday dinner soon."

Shawn's face relaxes into a grin. "Absolutely, Mrs. Milsom. Thank you so much."

As he leads me to the table, all thoughts of the pending disaster with Hailey dissipate. All our friends are here, dressed to the nines. And Shawn, in his black suit with his firm hand on my back, has butterflies taking flight in my stomach.

"You look absolutely stunning in this green dress, Red, I'm not going to lie," he whispers into my ear, then brushes a kiss to my shoulder. He slides out my chair and adds, "But I can't wait to see it on the floor." He nips at my neck before pulling away, and my entire body shudders.

I take a deep breath and greet our friends. Beside me, Charlotte grabs my arm. She's wearing a deep red velvet dress, and her chestnut hair is pulled back off her face. Her smoky eye makeup leaves her looking like a 1920s model. "You look absolutely gorgeous," I tell her, giving her hand a squeeze.

"Oh, stop it. Everyone does! We sure do clean up well, friends," she says in her ever-present cheerful kindergarten teacher voice. Like Shawn, she's always going out of her way for her friends. She's always kind and always outgoing.

"How were the kittens this week, Shawn?" Charlotte asks over my head. I turn to look at Shawn, confused by her question.

He shakes his head, and Colby, who is sitting across from me, catches my attention when he replies, "They were freaking adorable. But no one loved them as much as Mason."

Now we all spin in his direction. It's like a damn pinball machine, our attention darting from one person to another.

Mason grimaces. "They're cute," he says simply. Then, as if he can't help himself, he pulls out his phone and slides it across the table to me.

On it I find a picture of Prancer with four kittens curled up on his back. "What is this?" I coo, turning the photo so that Charlotte can see. Suddenly, she's screeching.

Mason grumbles, "Ah, give me that back."

But before he can grab it, Shawn takes the phone and examines the photo. When he looks back up, he smirks at Mason. "You realize he has to go back to the farm in New Hampshire next week, right?"

Mason sighs.

"Mason," I say softly, waiting for him to meet my eyes. "Are you getting attached to a reindeer?"

"I'm not attached," he grunts, holding out his hand. When Shawn passes his phone back, Mason pockets it and looks back up at us. "But the kittens are."

"Can someone explain the kittens to me, please?" I ask.

Beside me, Charlotte chortles. "Yes, brother. Please tell darling Jules about how you managed to get all the firefighters to pose with kittens for the Christmas calendar so that Jules could—"

Shawn clears his throat then, and Charlotte puts a hand to her lips, but she doesn't continue her thought.

"So I could what?"

He sighs. "Ya know, Charlotte, for a woman who went on a trip with a stranger and fell in love, you really don't get how romance works."

I can't help the smile that graces my lips. I angle closer. "Shawn, you do realize you're not an actual book boyfriend, right? You're not required to always be so perfect."

He sighs and presses his lips together. "Can we just forget my sister mentioned anything if I promise to get you a copy of the calendar?"

I slip my hands onto his cheeks and admire him for a moment. "Shawn Chase…"

"What?" he grumbles, staring back, all doe-eyed.

I press a kiss to his lips. "You're better than a book boyfriend."

He tilts his head into my hands and smiles. "Thanks, sweetheart."

"But if you don't show me the outtakes of this photo shoot, you'll go to bed alone tonight," I tease.

He laughs and pulls me onto his lap, and that's where I remain all through cocktail hour.

CHAPTER 60

HAILEY

Unlike the rest of the town, I'm stuck at the bar—a place that used to be my sanctuary. But the kitchen needs updating, the electrical needs work, our bartenders are all off enjoying their new lives, and I'm here, waiting in the empty dining space for the inevitable crowd to filter in after the Christmas ball.

It's why, when the door opens and a cold burst of air hits me, I immediately turn to greet my customer. It's still early—only nine p.m. The ball doesn't end until eleven, so most people won't be turning up for a few hours. But instead of a patron, I find my grandmother marching in with a scowl on her face.

Oh brother. What did I do now?

"Hi Grandmama," I say, sliding a coaster in front of where she's standing. "What can I get ya?"

She's wearing a mink coat that swallows her small frame, and her steely eyes remain fixed on me

"Why aren't you living with Jules?" she asks, getting straight to the point.

I let out a long breath, tired of her games. And just plain tired in general. I've been trying really hard. Trying to keep this place afloat, trying to nurse my dad back to health, trying to ignore my attraction to his doctor and my sister's best friend Maddox. And most of all, trying to get to know my twin because everyone tells me it's the right thing to do. But right about now, after she's clearly spilled to this woman, even though she knew it could cost me the bar, I'm not feeling like I want to try too hard anymore.

"I'm not…but—" I try.

My grandmother interrupts me. "Hailey, you knew the terms. I honestly thought you'd grown up."

I bite my lip to keep from saying things that would get us nowhere. "If you'd let me speak—"

"*Enough*. Your father gave you a lot of rope because he felt bad that you grew up without a mother. But so did Caris, and you don't see her messing up at every turn. And Jules. She's only been here a month, and she's settling into this town. Attending dinners. Trying. And she didn't have the benefit of your father because your mother stole her."

My mind is reeling from all the insults my grandmother just threw at me, but my focus turns to her last words. "She what?"

"Oh, Hailey, really. Do you think your father would split you two up? Just give up on one of his children? A baby at that? Of course not. Your mother grabbed Jules out of her crib and disappeared. When he finally tracked them down, she said she'd sue for full custody of all of you if he didn't back off. He didn't like it, but he was too scared he'd lose you and Caris Too. Your mother had met a man who had a lot of money and had access to the best attorneys in the area. But your father was an idiot. He gave up out of fear. I could have taken her down. And I will if I ever see her again." Anger turns my grandmother's face red, and her hands shake.

Even faced with the truth of how awful my mother was, relief washes over me. My father didn't choose to split Jules and me up like we were puppies on a farm. He isn't that kind of person. And I'm sure he's lived with the guilt of not fighting for my sister all those years ago.

"Poor Dad," I say quietly.

My grandmother continues. "I had hoped that since he raised you, you'd be more like him. But lately, I'm seeing more of your mother in you. And until you prove to me that's not who you are, I'm cutting you off."

"Grams," I try, suddenly desperate to get through to her.

She holds up her hand. "Bond with your sister, meet a nice man, settle down, get married. That's when you'll get your inheritance. Until then, we're done." She spins on her heel and walks out.

I flop my head and arms onto the bar. "How the hell is this my life?"

JULES
ICE CREAM
SUPER PREMIUM ICE CREAM
SUPER PREMIUM ICE CREAM

CHAPTER 61

JULES

The biggest surprise of the night happens when Mariah Carey's "All I Want for Christmas" starts playing. One by one, firefighters from different tables jump up. It takes me a moment to realize that they're all doing the same dance. One after another, they head to the dance floor in synchronized moves. Beside me, Charlotte screeches. "Oh my god, it's a flash mob!"

I tilt my head and look at Shawn. "I mean, I guess."

He winks at me before grabbing my hand and pulling me to my feet. "Crossing off another wish, Red."

"What?" I stutter as he pulls me toward the dance floor. "But I don't know the moves."

Turns out I'm wrong. Because they're all doing the moves we've done countless times in our Zumba class. That little stinker. I grin in Shawn's direction, and he beams and slides across the dance floor toward me like Michael Bublé in concert. The man is smooth. Then he grabs my hand and spins me, all while singing the words along with Mariah.

"You're nuts. You know that, right?" I shout over the music, getting back to the Zumba moves along with the rest of the firefighters.

"I'd do anything for that look right there, Red," he says, pointing to my face.

My insides dance along with my feet. I feel brighter, lighter, than I ever have.

"That smile right there, Red. It's everything."

As soon as the song is over, I grab my man and head for the door, waving at everyone as we go.

Shawn laughs. "Don't you want to stay for dessert?"

I shake my head. "Nope." I lean against him. "You said it's covered, so it's covered. Take me home, *Babe*."

JULES
ICE CREAM
SUPER PREMIUM ICE CREAM
SUPER PREMIUM ICE CREAM

CHAPTER 62

JULES

C hristmas is only a week away, and since the ball, I've had calls coming in for Christmas eve orders almost every few minutes all day long. Shawn and I hung wreaths on the front doors, and Christmas lights glitter around the shop. I wipe down the old-fashioned red cash register my grandmother surprised me with the day after the ball and smile to myself. Although I'm so busy I can barely see straight and I haven't slept past four a.m. any day this week, I'm the happiest I've ever been. And it's all because of this beautiful bakery, our little town, my new friends, and Shawn.

When my mother calls, I decide that not even she can ruin my mood, so I pick up. "Hey, Mom," I say, setting the rag down and sliding to the floor behind the counter. The closed sign is already in the window, and Shawn is at the fire station, so I doubt anyone will come looking for me.

"Juliana Marie Kingsl—"

"Milsom," I retort. I don't even know why I said it. Lord knows I don't feel like a Milsom, even if my grandmother has welcomed me into the family. My father has been kind, and Caris and Hailey have been more open to real relationships, but I don't know that I'll ever stop feeling like an outsider in my own family. But the way she thinks she can scold me irks me. As if *I've* done something wrong.

She sucks in a breath.

"I'm sorry, Mom," I say immediately. I'm not in the wrong here, but the jab wasn't necessary.

"I knew they would make you hate me. It's Eveline, isn't it? She never liked me. I was never good enough for her son."

"Mom, please. No one has said a thing about you." I press my head into my hands, hiding my groan.

"Right. I'm sure that wasn't the first thing they did. Throw me under the bus for how I handled things. I did what I thought was best. I couldn't handle three kids. Your father wanted joint custody, and what? I'd have to stay in Rhode Island and have three kids half the time? By myself? That's insanity. I did what was best for us, honey. I took you and gave you a good life in Los Angeles."

I swallow gulps of air. She what? "Wait. Back up, Mom."

But she just keeps prattling on. "And now they're poisoning you against me. You should be here with me. Not working until all hours of the night and ignoring my phone calls, doing God knows what in that little podunk town! You were meant for more, Juliana."

Tears pour down my face at the implication here. My mother really did kidnap me. She stole me from my father. From my sisters. She robbed me of a childhood in this town. Of memories with my grandmother. Of a family. All because, what, she wanted to be an actress?

"Meant for more?" I seethe. "Am I just supposed to get married, pop out two kids, and live comfortably for the rest of my life on my husband's dime? I mean, sure, it would be great not having to work long hours in the bakery. I won't have to pretend I care about the people in this town. I won't have to spend time with my new family. Yeah, sounds like a perfect idea," I huff sarcastically.

"What's so bad about that, Juliana? Did you not feel loved as a child? I loved you every day. I put everything I had into raising you. If

I'd had three kids, you would have had a third of the attention."

"But you did have three kids, Mom. *You do.* You just *left* them here. And you stole me. You stole my memories. All my time. I'll be lucky to have some semblance of a relationship with my twin," I sob. "Don't you get it? I want this. The bakery. This life. I want my sisters and my family and this town. I want this crazy community that does Zumba dances to make me smile, that buys up all my pastries because they want to support me, the people who show up and bake with me so I can get my name out into the community." I wipe a hand under my nose, wishing I didn't cry when I was angry.

"I want the crazy old ladies who sit by the water and gossip while they drink their coffee but love planning events. I want the Christmas tree farm with the grumpiest owner in the world who loves a reindeer and four kittens more than he likes people."

I clear my throat and sit a little straighter. "I want the man who cooks with me and reads to me every night. I want to raise kids with him and live in this town and do all the things with him because *he* makes me happy. And running this bakery makes me happy. I'm sorry you don't understand that. I'm sorry you weren't happy here. But I am," I say, taking a deep breath.

Clarity is finally seeping in. Every word I spoke to my mother was true. I just hadn't realized how much I truly love this town—how deep my feelings for Shawn had grown—until this very moment. There is no doubt I am in love with that man. I want everything with him. And I can't wait to tell him.

Perhaps shocked by my outburst, my mother is silent on the other end of the phone. But I'm spent from crying. So rather than apologizing for my feelings, rather than feeling guilty for being happy, I hit the End button and let the phone slip out of my hand. And then I turn off the lights, climb the stairs slowly, and put myself to bed.

CHAPTER 63

SHAWN

"Mrs. Prenderson, please make sure you water your tree. Christmas trees are the biggest causes of fires this time of year," I warn as we cart the dead tree down her front steps. Of course, I couldn't let the woman go without a tree a week before Christmas, so Mason delivered a fresh balsam fir, and we've spent the last two hours decorating it instead of eating dinner at the station with the guys.

"Of course, Shawn. Thank you again for all your help," she says, looking back toward her much bigger, much prettier tree. If I didn't know better, I'd think she did this for a little attention and a better tree.

I chuckle as I walk down the sidewalk and toss the blue spruce into the back of Mason's pickup truck. A fire truck seemed like overkill for this call, and I'm glad we didn't drag the big boy out for this stop. "Wanna grab burgers at Thames to bring back to the station? I'm starving," I grumble, hauling myself into his truck.

Mason grunts a yes, and we head toward town.

"How's Prancer?" I rib him.

He glances at me and grunts again. "Fine."

"You going to give him back?" I ask, giving him a shit-eating grin.

Mason shrugs a shoulder, bringing an elbow up along with it while keeping his hand on the wheel. "Dunno."

I laugh. "You're really thinking of keeping the reindeer?"

He sighs heavily. "He makes the kittens happy."

I shake my head and look out the window. Our town is lit up. Tomorrow night, there will be Christmas carolers strolling down the street while the stores open for the Sip and Stroll. Jules and I will have Christmas margaritas to serve with her fresh churros. We figure the nontraditional choice will keep people warm and once again make her shop stand out against others. Not that she doesn't already stand out. The woman is in a class of her own. And tomorrow, when we close up shop and stroll together to the tree lighting ceremony, where the entire town will sing around the Christmas tree like we're whos in Whoville, I'm going to tell Jules that I love her. That I'm *in love* with her. I can't hold it in anymore. It slipped out last week, and I was able to cover it up, but I don't *want* to cover it up. It may be too soon. It may seem crazy, but it feels right. *She* feels right, and most importantly, when I'm with her, *I* feel right.

I don't need some predetermined timeline approved by society to know that Jules is it for me. When you love someone, you tell them. You leave nothing left unsaid. Life is too short to do anything but that.

In the restaurant, we find Hailey behind the bar, her eyes unfocused and a frown marring her face.

When she doesn't look our way after a moment, I nod to Mason. "I'm just gonna take her in the back to see what's going on. Can you watch the bar?"

Mason doesn't hesitate, moving behind the bar as if he belongs there. He may not talk a lot, but he's the most reliable person I've ever met.

"Hey, Hailes," I say softly, pulling her from the thoughts eating at her. "You okay?"

She raises her eyes, as if she's just seeing me. "Uh, yeah. Wait, what are you guys doing behind the bar?" she asks, although there's no fight to her words. Just defeat.

I grab her by the elbow and lead her away from the customers. I know something is wrong when she doesn't argue. I guide her toward the stairs to her apartment and then hold out my arm to motion for her to lead us up. She goes without hesitation.

Once in her apartment, she heads straight to the kitchen and grabs a bottle of tequila. "Shot?" she asks, holding up two shot glasses.

I shake my head. "On the job. Gotta go back to the station. What's going on?"

She sighs. "You're gonna wish you could have something to numb the burn of what I'm about to tell you."

"You're scaring me, Hailey. What's going on?" My mind races. What could have her so shaken? Is it her dad? I look around the space as I wait for her to sit with me. Unlike our apartment, she has no decorations. No Christmas tree, not a single string of lights, no indication whatsoever that it's winter, let alone the week before Christmas. There are dishes piled up in her sink, clothes sprawled on her floor, a wet towel by the bathroom door, and dust accumulating on the table in front of me. It's a mess. Which isn't Hailey. She's not a neat freak, but she's not a slob either. I've been busy with the fire department and Jules, but has anyone been checking on Hailey?

She settles next to me on the couch and pours tequila into both shot glasses.

I object. "I told you—"

"It's for me. Believe me, I'm going to need it," she interrupts. She throws one back and holds the other one in preparation. "Jules isn't who we thought she was."

I sit a little straighter and wait for her to continue.

"She's using you. *Us.* All of us. This town. This place...but mostly you. For your money," she says quietly.

If she didn't look so distraught, I would actually laugh. There isn't a cruel bone in Jules's body. She couldn't *use* someone if she tried. Hell, she named the damn spider in our shower despite hating the species, and she carries on conversations with it while she showers so the thing won't jump on her. She's not just a good person. She's *the best* person I know. My favorite person.

I sigh. "What are you talking about, Hailey? Your sister has done nothing but try with you. Is this about us?" I start, really hoping it's not. It's been months since I've thought of her like that. And I don't think the feeling was ever mutual.

We're friends. She's my girlfriend's sister. Her *twin* sister. What is she thinking?

Hailey scoffs. "Of course you believe her over me. Well, I heard it straight from her."

I throw my head back, the tension building in my neck. "What did you hear?"

"How she just wants to get married so she doesn't have to work. How much she hates this town. Hates having to fake relationships with all of us…how she's marrying you for your money."

I roll my eyes and shake my head. "Hailey," I pull her closer and hug her, "whatever you heard must have been a misunderstanding." I stroke her hair, and she sinks against me, her breathing coming out harder while she tries to hold back tears. The girl never lets go. She must be exhausted from running this place on her own. From dealing with her father. Her new sister. And on top of all of that, her best friend all but disappeared months ago. I had to do it. Our relationship wasn't healthy. I was looking at her like she hung the moon, and she didn't even see me. But that doesn't make it easier knowing that I wasn't here when she needed me the most.

"Why do you believe her without even flinching? I'm telling you what I heard," she huffs, pulling away from me.

I lean back and give her my full attention. "Because I know her. Because that's what trust is. Knowing that the person you love is the person you believe them to be because that's what they've shown you time and time again."

She shakes her head. "But I heard her——" she starts.

I silence her lips with my fingers. "This happens in every book."

Hailey looks at me as if I have two heads. "What?"

"Romance books. I read them," I say, breezing past the information as if it's no big deal. More men should read them. They're good for more than just turning my girlfriend on.

"In every book, there comes a point when there is some miscommunication. It's extremely aggravating to read because if people just sat down and had a conversation, everything would get worked out. Talk to your sister. Ask her about what you heard. Don't attack. Don't assume. And don't tell me that I don't know the woman I love. Because I do. And I promise you, whatever you heard, it was something else completely." I rub her arm. "Now, I have to go Hailes, but you need to get some rest. You need help at the bar. You need a cleaning lady." I survey the room pointedly. "You're struggling, and you need to speak up. I promise, if you ask Jules to help, she'll be here in an instant. As will Caris. And me," I remind her. I lean in and kiss her forehead, then give her a stern look. "I may love Jules—hell, she's everything to me—but you'll always be my friend. Hear me?" I stand and watch her, waiting for a response.

When she nods, I head for the door. As I swing it open, she calls out, "You really love her?"

I grin back at her. "She's my person."

Hailey gives me a crooked, teary smile. "I'm happy for you," she whispers.

"Thanks. Now get some rest. And tomorrow, call your sister," I say with another stern glare.

She smiles. "Go. I'll call Amelia and see if she can come down and help tonight."

"Good girl."

I blow out a breath and take two stairs at a time. I've now told Mason and Hailey I'm in love with Jules. I can't wait to finally tell her.

JULES
ICE CREAM
SUPER PREMIUM ICE CREAM
SUPER PREMIUM ICE CREAM

CHAPTER 64

JULES

The heat from the wax makes my toes curl. Shawn watches me, biting his lip as I groan and shift my hips when the wax drips onto my skin, my body begging for his touch. I keep trying to lift my hands, but they must be restrained because I can't get them to move. "Please," I beg. But it's like he doesn't hear me. The heat grows stronger, and the burning smell scares me. We've used this candle before, and it's never gotten this hot. "Please," I say again, ready to use my safe word for real this time.

When Shawn's face morphs and melts in front of me, my eyes fly open. "Oh, thank God. It's just a dream," I mutter. But as I try to lift my hands, they're weighed down, almost like I'm drunk. My reactions are slow, my movements stilted.

And the heat. It feels like there's a wood-burning stove in the room. Or like I fell asleep in the sauna after an intense workout. The sweat drips down my skin, and I frown in confusion. "What is going on?"

A beeping sounds in the distance. I recognize the noise, I think. Maybe. I search for my phone, but the room is hazy and I can't see it.

"Shawn!" I call out, starting to panic. But he's not here. He's working tonight, I remind myself. At the fire station. And that's when it hits me.

Fire. There's a fire.

Oh fudge. I have to get out of here.

CHAPTER 65

HAILEY

Looking around my apartment, I can't help but think how right Shawn was. This place was disgusting. It took me four hours to clean it, and now I can finally breathe again. And with the mess gone and a little less stress on my shoulders, I can see that I might have flown off the handle tonight.

What is wrong with me?

I'm not the type of person to think this nonsensically. Even a blind person could see what Jules and Shawn have. It's the way they make the people around them feel. Like we're bearing witness to honest, genuine love and devotion. And I'm not a bit surprised at how Shawn so freely admitted his feelings. He's always worn his heart on his sleeve. He's a good friend, and I'm lucky he found me before I confronted Jules. I can't imagine how she would have handled my accusations.

I settle myself into bed and stare up at the ceiling. What am I going to do? This bar needs so much work, and my grandmother is cutting me off. I need to find a husband. But I want what Jules and Shawn have. Not just a relationship so I can keep my business. I want it all. I want the *can't eat, can't sleep, just want to stay up all night and kiss* kind of love. But what would I even know about that? I'm the girl who's barely been kissed.

Even if I talk a big game.

I can't imagine what everyone would think if they knew the truth. That I, Hailey Milsom, resident flirt and tease, am a bona fide twenty-eight-year-old virgin.

My mind drifts to the one man I'd give it all to. My heart, my body, and all my tomorrows. If only he knew I existed.

I'm woken by the feeling of heat on my skin. My heart pounds in my chest and my eyes fly open.

Jules.

I'm out of my bed in seconds, reaching for my phone to call Shawn. I don't know what it is or how I know, but something is wrong.

Before I have a chance to dial, the security system app on my phone dings, alerting me to a problem at one of my family's properties. I don't have to click on the notification to know that it's the ice cream shop. Slipping on my shoes, I grab my keys and dial 911. According to the alert, the smoke detector is going off. I don't care if I find Jules standing in a cloud of smoke in her new kitchen. I don't care if I've just alerted both the police and fire departments to a false alarm. I'm not taking a chance.

I can see the flames from outside the bar, and that pushes me to pick up my pace. It only takes me two minutes to get to the building. I climb out of the car, my heart beating out of my chest. It's a blazing inferno. Without thinking, I do the only thing I can. I run into the building in search of my sister.

CHAPTER 66

SHAWN

"**F**uck! You win again!" I groan when Colby throws down an ace.

"What can I say? I'm just better than you, old man!" he teases.

I'm not really mad. I can't be mad. I walk around with a perpetual smile lately because Jules makes me the happiest motherfucker this side of the Mason-Dixon.

"All right, I'm gonna get some sleep," I say and stand.

Colby scoffs. "All right, old man. Go get your rest."

I grin. "Call me whatever you want. I'm just making sure I'm well rested for my night with Jules." I waggle my eyebrows.

Mason groans from the other side of the table. "Shawn, no."

I roll my eyes. "I didn't mean like that." Then I laugh. "Although…" I drawl.

Just then, the alarm sounds in the station. Without thinking, we move to the bay to throw on our gear and hop in the truck. The actions are ingrained. When that alarm rings, we go. It isn't until we're a few blocks down the street that the captain rattles off the address. He looks at me as he says it, gauging my reaction. When it clicks, my stomach drops.

BRITTANÉE NICOLE

My address. The shop. Where Jules is currently sleeping.

My vision blurs and my dinner churns in my stomach.

Mason grabs my leg. "She'll be okay. We got her." His tone is one of reassurance, but I know better. I know that by the time someone spotted the flames, by the time they called the fire department, the smoke could have already killed her.

It's a four-minute ride, but it's the longest ride of my life. As we pull up to my building, which is engulfed in flames—the windows blown out, and glass everywhere—I push past my crew and bolt out of the truck. I don't stop until I'm running into the building, but that's when I hear her shouts.

"Shawn!"

I whip around to the right and spot her standing in the grass, shivering, her phone in her hand, my sweatshirt swallowing her up. Her bare legs buckle as I pull her into my chest.

"Jules, baby. Are you okay?" I ask, running my hands up and down her arms, checking her for bumps and bruises and knocking her phone to the ground in the process. I search her eyes for signs of a concussion. Pull her mouth open, looking for evidence of smoke inhalation. But I can't see through the blur of tears. "We need a medic!" I scream.

She grabs at my face, her palms flat against my cheeks. "Shawn, I'm fine. I got out in time. I'm fine."

I shake my head. No. It's just like last time. I was so close to getting him out. I thought we'd be fine, and then I lost everything…

"Shawn, look at me. I'm fine…I'm completely fine."

Snap out of it. Be in the moment. Focus, I remind myself.

"Medic!" I shout again.

Tim runs up with his bag. Around me, my guys unload the hose. They spray down the building, they shout, they run, they fight the goddamn fire. And I stand, staring, lost, drowning.

"I'm fine!" Jules shouts again. "But please check on my sister. She ran into the building…"

I spin in the direction Jules is pointing. On the sidewalk, with her head between her knees, Hailey is breathing heavily. She's wrapped in a wet blanket, shivering.

Tim motions for Jules to follow him. "Why don't you sit next to your sister, and I'll check you both out," he instructs.

Jules lowers herself to the concrete next to Hailey, and the two of them link hands, twining them together and leaning their heads into one another. I've always kept my emotions inside, refusing to show them to others, but seeing the two women I'm closest to finally find one another, seeing the woman I love finally have the love she so desperately wanted from her twin, it's too much.

"What happened?" Tim asks. He gestures for Jules to open her mouth. After he shines his light into her throat and gives her the all-clear, he turns to Hailey, waiting for her response.

"I—" she coughs.

Tim shuffles on his knees so he's next to her and repeats the steps he just finished with Jules. When he confirms that it's not smoke related, he hands her a bottle of water.

She takes a sip and clears her throat. "I have an alarm on my phone. It monitors all our properties. If an alarm goes off, burglar…fire," she whispers the last word. She shakes her head, and Jules squeezes her hand tight. "I heard the alarm and knew you were working, so I got in my car, dialed 911, and got here as fast as I could. When I pulled up, the building was already in flames, but I didn't see Jules anywhere—"

Jules finishes for her. "So she grabbed the tablecloth I'd used in the window display as fake snow, wet it down, and ran upstairs to get me out."

Tim and I suck in breaths simultaneously, and I gulp my surprise. "You ran into a burning building?"

Hailey looks at Jules when she replies. "She's my *sister*." Her voice breaks on the admission and tears fill both their eyes.

CHAPTER 67

SHAWN

She's going to leave.

It's all I can think about as I take in the burned-out building that once housed everything that mattered to Jules.

She's going to leave. There's not enough left here for her. I worked so hard to make the bakery perfect so she'd stay. It was her dream... and now it's gone.

"Come to my house, man. You can stay in the guest room," Dane offers.

He's freshly showered. Everyone is freshly showered but me. After the fire was put out, I followed Jules to the hospital, waited with her to get checked out, and didn't leave until they kicked me out of the room. She and Hailey were together, and they gently requested time alone.

Don't get me wrong, I'm happy Hailey and Jules have each other. I'm ecstatic that they finally connected...but is it enough? Will her family be enough to keep her here?

I shake my head. "I'm gonna head back to the hospital."

Dane puts his hand on my shoulder. "You need to shower. You need to sleep. And so does she. She doesn't need to see you like this. Stressed. On the edge. She's okay, Shawn," he urges.

I scrub my hands through my hair. They're still black from the smoke and the charred remains. I can't stop picking at what's left. As if, under the rubble, I'll find a reason to make Jules stay. "I almost lost her…" My voice cracks. And I still might.

"But you didn't. Hailey got there in time. Jules is safe. The fire is out. Your job is done," Dane says, his words forceful.

I shake my head. "If I'd been there…"

"Stop." He looks me dead in the eye. "We aren't going there. You have a job, and you were doing it. You can't put the ones you love in a bubble. No matter what we do, we can't be everywhere all the time. She's safe. You're safe. That's all that matters."

I blow out a breath. It plumes in front of me in the cold December air. I don't feel the cold though. I'm burning up inside. I should have been there. I should have been the one to save her.

She's going to leave.

JULES
ICE CREAM
SUPER PREMIUM ICE CREAM
SUPER PREMIUM ICE CREAM

CHAPTER 68

JULES

The building is marked off with yellow tape. The Christmas lights lie charred on the ground, the green wire singed open in multiple places, and each tiny light is blown out, leaving colored glass littering the floor.

All the work we've spent the last few weeks on literally went up in flames.

Shawn walks out holding the remnants of the pink Jules sign. "I'm so sorry, sweetheart," he says. "I'll get you a new one. We'll rebuild. I promise." The stress is radiating off him. He's been so quiet, so wound tight, and I can't blame him.

I take a deep breath. An exhausted breath. It feels like we haven't stopped since the fire. And it was only forty-eight hours ago. The town canceled the Sip and Stroll. Hailey and I spent the night in the hospital beside one another. And although it was a scary, stressful night and I lost literally everything I owned, it was the first night I'd ever spent beside my sister, and I found myself smiling as we got to really know one another.

"Coffee?" she asks.

"With sugar and creamer."

She laughs and rolls her eyes. "Of course, Ms. Sugar," she teases.

"If I'm Ms. Sugar, what are you?"

"Ms. Spice," she cackles. "Duh."

"Okay, so what? You like spicy coffee?"

"No, black. Like my soul," she says darkly with wide eyes.

We both burst into giggles at that.

"Pizza?" I ask.

"Cheese...the OG!"

I smile. "Same."

Eventually, the nurse had to come in and tell us to get some sleep. Apparently we were keeping the whole floor awake.

"You okay, Red?" Shawn murmurs, pulling me against his chest.

"I'm fine. Really, I am." I hug him tight. "Are you okay?"

Even though he's holding me, I can't help but feel like he's a million miles away. Is it possible for me to miss someone who's standing right beside me?

"Don't worry about me," he says quickly, his mouth dipping into a frown. "I'm going to check upstairs. There's less damage up there, but I don't want you going in. The building isn't safe."

"Can you check on Charlotte?" I ask like a complete lunatic. Yes, I want to know if the spider I despise is alive. It's insane.

Shawn almost smiles at that. "Of course, sweetheart. Do you want me to bring her down if she's alive?" he teases.

I giggle. There's my Shawn. We're fine. He's fine. We're just adjusting. "You know what? Don't tell me either way. Probably better if I believe she just wandered out into the cold, looking for a new shower to hang out in." I pause and squeeze him to me. "Be careful," I say softly.

Shawn leans down and presses his lips softly against mine. "Always, Red."

I stand outside in the cold winter air, my breath blowing hot puffs that I focus on rather than the charred remains of my business and home.

"What a pity," a voice says behind me.

When I turn, I spot Lucy sauntering toward me, a black hat covering her red hair and a big puffy coat that is the opposite of flattering.

"Hi, Lucy," I say, feigning cheer. I'm exhausted, but my mother raised me to smile regardless.

"After all the work those boys did," she says, shaking her head and inspecting the rubble that used to be my bakery. My home. "And Shawn. How he got the whole town to support your bakery. Just… what a waste."

I can't help but roll my eyes at her insincerity. Also, while I appreciate what the guys did, my friends and I also put in a lot of work here. Work, sweat, and tears. But it's pointless to argue about it.

I sigh. "We'll rebuild." I look back up at what's left of my business. "It will just take a while."

"Yes. But I'm sure by the time you get around to it, someone else will have filled that need. You're not the only bakery in town. After all, Shawn's persistence was the reason you were chosen for the ball." She presses her lips together in fake pity.

My hands shake as I try to control my anger. "What do you mean it's because of Shawn?"

She fluffs the hair under her hat like she's gearing up to give a performance. "Oh, he didn't tell you?"

I huff out my annoyance. It's been a long forty-eight hours. "Out with it."

"The only reason the committee chose you to make the desserts was because Shawn offered up the help of the fire department for the festival. And the calendars, of course."

I suck my bottom lip into my mouth as I consider this new information. Shawn did go to great lengths to get everyone to welcome me. He delivered pastries and touted me around town as the best thing since sliced bread.

I'd like to think that my baking stood out on its own, without the sexy fireman selling it. I so wanted to be part of this community, to be welcomed, to belong.

On the other hand, Shawn's motives were pure, and I love him for it.

Deciding that I'd rather be grateful for the love I've been given than upset over how it came about, I smile. "I'd say I'm pretty lucky then, huh?"

The woman almost falls over as her mouth opens wide. "Huh?"

My smile grows as I study the sign in my hand. A gift from Shawn. The one he promised to replace.

We will rebuild. I'm building a life here. In this town. Within this community. With my sisters by my side. And I'm alive. Those are reasons enough to smile.

I shrug as I breathe new life into my spirits. "We'll rebuild. I'm lucky to have found a place where people stood beside me when I opened the first time and to have found the love of a man who would go to all that trouble for me."

"He's not the only one who loves you," a voice says from behind me. When I spin, I find Carmella, Belle, Charlotte, Amelia, and Hailey bundled up and holding coffees. Carmella speaks again as my twin hands me a to-go cup and squares off in front of Lucy. "You've got us. We'll help you rebuild. We'll be here to lift you up. And you're lucky, because these cups aren't full of coffee."

I laugh as I take a sip and choke on the sweet liquid. *Limoncello*! I should have known. "Warn a girl!" I tease.

Belle shakes her head with a knowing smile, and Carmella just lifts her shoulders in mock apology.

Lucy sputters, "Of course the town will help her. I was just telling her that."

She isn't fooling anyone, least of all Hailey. "Well, this has been fun, but my sister needs to get some rest. Come on, Red, you're staying with me."

"I am?" I ask in complete shock.

Amelia scoffs. "Only if you want to get a disease."

Hailey glares at her. "I'm trying to be sisterly."

Amelia laughs. "Then let her stay with Charlotte and Jack, as Shawn suggested."

"He did?" I say, surprised again. The back and forth is giving me whiplash.

"But I'm her sister," Hailey whines.

"Well, one day I will be too," Charlotte retorts, and we all turn to her with our mouths wide open. "What? I've seen how my brother looks at you. Mark my words—you're next."

"As fun as this is," Amelia says with a roll of her eyes, "I'm freezing. Can we just pick a place? And I'm with Charlotte on this one. She has a house. She's domesticated, and Shawn and Jules will totally be more comfortable there. Hailes, you get brownie points for offering, but let poor Jules have the picture-perfect Christmas she deserves."

Tears well in my eyes as I listen to these women fight over who gets to spend Christmas with me. I loop my arm through Hailey's as she replies, "I'm not looking for brownie points. I really *wanted* to spend time with you."

I smile. "I know, but you also like your own space."

She rolls her eyes. "Well, yeah. But I totally would have stayed on the couch and given you and Shawn my bedroom."

Charlotte laughs. "Yeah, I'm not giving up my bed for you. But I do have a guest bedroom."

"How about we head to Charlotte's and finish this conversation when Shawn gets home?" I suggest.

Hailey looks at me for a couple of beats, and I almost feel bad that I'm not immediately agreeing to live with her. But really, it's better for our sister relationship if I'm not in her space. And as long as I can convince her that I appreciate her gesture, I think she'll agree.

"Fine," she says, pulling me along. "But you better come to Grandmama's on Christmas day or I'll never forgive you."

I laugh and snuggle in closer to her. I can only imagine how much our grandmother hates that nickname. I love it. "I wouldn't want to be anywhere else."

CHAPTER 69

SHAWN

I'm hanging by a thread. I can feel the spiral, the tug of depression, the fear of coming so close to having everything only for it to be taken away again. And yet, I can't voice my thoughts. Instead, I wake up every day in my sister's basement, with my girlfriend by my side, and try to smile, crack jokes, work through what needs to be done to rebuild the bakery and our life so that I won't lose her.

It's been a week since the fire. Last year on Christmas Eve, I woke up in Tahoe and had nothing going for me. Now I've found my person. A community. Friends. A new job. To say I'm lucky would be an understatement. After my accident, I never thought I'd feel this whole again. For a year, I lived in Tahoe and watched couple after couple find their happily ever after. I watched person after person make their wish on a dollar—plaster their hopes and dreams to the wall of the bar where I worked. And for so long, I thought it was nonsense. Until I watched Ryan win over his best friend since childhood. After that, I knew I needed a change. A mix-up.

And what a mix-up it was.

But I'm scared to death that it will all slip through my fingertips.

I tug Jules closer and kiss her forehead. I can't believe I almost lost her. And Hailey. She saved her life. The phone beside me vibrates on the nightstand. I grab for it and read the text on the lock screen before I realize the phone isn't mine.

I stare at the message with a lump in my throat. I didn't mean to pick up her phone. But now that I've looked, I can't unsee the words.

Jared: I left my wife. The bakery is yours. Come home, Jules. I miss you.

Unable to help myself, I look at her phone log. She got a call from him recently. It didn't last long, but the log shows they were connected long enough to communicate at least a little. I look from the phone back to Jules. She's sleeping beside me. Peacefully. Completely unaware that I'm violating her privacy right now.

Part of me wants to delete the message. Block his phone number. So he can't steal her from me. So she doesn't have the option to pick him.

But I can't.

I can rebuild her bakery. I can love her like she's my everything. I can give her everything she's ever wanted.

But I can't make her choose me.

Not like this.

I sigh and lean back against the headboard. It'll take months to rebuild her bakery. Months for us to be back in our own place. And what if that's not what she wants? What if what she wants is the man on the other end of the phone? What if she wants California? Her old life—her other friends?

And on top of that, we've now confirmed that the fire in the bakery wasn't an accident. Someone is burning down buildings in this town. Someone almost *killed* my girlfriend. Is she even safe here?

"Everything okay?" she asks, her voice scratchy from sleep.

I try to smile but just can't muster it today. Rather than saying anything, I just hand her the phone. She doesn't look at it. She just stares at me. "What's wrong?"

"When was the last time you talked to your ex?" I ask quietly, not daring to look at her.

"I haven't…" she sputters, finally taking the phone from my hands.

She scoffs as she reads the words, and I finally have the courage to look at her. She's angry. "Ugh, idiot," she mutters, shaking her head.

"If this is what you want," I whisper—it's all I can manage, "if *he's* what you want…you need to tell me now, Red. It's okay if it is. I'll understand…but if there is any chance that you want him…that his offer interests you, let me go before…" My voice cracks. I can't do this again. I can't lose *everything* again.

Jules sits up in bed and drops her phone. Her tiny hands pull at my face until I'm looking her in the eye. "Before what?"

"Before I fall…" I get lost in those green depths of hers, wishing I was enough for the woman who's stolen my heart.

A sweet smile spreads across her face. "You haven't fallen yet?" she teases. She hooks a leg over me and straddles my hips, her hair a curtain around us.

I huff out a breath, even as my hands go to her hips, holding her in place. Willing her to want only me. "That obvious?" I ask.

"You convinced the town to welcome me. You gave me every Christmas memory I ever wanted. You gave me a relationship with my sisters. Built me a bakery. Got me a reindeer! It was all you." She rubs my cheek, scrutinizing me with what I hope is a look of awe on her face. "Of course it's obvious."

"I just wanted to make you happy," I admit. And then, because I need her to know that I'll let her go if that's what she wants, I offer her the out. "And if California will make you happy—"

She presses a finger to my lips. "Shh. *You* make me happy. The bakery, the town, my sisters, our friends. Even without *all* that, I'd choose *you*. Every day. No contest. *You* are enough, Shawn. *You* are what I want. You're everything."

My heart hammers in my chest. It's almost impossible to breathe. "I'm scared, sweetheart. I—I'm spiraling," I admit. It's hard to ask for help. It's hard to admit that I need her in this way. I want to be everything for her like she says I am, but—

Jules presses her body against mine and interrupts my thoughts. "What can I do to make it better?" But she already knows that answer. She's already squeezing me tighter. I need the pressure to quiet my mind. I need her touch to remind me that she's still here. I need *her*.

Jules's green eyes meet mine, and she bites her lip. "Do you want to tie me up? Would that help?"

I shake my head. "Would you—" I stop myself and look away. Will this freak her out?

"Do you want me…Do you want me to tie you up?" she asks softly, her eyes wide and open, clear of judgment.

I swallow hard, unable to take my eyes off this gorgeous woman who just *gets* me. I nod, finally letting go. Finally allowing myself to ask for what I need. Isn't this what I tell my friends? That they only need to ask for help? To make their needs known—my best friend Ryan, Amelia, Charlotte, Hailey, Jules…But I'd been too afraid to do it myself.

Jules smiles. "Well, why didn't you say so? I'd *love* to tie you up." Her eyes glow with excitement, a hunger evident as she searches for the new red rope I used on her only a few hours ago.

When she returns to the bed with it, she nibbles her bottom lip. "You're going to have to talk me through this," she whispers, rolling the rope back and forth between her fingers. My breath hitches in my throat when she looks at me. She's so damn beautiful. So damn perfect for me. And so damn mine.

"I love you," I say without hesitation.

Her green eyes light up. She smiles, then closes her eyes as she touches her heart.

I say it again. "I love you so much, sweetheart. You're everything to me."

Jules crawls up the bed, her movements slow, the rope still in one hand. And she doesn't stop until she's straddling me. Her pelvis rubs gently against mine when she reaches for my shirt and tugs it over my head.

With her palms pressed against my chest, she looks down at me. "I love you, too, Shawn. Now give me those lips please," she says sweetly, holding out the rope. I lean up and kiss her as she winds the rope around my waist, just like I do to her. With each sweep of her fingers across my skin, I breathe easier. The light pressure from the rope frees me from my anxiety, the scrape of her nails reminding me she's still here. And her gentle kisses against my chest as she works tell me without words just how much she loves me.

When she finally finishes the knot—a simple one she's seen me do dozens of times—she looks down at me with pride. "Is that better?" she asks, studying my reaction.

I sigh in relief. "So much."

"Would anything else make it better?" she asks coyly, slipping her pajama top over her head, exposing her pretty pink nipples.

"Take off your pants, Red," I tell her.

Even tied up, I'm still in charge—she knows that—and her eyes melt at my command. She strips until she's bare, straddling me and waiting for my instruction.

"Now mine, sweetheart."

She smiles as she shimmies my shorts down my legs.

"I need to be inside you, baby," I admit, once again asking for what I need.

Jules exhales. "Oh, thank God," she whispers. She lines herself up above me and stares down. "I'm on birth control. Is this okay?"

I nod. "It's just you and me," I promise. As soon as she slides down over my erection and her heat surrounds me, my entire body deflates. All the knots of anxiety loosen and the fear melts away. "Closer," I beg.

She presses against me, skin to skin, and brings her lips close. "Like this?"

I nod as I bite her bottom lip and pull her to me, kissing her through a gasp. When she starts to move, I open my eyes to watch her. "I love you," I say again, unable to help myself.

It doesn't take long for her to grip the rope and pull, using it for leverage to chase both our orgasms. I love watching her. Love feeling the tightness of the rope as she tugs, knowing she's marking me, that I'll feel her even after she's left me. She harnesses me, rides me, and I revel in the feeling of it. And when she squeezes me and kisses me as we both go over the edge, I pour into her, knowing she's mine.

When we're cuddled up and she's untied the knot, kissing each mark just like I do with her, I look down at her in wonder. "You're really staying in Bristol, Red?"

She grins up at me from under my arm. "Are you staying here?"

I nod. After feeling restless for over a year, wondering where I belong, I've finally found my home.

"Then yes. Wherever you are, that's where I belong."

I blow out a breath. "That's a good answer because I have a surprise for you tonight, and if you were leaving, it really would have sucked."

Jules grins, then she shakes her head and presses her lips to mine again. "You and your surprises."

I pull the box from under the tree, sneaking a peek at Jules. She's on the couch, sitting beside my sister. Her eyes dance while she listens to a story Charlotte shares about when she first met Jack.

I thought my sister was crazy when she told me about meeting her fiancé years ago, long before they reconnected. The way she described him as a perfect man she spent one perfect night with seemed ridiculous—and it was far more information than she needed to share with me.

That a spark like that could ignite after only one night, how they *just knew*…it was crazy. Or so it seemed. But then I saw Jules on the docks.

It may have been a mix-up, but if it really had been Hailey like I thought, I'm confident that I wouldn't have kissed her.

It was *because* it was Jules. The way she stood there, the way she looked at me, when our eyes met, I just knew I *had* to kiss her.

I'd never felt that mind-blowing connection with anyone.

And all of that led me to this crazy moment. Sitting below the tree, ready to hand her a box and make another one of her Christmas wishes come true.

"Hey, Red," I say, grabbing her attention. She turns my way, her brows drawing together as she looks at the box. I hold it up and wiggle it in the air. "Time for the first Christmas present."

My sister claps and whoops in excitement. "I love the first Christmas present. Jack, come here. It's time!"

She hops down onto the floor next to me and grabs Jack's box. It's their first Christmas together too. Despite losing my home, I'm happy to be sharing this moment with my sister.

Jack holds out his hands, and Charlotte, of course, hops back up and jumps into his lap. He laughs as he falls back but works the wrapping paper with both arms wrapped around my sister.

I hand Jules her gift, sitting at her feet, reveling in the sight of the gorgeous woman who owns my heart. She bites her lip as she carefully opens the wrapping paper. She gently, painstakingly, eases the tape off each end like destroying the wrapping paper isn't half the fun. Impatient, I huff and reach up to tear at it. "Come on, Jules. Ya gotta get in there and really take it apart."

She laughs and rips at it then, her normally poised resolve melting. When she finally gets the box open, she gasps. She gingerly touches the soft fabric with her fingers, pulling out the reindeer-covered pajamas.

Jack laughs beside her, kissing Charlotte on the cheek. "Ya want me to wear this onesie covered in little reindeer, Sas?"

She jumps up and grabs the matching pairs we have below the tree. "Don't worry, Shawn has a pair too!"

Jules raises her eyes to meet mine and gives me a watery smile. "Matching pajamas on Christmas…." Her voice breaks, and a tear slips down her face.

I push up on my knees and swipe at it before it can fall. "No crying on Christmas, baby." I press a soft kiss against her lips and feel another tear hit my nose. "Sweetheart, no," I say, swiping it away as I cradle her face. "Was this not good?"

She smiles and shakes her head. "It's perfect. The only thing that would make it more perfect was if my sisters were here too," she admits quietly.

I press my lips together. "I know, baby." I kiss another tear from her cheek.

She nods and takes a deep breath. "Okay. Enough of feeling all the emotions. I wanna see you in your reindeer jammies."

Jules and I walk hand in hand down Hope Street toward the Christmas tree. Although it's Christmas Eve and this was a last-minute request, the entire department has shown.

With the Sip and Stroll having been canceled, it was easy to convince those who are in town for the holiday to come for a special Christmas Eve tree stroll. And most of the town showed up. They've shown up for Jules and for me—two outsiders they've welcomed with open arms and pajamas.

Because yeah…everyone is wearing them.

Carmella passes out warm cookies and hot chocolate with Belle, Luca, and his sister Stella, while the guys from the fire department walk around with buckets collecting money.

Nate gets out his guitar, and with Amelia by his side, he strums a few lines to get everyone's attention.

"Thank you all for coming. I know I can speak for all of our families when I say we are so happy that, as always, this town has shown up for another one of our own."

Jules looks up at me. "What's he talking about?"

"Shh," I say, squeezing her hand. We're all bundled up in jackets and gloves and scarves, but pajama pants peek out from below long coats and above coat collars. I can't wait to see Jules's expression when she catches on.

"So, if you guys don't mind, let's get this singing for Jules started. You know how this works. Pick a song, and for a donation, Ames and I will sing it. But you gotta make sure the dollar bills have your Christmas wishes on them. Right, Shawn?"

When I nod, Nate continues. "And all the money will go to help our favorite new bakery rebuild."

Jules sucks in a breath. "What is he talking about?"

Sure, insurance will cover a lot of the rebuild. And if it didn't, her grandmother and I would have. There are plenty of people willing to step in to make Jules's dream come true. But I want her to see how the town will step up too. To know what it feels like to allow others to show up for her. To know that she's a Bristolian. She belongs here. Just like her sister.

I smile at her as Nate goes on. "Oh, and before I forget—Hailey, can you come out here?"

Hailey and Caris walk out from behind the tree, wearing pajamas that match ours. Jules squeals beside me and hugs me tight.

"Go on up there," I say, pushing my girl forward. "Time for some more Christmas memories." She moves forward but doesn't let go of me. Charlotte follows behind us, pulling Jack.

As we stand in front of the tree with Nate, Amelia, Charlotte, Jack, Hailey, and Caris, we watch as the entire group in front of us unzips their coats, revealing their Christmas pajamas. Jules laughs as tears stream down her face, and Nate starts to sing, "Have Yourself a Merry Little Christmas."

The whole crowd sings along, and I sway with my girl in my arms, decked out in Christmas pajamas, looking out at the town that chose us. Without a doubt, I'm exactly where I'm meant to be with my person by my side.

And as the dollar bills flutter into the bucket, I gotta be honest—it feels a lot like magic.

JULES
ICE CREAM
SUPER PREMIUM ICE CREAM
SUPER PREMIUM ICE CREAM

EPILOGUE

JULES

SEVEN MONTHS LATER

There's magic in the quiet moments. Sure, big days have magic. I'm sure the day Shawn proposes will be magical. And the day we get married. The day we have our first child. These are things I know will happen someday. We talk about our future often. Shawn's like that. He doesn't hide his feelings or his dreams from me.

But our dreams are filled with a lot more than those big moments. They're filled with love notes left by the coffee pot. Mistletoe hanging in the kitchen. Blueberry donuts on a Sunday morning. Margaritas on the front porch at sunset. Speedy showers with Charlotte. Ropes and wax in the bedroom. Glasses that slide down Shawn's nose when he leans in for a kiss. Sugar and fudge when I've had a bad day. Sister sleepovers with matching pajamas. And, of course, kittens cuddled up on a reindeer.

Today though. Today is a big day. It's taken months and months of hard work, an absurd amount of money, and quite a few tears to get to this point. But when I walk down the steps and flip on the Christmas lights Dane hardwired into the kitchen, I can't help but feel the magic.

Sure, it's three a.m. and I should be exhausted. I should be yawning, not smiling, as I hum a Christmas song in the middle of July.

I shuffle over to the coffee pot and smile at the note stuck to it as I switch it on.

Happy first day, sweetheart. I'm so proud of you. I can't wait to be your first customer. See you in a few hours. I love you.

XOXO,

Shawn

I try to contain my grin, but it breaks out in full force. As always, Shawn earns all my smiles.

I settle into my new routine, prepping for the morning crowd— something I can only hope is a reality. But even as the insecurity niggles at my insides and I find myself pressing on my thumb, I focus on the pink sign hanging above the oven—*Jules Bakery*, with the three little ice cream scoops in pink, teal, and yellow—and I smile.

My people will show up.

Carmella will likely be here before the doors open. Belle and Charlotte will be quick to follow. Amelia gave birth to a baby girl only a week ago, so she won't be stopping by, but I'm sure Nate will be in to pick up something with chocolate in it. Or a chocolate chip cookie. That seems to be her thing. And Caris will come barreling in sometime midmorning. She'll probably buy me out of every dessert I have and claim she needs them for the new hotel, even though we both know she has dessert chefs who provide more than she needs.

The firefighters will filter in throughout the morning, and possibly even some of the women from Zumba. My grandmother will force Bernard to drive her over here, and she'll fawn all over me and this shop.

I have a community here. People who love me. People who show up for me. Not because they're related by blood—although some are—but because they want to be.

"Hey, Jules," my twin sister says, rolling in with a cup of coffee in her hand and bags under her eyes. I have two employees who will get here in a few hours, but Hailey wanted to be here with me at the crack of dawn.

"You really made it here early," I say.

Hailey gives me a haughty laugh and puts her hand on her hip. "You thought I wouldn't make it?"

I shrug. "I mean, the bar closed like two hours ago."

"Yeah, I haven't slept yet. Grandmama is driving me nuts. Since she cut me off, I don't have the money to pay for the work that needs to be done to update the kitchen. And believe me, those updates need to get done!"

I wince. I can't believe our grandmother is still holding Hailey not living with me over her head. "If you need money—"

Hailey holds up her hand. "Do not finish that sentence. It will be fine. I just…" She looks away from me, sighs, and meets my gaze again. "I just need a few more good nights at the bar, and then we should be able to cover it."

I nod.

"Or a husband," she jokes, rolling her eyes.

"I mean…" I say, gauging her opinion on the subject.

Hailey side-eyes me. "*Stop.* I'm not even dating anyone. Who wants to deal with this hot mess?" she adds, waving a hand and gesturing to herself.

I can't stand that she sees herself that way. I grab her in a side hug. "There are very few men who deserve you, Hailes. But seriously, Shawn and I would be happy to help," I add, knowing Shawn would do anything for anyone, especially my twin.

Hailey smiles. "Yes, we all know Shawn is perfect. Lucky girl you are," she teases. "Now put me to work. What do we need to do to prepare for your first day?"

Hours later, a line loops around the corner, and I look back at Hailey in shock before flipping the sign to open and greeting our customers. As promised, Shawn stands in the front of the line.

My first customer.

"Get in here, you," I tease and pull him inside. He lifts me up in his arms and spins me around while I laugh into his neck.

"Happy first day, Red. Hell of a line you got out there," he teases, as if he didn't have anything to do with it.

I fold in my lips to hide my smile and shake my head. "You are something else, *Babe*."

He pushes me behind the counter to wait on him. "I'll take two dozen blueberry donuts, a dozen margarita cupcakes, and a cup of coffee to go, please," he says with a grin.

"Shawn, you don't have to buy all of that," I object.

He narrows his eyes. "I'm aware of what I do and don't have to do, Red. Now box up my treats. The ladies are waiting down by the docks."

I shake my head. Once a week, my sweet boyfriend meets with the cougars and Carmella to plan town events. Apparently, he loved doing all the events for the Christmas festival so much that he wanted to help out year-round.

I find the entire thing suspicious.

I believe it has more to do with the permit we needed to rush along the rebuild and how Mitzy's husband is the head of Zoning. Shawn will never admit that he's stuck with the ladies once a week for the next year because he wanted to help me out though. He knows I'd feel guilty, so instead, I allow him his white lie.

I box up his treats and wave him off when he tries to pay. "Your money is no good here," I tell him.

Shawn glares. "I'll eat all your profits, sweetheart. Take the money." He slides a crisp one-hundred-dollar bill across the counter.

I roll my eyes, but as I grab it to make change, it's what's beneath it that has me pausing.

In big black letters across a one-dollar bill are the words **I wish for my best friend to have the best first day in her new bakery.**

I smile and read the message again, then look back up at my boyfriend. "Aw, you got me a wish just like the ones you had in Tahoe."

Shawn grins. "Put it up on the wall, Red. It's tradition."

I lean across the counter and plant a kiss on his lips before doing just that. Shawn grabs his boxes, winks at me, and then he's gone, and I'm turning to my next customer.

Carmella smiles and peruses the menu. "I think I'll take a croissant and a cappuccino for here, my dear."

"Of course. That will be seven dollars," I say, ringing her up while Hailey grabs her croissant. She smiles as she hands me a ten. I slide it across the counter, but once again, when I lift it up, another dollar sits below it. I spot the black writing and bring it closer to inspect what it says.

I wish my girl never has a reason to frown.

I scratch my head in confusion. "Carmella, what is this?"

It may seem dumb, but this really looks like Shawn's handwriting.

Carmella shrugs. "Shawn gave it to me. What does it say?"

My shoulders drop in confusion. Why did Shawn give her this dollar? I shake my head of the thoughts, though, because I have a line out the door and limited help. "No worries," I say and set the dollar aside so that I remember to ask Shawn about it later.

The next person in line is Dane. He's come in with his twin sons, who are practically salivating as they wander back and forth, staring at the display shelves. "Place looks great," he says while he waits on them to pick what they want.

"Couldn't have done it without you," I reply. And it's true. Shawn and the guys got this place up and running in a matter of weeks once the construction was finished.

"This is on the house," I say when I hand over the donuts the boys have picked.

Dane shakes his head. "Your boy would kill me." He slides a twenty over with a wink. "Keep the change."

I laugh and thank him, but when I go to slide the twenty into the cash register to make change for the tip drawer, I spot another dollar with black writing on it.

I wish that my best friend never has spiders in her showers. But if she does, I hope I'm there to witness it.

A loud laugh escapes as I read it a second time and put it next to Carmella's. The morning proceeds like that. Each customer has a dollar bill with another one of Shawn's notes. That man. He really knows how to let a girl know he cares.

I wish that my girl never goes to bed angry.

I wish that my best friend never runs out of rope.

I wish that my girl always has a real Christmas tree.

I wish that my best friend is never sad.

I wish that my girl always believes in magic.

I wish that my girl never has a reason to be anxious.

I wish that my girl only knows good days.

I wish that my girl always finds someone to Zumba with.

I wish that I never wake without my best friend by my side.

I wish that my girl reads with me every night.

When I get to the one that says **I wish that my best friend gets to have matching pajamas with her children,** I start to cry.

A VERY MERRY MARGARITA MIX-UP

As I look up at the next customer in line, the tears come down even harder. "What the heck are you doing here?" I ask Amy on a sob.

My other best friend gives me a watery smile.

"Don't just stand there. Come over here and hug me," I say, coming around the counter and grabbing my best friend in my arms.

"This place is amazing," she whispers through her tears.

I look at her and then glance around at the shop. Hailey is on the other side of the counter with a smirk. "You knew about this?" I ask her.

She nods. "But it was all Shawn."

I heave in a heavy breath, trying to keep the tears at bay. "Of course it was. So do you have one?" I ask, looking at her hands, anxious for the next dollar.

Amy's brows furrow in confusion. "Have one what?"

My mood deflates a little. "Never mind. I'm just so happy you're here. Let me get you something to eat and a coffee, and we can sit for a bit. It looks like the crowd is finally under control."

The bakery is loud and full of all our friends, who are at tables relaxing and eating. Even Amelia came down with Nate and baby Pauline in her stroller. A week old and absolute perfection. Amelia looks up at me with a warm smile from her spot next to her husband, a chocolate croissant in her hand.

"Oh, did you mean do I have one of these?" Amy says, waving the bill like I'm a bull about to charge her. I just might with how anxious I am to grab that dollar.

"Gimme," I say and reach for it.

She laughs and hands it over.

I wish my best friend is always surrounded by her best friends.

"That's a good one," I murmur.

"Hmm," Amy hums, smiling at me.

"Well, what I really wish is that Shawn didn't have to work so you could finally meet him," I say, frustrated that I can't just kiss him right now. Where's the mistletoe and a hot boyfriend when you need them?

"Plenty of time for that," Amy supplies as she accepts the coffee Hailey hands her. She shakes her head, looking back and forth between the two of us. "You two really are identical."

Hailey laughs. "And yet everyone can tell us apart *except* her boyfriend-slash-my best friend, who mistook me for her."

I glare at Hailey.

"Too soon?" she teases. "Will this make up for it?" She waves another greenback in my face.

"Gimme that!" I grab for it, causing both Amy and Hailey to laugh. I take a deep breath before reading it.

I wish that my best friend is always surrounded by her family.

Warmth pools in my chest when Caris and my grandmother enter the shop. Hailey sighs beside me, and I squeeze her hand. Jack and Charlotte follow behind them with Shawn and Charlotte's parents. It really is a friends-and-family affair.

I excuse myself to say hello and take their orders, nervous and a bit excited to see what wish Charlotte will hand me. When I lift her twenty up, though, there's nothing beneath it. I school my expression, but she doesn't miss the disappointment on my face. "I have the last dollar, but you can't look at it until you go outside," she says with a whimsical expression.

I bite my lip and nod, unable to find my voice.

I feel all eyes on me as I walk toward the bakery door, the jangle of the bell ringing out when I open it and focus on the sight before me. Prancer in front of a sled—on wheels—with Mason by his side.

"What?" I say in wonder.

Snow flutters around me and hits the pavement in big drops. "Kinda hard to keep it frozen," Shawn's booming voice says from the corner. I spin to find him walking toward me on the porch. "Last

Christmas, you wished for a sleigh ride, snow, and reindeer. I realized you only got one of the three."

I shake my head, but my smile remains. I'm so very confused. "Why is Prancer tied to a sleigh, Shawn? It's July."

He grins. One of the cocky ones I love so much. "Turn over the dollar bill, Red."

I take a deep breath and flip it.

I wish that all of your wishes always come true.

"And if they don't, I'll make them come true, sweetheart," he says, stepping in close.

I look up at him. "What's going on?"

"I could have written a million more wishes for you, Jules. You deserve everything."

My tears fall at the look of sincerity on his face. How did I manage to get so lucky?

He swipes them away and continues. "But I only have one wish for myself, and only you can make it come true."

I take a deep breath, trying to calm my racing heart. "And what is that?"

He reaches into his back pocket and pulls out another dollar bill. I take it and study it, the tears making it almost impossible to read. "I wish my best friend would agree to be my wife," I whisper the words scrawled across the dollar bill.

Shawn drops to his knee, and a diamond ring materializes in front of me. He holds it up between his fingers. "Marry me, Red? Make my wish come true and marry me, and I promise I'll do everything in my power to make all *your* wishes come true."

I drop to my knees and take Shawn's face in my hands, pulling his lips to mine in a desperate kiss. He wraps me up in a hug as my tears continue to fall, but our lips don't break apart.

"Is that a yes?" he whispers through another kiss.

I laugh. "Yes, Shawn. I'll marry you."

Behind us, Hailey shouts, "she said yes!" and our friends' cheers flood the bakery.

Shawn grabs my left hand and slips the diamond ring onto my finger. My goofy smile matches his.

"Is this for real?" I ask, looking into his chocolaty eyes, the eyes that make me melt on a daily basis.

"Yeah, sweetheart. It's real. And you know what all the books say?"

I grin. "What?"

His eyes light up with a glint of mischief. "And they lived happily ever after. The end."

I shake my head and kiss him again. "No, Babe, you've got it all wrong. This is just our beginning."

THE END

ACKNOWLEDGEMENTS

First and foremost, to my readers, thank you so much for this wildride of a year. This is my last book to be published in 2022-which makes seven books this year! I would not have kept writing if not for the fact that you read my work. Your enthusiasm and love for my characters makes this quite simply a joy to do. So thank you!

To my team at Cover 2 Cover Author Services, I couldn't do it without you. Above all, thank you for your friendship.

To my Beta Readers, especially Katherine Jay, Brittni Van and Jenni Bara, you made this book better. Thank you! And to my street team, I have no idea how I got so lucky to have you Bookstagram and Booktok Queens behind me, but I thank my lucky stars everyday. Your friendship, encouragement, excitement and support is something dreams are made of.

A special thanks to my author besties, Elyse Kelly, Daphne Elliot, Jenni Bara, Swati M.H. and S.J. Tilly who are always willing to listen to my questions or my rants. This is all more fun because of you.

To my lovely editor Beth, thank you for taking my words and making them better. Your dedication and love for my characters shines through in this book and I can't praise you enough!

Last but certainly not least, my family. I spend a tremendous amount of time with my characters, with my readers and on Tiktok, but your love and support means the world to me.

Writing has become my outlet. I think as mothers, wives,

daughters, friends, workers, etc. we all need something that is for us. For me that is reading and writing. I adore this community.

If you are wondering what is coming next, follow me on Instagram, join my awesome Facebook group, sign-up for my newsletter and follow me on TikTok. Much love to you all!

OTHER BOOKS BY BRITTANÉE NICOLE

BRISTOL BAY SERIES

SHE LIKES PINA COLADAS
KISSES SWEET LIKE WINE
OVER THE RAINBOW
LOVE & TEQUILA MAKE HER CRAZY

BOSTON BILLIONAIRES

WHISKEY LIES
LOVING WHISKEY
WISHING FOR CHAMPAGNE KISSES

COMING SOON

EXTRA DIRTY
DEADLY GOSSIP

Made in the USA
Coppell, TX
09 December 2022

88353372R00254